JONAH'S BELLY

a novel by

ANTHONY WITTWER

BIG GRUFF BOOKS

JONAH'S BELLY
Published by Big Gruff Books.

Copyright © 2013 by Anthony Wittwer
www.anthonywittwer.com

Author services by Pedernales Publishing, LLC.
www.pedernalespublishing.com

Cover Art & Author Photo: Meg Wittwer
Big Gruff Books Illustration: James Wittwer

Library of Congress Control Number: 2014904464

ISBN 978-0-9916060-9-2 Paperback Edition
ISBN 978-0-9916060-8-5 Hardcover Edition
ISBN 978-0-9916060-7-8 Digital Edition

Printed in the United States of America

For Elissa.
Our life together is my favorite story.

The question is not what you look at,
but what you see.

—Henry David Thoreau

PROLOGUE

I WILL NOT SLEEP TONIGHT.

It is only fair.

I am the one usually woken by nightmares, the one whose memories tear me from sleep—and it is always Elissa who comforts me, always Elissa who calms me and leads me back to safe dreams.

But not tonight.

Tonight, I am the one who will stay awake. Tonight, I will comfort her. I will talk to her until she drifts to sleep. I will hold her until her cries quiet, until her tears dry. And then I will hold her more.

I will not sleep tonight.

It is only fair.

FEELING HER SHAKING, knowing she hurts, I raise my hand to her face. My fingertips stroke her forehead, touch her cheek, brush her closed eyes. And I almost murmur the same words that I've heard her murmur so many times before, almost say to her what she's always said to all of the small, hurt animals that she's cradled in her arms, her fingertips stroking their foreheads, touching their cheeks, brushing their closed eyes as she whispers her soothing, familiar song. "Sleepy eyes," I almost say. "You've got such sleepy eyes"— but I stop before I speak, realizing how those words—tonight, at this moment—would hurt her even more than she is already hurt, would wound her even worse than she is already wounded. So I do not say those words.

Instead, I whisper other words: "I love you. I love you. I love you."

And I try thinking only of the woman I hold.

And not the blood outside our door.

BLUE

1

I ENTERED THE WORLD wearing a dark mask of membrane, a shadow-veined caul that covered my head like an opaque executioner's hood. Seconds after I was born, Ebeneezer, the big ball of gray-striped Manx cat my mother carried everywhere—including into the delivery room of my birth—crawled into my crib and licked the caul from my wrinkled, wet face. I still remember that first cleaning: the pink sandpaper pressure of Ebeneezer's tongue, the bump of his pointed feline teeth against my face, the soft brush of rumbling fur, the gentle push and pull of his padded paws kneading my baby skin.

Neither Ebeneezer nor my mother—the Gypsy fortune-teller, Callista Marie—was to be present for the rest of my childhood. Both, however, touched me for forever in those first few squalling, newborn seconds—

Ebeneezer the Cat: Lying innocent and quivering in my crib, being bathed and comforted by the Manx cat's careful ministrations, I bonded with Ebeneezer before I was cradled in Callista's lithe arms. Consequently, for all of my life I've held a deep abiding love of gray, tiger-striped cats. As evidence of this, for the last four years one of my closest companions has been Grendel, a wild Canada lynx. He is fifty-eight pounds of gray-striped muscle and good nature, and few people I know are blessed with as fine a friend.

My Mother, Callista Marie the Gypsy: Cally's tambourine-tuned body, rolling the mystic dice of heredity and chance within her womb, threw a seven and won a cache of wonderments, one of which was the caul she then draped over my developing eyes. True to the superstition of being born with a caul, I have a loving awe of the everyday magic that's nestled into the warm, woven folds of every second, that's tuck-pointed and troweled like precious mortar into the wet furrows of our brains. The magic that's enfolding, alive, and everywhere, gliding unseen across our paths and following us along walkways. The magic that strokes our temples with alchemist's fingers, whispering into our ears, "…from ordinary, to dreams…to dreams."

IT ISN'T ONLY that I wore a caul that has influenced my life—it is also that my twin brother did not. Cally's womb, although a warm and safe haven, was also a crowded one, shared by me and my identical-fraternal twin.

My older brother—born two minutes before me and christened Garrett James, then quickly renamed Alassadir by the band of Gypsies who immediately took him away as their king (which, according to my father, was *exactly* the deal he'd arranged). However, soon after taking my brother, the Gypsies again returned and also took away my mother and Ebeneezer (which, according to my father, was *not at all* the deal he'd arranged).

Caul, cat, and Gypsies: There have been more usual births.

AS A CHILD, I used to ask my father, "Why this brother I never knew? Why is he now King of the Gypsies, and I am not? Why did you choose him?"

"It wasn't because he was first-born, Blue," my father answered. "It wasn't that at all."

Nor was it our appearance.

Looking at us lying side by side, both babies new and splotchy with the exertions of birth, my father couldn't see a single difference

2

between the two. He saw the exact same hair, the exact same face, the exact same fingers and toes. To him, the magnificence of birth had wrapped both my brother and me in the same swaddling cloth, making us identical halves of the same miracle and blinding him to any differences.

"Right then," he always said, "with both of you in front of me, you both looked exactly the same. Of course, I was wrong. You weren't identical twins, you were fraternal. But to me, right then, you both looked exactly alike. Right then, the two of you were the world's first identical-fraternal twins."

I EVENTUALLY learned why my brother, and not I, was given to the Gypsies as their king. I learned that the reasons for my father's choice were decided when he was six years old, when his dog Warlock was killed by a lightning strike that left behind only a charred stick of tail and a melted nugget of the silver dog tag that had attracted the lethal electric bolt.

THE DOG TAG was a wide, dangling silver totem.

As a boy, my father had crafted it at a stamping booth exhibition during a family trip to the Indianapolis State Fair. Beneath a sign proclaiming "50 CENTS PRINTS ANY MESSAGE!" my father dropped two quarters into an industrial-green metal box and began turning a large, black-lettered dial. Letter by letter, he spun the dial back and forth through the alphabet, directing hydraulically-driven steel stamping punches at the edge of a blank, round emblem held clamped in vises behind the thick glass of the exhibit's display. Working slowly, biting the inside of his cheek in concentration, he filled the empty spaces around the silver tag's circumference, encircling it with the legend: WARLOCK, DEAR & PROVEN FRIEND OF THE WITTWERS. Hitting the display's red, mushroom cap-shaped FINISH button, he reached down as the round medal dropped first into the machine's internal darkness, then rolled out through a narrow slot and into his cupped hands.

Lifting the tag to eye-level for inspection, it felt good against his palm. The medal's heft was substantial and reassuring, its metal bright from the stamping. The silver token's newly struck edges caught the sun and hurled back the light like a warrior's polished shield. Looking at it, my father smiled. Slipping the medal into the deep boy-pockets of his corduroys, he then shuffled down the rows of other booths to enjoy the rest of the fair.

At home the next day, with a single hammer-swing at a ten-penny nail, he struck a hole through the tag. Then, with much ceremony, he attached the medal—as an amulet of loyalty and friendship—to the wide brown leather collar that circled Warlock's massive neck. Warlock, a chocolate Labrador retriever, full of keen intelligence and unrelenting love, walked proudly back and forth displaying his new gift. The dog gazed at my father in unquestioning adoration, his muzzle lifting as he barked deep woofs of canine joy.

WEEKS LATER, while searching nearby farm fields for plowed-up arrowheads, my father and Warlock were walking through open acres of just-harvested corn. As they walked, broken cornstalks reached up to them from the ground like skeletal, beckoning arms. Suddenly, without warning, an Indiana thunderstorm purpled the air around them and filled the sky with circular stair-steps of black clouds.

Feeling the storm's coming violence, boy and dog began running home. Within moments the storm was upon them. Torrential, rushing brooms of wind and rain soon swept away my father's yells and Warlock's mournful howls. White pebbles of hail began striking and stinging them as they ran through the open field.

WHAT HAPPENED next wasn't the clearest detail in my father's memory of the storm. Like an old movie that suddenly skips whole scenes ahead, my father recalled only a momentary, startling absence of sound and then a thick, soppy sense of sluggardly movement, as though he were swimming in a lake of honey. In fact, his memory was not so far from the truth. When found by his father after the storm, my lightning-struck, almost-unconscious father—his eyes closed, his clothing smoking and torn—was crawling like a dazed, scorched mole through the wet field's deep, sloppy mud.

RECOVERING IN HIS BED, my father learned the reason he was alive was because the lightning bolt that hit him had first struck and killed Warlock. The electrical strike had been drawn to the metal talisman on the big Lab's collar. The dog's electrocuted body had already been buried in the field where he died. The only remaining bits of my father's lifelong friend were a blackened stub of Warlock's burnt tail and the smelted, silver tag. Crying, holding the tag close, my father began to understand the universe's darker, malevolent forces. This understanding was greatly increased when he saw that the lightning had not entirely destroyed the medal's motto, but had instead, with malicious glee, erased and folded the letters into a grotesque, mocking epitaph: WARLOCK, DEAP FRIED HE IS. Reading this, my father trembled with the pure, clean rage of a six-year-old. Shaking his clenched child-fist at whatever powers had conspired to do this, he suddenly understood that eternal battle lines had indeed been drawn. From that day forward, he kept the metal nugget with him always, only parting with it when, as a reminder of love and evil, he gave it to me before he died. I still carry it in the small leather bag I wear around my neck.

ONE MONTH after the storm, hoping to draw my father out from the sepulchral mood that continued to cloak him like tightly wrapped black sheets, his father took him for a ride in the country. The direction of their ride was random, an unplanned afternoon drive along rural dirt roads. Random drive or not, however, they eventually came across something as predictably sure to happen as the seventeen-year locust swarm. Approaching an isolated farm, they saw a large plywood sign propped against the home's roadside mailbox. Freshly painted in tall, barn-red letters, the sign was a simple, pithy one: PUPPIES. FREE.

Despite his determined loyalty to Warlock's memory, six years old *is* six years old, and a pen of scrabbling, yelping puppies makes a heady music that quickly courses through a child's bloodstream and into his heart. For my father, it soon became only a question of choice, the most important choice of all: which pup to pick?

Looking to his father for help, my father then learned—and buried as absolute truth deep inside his brain—one of the tidbits of arcane knowledge that families pass down through generations. Looking into my father's eyes, his father conveyed to him a gem of mysterious wisdom: "Choose the pup with the darkest roof-color in its mouth," he said. "The darker the better. That'll be the pick of the litter, son. That'll be the keeper."

With those words— with that single lesson so reverently imparted to his excited, believing son—my father's father, as surely as if he'd known what he was doing, determined that I was not to be the Gypsies' king.

FACED WITH THE SURPRISE of twin sons when only one baby had been expected, my father needed to choose which child to give the Gypsies and which to keep. Perhaps not even understanding or remembering why he did it, he opened Garrett's mouth and peered inside, delicately pulling back the tiny lips to more clearly look at the toothless gums and nub of tongue.

Next, he did the same to me.

Then, without hesitation, full of the same confidence he'd felt while picking out a new puppy all those years ago, my father handed Garrett James to the Gypsies to be their king. And kept me as his son.

"So you see, Blue," my father later explained, "it wasn't because your brother was first-born. I gave him to the Gypsies because *you* were the pick of the litter. You were the one I had to keep."

AFTER PROVIDING a home for two new souls and then crocheting a caul to warm my face, it seemed that Cally's body was not quite done. Her restless creative nature next picked up a paintbrush and, with an artist's deliberate stroke, began coloring my palate—the roof of my mouth resembles a smudge of indigo ink, the shadowy hue of a blue-black night. ("This one, Dad," my father had said so many years ago, absolutely sure of his pick as he clutched the squirming puppy in his arms. The dog's pink tongue was bright against the black cave of its mouth. "I'll take this one.")

On the day of my birth, as the Gypsies held my twin brother above their heads and danced to the chanted music of his new Gypsy name, "*Alassadir. Alassadir. Alassadir,*" my father watched me in my crib and listened to me gurgle as Ebeneezer purred and nuzzled my head. "This one," my father whispered, "I'll take this one." And in rhythm with the Gypsies' song for my brother, my father also softly sang, singing my new name to the world: "*Blue. Blue. Blue.*"

BLUE. THE CIRCLE

THERE IS ANOTHER Stonehenge. Another tall staggered Circle of weathered, white limestone pillars. A place pregnant with magic—ancient, holy, hidden, secret. A ring of forgotten Stones standing in the soft, gray blanket of mists that cover the wooded hills of Brown County, Indiana.

It is a quiet, sacred place. Full of life and warm comfort.

Like the green eyes of my Elissa.

WHEN I FIRST FOUND the Stone Circle, I softly walked around its circumference. With the reverence of a new father feeling his infant's first pink breaths, I moved from Stone to Stone. As I walked, I counted—eleven tall straight Stones and one Stone tilting inward, steeply leaning toward the Circle's center.

On the day of discovery, I stayed for hours, murmuring thankful prayers, caught somewhere between joy and fearful awe. I wanted to touch the Circle, to rejoice at its finding. Yet was afraid to move too close, was certain I'd be found out, that the accident of its revelation would be corrected and the Circle dissolved. Fearfully, I reached my hands out to the Stones. I reached slowly, carefully—

—pressed my open palms against one of the limestone pillars. Felt its surface, electric and cool—

And the Circle remained.

THE TWELVE STONES stand on the hill called Jonah's Belly.

Like old friends, their fellowship is hushed and filled with long pauses. They are motionless in most of the sweeping weather that touches them. Are unmoved when quick, snapping winds fill the air with leaves that swirl like drunken birds. And they stand firm in the sudden drenching storms that groove and cut the ground with sluicing, downhill rushes of water.

The Stones: Strong. Mute. Stationary. Except—

In a certain rain…the fine, beaded rain that glistens gently on the air before slipping down to earth…in this rain…magic.

In this rain, the Stones dance.

The dance is a slow minuet of slight degrees, an almost imperceptible pattern of rhythm and time. The Stones sway as if nudged by whispers, leaning from side to side as though brushed and moved by the touch of unseen wings.

And there are songs…

…though sung by Stones, the songs come from deep within some large and crimson heart, pulsing with life and love. The songs are a low hum of rising and falling notes, like the dozing, winter breath-chant of a hibernating family of massive bears. The songs are filled with memories of long-ago times—times when the warrior, Always One More Arrow, knelt within the Circle, suckled on its magic, and blessed it as *aalhsoohkaani waal*…consecrated ground.

The songs make me tremble when I hear them. I listen quietly, often crying—my tears mixing with the fine rain, then falling to the earth. As I listen, I sway slowly from side to side, dancing with the pillars.

THE STONE CIRCLE soon claims me. It catches me in its full, swelling tide of magic, rushing over, around, and through me. I feel it everywhere. Like an ocean, beneath its surface there's an undertow, a force drawing me through the depths, pulling me to its center, sweeping me along. In the curl of this rolling wave, it seems that all my paths begin leading back to the pillars. No matter in which direction my trips begin, I'm somehow always returned to the Circle's heart. The Stones capture and bring me to them. As surely as a long-forgotten, dried flower will fall from a dusty, opened book of poems, I begin falling just as surely toward the Stones.

AT HOME in our cabin, I decide to test the Circle, to learn the strength of its magnetic draw.

As an experiment, I ask Elissa to watch me from a chair. I explain, somewhat sheepishly—my magic is usually more subtle than this, more unassuming—that I'm practicing *something new*. She laughs and sips her lemonade, the ice ringing like tiny church bells against the clear glass as she tips it back to drink, then holds it out to me in questioning salute.

"Should I put on my sequined tutu and be your assistant?" she asks, grinning as she stands and kisses me. With her lips pressed gently against mine, she pops an ice cube, half-melted from her warmth and tasting of sweet lemons, into my mouth.

I return her kiss—now thinking thoughts of things other than the Circle, wondering about the possibilities of a sequined tutu—when suddenly she sits back down, saying, "No, your magic is important. Practice. I'll be here when you're done, Blue. Just hurry back." She looks at me and nods, understanding how much I love her for her words. Understanding how important her belief is to me.

"Back soon," I answer, then turn and walk into one of the cabin's long, narrow closets. And almost immediately, there inside the closet, the Circle asserts itself: the path is made. Like the enchanted wardrobe of *The Chronicles of Narnia*, once I've edged past a tangle of clothes hangers and no-longer-worn business suits, I find myself, only seconds later, standing on Jonah's Belly, staring at the Stones. And in that moment's quiet pause, I feel frightened and happy and anxious, because now I know for certain: *something is going to happen. Something soon—*

Why else this brandishing of power?

A FEW NIGHTS LATER I fall asleep, tangled with Elissa in a warm naked knot on our sheets. I dream strange bits of dreams, of shadows moving, of a bearded Indian, of old men screaming, their limbs bloody and bound—

—then I awaken at the Stones, brought to them as though each dream had been an opaque, climbing wisp of stairs leading me to the Circle.

I lie there, feeling disoriented. Unsettled. Not because I'm at the Circle, but because of something else. Something unfamiliar. After a moment, I realize what it is: I have never been inside the Circle before; I have never looked outward at the hill from the center of the Stones. Until now, I have always stayed outside the ring like an anxious suitor, arms full of candy and roses, waiting to be invited off of the front porch and into the sitting room.

The night around me is warm, warmer even than the moments before when Elissa and I lay curled together like two sun-freckles. Even in the Circle, the faint, loving odors of our bed are still around me like an ethereal, scented flesh.

The grass I've woken on is soft against my back. Above me, a loose web of clouds drifts free of the moon, and a sudden spill of moonlight pours down the hill, painting my body the same gleaming color as the white limestone monoliths that surround me. I remain perfectly still, a single glowing spoke within a wheel of tall Stones.

That's when I hear it—

The sound that knifes through me.

The sound that I know has called me here.

HOURS LATER, skin scratched and burrs sticking to the fine hairs of my legs, I walk back home from the Circle. The night is bright. For a moment, when I first see the cabin through the woods, the reflections of the moon in the two large front windows looks like a pair of white, pupil-less eyes emptily regarding my approach.

I step inside, try to slip quietly back into bed, but don't quite make it as Elissa rolls close and whispers, "Practicing again?" then wraps her arms around me, pulling me into the sweeping nutmeg and cinnamon wash of her skin.

"Poetry," I answer, carried away in her river.

EARLY THE NEXT MORNING. I'm awake. Feeling guilty. Sitting alone at the window. Watching the night draw slowly back, revealing an inching conjuring of dawn, all pink and frothy gold. Coffee steam keeping me company, curling out of the mug and around my fingers.

Sitting. Watching. And wondering. *Should I have told her?*

If there is one thing—only one single thing—that I could change about the time I've shared with the woman-treasure sleeping in my bed, it would be none of our moments or minutes or memories. Not a single one of our differing ideas. Not even the arguments that she shouts at me on occasion. None of it. Not one second. Except—

Except for the "almost family."

The "almost family" that we almost were, with the son we almost had. A boy who would now be ten months old. A boy who'd be sitting in his highchair, burbling in sweet child-talk about the wonders of everything new. A son who'd play with the still-untouched roomful of boxed and packed-away toys—with the tricycle, the soccer ball, and the three huge stuffed animals in the corner *(a massive lion, tiger, and bear from the LAND OF OZ COLLECTOR SET, ALL WITH NIGHTGLOW EYES!).* A boy who would have opened all of the child-riches still wrapped and waiting in their untorn labels of Fisher-Price, Mattel, and Johnson & Johnson.

A son who almost was. Part of the family we almost were. A family filled full of dreamed futures for the torn, dented body of our boy. Born at only eight months. Born with no fire, with no light or saving magic. And with no chance. Our baby boy—punched out from Elissa's body in a single crushing moment. Dead—

For a reason she thinks was an accident.

For a reason I know was not.

Through the window, the sun is now flooding the ground, its light quickly rising.

I give thank-yous to heaven for each day that passes, for each day that gives us the balm of more time and more healing, for each day when the hurt is further soothed. And although full forgetting is not what I want, I am grateful that the *almost family* is finally *almost gone*. I truly believe that Elissa is now almost able to not think about it when we hear the back-and-forth creak of a child's swing set. Or eat cotton candy. Or bake snickerdoodle cookies.

She can almost not think about it at all—

Almost.

So now I'm awake. Feeling guilty. And wondering: Should I have told her? Because even though I told her about last night's adventure—about my dreams, about waking at the Circle, about my naked walk back home—I told her nothing about what I heard only seconds after I'd awoken within the Stone Circle. And said nothing about what I still heard minutes later, after assuring myself that I was awake. Because if I told her what I'd heard, then how could she not hurt again? How could she not wonder, and dwell on, and then how could she not go searching after—

The child I heard crying.

The child I looked for and could not find.

The child crying on Jonah's Belly.

THE WARRIOR, ALWAYS ONE MORE ARROW

NIGHT.

He sits in the darkness, wearing only moonlight. The moon cloaks his shoulders, draping his back in a fine silver cape. He hears the songs sung by the Circle of Stones. Hears their warnings, senses their sorrow. And he knows what approaches. Knows, but cannot see. Not yet, not clearly. Still, though, he knows. *Time again,* he thinks. *The path is built. The way is open.*

A familiar, twisting spasm runs along his hunched back. At the first wrenching pain, he sucks a quick, hissing stream of air through his ivory-yellow teeth. He grunts. Shakes his head. Feels his eyes tearing. He waits for the clenching pain to recede. Thinks, *Try not to squeal. Try not to moan.*

When the hurt is finally gone, he thinks again of the songs and the Stones. *Still here,* he thinks. He looks down at his wrinkled hands. Again shakes his head and grins, thinking the same thoughts about himself. *Still here—still here watching, still here waiting. Still here, circling in the darkness.*

He is surprised to be "still here." Surprised and grateful. But he feels old inside this skin. Old and weak. Sitting quietly, looking at the moon, he absent-mindedly scratches his shoulder, his black fingernails scraping across a fresh rash of small, itching bites. *Wonderful,* he thinks, scratching the tiny bumps. *More fleas.*

HE SETTLES INTO HIMSELF. Closes his eyes. Clears his mind. Calms his thoughts. Then looks outward, sending his sight…away. Sending it down the streets. Over the hills. Searching. Searching until he sees the Stones. He sees them moving, dancing in the rain that's now falling on the hill, falling as lightly as a brown sparrow's tears.

He sees that the man is there again. The man now so often at the Circle. The man who has become a part of things. *Yes*, he thinks. *Time once again. Soon. The same as it always was. The same as it always will be: Blood builds the path. Blood opens the way.*

He watches the man. Listens to the Circle's song. Feels the blood stirring within him. He stretches his hands toward the stars that look like uncounted glittering minnows against the blackest river-clay of night. He leans his head back and starts singing with the Circle, singing in a growl from deep within his throat. Singing a song of older times, of times when the hill was *Ninkya*—Mother— to all those living on and within her. Of the time when he wore his first skin, the warrior Always One More Arrow. A time when he waited at the Stones, watching and circling—a time when blood built the path, when blood opened the way.

He sings, then grows quiet and pauses. Listens again to the pillars' song, listens and hears…something else. Something not heard before—

A child. Crying.

He tugs his thick beard. Grunts in puzzlement. Listens to the fragile, broken crying. Then he searches for the child, looking, but not finding. Searching until he is nestled and drowsing in the soft patchwork of sleep that Mother Moon throws down upon him.

A child, he thinks from almost-dreams.

A child on Jonah's Belly.

STACY B. THE MATCHMAN

*F*LAT TIRE, she thought, *the front right—*

—and screamed, "Shit! Shit! Shit!" as the car pulled fast to the side, straight at the trees, straight at the BIG ROLL DOWN THE HILL, and she screamed again and yanked the wheel left, turning it too hard, turning it too far, wanting to get away from the sharp drop-off that fell downhill forever into the trees and vines and darkness, and the car jerked and swung hard left—

—back to the road, away from the ravine, but now the rear tires' traction broke free and the car's back end started sliding across the loose road gravel, back toward the drop-off, back to the BIG ROLL DOWN. *And oh, Stacy B.,* she thought, *don't fall down there, don't disappear,* and she—

—hard-steered right, pumping the brake again and again and again and, god, why was she driving so fast she'd been so stupid and the car was shuddering and should she keep pumping the brakes or keep steady pressure on and now the car fishtailed, swerving fast across the road, the back-left tire swinging over the road's edge, the loose edge-rocks under the tire starting to crumble and give way, and she could hear the spinning tires firing machine-gun gravel sprays under the car, the tiny thrown stones ringing *tat-tat-tat-tat* against the metal, and she sensed gravity shifting and felt the car's rear end slanting down, slipping through the collapsing edge as the front end started tilting up, lifting off the road—

—and she stopped pushing on the brakes and instead quick-gunned the engine, praying, *please baby please baby please*, but the car's rear kept slanting down, kept falling toward the deep dark place below, then she—

—pulled the wheel left, into the spin, pulling hard but not too hard, pulling just enough, and she lightly tapped the brake twice, then let her foot slip to the gas and pressed softly, pressed gently, pressed oh-so-hardly at all. Wanting traction. Wanting control. Wanting to GO FORWARD NOW. And she prayed out loud, praying, "Please don't spin, please don't spin, please don't spin," but she felt the tires spinning and spinning, but then felt them—

Gripping.

Then pulling.

Then edging. Forward. Slowly.

Onto the road.

And she started braking.

And the car started slowing.

And then—

It stopped.

Her hand slow-floated down to the key. Turned off the car. And suddenly—

Nothing.

No spinning wheels. No shooting stones.

Nothing.

She looked around. Saw hardly any hint at all that she'd just about shuffled off this mortal coil. Well, not so much "shuffled" as rolled end-over-end ("ass-over-eyeballs" is what her dad would have said) all the way down hill-and-damn-dale. *I mean, really,* she thought, letting out the explosion of breath she'd been holding, *just look at all of the green nothing down there...*

Still gripping the steering wheel—adrenaline still filling her veins, little shake and tremor aftershocks still rippling through her—she watched a floating swirl of gravel dust settle on the ground. *So much for the morning's quest for peace and quiet,* she thought. *So much for inner reflection and soothing thoughts.*

Screw all that. She didn't need those anymore—

—what she needed now was to get a tire changed. *And that was truly going to make for an interesting rest of the morning, wasn't it, Stacy B?* Because even though she *could* change a tire, she wouldn't—not here. Not on top this steep dangerous ridge of dirt and gravel road. Because—besides knowing how to change a tire—she also knew how to call KarKlub. *"Car troubles? Klub 'em with KarKlub!"*—it was printed right there on the "dues-fully-paid" membership card in her purse. The same purse holding her cell phone. All of which meant, really, that there was just one remaining problem—

The scenery.

The scenery was a big problem—

—all of the incredible damn beauty around her: the pretty hills, the dense growth of trees, the deep valleys. But mostly the hills. It was the pretty hills that were truly screwing her, all of them so green and rolling, sharply up and quickly down, as far as she could see. Hills with views that were disturbed in no way at all—not by billboards, not by buildings, not by houses, and—*this one's the important one, Stacy B., she thought,* looking at her phone's blank display, *this is the one that really makes it really rich*—not by cell towers. She did the quick math in her head—

No towers, which meant—

No signal, which meant—

No service, which meant—

No calls.

Not a single antenna line showed on her phone. *Officially fucked, and officially stucked,* she said to herself. *But really and truly especially stucked.* Stranded on top of an unknown hill, on a road with no other cars, with a phone that didn't phone, she was ab-so-certainly royally and officially—

Wait!—

Something? A phone-flicker? A shadow-line? Maybe a signal?

—then gone.

She waited. Whispered, "Come on, come on, come on, come on—"

—nothing.

Then there again. And still there, still there, still—

—then flicker and fade.

Back again.

—staying? Long enough? Maybe?

Yes!

"Now you're working with me!" she shouted. "Now we can deal!"

She wouldn't have much talk-time, not with the flakey in-and-out signal. Unfortunately, the sketchy reception took KarKlub off her list of possible calls (*"Car Problems? Klub 'em with KarKlub. May I have your membership number, please? Hello? Hello?"*) Even if she called back every time the connection broke, a different KarKlub person would answer each time, making her need to start her explanation all over again. Besides, what was she going to tell somebody at "1-800-Probably-A-Foreign-Call-Center," anyway? That she didn't know where she was? That she didn't have a damn clue? Or, even better, that getting turned around and lost had actually been a part of her plan all along...a plan of trying to relax, of getting away for the day. And the plan had been working perfectly fine, thank you so very much—

Until now.

She nodded, one hand holding the phone, the other arm propped on the steering wheel, her fingers lightly drumming against her cheek. She knew the answer. Knew it was the only answer. But she needed a different one. Wanted a different one. Because, after all, she was smart. And capable. And, damn it, she should have a different answer. An answer that wouldn't worry him. Because he already worried too much. Had already loved and worried about her every day for twenty-six years.

And now she could think of only one good answer: Worry him some more.

She needed to call Dad. Loving, sad Dad. Loving for the entire twenty-six years of her entire life. Sad for the same twenty-six years since losing her mom. Dad: watchful and protective every single moment since his long-ago attendance at the worst-of-all-days' hospital version of Let's Make A Deal. (*"Ok, Frank, we've got your wife behind curtain number one! And, Frank, as a special surprise: WE'RE KEEPING HER FOREVER! But, Frank, in appreciation for playing our game, you've won this brand-spanking-new BABY GIRL to raise alone! With no help or support at all! All prizes are final! Thank you so much for playing our game."*)

Call Dad. Worry him one more time.

It was Saturday morning. He'd be at his office. No matter how many times the connection broke, she could keep calling until he had the whole message. She'd tell him that she was on a high ridge "—somewhere north of Plum Creek Road, but with no idea how far or close I am to anywhere I'd recognize." Then she'd ask him to call the sheriff's department, tell them to send a car out to look for her, that she'd honk every few minutes to help them find her. And once she'd finally been found, once she knew where the hell she really was, *then* she'd work out the details with KarKlub—

And she'd tell him not to worry. Would tell him she'd be back in the city tonight. That she'd come over and they'd get some dinner together. Her treat. Make him promise to let her pay—

It was a good plan.

She dialed. Discovered that her prediction was right: he was working at the office. Was already talking on the phone, the busy signal loud, strong and clear in her ear. She hit *End*, quickly hit *Send* again.

Still busy.

She spent the next twenty-five minutes doing the same back-and-forth finger move between the two buttons. Then had an idea: She hit *Auto Redial* and watched to see what happened—now remembering that as long as the connection held *(Please oh please, oh please)* the phone would keep dialing until the call finally went through. And once her dad's phone rang, her phone would ring, too, letting her know that she'd finally—really and truly—reached out and touched someone (*Hallelujah!*).

Then she saw it.

A black car—

—she looked up from her phone, looked in the rearview mirror, then swung around and stared, startled by its all-of-a-sudden appearance. Parked behind her. Just sitting there. Twenty feet away. No cloud of "just-stopped" dust falling to the ground around it. The air now settled and still. *Meaning the car had been there...how long? Watching me? What the hell, Stacy B?* she thought. *What the holy hell?*

THE BLACK CAR'S hood was painted with flame-blue lettering, the blue letters tipped with yellow and orange, reading *NOW YOU'RE COOKING WITH GAS!* The rising sun angled through the black car's rear window. *The sun rises in the east,* she thought, looking at the light. *Meaning: I'm pointing west. I can tell that to Dad, can tell him I'm on a road heading east to west.* The sunlight backlit the inside of the black car, revealing the silhouette of a dark man-shape behind the wheel, a shape that now moved, its shoulder dipping toward the door.

The car's door opened quietly. In fact, she noticed, everything was quiet. *Where are the sounds?* she wondered. *I'm in the woods. There are supposed to be sounds.* But there weren't any sounds. The silence was full, complete, pressing—

—then was suddenly shattered by a vibrating, growling roar. A deep, primal reverberation rising from somewhere far down the steep ravine. *From where I almost went over the edge. From where I almost rolled ass-over-eyeballs.*

She listened to the sound. Thought, *Roaring? A lion? Here?* Then thought only about the driver getting out of the black car and walking slowly toward her. A tall, narrow man. His suit blacker than the car. A torch of bright red hair. Despite the distance, she could see the lit-blue circles of his eyes. *He looks like a match,* she thought. *Like a matchman.*

Then, and even as she saw it, she knew she couldn't have seen it—

He flickered.

Shimmer-faded out, then shimmered back again—

—but I couldn't have seen that. Not really. Not truly. And, hey, Stacy B., she told herself, *let's be honest and tell the viewing audience what else you don't think you really saw: that the Matchman didn't just flicker and fade. No, he flickered and became... something else. Something quivering and bunched and large. Something you saw for just a dust-speck of time before he was back again, before he was solidly here. Here and walking toward you.*

No, she thought. *I couldn't have seen that. I didn't see that. Not really. Not truly.*

HE STOPPED beside her door. Bent his knees and sank down till he was looking at her, his elbows resting on the open window. "Looks fun," he said.

"Not really," she whispered. "Not much"—and didn't know when she'd started crying (was still thinking, *I didn't see that. Not really. Not truly*), but could feel the hot tears on her cheeks.

"Oh, now, kitten," he said. "It's not so bad. Just a flat tire. We'll get it fixed up."

"Really?" she said, feeling a small hope. And even though her voice was still quivering (but only a little, only the smallest bit), and even though she still felt tear tracks on her cheeks (but they were already drying, were hardly there at all), she started feeling better. Started understanding what had happened—that she'd seen a trick of dust and light, a blurry blink of nerves and emotion.

"Really and truly," he said. "Stay in the car and pop the trunk. I've got it from there."

"Sure?"

"Sure."

She pushed the button. Heard the trunk open. The trunk lid lifted higher than the back window, blocking the sunlight behind the car and darkening the inside, leaving her in a twilight murk. He tapped his hands against the doorframe. Stood straight and turned. Said over his shoulder, "Don't worry. You're gonna be cooking with gas."

She watched him in the side mirror. Saw him disappear behind the car. Couldn't see him, but heard the muffled shuffle-slide of things shifting inside the trunk. The car rocked as things were pushed and pulled. Then she saw him in the side mirror again, dropping the spare tire onto the road. The tire bounced twice and fell over, smacking into the gravel and raising a powdery smoke-ring halo up from the road. He came back to her window holding the car jack and tire iron in his hands.

"Just sit still," he said. "Don't—" and then he paused, interrupted by another rumbling roar. Louder this time. From somewhere closer in the green vines and branches. And then—

He shimmered again—

—*it happened so fast that if she didn't want to, she didn't have to believe what she saw. Didn't have to believe all of the teeth, all the bulk of raw, folded, yellow skin and scales. Didn't have to believe any of it because ever-so-quick it was him again. It was only the Matchman.*

He stood still. Eyes half-closed, looking toward the sound. Breathing quickly in and out through his nose.

He's sniffing, she thought. *Sniffing the air, searching for the scent.*

After a moment he looked back at her. "That's some kitty-kitty out there. That's some puss-puss," and he made a kissing noise in the air, like inviting a cat to play. He listened again. She listened, too, hoping to hear a sound, any sound at all. But heard nothing. Only quiet.

He shook his head. Looked at her. "Well," he said. Tilted his head and grinned. Said it again. "Well."

"Please," she said, not knowing exactly why (and heard her voice quiver again, felt her tears falling again). "Please."

He walked to the front of the car and squatted down near the flat tire, where she could only see the top of his red hair. He raised his head high enough to see her and saw she was looking straight at him. He smiled. Stared back at her over the expanse of the hood. Made the same *kiss-kiss* noise he'd made before, only this time made it to her. Then ducked his head down again.

She felt the clanking bump of metal on metal as he put the jack under the car, then felt the first lurching sensation as the car began lifting, and she heard the *click-click-click* of the jack notching up and felt the car keep rising. Rising high enough now that she couldn't see his hair.

Rising higher.

Still higher.

Too high.

She looked out the window. Saw a tilting view of the ravine. Looking down, she thought, *The woods are lovely, dark and deep.* And as the car lifted even higher, she knew that she was done. Knew she was done because, looking over the hood, she knew that she saw (really, truly) a leathery hand with black claws gripping the car. Pushing the car up. Pushing it over—

—and she knew she was still crying, but also knew she wasn't screaming. Knew she wasn't making any sound at all. Instead, she just stared down, down to where she'd soon fall. She watched, silence surrounding her. Hearing only the *click-click-click* of the jack still rising. Hearing only the ringing phone—

Ringing phone?—

—on the tilting seat beside her, the phone had started ringing. She reached for it, thinking, *Daddy?* and pushed *Call.* Then heard a distant voice. "Stacia? Stacy?" and she started screaming then, screaming "Daddy! Daddy! Daddy!" into the phone, because now the car was tipping. Tipping. And rolling. And falling. And now up was down, and down was up as she tumbled over and over, falling into the deep, green and black place far below.

FINALLY STOPPING.

Still alive.

Dazed. Making small, hurt noises. Seeing through one open eye. Her left arm not working. Her right arm raking open as she dragged it across the jagged jigsaw of window glass in her lap.

Her hand found the door handle. Pulled at it weakly.

Then she heard it. A snuffling, slobbering noise. Calling thickly to her in a muffled, grunting croak. Calling, "Here, kitty-kitty. Here, kitty-kitty." Walking heavily through the brush. Getting closer. And closer.

She heard it stop beside her. But couldn't lift her head. Couldn't see what was standing there. Could only feel blood dripping off of her chin, falling onto the glass in her lap. Then she sensed the shadow of something reaching in. Felt the touch of scaly hide on her face. Heard "Hey, puss-puss." Then felt the first curved claw. Felt it pushing slowly into her open eye. Then the eye burst open and spilled like an eggcup of warm dew across the glass and blood already in her lap—

—and she felt the claw reach deeper. Felt it snag behind the cartilage of her nose and pull, dragging her out of the car. Then felt a second claw. Slicing through her belly. Dragging along her spine. Felt it snag on her backbone and lift.

At the very last—from somewhere very, very far away—she heard the chuckling *kiss-kiss* sound again. And heard the thing's noisy savoring of smells and meat as its snout pushed through the open bowl of her ruined flesh. And then she was gone. Really and truly. Gone so far away that she didn't feel the final pull and tug of its teeth. Gone so far away that she didn't feel the chewing.

ELISSA. GORDY. THE GLAMMERYS. GRENDEL

*L*OOKING AT *Gordy, Elissa wonders again at the feeling she has when he's around, the feeling that she's safe, that anything bad would have to go through him first to get at her or Blue. Maybe feeling that way because Gordy already saved them once before, at the accident. Or maybe because he's one of the few people that Blue loves, a part of Blue's small family of people and beasts. She knows that Gordy loves her and Blue, too. That they're also a part of his small family...maybe even all of it. The thing is, with Gordy it's simple—no matter what, he'll be there for them, always, and then some after that. With him, it's not complicated: Once he's in, he's in all the way.*

SHE SITS at the top of the porch steps, watching him sip his lemonade. Gordy's on the red porch swing, looking out over the cabin's railing. He stares into the woods, seeming to calculate the plusses and minuses of adding to what he's already said. He takes another drink, using the time to do a few more mental calculations before he looks at her.

"Blue's told you about the Glammerys, right?"

"A little, I guess. Some." She stands. Walks over. Sits beside him on the swing. "Not much, though. Not really."

"As careful as he is," he says, "seems he would have told you more than just a little."

"Why? What do the Glammerys have to do with being careful?"

Gordy sets the tall glass on his knee, holds it there with his fingers cupped over the top. Legs of cold water run down the outside of the glass and soak into his uniform, forming the shape of sunrays on his leg. His feet push against the porch floor, just enough to keep the swing moving slowly back and forth. "Some things are just good to know," he says. "Doesn't mean anything bad will happen if you don't know. Just means you'll know how to act when you need to. Most of the time, it's good knowing what to expect from certain things. Like knowing that making noise in the woods will scare rattlesnakes away, but those same noises will tell the copperheads where to come looking for you."

"Gordy, I'm sorry, but you're losing me—I'm not following what you mean. Blue said the Glammerys were the reason you two became friends. That they were how you two got to know each other."

"True enough…they're how we all got together."

"You and Blue?"

"Blue. Me. Everybody—Creel Glammery, Simon Glammery, Sarah Murphy. Of course she's dead now, Sarah is."

Elissa watches him talk. Sees his mouth draw tighter when he says "Sarah." "Blue said you two got into it with the Glammerys when you were younger," she says. "I remember there was a girl, but didn't know her name—Sarah. He said that all he did was watch after the girl. That—whatever happened—you handled the Glammerys."

Gordy looks at her. She senses his amusement. "That's what he said? That I took care of the Glammerys? That he took care of the girl?" He smiles. Says softly, "You know, sometimes our Blue decides to remember things a little differently than everybody else. That's not always a bad thing; hell, I usually like his version best of all. Sometimes though…sometimes I think the actual black-and-white of things is how they're supposed to be, that it's exactly the way they shouldn't be forgotten. Sometimes, I think…" The sentence drifts off as he looks somewhere else, somewhere she knows that she can't see.

AFTER THE ACCIDENT, Gordy was wherever he needed to be—doing whatever he needed to do to save her and Blue. First at the stream. Then the hospital. Then at the cabin. He took care of the two of them, helping them to heal. Making sure that nothing else happened. She knew that he'd been standing guard over them. That he'd been protecting his family.

Even now, though, as comfortable and safe as she feels around him, even knowing how much he loves them…sometimes he makes her feel anxious. Maybe even a little afraid. The fear seems easy enough to understand: Gordy is a big man who wears a badge and carries a big, loaded weapon to work. And he's good at his job—a job where he spends large amounts of time alone in the woods, trying to catch people who'd gladly shoot him. But those things aren't why she feels nervous. She's thought about it and thinks she's finally figured it out. It's because Gordy *is* a gun. He's quiet, efficient, strong. By design, he's easy to understand—like aiming and firing. He doesn't say much, but doesn't need to. And, like a gun, there's a certain responsibility which needs to be recognized when he's around, a recognition of certain facts—like the fact that once something starts, Gordy will be there until it's done, no matter how it turns out. He doesn't have a stop button. Once something bad starts to happen, it'll end like it ends—but it will definitely end… and he'll have the final word. He'll make sure of it.

She knows that he sees events as moments of simple flowing logic—from this to this to this, all the way to the end. It's probably why he's so good at his job. Probably why things work out okay for him when he's dealing with the kind of people he deals with—because they know, too. Because when they look at him and listen to him, they know that he'll go as far as he needs to go—that he's already made all his decisions about everything that might happen along the way. Maybe that's what makes them think twice about causing him any trouble—because maybe they aren't as certain about how far they're willing to go, because maybe they aren't so willing to take it to the end.

SHE CAN TELL, whatever questions he's been worrying about, he's found his answers. He quits pushing against the porch. Lets the swing come to a slow, floating stop. Says, "I'm going to tell you about the Glammerys, the way I remember it happening when Blue and I met." His gaze moves from the woods to her eyes. "Some of what I tell will sound different from the Blue you know. But not bad different, at least not to me. Not to you either, I'd guess."

He looks at her then. Waiting for her agreement. Waiting for her nod before he starts.

She nods.

"SOME OF THIS is *then*, and some of it's *now*. With the Glammerys, it's easy moving back and forth like that, getting everything mixed up. I don't think time really matters to the Glammerys, because not a lot ever changes in the shithole where they live.

"Years ago, one of the reasons I chose my job was so that I could keep seeing the same places I saw growing up—every gully, every ridge, every creek and trail. I grew up exploring it all, knowing even then how special it all was, how lucky I was to have it.

"There are so many places around here that are sun-drenched and warm. High-ridged places where the view opens up to miles of treetops and color. Where redbud and dogwood trees blossoms make you feel like you're walking in clouds made of flowers. Where the correct feeling is simple gratitude for being allowed to be part of it all—"

He paused a minute, then, "But the Glammerys don't live in one of those places.

"They live in a place that's just...wrong. A place that the sun almost absolutely misses. Hell, the little light that does shine in their hole, they hide from it, crouching inside their collection of dented trailers and broken school busses, turning themselves into a clan of withered, gray people. That's what they are, really—a shitty nest of nasty, gray people.

"You have to work to find it, but there's a rough gravel road that leads to a dirt rut, then the rut leads up a steep fold of narrow hills. Those hills form an enclosed wall around a damn hole that looks like a sharp sucker punch straight down into the earth. Funny thing, though, those hills aren't half as tall as the hole is deep. The hole just keeps twisting down and in, sinking deeper and deeper into the shadows, getting so dark it's hard to see the bottom....

"But I've seen it.

"Actually, finding the Glammerys isn't that hard. All you have to do is follow their trash trucks home. They run a trash route. For a little money, they'll haul away whatever crap you put out by the road. Truth is, even without the fee, they'll still take your trash. Then, feeling like it's Christmas morning, they beeline straight back home—because that's where they take every scrap of shit they collect. Right back home. Then, sitting there—parked at the top of their pit—they sort through all the trash that's piled high in their trucks, looking through it for 'the good stuff.' After they find all the things they want to keep—everything they think they might use one day—it all gets pitched down the hill, bouncing and rolling to the bottom. Everywhere else in this county, the hills are a picture of trees and rocks and water and vines. But not at the Glammerys'. Their hills are a tumbling dump of washers and dryers and broken furniture and machines, all of it rusting and rotting and broken.

"Almost nothing except the Glammerys lives in that hole. Whenever I've walked through, there's no sign of anything. Nothing. No squirrels, no deer, not even birds. The only other thing living there is a herd of skinny, mean goats walking up and down the hillsides, eating whatever they find growing around the trash piles.

"At the bottom of the hole, along with all the junk that's been pitched down that far, it looks like somebody rolled down eight busted-up trailers and two bent-up school buses. Some of the trailers and buses have plywood tunnels built between them, connecting together like the little plastic tubes that join gerbil cages together...and this is where the Glammerys live. This is their home-sweet-hole."

Gordy laughs. "It's a hell of a picture. Dirty goats and dirtier Glammerys. Two filthy herds living together. Each one watching the other. Everybody feeling hungry.

"Speaking of food, I don't know what the Glammerys eat. I've asked Bill Shepard about it. Bill manages the Hungry Sack store. He says they've never been in his store. Not even for beer or gum. I think they've got two ways of getting food. One way's poaching—which, of course, is the reason I enjoy my continuing association with their fine little family. I've had more than a few of those tussles with them—the kind of things where if I hadn't won, I'm sure I'd have ended up as little pieces of goat kibble.

"Their other food is fresh road kill, mostly the deer that people hit and call them about. I don't know how it started, but when a car hits a deer around here, the Glammerys usually get the call. And once that roadside dinner bell rings, they get there quick, usually Creel and Simon. From what I've heard, by the time someone makes the call and drives back to where the deer was, often as not it's already gone, with maybe only a drying puddle of blood and a few sticky wads of Creel's *calling cards* left around to step in...I'll get back to those 'calling cards' in a minute."

GORDY SETTLES himself more comfortably. "As small as Brown County is, it's hard to believe but there are three separate elementary schools, each one going to eighth grade. After that, everybody goes to the same high school. So even though Blue and I both grew up in Brown County, we didn't know each other till ninth grade. High school. Since the Glammerys went to my elementary school, Blue never had the early pleasure of their company that I'd already enjoyed every single school year.

"There are five Glammery children, all boys—each one a different point on the family pentagram. The oldest one is Creel. Then Simon. Both were in my class. That's how it was with them: two in my class, two in the next class—Renny and Harlan—then Merl, the last one. It wasn't that any of them were held back, or that any were smart enough to be moved ahead so that two Glammerys were in two classrooms at the same time—it's that there are always at least four women living in those trailers and buses at the bottom of the hole. Some have their own place. Some shack up with the boys. But no matter where the women stay—alone or with the boys—their daddy, Clete, visits whenever he wants. I don't know what kind of woman gets collected by a Glammery, but I do know that once they fall down the hole, not many climb back out. Still, there always seems to be a new face or two. And years ago, two of those women at a time were delivering Clete's demon children into the world."

GORDY SHAKES his head. "As dirty and feral as Clete is, his boys are worse. Creel and Simon are the meanest. With those two, every school day was a chance to hurt someone in a brand new way. One year they carried baling twine in their pockets. They used it to give out what they called 'class rings.' The way they'd do it, they'd catch someone in one of the usual places that people and animals get brought down by predators—around watering spots, or accidentally separated from the herd. One Glammery would hold the captured kid's arms while the other one looped a circle of twine around the kid's wrist. They'd pull the twine back and forth across the skin, like a little rope saw blade. When they were done, the wrist was a circle of blood and raw flesh.

"There are people around town today who still have a white circle of scar tissue on their arm. It's their own special class ring, a personal memento of their golden school days with Creel and Simon.

"I'D LIKE TO TELL YOU that I protected everyone from Creel and Simon back then, but it wouldn't be true. I just didn't pay much attention to the Glammerys or to anybody else. All I thought about was spending every moment I could in the woods. Even in grade school, I was big and I was strong, and not much of anything frightened me. I wasn't easy prey, and the Glammerys knew it. By spending so much time alone, I didn't make many friends, so, as long as they weren't involving themselves with me, I didn't involve myself with the Glammerys or what they were doing.

"Of course, that changed later.

"For as long as I knew them, one thing never changed. From the very first days, Creel always had a wad of chewing tobacco and bubble gum soaking in his mouth. A big brown mess that bulged in his cheek like a wad of dripping mulch. He didn't spit out the juice, so he must have swallowed most of it. Little brown-green streams of it were always leaking out of the corners of his mouth, running down onto his chin and T-shirts. He had a habit of pulling little pieces of the wad out of his mouth and sticking them to things—those were his *calling cards*. Call it what you want, either marking his territory or just one more dirty way to pollute the world around him, but you could track Creel's movements by following his trail of dripping, sticking, messy gobs. Whenever he stayed in any one place long enough, a perimeter of the shit would build up around him. At the end of every year, Creel's desk was a brown, barnacled mass of mouth-slime, tobacco, and bubble gum."

"IN THE FIRST YEAR of high-school, in the first week of ninth grade, I fell in love for the first time. With Sarah Murphy. Even knowing how silly it sounds, I swear I can still feel it. Maybe because she was the first girl I'd ever felt that way about. Or maybe because it was a crush I never had the chance to grow out of. Either way, we shared enough classes that I could sit and stare at her for most of each day. And she looked back just enough times—with just enough of a smile—for me to believe I might actually be able to talk to her. By the end of the week, all I could think of was her long, light red hair and brown eyes.

"Before saying one word to her, I was already planning all the places in the woods that I couldn't wait to show her. Places where I'd pick her a bouquet of wildflowers. Places where we'd watch a pack of coyotes playing in a field."

GORDY PAUSES a moment. Lingers in his memories. Shakes his head and sighs. "High school was the first real chance for all the county's kids to meet and feel each other out. By the time students from the three elementary schools and the students already at the high school were all blended together, there were a lot of new people to get to know. And a lot to figure out about where you belonged in the mix.

"While I was spending my first week trying to learn about Sarah, the rest of school was getting to know the Glammerys. It wasn't an easy introduction. Creel and Simon had learned a new trick over the summer, something they called Dots and Plugs.

"Working together, they'd pick a victim for their game. First they'd knock the person down. Then they'd give 'dots.' Simon would sit on the person's chest and hold them down. Creel would kneel near their head. He'd crouch there, winding coils of the kid's hair around his index fingers. Then he'd yell, 'Dots!' and rip up with his fingers. Almost-perfect circles of hair and scalp would tear off of the kid's head. After that, when the blood started flowing, Simon would yell, 'Plugs!' and Creel would pull a big, sticky dripping 'calling card' out of his mouth. He'd split the wet brown ball in half, then squash the two gobs down onto the kid's bleeding scalp. By then, Simon would already be punching the screaming kid, warning him not to tell anybody or else they'd make sure to 'get even.'

"So nobody told. Not a single person. Because no one knew—and no one wanted to know—what Creel and Simon might do if they decided to 'get even.' You'd think that someone in charge might have asked a few questions about all the students walking around with smears of greasy ointment on raw, red, bald spots. But no one asked anything.

"Instead, in the grotesque way of things, what happened was that the Glammerys attracted a group of fans. Some were like-minded wannabes. Others were just scared kids who'd rather side with a bully than risk his wrath. The fan-boy group began to surround the assaults, chanting, 'Dots! Dots! Dots!' and 'Plugs! Plugs! Plugs!' at the right points in the game.

"It was clear the Glammerys were quickly becoming the kings of their new castle, and they found it much to their liking—especially with all of the village peasants acting so properly terrified. For almost everyone, Creel and Simon were a new kind of fear that they had no idea how to handle. It seemed the Glammerys were going to keep playing their games for the rest of the year, maybe even all through high school. And it might have gone on that long... except for what happened on Monday of the third week."

GORDY SHIFTS his posture. Thinks for a minute. Takes another sip of tea. Continues his story. "Truthfully, by the end of the first week, I'd spent the whole weekend practicing: practicing where I planned to take Sarah, practicing what I'd say along the way. It's embarrassing, but I actually made a little map of the places we'd go. Even drew little pictures on the map of all the 'treasures' we'd see—pictures of deer, a fox den, pine trees, a stream full of broken geodes. (I remember drawing them so their crystal interiors reflected the sunshine like gold.) Silly things like that. I also went to an outcropping of dark flint I'd found, the kind the Indians used to make the best arrowheads. I picked out a piece the right size to make a perfect heart-shape. I chipped and shaped the stone, making sure it was exactly right. Then, being careful not to shatter the heart, I drilled a small hole in it and threaded a soft piece of leather lace through to make a necklace.

"The whole time that I was making the map and necklace, I was planning my conversation with her. Figuring out what I'd say first, then what she'd say back. Planning every word with all of the weird, wonderful focus of first love.

"IT TURNS OUT, I was wrong to think that I wasn't afraid of anything: I was terrified of talking to Sarah. During the second week, every time I saw her, the conversation I'd planned flew right out of my mind, leaving me sitting mute behind her in class. Or dipping my head and ignoring her when she walked by me in the hall. All I was able to do was wrap the heart necklace inside of the treasure map and push it into her hands as she stood by her locker one day. Then I stumbled away, not able to think of anything else after telling her, 'Here, this is yours.' I couldn't even stay to watch her open the paper. Was certain she'd start laughing at what she saw.

"The next day though, the last day of the second week, I didn't hear a single thing that anyone said in any of my classes. All I could do was stare at the most beautiful girl I'd ever seen. The girl wearing a necklace of heart-shaped stone. And when she smiled at me and mouthed, 'Hello!' I was so thrilled I could only smile back before looking away in uncertain joy—not knowing what to do next except promise myself that next Monday, on the first day of the third week, I would definitely talk to her then.

"MONDAY CAME. Sarah was wearing a dress covered with a pattern of strewn daisies. Her red hair looked like early morning sunlight on a straw-covered field. She was beautiful. But, once again I couldn't bring myself to talk with her. I told myself I'd wait till the day was over. That I'd talk to her then, right after school.

"Those hopeful thoughts filled my head through the rest of my classes. They're what I was thinking at the end of the day as I left the building, my head down until I heard the chorus of 'Dots! Dots! Dots!' coming from the side of the school. Drawn by the noise, I walked over and looked around the corner.

"I saw Simon on the ground. Creel was kneeling. Their fan club was circled around them. Through the spaces between the legs, I saw a quick jumble of confusing images. I remember thinking, *Digging up a garden?* That's what it looked like to me. Like they were digging up a flower garden. Their hands were moving deep in the plants, pulling and grabbing. Then I saw that Creel's hands were wrapped with red hair—hair the color of sunlight in the morning. And I saw that Simon was pawing at a field of daisies with one hand and holding someone's mouth closed with his other.

"Sarah.

"Simon was sitting on her, his knees holding down her arms while he grabbed at her. Over the chanting of 'Dot! Dots! Dots!' I heard myself yelling then. And felt my legs and arms moving, charging at the group. And knew I was going to kill them.

"As I covered the distance, I heard a new sound. Not my yelling. Not the crowd's. Something else—a sound not supposed to be heard where people are found. It was an animal's hunting scream—a bellowing, growling roar. The sound froze everything—hell, it even made the fan club shut up. In the middle of the sound was a furious movement—a body hurtling, low to the ground, launching through the crowd and into Simon, wrapping its arms around his neck and lifting him off Sarah with the strength of its spring. Then I saw that it wasn't a lion or a tiger.

"It was something worse for the Glammerys: it was Blue.

"He landed in a crouch on Simon. One foot on Simon's throat, the other on his chest. He was facing Creel. I saw his body tense and coil for the next attack. Creel was staring at Blue and—I actually saw this thought register on his face—somewhere in Creel's wrinkled brain he realized (hell, we all realized) that this wasn't like anything he'd ever seen before.

"Simon was lying stunned under Blue. He wasn't moving. Hadn't moved since his back slammed into the earth. Creel, though, he was still kneeling by Sarah's head. He tried to stand up, but he tripped and fell over backward. When he hit the ground, he drew his legs up to cover himself and threw his hands up to cover his neck. Blue roared again, still nothing in his voice or eyes that anyone recognized as human. Only this time, the sound broke the crowd's frozen fear and everyone scattered. Still crouched on Simon, Blue stood up and gave a light, crunching jump, up and down, making something crack and pushing a thick wheezing noise out of Simon's mouth. Blue looked over at me—his head tilted, like a cat asking a question. I looked at him, then down at Sarah. He nodded, somehow understanding, and I moved to Sarah's side. She was crying, and she folded into me. I brushed her red hair with my hands.

"Then Blue stepped off Simon and moved toward Creel. Creel started making his own strange, afraid kind of noises—some sort of *whmm, whmm, whmm* sound. He tried scooting away, shuffling backward on his shoulders. Blue crouched a bit, then there was a blur—I've never seen anyone move so fast—and suddenly Blue was sitting behind Creel, with Creel's head almost lifted into his lap. His legs were scissor-locked around Creel's neck, squeezing his breath out. Creel reached backward, his hands scrabbling, trying to grab Blue's face—which was when Blue, staring at the top of Creel's head like he'd found an unfamiliar bug, drew his arm back and then pistoned it forward, driving his fist into the crown of Creel's skull.

"Creel's mouth popped open. His greasy cud of tobacco and gum rolled onto his chest, and his head settled down into Blue's lap. His arms dropped down, too, and his body sagged a few inches deeper into the earth. That was when Blue coiled two thick wraps of Creel's hair around his fingers. Then he whispered, 'Dots.' And then he pulled.

"Then said 'Dots' again.

"Then pulled again.

"And again.

"And again."

Gordy stops for a minute. When he resumes, his voice is different. Thoughtful. "When he was done, when something normal—something human—put itself back in the driver's seat behind Blue's eyes, back in control of the little levers and switches in his head, he looked over at me.

"'Hey,' he said.

"'Hey,' I said back.

"THE GLAMMERYS didn't come back to school after that. Simon's ribs were broken. His throat was so hurt and swollen that he couldn't talk for most of a month—and for weeks after that, he could only make dry, squeaking sounds. Even now, all these years later, his voice still isn't right. And Creel's concussion kept him in the hospital for most of a week, his head swathed in a turban of bandages and black salve. The salve was supposed to help heal the hairless, seeping skullcap he was wearing. Some hair eventually grew back, but it came in unevenly, in unconnected tufts, like a bunch of matted, mossy humps.

"With Simon and Creel confined to a hospital, the other students began reporting the horrors of their first ten days at the Glammerys' hands. Sarah's parents had a number of private meetings with the school officials, then took her out of the school. Then they moved away. In the end, that's what happened to everything. It all just went away. The Glammerys went away. Sarah went away. Blue didn't get into trouble. And as simply as that, it was over. By the end of the next week, the daily routine of Brown

County High School became a wonderful pattern of uneventful and predictable tedium.

"FOR THE NEXT four years, on weekends and after school, Blue and I roamed these hills together. We both had the kinds of family stories that make a person hesitant about sharing them with anyone. Because of that, neither of us ever really had a close friend. But after that day, more than being friends, it seemed like we were brothers. Like we'd adopted each other."

Gordy stops talking. Elissa lets the quiet settle. They listen awhile to the creaking of the porch swing. Then he looks at her. "I grew up mostly alone, and mostly in the woods," he says. "Usually, if there's a fight, I'm the hunter, the one who's in pursuit. But truthfully, if I knew Blue was after me—if I knew he was hunting me...I believe it would scare me shitless."

SHE CAN TELL it is the end of his story. She feels the sadness it left in him, some sorrow still there from long ago. She touches his shoulder.

"He loves you, Gordy. I love you."

She sees him trying to shake off the mood, trying to leave it behind with his memories.

"I know," he says. Then asks, "You all right?"

She knows he's asking if it was okay that he'd told her the story. That he wondered if she had any questions. She does.

"Gordy, what happened to Sarah? You said she died?"

His eyes flick to the woods again. "Let me tell you about that some other time. I'll tell you...just later, okay?"

"Okay," she answers, knowing she's found what is making him sad. Reaching over, she intertwines the thumb and three fingers of her left hand into his right hand. Holding his hand, she knows that he can feel the small bump of bone where her pinky finger used to be.

They sip their drinks, drinking down to the bottom where the unmelted sugar makes the ice taste like candy. Their feet nudge the swing back and forth.

"The Glammerys," she says flatly.

"Yes—Glammerys."

"Why'd you tell me about them?"

"Because I don't know where Creel and Simon are. They're missing. And as happy as that makes me, it also means I need to find them. Blue knows they're missing, too. Knows I've been looking for them for a while now. I'm just letting him know—and now you— we still haven't found them. That we're still looking."

"Why, though? Why even look?"

"Curiosity. Caution. A little of both. I don't like not knowing where they are. It's not good for any of us. They've been missing almost a year, and the rest of the clan isn't very happy about their absence. As a group, the Glammerys don't have a lot of things to focus on, and that can be a problem. I just want to make sure they stay down in their little hole, no matter how worked up they get themselves. I'm not worried about it…but…still, I want to keep Blue aware of things. Like I said earlier, with the Glammerys 'then' and 'now' don't really have a lot of meaning. I don't trust them to think logically. Given the history between Creel and Simon and Blue and me—and as upset as the rest of the Glammerys are—there's a chance they'll start dwelling *now* on things from back *then*. See?"

Elissa is silent. Doesn't want to ask, but has to. "Gordy, you said they disappeared about a year ago?"

"Yeah. About then."

"But…a year ago," she says, voice faltering. "That's when… when…"

"I know," he answers. "I know." He puts his arm across her shoulder. Feels her shaking. Knows she is trying not to remember. He wonders if she realizes she's pulled her hand away and is now pressing it against her stomach, pressing where her son had once turned and moved and kicked and grown.

He reaches out. Gently takes back her hand. "Hey," he says.

She does a slow, quiet exhale. Pulling her thoughts back, gathering things together from her own sad place. Gives it another half-beat to be sure, then looks at him. "Hey," she says back.

They sit. Watching the woods.

THE BRAMBLE of tall grasses and curled vines beside the cabin begins moving, rustling as something large walks through them. Elissa and Gordy watch a low break in the green growth that offers the hint of a narrow, well-worn trail beyond.

"Grendel?" Gordy asks.

Elissa nods, staring at the spot she knows he'll come through. "And maybe a friend, too."

A large inverted triangle of a furred head pushes through the brush. The head's tufted ears are tall and pointed. A lush Fu-Manchu mustache of drooping fur and whiskers outlines the mouth. The cat's golden eyes stare at them. His lips are drawn back, revealing a sharp, curved clamp of feline incisors—and also a small black-and-white puppy limply dangling from between the lynx's teeth, blood dripping down the little dog's foreleg.

Gordy follows Elissa off the porch, mumbling as much to himself as to her. "You do know that *I am* a conservation officer. *I am* supposed to pay attention to certain things like the Endangered Species Act. I mean, *he is* a wild animal. And *I am*—*aw, shit!*" He kneels beside Elissa. Looks at the hurt pup in Grendel's jaws. "What's this one? A little Border collie?"

"Mostly. Maybe some Lab, too," Elissa answers, then murmurs soft words to Grendel.

The cat purrs soft sounds back.

Elissa eases her hands around the pup's ribs, then lifts the dog's weight from Grendel's mouth. Grendel opens his jaws wider, releasing his hold on the puppy, then settles back on his tawny and gray-speckled haunches, his long hind legs folding deftly beneath him. His golden eyes watch Elissa as she chants a stream of low, comforting tones, talking to Grendel and soothing the pup, saying, "I've got her, Gren. I've got her now, thank you, boy, that's a good pup, that's a good girl, you'll be okay, you're a good girl." She carefully lays the pup on the ground. "Hit by a car, you think?" she asks Gordy, her hands stroking the pup, lightly touching its limbs, gently manipulating its flesh, feeling for injuries. The pup's eyes flutter half-open. A little cry-whimper escapes its throat. "Broken shoulder," Elissa says. "A few ribs. A cut on its leg." She cups the dog's head. "The vet will tell us what's going on inside." As she speaks, Grendel inches forward on his massive furred paws, getting close enough to start licking the pup's wounded leg.

Gordy watches the big cat care for the dog. "How many does that make this month?"

Elissa thinks for a moment. "It's been more than usual. Two other dogs. A fawn. A raccoon. A big hawk. Two rabbits. He carried them all in like kittens. Except for the raccoon, they all made it. The bunnies are living in the hutches out back. The others went to the wildlife sanctuary. All of them were like this one, each one hurt in some way."

Gordy shakes his head. "I'm surprised he didn't eat the rabbits. Actually, I'm surprised he doesn't eat all your rabbits, not because he's a bad cat, but because that's what cats do. These big cats love the taste of rabbit."

"Gordy, he probably *does* eat rabbits. Probably lots of them. But he brings home the broken things. And he's never bothered the hutches. I think he just knows…everybody here is family."

The big cat nuzzles the pup with his moist buckwheat-brown nose.

Keeping one hand on the dog, Elissa reaches out her other hand, scratching Grendel between the ears and rubbing his broad forehead. He presses his head against her hand, his eyes starting to haze and close. "Sleeeeepy-eyes," Elissa murmurs. "You've got such sleeeeeepy-eyes." The cat's head starts sinking downward, dozy from the petting and the soft, hypnotic words. Then he stands up and shakes himself. He looks at Elissa and Gordy. Seems to say, *Okay, I'm trusting you two to handle this now*. Then turns and pads back into the woods. His small, black, tail stub, held straight up, disappears last.

Gordy and Elissa watch Grendel's silent exit.

"Un-damn-believable," says Gordy. "And that's the only reason I don't do anything about it. Who'd believe me?"

GORDY WALKS to the back of his truck and pulls out a soft carry-blanket, then comes back and squats beside Elissa. He helps her bundle the pup into the blanket's pillowy folds.

"Time to go," he tells the ball of black-and-white fur. "Time to meet the vet."

They both stand at the same time, lifting the blanket and its patient. As they walk toward the truck, the dog pushes its cut leg outward, free of the blanket. The injured leg brushes across Elissa's abdomen, smearing a wet crescent of blood onto her blouse, above where the shirt is covering her stomach's puckered, scarred flesh. Elissa looks down. Sees the smudged, dripping red streak across her belly and feels the ground shift as a dark weight of sudden memories pull at her heart. Her breath hitches in her throat. Gordy feels a brief, halting tilt in her step. The abrupt moment of unevenness causes the small dog pain. It cries out and starts biting at its own leg, attacking the hurt.

They stop walking.

Elissa closes her eyes. Catches her breath.

After the slightest pause, she leans close to the pup and looks into its frightened eyes. She begins murmuring. Begins hushing away its worry. Keeps talking till it's calmed.

The pup quiets.
Elissa's breath evens.
After a while, they continue their careful walk to the truck.

THE BLACK CARS

THERE ARE FIVE black cars. Blue and yellow-flame lettering is painted across their hoods and doors. It is early morning. The cars are beaded with drops of night-chill. The drops slide down the sleek metal like cold, black sweat.

The cars are parked close together in a grouping that looks like a wet black stain at the bottom of the deep hole where they're gathered. The stain is bordered by a half-moon of sagging mobile homes and rusted school buses that also rest on the hole's earthen floor. Morning's light has not yet fallen far enough into the hole to touch the black cars.

When the cars begin moving, the black stain unwinds, becoming a dark snaking ribbon. The slinking ribbon unfurls slowly, then begins crawling up the steep, rough-cut path that leads in and out of the hole. Halfway up, the black cars move through a pool of sunlight and their flame-lettered slogans shine. Each car bears a different phrase.

At the path's top, the cars creep over the hole's angled lip like iridescent beetles spilling up from a crack in the floor. They drive onto a dirt and gravel road that is more rut than road. The rut's serpentine curves lead down the outside wall of the hill. The cars begin descending, again becoming a black ribbon that now uncurls down the hillside. Near the bottom, the rut crosses other roads at infrequent, unmarked intersections. At the third of these crossroads, the black ribbon tears. Then tears again at the next crossroad. And again at the next. One by one, the cars separate, each one turning down a different road.

THE CARS TRAVEL in separate directions. Moving slowly. Deliberately. Coursing with the stealth of predators, careful not to disturb the underbrush, intent not to alert the prey. By mid-morning, each black car is in a different area, hunting on its own ground. They move quietly. Drifting. Prowling. Traveling back and forth. Pausing near private drives, slowing by secluded homes.

Watching.

Considering.

Four of the cars roam within borders that only they can sense, each one keeping to its own territory, moving to the edge and then back between those unseen boundaries. The boundaries are simple things, the four primary directions of a map: north, east, south, west…the needle points of a small, imagined compass. If laid over the map, the compass' center would float on a tall earthen pivot of a hill. And the needle, perfectly balanced, would rest on a Circle of Stones.

THE FIFTH CAR.

It rolls through the quiet mornings. Down Main Street. Onto side streets. Then out of town, to the narrow roads bordering the hill. Following the circling stream.

Watching.

Considering.

The car's black paint is a deep, dark mirror, reflecting the images it slowly passes—

—a tall, round cage…a monkey and an Indian slumbering within.

—a mail truck…a body slumped in the back, legs dangling over the bumper.

—a field of grass and wildflowers…filled with vases of bright red geraniums.

—a cabin on the hill, its large front windows lit from within…an outline of someone inside, watching the morning sun rising.

—a white wicker flying chair…resting on a cloud of rising mist.

—a small boy, crouched in a stream…a man, arms upraised, stands over the boy…the man's hands hold large, heavy rocks.

AT NIGHT, the cars return. They slip back over the edge of the road and into the hole. Crawling to the bottom, they gather again in a dark cluster. Four drivers leave their cars. They walk silently to one of the trailers. They step up a ramp of stacked cement blocks, then disappear through a canted, dented door. No sounds are made. No light is lit. Nothing stirs within.

The fifth driver remains standing beside his car. His red hair and blue eyes are bright points of color in the falling night. He watches the others walk away. Sees them disappear into the metal box. He stands silently while the hole fills with an oily subterranean darkness—the darkness of caves and seeping tombs. The blackness slides down the walls of the hole, puddling into a deep, inky pool. The cars are folded into the darkness, like black bones sinking into tar. Everything is swallowed—the crescent fan of rotting mobile homes and the broken-windowed school buses; the steep, narrow trail; even the hole's scraped-earth walls disappear, giving the sense of limitless void. Of emptiness. Of endless nothing. And in that nothingness, the red-haired driver smiles. Then he turns and walks into the darkness. He holds his hands out in embrace, bringing the night closer to him.

BLUE 7

RETURNING from another trip to the Circle, I'm surprised to see the cabin door standing open. The open door sends a percussion tap of fear through me, my instincts screaming, *Stop! Wait! Something's different! Something's bad!*

Today, though, there is nothing to fear. Nothing is wrong. The door is open, the windows are up, a late spring breeze is moving through the cabin. I hear Elissa talking to the rabbits she keeps in the hutches behind the cabin. I walk quietly up the porch stairs and through our home. Looking through the back door, I watch her work *her* magic.

She has five rabbits: Fee, Fi, Fo, Fum, and Troll. Each one arrived broken and bleeding at our home. Through the door, I see her cradling Troll. The rabbit is a picture of complete relaxation, lying on his back, loosely stretched along the length of Elissa's arm. His short, scarred legs are sticking straight up in the air, and his long ears—tattooed with a bas-relief pattern of healed bites and jagged tears—are tilted toward the gentle music of Elissa's voice. His half-open eyes are heavy-lidded with contentment as Elissa's fingers stroke his face. As she holds him, Elissa's body rocks in a lullaby cadence. "Sleepy eyes," she whispers. "You've got such sleeeepy eyes…sleeepy eyyyes." Her fingertips lightly brush against the rabbit's slowly closing eyes, her voice growing even softer. "Sleepy eyes…" I can see the moment that sleep overtakes the rabbit. I see his legs relax and his ears lean forward as his head falls deeper into the pillow of his chest.

Elissa stands quietly, still rocking. Then, leaning down, she presses her lips against the white drop of fur between his ears.

"SLEEEPYY EYES. *You've got such sleeeepy eyyyes.*" It is a hypnotic chant. A balm of warm tones. No matter which animal she's holding, no matter how broken or frightened, Elissa's words wrap each creature in a calm blanket of safety, giving it a place to find comfort and rest, and eventually, always, a place to sleep. "And sleep," she says, "is one of the best places to be. The place where one feels simply 'there.' The place where all is well."

"Sleepy eyes" she murmurs, holding an animal in her arms. And the animal pauses, breathing Elissa's breath, feeling the beat of Elissa's heart, quieting in the light of Elissa's eyes. Then, drifting asleep, the animal finds the still, healing moment in which it feels simply 'there,' the place where it feels that all is well.

She is right. It is, indeed, one of the best places to be.

I RETURNED to Brown County five years ago and began walking these green hills, trying to rid myself of the gray city-skin I had grown during the years before—a spongy covering that felt stuck on with gritty little balls of rubber cement and envelope glue.

As I walked, I inhaled the many wonderful names of this place like they were a medicated vapor of steam and exotic oils, letting them purify my lungs and mind with their magic and cleansing power. The names are a powerful incantation of old stories and imagined histories: Nineveh, Gnaw Bone, Bear Wallow, Greasy Creek, Stony Lonesome, Milk-Sick Bottoms, Needmore, Three Story Hill, Annie Smith Hollow, Lost Ones Ridge. While contemplating these names, I washed away the soulless corporate existence I'd just left, spent in a place where there were no names—not real names, at least. A place where buildings and meetings were only identified by numbers and times. A place where whole years are reduced to scribbled documentation of wasted minutes spent in designated conference rooms at noted addresses, discussing meaningless percentages. It was a place where I spent time talking with people I did not like about things which were not interesting, in pursuit of things that did not matter.

There was no sense of wonder in that place. No pulse of joy. No rumpled hints of things eternal. So I came home. And now, with every breath of air and every touch of rain, with every kiss and dream and step, I scour more of that dead place and time from my brain and heart: I am almost clean.

I'd left Brown County years ago, soon after my father died. When I left, I went to search for *something sure*. To look for *something black* and *something white*. I was seeking a place that spoke in short declarative statements. A place where the answers to my questions had large, final periods at the end of their sentences, not my father's question marks or open-ended, reflective silences. I left Brown County intending to leave behind the undefined, open-prose format of my childhood. I was tired of my father's tangled answers to my questions. Tired of the never-finished, rambling mysteries given to me by the poor, drunken poet who was my dad. I was tired of the sense that we were always waiting…but never knowing what we were waiting for. With my father's death, I felt a hunger for absolute conclusions and clear definitions. So I went searching for things that were certain.

What I found was a surprise.

Rather than enjoying the easy embrace of black and white conclusions and clear, unambiguous definitions—the things I'd thought I wanted—I felt myself dying. Contrary to what I'd believed when I first left Brown County, I discovered that my father had taught me a deep love of things uncertain—of things unknown, of unhurried wandering, of interesting questions to ponder. Only after trying to escape from him did I learn that I was my father's son.

I discovered that I didn't care for small rooms with small desks where numbers always added perfectly up to expected answers. And I learned that I didn't trust those calculated answers. I'd left Brown County believing that the thick black line of a carpenter's pencil would be better used to draft mechanical blueprints than to shape the poems of an old, dream-filled man. I was wrong. I discovered that poems are the best blueprints—they are the skeletons upon which we should drape our flesh, the nerves and muscles that support and move us. They are the designs from which we should build our dreams.

I'd left Brown County believing I was tired of many things: tired of the place, tired of my father, tired of my own thoughts. Later, though, I realized that *I'd simply been tired*. My father's dying had exhausted us both. With this realization, I knew it was time to return home. While in the city, I'd been good at what I did and was well rewarded. I returned to Brown County with enough money to buy the cabin and land where I intend to stay forever, and where I plan to do only those things that I wish to do—

To love Elissa.

To write my stories and poems.

To walk these hills every day.

And to treasure things uncertain.

MAGIC AND SERENDIPITY are the touchstones of my life, the magnetic poles by which I navigate my world. Each of the shaping events, major occurrences, and discoveries of note in my life has been either the result of a glorious, blessed accident or foretold by personal omen, with both circumstances—accidents and omens—being equally treasured and powerful forces.

Blessed accident: After incorrectly completing a course registration at Indiana University, a nearby school where I sometimes take classes, I found myself assigned to a foreign land, a world where I was the stereotypical arrogant tourist—a traveler ignorant of local customs and unwilling to learn the language: I was lost in the exotic country of computers.

Corresponding major occurrence: The computer course was taught by a woman who possessed all of the magic that the surrounding machinery lacked. A woman whose eyes are a rare green potion of haunting, flickering marsh fire and amber depths. A woman with whom I find poetry in even her smallest words, in even our quietest conversations.

<u>Morning Song</u>

Morning, hon.
Mornin', babe.
Coffee's made.
Mmmm.
Slept good.
Workin' so hard,
knew you would.
A little chilly.
Fall soon.
Going so fast.
That's true.
Refill?
Please.
Love you.
Love you, too.

I dropped the course. And brought the girl home to Brown County to stay.

LATER THAT NIGHT, lying outside on a cushion of sleeping bags and pillows, we are sprawled near the rock-bordered fire ring. The snapping and burning hickory and sassafras logs provide the only light. One side of me is near enough to the fire to feel the heat on my shoulder and hip bones. It's hot enough that I'd normally move away...if I weren't so otherwise completely comfortable. And if the stars weren't so brightly and perfectly flung above me. And if Elissa wasn't so correctly tucked into my other shoulder and hip. And if Grendel hadn't fallen asleep like a cast-iron, feline anchor across our ankles, pinning us down while his cat snores mixed with the hushed night sounds of the woods around us.

Elissa had told me about the black-and-white pup that Grendel had brought home. She'd also talked about Gordon's visit. And now she asks a question that I—mostly—answer (hoping she doesn't feel the coil of tension that ratchets my ribs down tight, that turns the air in my chest into a charcoal lump).

"Blue, have I ever met the Glammerys?" she asks. "Have I ever seen them?"

"You saw them. Once. At Gatesville Park."

Elissa shifts, moving just enough that her shoulder and hip no longer fit into mine. She props herself up on an elbow. "At Gatesville? When?"

"About two years ago. When we were having a picnic." I try to speak normally, but suddenly realize I can't see the stars anymore. All I see is a black curtain of rage unfurling in front of my eyes. I try pulling it back, wanting to tame it. Wanting to hide it from her.

Grendel raises his thick battering ram of a head and looks at us. Either because Elissa has moved or because he feels the change in my mood, he no longer finds our legs comfortable. He stands and stretches, his paws pressing four plate-sized depressions into the earth. Then he slips into the shadows outside the flame-light and becomes part of the darkness.

Staring at the woods where Grendel has disappeared, Elissa speaks with the distracted voice of someone sorting through memories, trying to find the one she's searching for. "I remember the picnic, but not them. Wait—were they the ones by the car?"

The charcoal in my chest ignites, its searing burn spreading into my guts. "If you mean the two greasy, illiterate assholes by the car—then, yes, that was them."

She isn't looking at the woods anymore. Now she's staring at me. "Blue?" she asks, moving closer, fitting her body back into mine. "You okay?"

I need to do better than this. Much better. "Sure," I answer. "Hey...I'm sorry." I pull her closer. "Gordy was right, though. There's nothing good about any of the Glammerys. And I should have told you about them. But it's just—well, they're not a part of where I want to live. I don't like even giving them the time of a single thought. I'd rather just think about...you. And us."

She's still staring at me, but the concerned edge leaves her eyes. It's replaced with something softer. "Hey, mister, that kind of talk won't get you in any trouble around here. It might even help you get a little lucky." She moves even closer. And I start to see the stars again. And start to hear the night's noises again. We listen to the sounds for a few minutes. When she asks, "That day at Gatesville. What did you talk with them about?" I answer so calmly that even I almost believe it. "Not a lot," I tell her. "We talked about small stuff. They weren't too bad that day. We visited. They left. That's it. The end."

"That's it, huh? That's all?"

I can tell she doesn't believe me. That she knows there's more. But she's willing to wait. Willing to give me time.

"Oohh, well, it must have been soooo awful for you then—'talking about small stuff and visiting' with them. How awful it must have been!" She's laughing now, pressed close enough that I feel her chuckle moving through me.

"It *was* awful," I answer. "It was! Soooo dreadfully awful." I roll my leg and arm over her, pinning her to the sleeping bag. "I'll give you awful." We're both laughing now, easing back into the spell of the fire and the stars, our own night sounds soon mixing with those from the woods.

I KNEW EXACTLY how long ago we'd seen the Glammerys. It wasn't simply "almost two years ago." It was nineteen months ago. In October. On Thursday. In late afternoon. When Elissa was one month pregnant. That's when she saw the Glammerys. That's when I'd talked with them. And the talk had been what all talks are like with the Glammerys. Not good. Not fun. *Bad*. But that day, it had only been bad. Not horrible. Not yet. Things eventually did get horrible. But not then. Horrible came later. Then it got worse.

SALT CREEK ROAD follows the miles of low ground around the base of Jonah's Belly, and for the most part Salt Creek does, too. The creek circles the hill like a jeweled necklace, sometimes meandering away from the road and disappearing into the woods and thickets for awhile, then returning. Along its wandering course, the stream has deep pools and shallow ones, wide banks and narrow bends, fast currents and slow drifts. It has places that are a wonder of bright, reflected sunlight and others that are a shaded cathedral of overhead branches, vines, and leaves. Some of its places are hidden, others are seen. One of the "seen" places is Gatesville.

Gatesville is one of my favorite towns. A place so small that visitors truly enter and exit at exactly the same time. It is a few park-like acres of lush grass and wildflowers, with Salt Creek cutting deeply through one side. The dirt banks leading down to the creek are tall, but slope gently to the water. A traffic sign is staked at the intersection of Salt Creek Road and Gatesville Road.

GATESVILLE
ENTERING/LEAVING
POPULATION "0"

At the northeast corner of the intersection, just a few steps off of Gatesville Road is a little gift for visitors: the Gatesville General Store. It's owned by a couple that I've never learned too much about, just the few small bits they're willing to share. Lee and Michelle. First names only. I find more hints about their earlier life in the things they don't say than in those they do. I have the sense they're refugees from a different sort of life. A life stressful enough to leave Lee with a permanent starburst of broken capillaries in his right eye. And a life that left Michelle unwilling to speak above more than a whisper, as though at some point she'd begun to dislike the sound of her own voice. In this present life, I notice that they hold each other a lot. And that they like to spend their time scattering small clay pots filled with bright red geraniums throughout the park. They also rent gold pans and shovels to the tourists and locals who want to spend a few hours "looking for color" in the creek. They surprise those same people with an in-the-middle-of-nowhere menu of incredible, fresh deli sandwiches and deep-dish pizzas. And every few years, they host a storytelling festival in the park. The festival makes no money, but is a wonder to all who attend.

Lee and Michele have made Gatesville more than an intersection. They've made it a gathering place.

NINETEEN MONTHS AGO.

Elissa and I couldn't stop celebrating. We celebrated every day for two straight weeks. Every day since we learned we were having a baby. Every day since finding out we were growing a family.

On that day, nineteen months ago, we went to Gatesville.

We were alone at the park. Somehow, no one else had thought to enjoy the afternoon in the same way we'd planned, like two drowsy cats with nothing to do but eat, nap, and feel the flannel touch of autumn sun on our limbs.

The park's only sounds were the music and song of the full, quick stream, the brush of dry summer grasses, the sharp *kree*-cry of a red-tailed hawk riding high above us on a warm, curling lift of air. As I half-dozed, I remember Elissa asking, a smile in her words, "Is that you I hear? Are you—purring?" And, truthfully, I was—

until I heard the skid of gravel in the parking area by the store, followed, minutes later, by broken, jeering voices floating to us over the park.

"Little Boy Bluuuue! Come blow my horn!"

"Hey, poem-boy, I gotta rhyme for you! There once was a pretty teacher from IU, when I saw her I wanted to screw—"

—and before the sentence ends, I'm already on my feet and walking. Have already told Elissa, "—will be right back, babe," and am too far away to answer when I hear her calling after me. "Blue? What are they saying? Who are they—?"

Glammerys.

Goddamned Glammerys.

Their pickup, parked between me and my car, was the only other vehicle in the lot. The truck bed was heaped full of scrub brush and branches.

They were standing on both sides of my car, Simon on the far side, leaning across the hood. Creel at the back.

"Oh, look out Simon," Creel called, "he's coming at us now! 'Course it's a little different when we're ready for him. Maybe now it's his turn to spend a little time on the ground."

"Maybe he'll tell us a PO-EHM and ask us to be good—"

I'm amazed. We haven't spoken a single word to each other in over fifteen years. The only contact we've had is occasionally seeing each other while driving through town. Yet they're still caught somewhere in that unforgettable, long-ago day at school. They're still holding on to it. Still feeling it. Still angry—

—and, more amazingly, I discover that I am, too.

Like a red-hot solder weld, our past and present are suddenly fused together. In the short space of sentences that Creel yelled across the park on an October day, the three of us have immediately time-traveled backward. Back to hunter and hunted. To predator and prey. Back to a place where we're joined together by remembered violence…*a place where I'm comfortable.*

The nearer I got, the more details I noticed. I've never learned the trick of recognizing different makes and models of automobiles, meaning I only have a few quick impressions of their vehicle. The truck was big. New. A crisp, white, paper license plate taped in the back window. The paint not covered by spattered mud looked factory-waxed and smooth, but a large dent pocked the center of the hood, with a sunburst of deep scratches radiating out from it.

Of course there was a gun rack. Two scoped rifles hang in the cab.

Walking by, I glanced inside the truck. A metal and cardboard carpet of crushed beer cans and ammo boxes covered the floor. On top of the litter was a cellophane layer of empty pork-rind bags (SO FIERY HOT THE PIGS DON'T WANT 'EM BACK!). Nestled in the cellophane were two high-power, camouflage-printed spotlights. Spread across the back seat was a fanned stack of folded-open skin magazines. There weren't any words on the pages, just blocks of flesh-colored photos. One picture was a half-page zoom-shot of a drooping, blue-veined breast with a pierced nipple—there's a small bullet dangling from the nipple-ring.

Up close, I saw I was wrong about the truck's load. It wasn't heaped full of branches—the leafy layer of scrub in the back was thrown over a lumpy pile of something else underneath that'd been covered with a brown plastic tarp. From a distance, the brown tarp was invisible beneath the branches. A thin red stream—channeled by the truck bed's rain grooves—was leaking out from the back corner of the tailgate, the drip-drip-drip trail flowing in a wet line down the bright expanse of chromed rear bumper and puddling on the gravel under the truck.

The brothers were drunk, with an acrid, musky stink around them. Rather than stopping at the middle of my car, positioned equally between them, I walked to the front of my car, closer to Simon—

—*I'm going to hit him first.* "Nice hair," *I say, looking back at Creel. His hair's never grown back right since that school day defeat.*

It looks like a light-and-dark jigsaw of knitted rags. "You comb that yourself?" I ask.

"Good seeing you, too, dickhead," Simon grunts. His broken voice sounds like a brittle rattle of saw blades. He starts to stand, rising from his slouch across the hood of my car. "Even better seeing your girl over—"

"Simon," I say, cutting him off. "You'll have to speak up. I can barely hear you. You don't sing in church with that voice, do you? Truly, that would be an offensive sound, even to God's ears." Then Creel starts moving toward me and Simon lurches up—

—and I feel my foot planting down, feel my hip beginning to pivot, know my elbow is going to drive into Simon's forehead and the heel of my foot is going to crush back against—

Wait.

Elissa.

She doesn't need this. Not now. Not today. Not in our park—

—hell, I don't need this—

—so when Creel is almost at my side, I say, "Too bad about your new vehicle." The words stop them for a second. In that pause, I nod at the rear of their truck. "You should probably get that thing to the hospital. Get it bandaged up."

I see Simon's hand moving to something—knife? gun?—beneath his overshirt—

—and I'm already relaxing into whatever is going to happen in the next seconds, already feel the moment-away snap of my elbow slamming into Simon's forehead, then spearing down into his collarbone—

—when Creel, pausing a few feet away, looks where I've nodded, then looks back. "Hospital?" he repeats. "Bandaged?" He shakes his head. "Blueboy, what the hell are you talking—?"

"It's bleeding," I answer. "Your truck. It's bleeding. Maybe you ought to make a phone call to Gordy? Maybe get it looked at?"

They stare at me. Simon's hand stops moving, then settles against his side.

"Shine on," I say, staring back at him. "Right, boys?"
Shine on.

JUDGING FROM the beer cans, food wrappers, and soiled stash of skin-mags, they'd probably been "shining" all night long—using spotlights to illegally freeze deer in their tracks, then shooting them while they stood transfixed and motionless in the light. From the smell of the two brothers, they'd slept in the truck, and then—after waking—kept right on shooting.

It looked like they'd been "whackin' and stackin'" for quite awhile, piling the carcasses in their truck, killing so many deer that the blood was still draining out onto the parking lot. They'd covered their haul with a brown plastic tarp, then covered the tarp with branches and brush, trying to hide the load by making it look like it was just another Glammery trash-run rather than a poacher's field day.

"I TOOK everything they had," Gordon had told me a few years earlier. We were sitting in a Department of Natural Resources bass boat. Drifting in the middle of a small, peaceful lake. Casting lines into water lily-covered shallows. "I took all of it. Every bit. Their shitty car. The two shitty rifles in the trunk. Their shitty boat. Their shitty boat-trailer. Their shitty fishing gear. The two pistols under the seats. Their tent. Their camping gear. I confiscated all of it after I caught them trespassing on private 'no trespassing'-posted land, fishing without fishing licenses in a private, stocked lake, with coolers full of too-small fish, and packing a couple of beaver they'd shot with the pistols.

"So, first, I took it all. Then I jailed 'em. Then I fined 'em. And then I explained to them that, were I so inclined, I could use the confiscated evidence to obtain a search warrant to also look through their shitty homes. And that if I did that—and then found anything that even remotely reminded me of poaching—well, then I could take everything else that was there, too. All of it, including their homes and property. But I didn't do that to them. I could have, but I didn't. Because I'm a nice guy, right? And, also, because who the hell wants to go inside one of their filthy homes?

"Shit," he said, taking a deep drink from his beer, then reeling in his line. "I don't know why they were so mad." He cast into the deep water. "Goddamned Glammerys. They've got no sense of humor. Anyway," he added, "I just thought I'd let you know—they seemed pissed about things, even when I was letting them out of jail." He shook his head, smiling a little at the memory.

We watched our lines for a few minutes, finishing our bottles and opening two more.

"Well...," he said later, reeling in for the next cast. "I'd guess the next time I catch them is going to really be fun...just as long as I see them first."

"It'd be a shame if it just died here." I nodded at the red-brown pool on the gravel. "A brand new truck bleeding out... drained of its life fluids, and all." I made a move toward the store. "Let's make a call—alert the proper authorities, get it some proper attention. Right now."

They were caught in a war of so many conflicting emotions that it was hard to read any single expression on their faces. *They're caught wanting to fight. Caught wanting to yell. Caught looking at Elissa and wanting to do more than just look. And caught with me in a moment that they've probably dreamed about for years. But mostly—*

They're just caught.

And they know it.

They know that one phone call to Gordy means their new truck will be taken. Along with the guns. And the spotlights. And the deer.

All of it. And they know that it might not stop there. It might follow them right back home and take that away, too.

Creel moves first. He looks at me. Then looks over my shoulder to Simon. "Get in the truck," he tells his brother. He looks at me again. "You do know we live here? You know that, right? All day and all night. So you know this ain't done. You do know that don't you, Blueboy?"

I look back at him. Everything's quiet. Even Simon is waiting.

"A bullfrog," I say. "Right?"

Creel squints, not tracking what I said. I repeat it, nodding at his head. "A bullfrog—when you connect all the little black and white hair dots. I'm guessing it's the shape of a bullfrog. Or maybe a nipple-ring with a bullet on it. But it's one of those two things, though, right?" I move in close to him. Close to the stink and the blood. I feel the hot-solder heat burning in my temples. "Now listen, Creel," I whisper. "You deer-poaching, speckle-headed, Appaloosa-wannabe—do you want me to call some medical help for that truck? Or do you think you can make it home on your own?"

THEY DROVE AWAY, leaving in a cliché of spinning tire-gravel and shouted insults. The dripping blood-stream followed them down the road. I watched the truck till it was gone. I remember thinking— just like Gordon had said years ago—*the next time is going to really be fun. As long as I see them first.*

BLUE. BROWN COUNTY, INDIANA. A SMALL SENSE OF THEN

S TAND WITH ME at the top of this hill and watch the dawn spill down. Stand here and think of land and souls—there is not much of either in Brown County, Indiana. When the morning sun cups the whole of the county in its hands, its encircled fingers hold very little. Three hundred and twenty-four square miles is the county's full measure. It is a small, wondrous thing, a study of detail more than volume. Though a slight sanctuary, there is solitude here. Isolation, even. No more than 15,000 live along the thin roads and ruts that weave the county's tenuous web of "from here to there." Much slips through the large holes of so loose a net, escaping both notice and capture.

Both millennia and men have crafted this place. This ground and its gifts are the fortunate result of three powerful forces: an inland salt sea, ice, and ink.

AN INLAND SALT SEA: 360 million years ago, a shallow and warm fertile sea covered the land that would become southern Indiana. Wild prehistoric rivers emptied into the sea, their tumbling sediment drifting in feathery curls to its bottom. Over millions of years, the growing weight of the settled silt pressed down upon itself and formed shale, siltstone, and a high delta.

The sea's waters were alive, swirling with a frothy abundance of shell and sea creatures. In this living salt-brew, animals lived and died a million, million times. And their shells and skeletons then settled atop earlier shell and skeleton deposits. Then the weight of this marine graveyard crushed down upon itself and hardened, becoming the limestone rock that veins the county.

Time passed and the sea receded. It disappeared, but even today, it is not so far away—its ancient salt waters still pool and move beneath this ground. Like blood pumping from some hidden heart, the rich salt brine still flows up and out from deep springs, pouring into the stream named, appropriately, Salt Creek.

In the county's frontier history, early pioneers burned great fires under huge iron kettles, boiling away the brine they'd pumped with wells sunk 300 feet into the earth. The smoke and flames from these kettle fires smudged the sky each day and cast a red glow against each night. Until they were closed and abandoned, three separate salt works operated for years along the banks of Salt Creek, burning their endless fires as they harvested the waters of a buried sea.

ICE: Look where we stand. This is Bean Blossom Ridge in the northernmost part of the county. This is the high stone wall that blocked the glacier that crept forward and then fell back more than two million years ago. Our feet rest on the old rock of the salt sea's delta. It is this stone that stopped the crush of glacial ice that pushed down from the north, leveling and smoothing the land. Look south into the county and see the untouched roll of green hills and the fall of valleys. Look north. See the rippled fields, planed flat beneath the glacier's frozen, grinding weight. Where we stand is the dividing line that was drawn so long ago. This is where the ice piled and pushed and strained against rock—and the rock held.

While pushing against the delta, the halted glacier sparkled with bright, crystal glitterings of snow and ice—and with the other things that glittered there, too. In the far north of British America, a thick braid of gold, silver, diamonds, topaz, garnets, and rubies had snagged in the folds of the traveling glacier's cold robes and been carried down into Indiana. As the Age of Ice ended, the glacier's cold cloak melted under a warming sun, and a rolling slush of water and earth poured over this high delta ridge. Roiling in this melting pour, the vagabond treasure of gems and precious metals was scuffed and scattered into the soil and streams of Brown County.

INK: The county's boundaries were drawn by the covenants of two separate Indian treaties offered for signature by the U.S. government. Unlike other lands that were recognized as the territory of one tribe or another, the Indians held this ground to be a shared place, a land full of magic and replenishment. A blessing for all. Accordingly, the two U.S. treaties bore the council marks of several tribes.

As was the pattern of things back then, after the signing of government treaties, the shared blessings of the area were soon no longer any tribes' to share. With a few simple pen strokes, all those who believed that mystery and spirits walked in these hills, all those who had found visions and wisdom and power within the contours of this ground—those people were driven away.

The same documents that evicted one population invited another one in. The pioneers who soon began arriving found few Indians in the area—and the few they found, they first attacked, then ignored. Rather than finding magic and blessings in these hills, the pioneers bored deep holes into the earth and pulled up the seawater that had rested there for eons. They boiled the salt water away in bright, ever-burning fires of freshly felled hardwood trees.

NOW, A FEW questions. Close your eyes and tell me: If the tribes are gone, but the contours, waters and woods remain—are there still visions and wisdom and mystery in these hills? Do spirits and powers still move in the quiet here? Do you feel these things? And if they are here, why do they remain? Over what do they keep watch? For what are they waiting?

FOR DECADES, tales were told of Indians who quietly returned to the area and then disappeared into the hills, slipping away like a cat's shadow. Untrackable by the curious pioneers, the Indians would reappear days later, quietly camping near a stream, and then, in the same silence that they'd arrived, they'd then depart. Year after year this occurred. Conjecture, rumor, and dark secrets were traded about these visits—hushed stories of hidden treasure left behind, of holy sacraments performed, of eternal vigils kept and magical signs interpreted.

The stories were abundant.

Some would chill the night.

And some were true.

AT THE BEGINNING of the end of 12,000 years of Indian habitation, Christian missionaries began moving among the Indiana tribes. Those who listened to the missionaries and believed what they heard were called "Jesus Indians." The missionaries told Bible tales to the Jesus Indians. And the Jesus Indians told and retold those same tales to others. Over the years—years of unintentional narrative revision and story blending—the old Bible stories slowly changed and became something new.

One of the new stories told of a warrior god named Jonah, a god who battled an enemy of vast emptiness. After waging a great war against the dark nothingness, the God Jonah defeated his enemy. Victorious, Jonah determined to fill the dark void with all manner of life so that his enemy might never find an abyss in which to hide.

Jonah first placed the sun in the sky, giving himself light by which to see his work. He next created the ocean, from whose depths he fashioned all life. He drank deeply from the ocean, mixing it in his stomach with his food, then spat out his creations. The first of Jonah's creations was a great fish upon which he could ride. While riding the fish through the ocean, he gave form to all other things.

He worked without stopping, making the heavens, the earth, the animals and plants. After seven days of creating, Jonah grew weary. He needed sleep. Not wanting to rest, he kneeled wearily at the shore and drank again from the ocean, intending to give life to other forms. But he was so sleepy that he drank almost all of the water and even swallowed the large fish he'd been riding. The weight in his stomach filled him, making him even more tired, and before he could create new creatures, sleep overtook him and he lay down—his stomach stretched tight and churning. During his sleep, the God Jonah dreamed of a perfect creation. While slumbering, he opened his mouth, and out walked the People.

The People were formed in Jonah's image. They began to worship him and celebrate his other creations. Waking, Jonah saw the People and was so contented and pleased with them that he lay back down, stretched out on his back, and continued sleeping. His large belly, still full of life and water and food, pointed to the heavens.

THE EUROPEAN and American explorers who followed the missionaries spent time with the many tribes and learned their different languages. On the maps they made, the explorers recorded the places they were shown and the stories they were told. On each map, no matter who was drawing or which tribe was visited, the high hill circled by the salty stream was always called by the same name. All called it Jonah's Belly.

WENDELL. CHICORY. THAD

HE THINKS the monkeys like their cage. They act like they do. It's a silo-shaped structure, twenty-five feet in diameter, thirty feet tall. Suspended by heavy cables in the high upper area are nests of sitting platforms, net beds, a big sleeping box, and webs of interconnected rope ladders. The cage sits outdoors on a thick concrete pad, butted up tight against a faded green building. Arching across the building's front is a sign with giant letters: SERPENTARIUM! STARE DEATH IN THE EYE! The sign's wavy, bright red and yellow letters curve over a peeling wall-sized painting of a tail-shaking, fangs-exposed, ready-to-strike rattlesnake. He'd painted the sign almost twelve years ago, and, even now, with the actual snakes long since gone, he still thinks, *That is one great sign.* At least once a day some tourist sees the sign, walks in the door, smells the ever-burning sage stick, sees his long-braided hair and hand-beaded shirt with its tribal design, and then says something really clever like, "Hey, Heap-Powerful Chief, I'm ready to see the snakes. I'm ready to STARE DEATH IN THE EYE!"

And he always answers, "Sorry, no more snakes. But do you like monkeys? I've got some great monkeys."

THREE YEARS ago there hadn't been any monkeys. There'd been snakes. Lots of snakes. But then he'd been given a vision and things had changed. *Hell, everything had changed. The vision was that powerful.* Three years ago, his name hadn't even been Chicory Dirtfoot. It had been Wendell Morris. And for $2 a ticket, Wendell had happily let people STARE DEATH IN THE EYE! all day long.

For a man who didn't need much, it had been a good living. The snakes were almost cost-free. Between the mice he trapped around his home and the feeder mice he raised in his extra bedroom, the snakes' food cost almost nothing. And fresh snake bedding— sawdust and dirt—only cost as much as, well, sawdust and dirt. So three years ago, with almost sixty people a day paying full ticket price to STARE DEATH IN THE EYE! he'd been doing A-OK. Was even building a little nest egg. Of course, it wasn't like he had a lot of places to spend his money. There certainly wasn't a woman to spend it on. In his experience, most women didn't consider a man who owned poisonous snakes and kept hundreds of mice in his home to be someone they wanted to play house with. Most women didn't want that at all—

But one did.

Once.

Once, in an Indianapolis bar—miles and miles from where anyone knew about his snakes and mice—once there'd been a girl, a girl who didn't mind the mice at all. A small, spike-haired girl who'd been sitting alone—

("Alone" was good.)

She'd let him sit beside her—

("Beside her" was very good.)

He'd started easing into a conversation—

(Which was also good, but it was nothing, *nothing*, compared to what happened next.)

He'd introduced himself. And she'd answered, telling him her name, saying—

(*And this wasn't GOOD, this was I-SHIT-YOU-NOT GREAT*)

"Mouse. Call me Mouse."

After a few drinks, when he felt things getting happy-fuzzy, he told her about his mice and snakes. Or maybe, when he tried remembering later, he hadn't really told her about the snakes. Maybe had only told her about the mice. And maybe hadn't actually told her what the mice were for. *But damn,* he thought, *her name was Mouse. What the hell was I supposed to tell her?*

Whatever the hell it was that he had actually said, the result had been—

Amazing.

Perfect.

Gold.

"You. Have. Mice. Oh. My. God." she'd said, staring into his eyes. Then said, "You gotta look at these," and—*no shit!*—started pulling off her shirt. Started stripping, right there in the bar, right there in front of him. He watched, not believing his luck, thinking, *Yes, oh yes, oh yes, oh yes.*

"Just look at these," she said, excited and happy. Somehow touching his arm and thigh at the same time she was peeling off her blouse. For a moment, her spiked hair caught on the cloth, snagging the shirt above her head like a hooked kite. "You look right here and then try telling me we weren't intended to meet tonight. Try telling me that this wasn't freakin' *intentional.*" She finally got the blouse untangled from her hair and pulled it completely off. There, sitting in front of him, still half-dressed in a high-cropped T-shirt that was now disappointingly revealed beneath her blouse, she pointed a narrow stick of finger down at the two tattoos inked on her abdomen.

Located inches beneath her two sharp nipple-points—both nipples still covered by the thin bit of cropped T-shirt—the first tattoo was a swell of curving script that flowed across the taut skin below her ribcage: **RODENTZZ RULE!** Curled beneath the words, a beady-eyed ink-mouse face twitched at Wendell. Its long ink-whiskers were attached to a pointed ink-nose.

And lower, just above Mouse's hips, a cartoonish, curved arrow tattoo pointed down. *Down there!* he thought. *Down there!* The arrow tip disappeared beneath the low waist of her torn, gray jeans.

Along the arrow's shaft, written in wavy red and yellow letters—*MY letters,* he thought, *my STARE DEATH IN THE EYE! letters*—the tattooed words **MOUSE HOUSE** arced unmistakably down. *Down there! Down there!*

He stared at the arrow. Thought about the secret, warm place where it pointed. Forgot all about STARING DEATH IN THE EYE! Forgot about anything but the possibilities of her soft, wet, open MOUSE HOUSE. Looking up from the tattoos, he saw her expectant, welcoming eyes. And he absolutely had to agree with what she'd said (*oh yes, oh yes, oh yes*): It was freekin' intentional that they met.

Later, back at his house, they fucked in the guest bedroom. On the mattress in the middle of the floor. Surrounded by mice-filled cages lining the walls. Watched by thousands of bright, tiny mice-eyes.

It didn't bother Wendell.

It *really* didn't bother Miss Mouse.

She stayed the next day. And the next. And the next. Stayed long enough that he began thinking of her as "there" when he thought of his home. But she wouldn't go near the snakes. Couldn't stand them. Which meant she wouldn't visit the Serpentarium. Instead, she stayed in the house all day, seemingly content to wait for his return. Always waiting for him in the guest bedroom. Always ready to fuck, but only in the guest bedroom. Never anywhere else—

Which didn't bother her.

But did bother him.

A little.

Two weeks later. The fourth straight day of rain. Not a "wash-the-streets-and-everything-glows" sort of rain. Not a "feel-the-gentle-mist-on-your-face" rain. A shitty rain. The fourth day of a creeping wet darkness that depressed everything, slowed everything down. That pushed down hard, stopping all movement. He sure didn't feel like moving. The snakes weren't moving. And the empty streets confirmed that the tourists certainly weren't moving. He hadn't sold a single ticket yesterday or the day before. And wasn't going to sell one today either.

Fuck this.

He hung his Closed sign on the door: *Don't Get RATTLED. Don't have a HISSY fit. We'll SLITHER open tomorrow. Unless we're fatally BIT!*

Went home early.

And was bothered.

A lot.

HE WENT to the guest bedroom. Found her naked and alone on the mattress. Her eyes closed. Making little, squeaky-moan sounds. Wearing only a rumpled fur blanket and a spray-on wardrobe of Cheez Whiz (he saw the words *Spicy Nacho!* on one of the four nozzle-topped cans on the floor).

Then the bumpy fur blanket moved. And moved. And moved. And the fine details of the blanket—*noses? whiskers? tails?*—formed in his mind.

It was mice.

Hundreds of them.

Nibbling and tunneling.

Enjoying a frenzied mouse-frolic in the Cheez Whiz clothing.

He saw he'd been wrong about her being the one making the little squeaky-moan sounds. Yes, she was the one doing the moaning—

—but the mice were doing the squeaking. At least the ones he could hear. There were others he couldn't hear. And even though he couldn't hear them, he knew they were there—

—he could see their little pink tails wriggling inside of her MOUSE HOUSE.

SHE FLED: standing, wiping, dressing, leaving in what seemed only seconds. Hours after she'd left, he still couldn't shake the pictures out of his mind...and he wanted them gone. Far, far-away gone. *Forever* gone. To make them go, he needed things to be more than just a little happy-fuzzy. He needed drinks. Many, many drinks. He needed to be out of the house. To be away from the mice. Away from all the damn mouses in their damn Mouse-Houses. Away from their little wriggling pink tails. And—most of all—away from his memory of them disappearing *down there*.

Which is how his night started.

And is why he was drunk when it ended.

And is why he ended up back at the Serpentarium.

And, in a way, is also how he ended up killing himself.

FIFTY-SEVEN years before Wendell Morris died, eight-year-old Thaddeus Prime fell in love at summer camp. His parents, the doctors Lenora and Benford Prime, had sent him to camp for many reasons. The first reason was to assure that the body housing Thad's brain was maintained in the highest health, that it might perform in perfect working order, so as to give the world the longest benefit of their son's superior mind.

Within months of Thad's birth, it had been clear to Lenora and Benford that A Special Gift had been given them by the Almighty. Something beyond any request they'd presumed to make in their nightly bedside prayers. Certainly they'd held a reasonable expectation that theirs would be an intelligent child; after all, they *were* doctors, each held in the highest individual esteem by their circle of colleagues. As individuals and as a team, they'd received accolades and honoraria for their work, their charity, and for their dedication to the progress of medical science. Yet, for all the peer adulation and jealousy directed their way—jealousy being as valid a recognition of professional success as any certificate—the doctors were, in all areas but

Thad, without conceit. As individuals, they were talented, but as a team, they were a wonder. And they had quietly hoped their combined efforts at intercourse would produce no less a successful result.

Their hopes had not been disappointed.

They had been surpassed.

Their child was brilliant.

Not bright. Bright was being first to recognize which square-shaped block went into which square-shaped hole. Bright was a baby who began walking a month before other babies walked. Bright simply arrived early where others would also eventually arrive. Bright was good. But bright was overrated.

Not clever. Clever was occasional. Undependable. Clever was a surprising turn-of-phrase. A moment of sly understanding. Clever was fun, but mostly, clever was an illusion—a mask, a trick, a shyster in fine clothing.

Not ingenious. Ingenious was a narrow talent. Ingenious was given directions to a house, discovered the door locked, didn't have a key, so found another way in. But ingenious didn't know why that specific house was important. Didn't even know the house's address. And once inside the house, ingenious didn't know what to look for. Maybe had even already forgotten how he had gotten there. Ingenious was good to have along on the trip, but you didn't want ingenious holding the map.

Their son was none of those things. Those things were ephemeral. Unfixed. Small trinkets to ease one's passage. Things without lasting value. No, those things were not their son.

Their son was *brilliant.*

"Our son—twice a gift," they agreed. "First, given to us, given from above. And second, from us, given to the world."

"Greatness—his destiny," they prophesied. Such obvious genius. Such focus and discipline. *And this, already, in one so young. Just think of the future, think of that which is yet to come! A blessing for us, a blessing for all.*

Yes, they were his parents. And, yes, being his parents, they were overly proud. And, as parents do, they were inclined to overestimate the abilities of their sole child. Were likely to overstate the progress of his development. As his parents, they were all of that.

And, still, they were correct.

At only two months old, they saw Thad's "look." A look demanding knowledge of every detail that caught his attention. A look that froze visitors with its intensity (*"Did you see the way he looked at me? Did you see him stare?"*) A look that was all the more disquieting because it was framed in the perfect circle of a baby's puddled face. A face that drooled like other babies, that puckered with hunger and cried with colic like other babies. But a face that gave a look most definitely not seen on other babies' faces (*"... like he was observing me! Like I was his subject! Uncomfortable, I tell you, it was damn uncomfortable. He's not a normal child! Not normal at all."*)

At five months, when most babies found joy in muscles just strong enough to propel themselves in a rolling maze of directions, Thaddeus moved in straight lines. He moved toward the things held fixed in his stare, toward the bits and pieces that already excited his infant curiosity. (*"...just stared at a basket, that's all he did, for twenty-five minutes! Pressing his face up close to it, not making a single sound, just staring. At a basket!"*)

At nine months, he walked. Took no pleasure in the balance and movement of walking itself. Instead, seemed only pleased to arrive more quickly at whatever had caught his attention. And seemed even more pleased to stand above the object, viewing it from a new perspective, happy to be able to better contemplate the entirety of "it," whatever "it" was at that particular day and hour. In the thrall of such study, held fascinated by whatever was gripping his mind, his infant concentration was unbroken by outside distractions...or even a parent's call. (*"...it's a flower, Thad, the same flower as before. Now see the pretty toy bear! See the—Thad! Thaddy-boy, look! Look, look at Mommy! It's a nice flower but now see the bear, now see—Thad!")*

Then, soon, talking. Not saying "Mommy" or "Daddy." But pointing at the singular objects of his interest and asking "This? What's this?" Then, after receiving an answer, pointing at a smaller detail and asking again, "This? What's this?" Then turning it over, pointing at another detail. Asking again, "This? This?"

Then reading. Starting small, of course. Simple books at first, pictures and single words. Then…not so simple. Reading from the time he woke till he slept at night. Sometimes carrying the book to a parent, pointing at a word or a picture, asking, "This? What's this?" Of course Lenora and Benford had intended to hire tutors. Eventually. And certainly they would now. But who could have expected it so soon? For a child only two years old?

And so there was a string of hiring disappointments. Individuals let go for not fully understanding that This Was Something Different. A quickly-terminated procession of people who couldn't properly guide or teach young Thad.

Until Dr. Jerry S. Stuelpe arrived. Ph.D. doctor. Not M.D. doctor. Newly graduated. Young, unemployed. No preset study plans to assist with teaching Thad. Had never actually taught before. Instead was filled with just one perfect feeling—curiosity. About everything. Had immediately intuited the right way to answer when Thad pointed at an apple on a tree, asking, as always, "This? What's this?"

Dr. Stuelpe reached up and plucked the apple from the branch. Held it beneath Thad's nose for him to smell. Gave it to Thad to hold. Held Thad's hand in his and drew Thad's fingers across the apple skin. Across the stem. Across the top leaf. Then picked another apple and, using a pocketknife, slowly circled the red fruit with the blade, letting the ribbon of peel curl into Thad's hands. As Thad slipped the peel back and forth through his fingers, Dr. Stuelpe sliced two apple wedges—one for Thad, one for himself. Then he cored the apple, delicately lifting each seed from the plug.

He cut the seeds open and handed them to Thad. Still was nowhere near done, hadn't even begun answering the entirety of "This? What's this?"—

—and was still excited and answering "This. What's this?" three weeks later. Was using Benford and Lenora's home library to find wonderful reference books with whole sections—*whole sections!*—about apples. Page after page of incredible, color photo-plates and diagrams, all showing so many kinds of apples, and so many apple shapes and so many apple names and apple colors.

First studying the books. Then using a microscope to let Thad see everything *so closely*. Spending whole days viewing the delicate veining of the apples' flesh. The juice-filled cells visible in the oh-so-thin slices of apple fruit of the slides. Studying the edges and bristles of the apple leaf. Marveling at the smoothness of the deep-brown teardrop seeds.

Then going to an orchard.

Then another orchard.

Wandering through rows and rows of apple trees, with their thick bushy branches and scaly, puzzle-piece bark. Seeing the orchards' ladders and baskets and crates and presses. Drinking cups of cider made fresh in front of their eyes. Eating apples from all the different farms. Then planting their collected apple seeds in small cups, watering them, and setting them to grow on sunny windowsills.

ONE NIGHT they carried armfuls of dried apple-wood to a backyard fire ring. They let the fire's sweet smoke drift and curl around them as they roasted the wild apples they'd skewered with long sharp sticks. A single bat flitted through the campfire smoke and disappeared again into the gray twilight. Thad watched it, his eyes staring where it had gone. He dropped the long stick he held in his hand. He pointed after the bat. Pointed into the shadows and darkness where it had flown. Said, "This? What's this?"

SINGLE TOPICS, one at a time, each one entirely explored. From main point to medium point, to small point, to related point, to minutiae. To how does it sound, and how does it feel, and how does it grow, and what's inside, and does it die, and how many are there, and where are they, and what do they do. And more and more and more.

Thad needed more information. Wanted more details. Asked more questions. Was utterly, wholly, enthralled with whatever he was learning—until the split-second moment that he wasn't enthralled anymore. Consuming every fact—every flake and crumb and speck— until he was suddenly and entirely full of a topic. In that exact instant, he was simply and completely done with whatever the subject had been, was already immersed in something entirely else. Immediately dropped whatever he'd been holding and now pointed eagerly at something else, asking, "This. What's this?" Instantaneously, absolutely, fiercely interested in only the new "This, what's this?"

Devouring knowledge. Insatiable for it.

Maybe even obsessed.

Drs. Lenora and Benford reassured one another. *Our son's brilliant affliction! It is a good thing, a very good thing! He is determined! Committed! Inquisitive! Passionate! Just think, Lenora, of what he'll contribute—of what he'll produce—when his interest turns to medicine! Think of the discoveries! Think of the progress! And Benford, she'd tell him, think of the studies he'll pursue! The thoughts he'll have! The insights he'll gain. His focus—so strong, so complete— it is a good thing! It must be a good thing!*

Except he only *took* information in.

He gave nothing back.

No comments. No conclusions.

Nothing.

He remembered everything. And his questions showed a master's touch of nuance, each one turned just a bit differently to provide a different play of interpretation and perspective on the answers he sought. But once received, the answers were only for him—stored in a vault into which only he could walk.

Still, his parents felt no dismay. *Already practicing a scholar's research, Benford. Already learning a scientist's process. Eventually, Lenora, eventually he'll conjecture. Hypothesize. Postulate. Eventually, Lenora! And then, my God! And then!*

The years passed. Topics were identified, explored, retired. During those years, the Primes worked hard to avoid the observations which were increasingly…observable.

Their son was brilliant, yes—

And friendless. *Not good. Not good at all! He must be able to interact! To communicate! How else to head an institute?*

And weak. *He must be strengthened, Benford. He must have vigor and health! How else to endure?*

And boring. *He must engage! He must interest and intrigue! And, yes, even entertain! How else to be sought out?*

So, in the summer of his eighth year, Thad was summoned to his parents' study. Smiling reassuringly, they sat him down. Then said a single word to him.

"Camp."

CAMP CLAY CREEK.

Tucked deep in the hills of Brown County, Indiana. Now long since closed, its rows of low-roofed camper cabins permanently shuttered and mold-blackened. But in Thad's day, it was once a child's Eden. A garden of wild woods, and animals, and play.

In this place, there were friends to find. And Thad found them.

In this place, there were activities to enjoy. And Thad enjoyed them.

And in this place, how could there not be love? And Thad found love.

He met Rose.

Certainly, he met others at camp—Shelby, Ruby, Bethany,

Harriet—but none like Rose. No one who so filled his mind. After the campers met her that first night, every one of them fell under the dangerous excitement of her spell. They all felt the energy of her presence. But none were so taken as Thad. He was overwhelmed by her beauty. Was hypnotized by her grace. Speechless, he watched her simplest movements. Felt the air pressed from his lungs under the weight of his immediate young love. For the next two weeks, he could not help himself, could not escape the thought of her. Could only stare in adoration as she ate and as she slept. He felt transfixed by her mouth. By her tongue. By her skin. And would have given everything to reach through the thick glass wall of her locked cage and feel his fingers brush against her cool, dry back. Or to hold the fanged triangle of her head in his hands.

CAMPERS ARRIVED mid-afternoon at Camp Clay Creek. They checked in at the main cabin on the first day of their two-week adventure. Checking in, they learned that a large hand-lettered chalkboard conveyed each day's planned agenda.

WELCOME TO CAMP CLAY CREEK
ACTIVITY PLAN

DAY 1
Assemble In Grand Hall Lodge—4:00

1. Welcome

2. Rules

3. Introductions

    A. Directors

    B. Counselors

C. Camp Clay Creek's Nature Friends

<u>SHELBY SQUIRREL</u>
<u>RUBY RACCOON</u>
<u>BETHANY BUNNY</u>
<u>HARRIET HAWK</u>
<u>ROSE RATTLESNAKE</u>

4. Cabin Assignments

5. Dinner—6:00

6. Go to Cabins—7:00

7. Gather for Bonfire—8:00

Thad spent almost no time in his cabin. And he saw no bonfire. He'd found the serpent in this Eden.
And he was enthralled.

IT DIDN'T PASS.

He didn't grow bored.

The snakes were all he needed.

As he grew, he collected them. Only rattlesnakes. Content to simply own them. Feed them. Be near them.

Finally, years later, Benford and Lenora conceded that their son would not move the mountains they'd foreseen him moving. That he wouldn't push back any curtains of ignorance. That he'd perform no great, ground-breaking research and resolve no points of intellectual controversy. That he'd draw no startling conclusions about ideas old or new. More simply, he'd attend no college, would court no woman, would pursue no occupation.

Instead, Thad watched snakes.

He spent all his time in the outbuilding that housed his

collection. The shelving along three of the walls was boxed with glass, making the rattlesnake-filled cages into which Thad stared each day. The fourth wall of the building was filled with glass cages filled with white feeder-mice raised only a few feet from the same creatures that would soon consume them. One afternoon, Benford walked into the building and saw Thad sitting cross-legged in the middle of the room. The world began spinning around him. Feeling a horrible shift in perspective, he saw that Thad— like the snakes and mice—was also surrounded by four glass walls. *My son has built himself a cage*, he thought, feeling the surprise of tears upon his face.

In a final sad surrender, recognizing the facts of their own elder years and their son's affliction (that's what they called it now, *Thad's affliction*), they determined to provide him with the security of a center-point, to give him stability when they'd passed. Absent interaction with his parents, they knew their son would seek no contact with others but would happily remain entirely alone with his snakes. And that was a thought too lonely and hard for them to bear.

A trust account was established. A fountain from which a measured stream of funds would flow—funds to sustain Thad, and funds to provide for the upkeep and maintenance of the building and small home they purchased for him. Both the home and building, within walking distance of each other, were in Nashville, Indiana. *A commercial endeavor, a business, his father explained to him. A chance to share your interests with the community.*

The home was nondescript. A two-bedroom cottage on a backstreet. The building—its walls and floor remodeled to suit the special needs of Thad's displays—was situated on the corner of Main Street and Washington Street. Like the home, it was a simple nondescript affair. Entirely unnoticeable. Identifiable only by the simple block lettering painted above the doorway: NASHVILLE SERPENTARIUM.

THAD'S TRUST fund ensured that the business need not flourish.

It didn't.

People who were sharp-eyed enough to see the small sign, then intrigued enough to open the door, and then surprised enough to gasp with awe upon finding themselves suddenly surrounded by hundreds of venomous rattlesnakes, were then amazed, only seconds later, to also find themselves—

Completely bored.

Entirely uninterested.

Almost sleepy.

Standing in the aisles, the visitors breathed in the room's warm air and looked at shelf after shelf of uniform glass cages. They observed the light from the two small windows disappearing into the room's brown-painted ceiling. And brown-painted floor. And brown-and-black snakes. Even observed it disappearing into the quiet man in the brown suit who sat at a brown counter in the center of the brown room. Faced with this brown and lightless world, visitors felt a sudden and overwhelming urge to nap.

Whatever enchantment it was that Thad found in snakes, he wasn't able to share it with anyone else. Was unable to communicate the passion which had so wholly captured him. Without understanding why, those who entered the Serpentarium later found themselves standing outside the brown-painted building, curiously unable to recall what had been inside, uncertain of any details, and already forgetting the ticket-man's face.

When Thad's parents died, he let the family's Indianapolis home sit empty.

He lived in Nashville, close to his love.

It lasted thirty-five years.

It might have lasted thirty-five more.

But it all ended one day. With suddenness and screaming. When the carnival came to town.

NINE YEARS before he died in a rattling fury of fangs and poison, Wendell Morris woke up every day knowing that something good—something *very* good—was coming his way. At twenty-two, he was exactly where he was supposed to be. It was fate. It had to be. *A setup this good didn't just happen. It was preordained. His goddamned destiny!*

There were so many ways that he might never have learned about his gift. So many paths that might have ended with him wearing a paper hat and staring into a hot basket of fries. Or maybe handing lottery tickets and cigarettes across a tall counter, with hand-lettered signs posted above his head making sure that everybody understood the situation: THE CLERK DOES NOT KNOW THE COMBINATION TO THE SAFE and THE CLERK DOES NOT HAVE ANY BILL LARGER THAN $20. Hell, they might as well put up another sign: THE CLERK IS A DUMB-ASS AND CAN'T BE TRUSTED. Or, THE CLERK HAS NO MONEY. IF YOU KILL THE CLERK, IT WILL ONLY BE FOR THE SHEER PLEASURE OF IT.

But—*thank you, universe!*—that wasn't how he'd ended up. Life had taken a happy turn for Wendell. He'd found his place, he'd found his home—

The carnival.

Midways, sideshows, game booths, rides.

He loved them all.

And he was good at them. No, that was wrong: He was *great* at them. So what did it matter that three years ago, it had taken the escalating attention of the law—*nothing serious, nothing dangerous. Damn, man: his drugs, his body, his money. What part of this equation didn't anyone understand?*—to persuade him that traveling with the GYPSY MOON ATTRACTIONS carnival was a wonderful and well-timed career opportunity. And that was fine. Was even more than fine. Because the carnival was where he discovered his gift, was where he found he could sell anything to anybody—to a crowd, to a couple, to a child with a dollar to spend. It was where he found that he intuitively knew—somehow he just knew—which buttons to push and which ropes to pull to move any conversation to a beneficial monetary conclusion. He knew when to press. When to challenge. When to mock. And when to invite. And those weren't things you learned. You either had it or you didn't…

And he *definitely had IT.*

IT was his gift.

IT was his ticket.

All he had to do was keep his eyes open. Watch the signs. Wait for his big turn to use *IT* in the universal rotation. He just needed to be ready. Something big was coming his way. Something really big. He knew, he just knew. But until the big stuff arrived, he was more than happy to enjoy all the little stuff that was already here.

Little stuff like coins. Handfuls of small change. *Small change, my ass*, he thought. Not everyone understood what he knew, that there was a deep, tinkling river of silver and copper flowing all around them. It was all part of the universal rotation, all part of the eternal cycle. A person just had to figure out where to dip his hat into the flowing river of found coinage. Once someone figured that out, he could tuck a tiny living into his pockets every day. There were coins to be found everywhere at the carnival. Spilling out of pockets and purses. Falling onto the seats and floors of the midway rides. Landing in the soft dirt near the ticket booths. They even jumped into the tip jar he always put out no matter which spot he was working that day, whether at the games, the sideshows, or the rides, it didn't matter. Wherever he put it down, the magical tip jar got filled up. He came to believe he could set a tip jar outside a Porta-Potty, leave it there for the day, then find a cupful of coins when he came back. He even knew what sign he'd put on the jar: TAKE A BIG SHIT! REALLY LET IT RIP! FIRST DROP A BIG LOAD! THEN DROP A BIG TIP!

Yeah, coins were great little stuff.

Jewelry was good stuff, too. All of the lost and found adornments of the flesh: finger rings, toe rings, earrings, bracelets, necklaces, chains, loops, studs, chokers, brooches, and pins. He found them, then sold or traded almost all of them.

But he kept his lucky pendant.

He'd found it, gift-wrapped in a small piece of burgundy velvet, on the metal step of his ratty-ass travel trailer. It was late at night and he'd been getting a little drinky-fuzzy. He'd stepped outside to pee and had almost stepped on the pendant, but at the last moment had seen there was something on the step and raised his foot before he crushed it. He'd unwrapped it from the velvet cloth and then looked around, wondering who'd put it there. Had hoped that maybe someone was trying to make nice-nice with the Morris-Man. But there'd been no one around. The only movement he saw was a small curtain-twitch in the trailer of the carnival's fortune-teller. But, damn, he hoped she wasn't the one leaving him gifts. No thank you, Mabel. He'd let the fortune-teller read his palm once. Had let her hold his hand and mumble some mystery words over it, waving her other hand over his while making sing-song noises, until he couldn't take it anymore and just got the hell up and left—

—yeah, that woman gave him a humping case of the cold willies. God knows what kind of voodoo gift-shit she'd leave on someone's step. Her booth sign said it all: MADAM C SEES! ALL YOU WANT TO KNOW. AND MORE YOU DON'T. Besides, she was old—creepy old. Even if she'd seen who left the little velvet bag, he sure wasn't asking her anything about it. It'd be a long time before he needed an answer that bad. He'd just wait. Someone would tell him. People didn't leave gifts for no reason. This kind of thing wasn't accidental. It was intentional. Someone would explain.

But no one did.

Meanwhile, he wore the pendant. At first he wore it to give the gift-giver a conversational opening, a chance to talk. Later he wore it because…well, because he liked it. It was a simple thing. A wire-wrapped, palm-sized cluster of sparkling geode crystals, bound together in the shape of a hanging arrowhead, hanging from a dark leather cord. The crystals were multi-hued shades of cloud, drizzle, and shadow. The weight of the crystals was substantial around his neck, but rather than being uncomfortable, the heaviness was reassuring. The gift was an interesting piece. No doubt about it. An attention-getter. And if the actual gift-giver didn't want to talk about it, well, that was more than fine—there were plenty of others who did, people who pointed at the pendant and commented on it. Paid him compliments. The pendant was a little thing, but—like the rides and games and sideshow booths—it felt...correct. Directed. Part of the things that were coming his way.

No doubt about it, Wendell was doing fine.

It was a good living.

It might have gone on forever.

But then GYPSY MOON ATTRACTIONS set up camp at the Nashville, Indiana, fairgrounds and sent its workers to hand out posters, flyers, and coupons telling everyone the news: The traveling show had arrived. The carnival had come to town.

WALKING THROUGH town, a stack of window posters in one hand and a sack of carnival coupons in the other, Wendell used his shoulder to push through the brown door of a brown building. Inside, he paused, the building's looming quiet and darkness making him think that something was wrong, that maybe he'd made a mistake, maybe accidentally gotten into a vacant building or a closed warehouse. In that strange second—feeling the guilty possibility he was somewhere he shouldn't be—he saw he was not alone, not alone at all, because someone was charging straight at him from the shadows of a far corner (*Security guard? Cop?*), rushing right at him, moving fast and angry—

—Wendell slammed back against the door, instinctively trying to escape the attack, wanting an extra second to explain what had happened, to let the guy know the door hadn't been locked, that he wasn't breaking in, that it was all a misunderstanding—

—but the extra second wasn't going to matter, not to the man coming at him fast, with both arms reaching out, both hands going straight for Wendell's throat as the guy started yelling and yelling and yelling and yelling.

THAD HEARD the door open and raised his eyes from the cage he was staring into. Looking up, he saw sunlight coming through the windows. And saw it bursting against something beautiful. Against something wonderful. Something that took in the light, turning and flashing—

—and he already knew. Could already tell: whatever it was, it was lovely.

It was perfect.

And he had to touch it now.

Had to be near it now.

Had to know the answer.

Had to know. Now.

Right now.

Now.

"THIS! WHAT'S THIS?" the man screamed in Wendell's face. The man's hands were at Wendell's neck. The suddenness of the attack froze him against the door, paralyzed him. His hands, white-knuckled and clenching carnival posters and coupons, were useless balls at the ends of his leaden arms. He lowered his chin. Closed his eyes. Turned his head and tensed his neck. Waited for—

"This! What's this?" the man repeated. Only this time not so loudly.

And Wendell was confused because the man wasn't looking at Wendell's face. He was staring somewhere else. Was staring—

At the pendant.

The man's hands were still reaching, but slowly now. Reverently. Wendell felt the pendant's weight lifted as the man cupped his fingers around it and raised it. He heard the man whispering. Whispering again and again: "This... This... This... What's this?"

THAD FELT the crystals in his hands. Felt the sharp, lovely points of crystal and the sculpted arrowhead shape, all brought together so perfectly with a roping of gold and copper wires. He felt it filling his mind. And already had so many questions. So many things he needed to learn. He wanted it. Wanted everything about it. Wanted it *so much*. But how to get it? How to get it now. Right now. Now.

Then he had an idea. An idea that pushed its way through the thoughts and questions he had about "this"—the "this" that had captured him. The "this" that threatened to overtake him before it was truly his.

The idea seemed so right to him. So correct. So inevitable.

He looked up from the pendant. Looked into the eyes of the boy wearing it. A boy like he had once been a boy, when he'd first opened his collection to the world.

"Snakes," he whispered to the boy. "Do you like snakes?"

IT TOOK Wendell several minutes to fully understand the offer. Then more minutes to grasp its entirety and believe it was true. To be convinced that the man wasn't just some crazy fuck, chock-full o' babble. And then to decide that the man *might* be crazy, but he wasn't full of babble. He was just a guy who wanted out. Out fast. A guy who wanted to be done with everything around him—done with snakes, done with the building, done with the little house that he led Wendell to.

He was also a guy who *really wanted* Wendell's lucky pendant. And, hey, could a pendant be any luckier than being the one you could trade for an entire house and a whole business? Could the universal cosmic cycle's message be any clearer? It looked like it was finally Wendell's turn at the big wheel. Like it was the chance he'd known was coming. So what if he didn't really like snakes? He didn't really dislike them, either. Looked at another way, it was simple, really: The snakes were just a show. An attraction. A ride.

He looked at the house. Then at the building. And his mind started filling with ideas. Started seeing not only *what was there*, but also seeing *what could be there*. He began sensing the possibilities. Began thinking about the buttons he could push. About the ropes he could pull.

It could all work. Could really, really work. He knew. He just knew it.

He handed the man his lucky pendant. Felt the excitement growing inside him.

Because he might not know a lot about snakes—

But, hot damn, he could carnival.

PRESENTATION—

That was the key.

The secret.

"It."

He didn't change much in the brown building. Just enhanced it. Figured out its proper presentation.

First he painted. Painted the whole thing. Got rid of the shit-brown color. Painted everything snake-green. Then painted his great rattlesnake picture and STARE DEATH IN THE EYE! sign on the outside wall.

Inside the building, his four best ideas: THE MOOD. THE STAREDOWN. THE STRIKE. And, best of all, THE PIT WALK.

THE MOOD: People didn't see this one. They heard it. He recorded his own hellish version of a "nature sounds" tape, one where an imagined walk through the woods stirred up angry rattlers at irregular intervals—not too many, but not too few. He hid small speakers in the floor. Played the tape all day. The effect was incredible. More than one person had been strolling along, looking at the caged snakes, feeling safe, maybe daydreaming a little—and then screamed holy hell, jumped back, and almost wet themselves when they suddenly heard the close, angry *trrrrrrrr, trrrrrrr* of a loose rattler about to strike at their ankles.

THE STAREDOWN: He replaced the glass on one wall of cages with magnifying glass. Then positioned some tall store cabinets so that people standing between the cabinets and the snakes were edged forward, pushed closer to the cages than usual. Standing there, they began to realize something had changed, something making their hearts beat faster as an adrenaline tingle began fast-dripping into their veins. Something making them erupt in a chorus of nervous laughter because their backs, literally, were up against a wall as they realized that the situation had somehow been horribly switched around. Suddenly they weren't looking at the snakes. No, instead, those rows of magnified FUCKING HUGE RATTLESNAKES were looking at them.

THE STRIKE: For an extra $1, a person could put their hand against the glass of a cage he kept near the cash register. MOST HAVE SCREAMED! A FEW HAVE CRIED! YOU MIGHT LIVE! A FEW HAVE DIED! *One Try Per Visit, Please!*

If a person could hold their hand perfectly still when the rattler inside struck the glass, Wendell refunded their $1 strike ticket *and* their $2 admission ticket. The screams were wonderful. The excitement was, too. And best of all were the contagious *Me too! Me too's!* that brought more people through the door, all of them wondering what was going on.

And finally—

THE PIT WALK: In the center of the room, situated behind where the original ticket counter had been, a long holding-box had been built into the floor. About two feet deep, three feet wide, eight feet long. The floor-box's sunken walls had pinhole ventilation mesh in them to provide air circulation for the snakes. A hinged wooden lid with four small porthole windows in it covered the length of the box, closing it flush with the floor. *Thad must have liked looking down at the snakes?* he wondered.

Wendell almost put flooring over the box, hiding it away. But then had another idea. He moved the counter away from the center of the room. Replaced the box's porthole-windowed wooden lid with a rectangle of the strongest, clearest, kick-ass acrylic (*scuff-resistant! perfect clarity!*) he could buy. After setting the new lid over the floor-box, he stood back. And had to admit that just looking at it gave him the bloodcurdling heebie-jeebies. The thing looked like a gaping open hole—like there was an exposed nest of rattlers coiled in the middle of the floor. Walking on it was like floating above certain death. He could almost feel the flick of snakes' tongues on his shoes. Could imagine the pierce of fangs sinking into his calf. He'd had to step off the clear lid because—no doubt about it—it was scary shit. Was some powerful mojo. And looking down at it he knew—*he just knew*—that yes, indeed, the carnival had come to town.

FOR NINE YEARS it had been a good living. Good money for a good show. He'd been able to afford getting a little drinky-fuzzy at night. Had been quietly and contentedly enjoying the small gifts that cycled through as this part of the universal rotation.

It had been more than A-OK: It had been great.

Until he met Miss Mouse.

Until his mice met her MOUSE HOUSE.

That night, he got more than a little drinky-fuzzy. Much more. *Planet Shitfaced, straight ahead,* he thought. *We are targeting Planet Shitfaced.* At 2 a.m., after successfully landing all his rockets on the planet, he made a decision. The mice had to go. All of them. *And they had to go now. Right now. That's right, boys! It was FEEDIN' TIME!*

Drunk and stumbling, he filled two empty liquor boxes with every little nacho-cheez-covered MOUSE HOUSE-fucker he could find. He carried the boxes through the dark town and into the SERPENTARIUM yelling "FEEDIN' TIME! IT'S FEEDIN' TIME!" as he opened the boxes and began dropping handfuls of mice into the snake cages. As he worked, the snakes began their serpentine dinner dance toward the screaming, squeaking rodents. When he finished throwing mice into the last wall-cage, the second liquor box was still half full. And suddenly Wendell was just so tired. Was ready to be done with it all. Just wanted to lie down and sleep. But first he had to get rid of the rest of these damn cheese-covered mice, every last one of them. Seeing THE PIT WALK, he decided to dump the rest of the squeaking bastards in all at once.

He held the mouse-filled box in one hand. Pulled THE PIT WALK's heavy acrylic lid up with his other hand. Tried stepping backward at the same time he bent forward to tip the box forward and pour out the mice—

—and the drunken gravity of Planet Shitfaced caught him in its tumbling orbit, pulling his alcohol-fueled body forward into the open PIT WALK. He fell face down into the coffin-like hole, landing on top of twenty rattlesnakes, the heavy lid slamming closed above him—

—and he felt the snakes moving. Moving under his neck and around his knees and over his thighs and on his hands and under his chin and he wanted to GET OUT! GET OUT! GET OUT! and he tried rising on his knees and palms, pushing up fast against the thick lid, and the lid popped up for a second as he felt fangs sinking into the backs of his hands and felt more fangs piercing his legs and the heavy acrylic lid dropped back down and cracked against his head, knocking him back down flat onto the writhing snakes, and he felt another bite…

And another.

And another.

Feedin' time! It's feedin' time, he thought.

Then darkness.

"YOU'RE GOING to be bitten," Thad had told him. "No matter how careful you are. Probably more than once, depending how long you do this. And when it happens, remember this: You are in a town. And the town has a medical clinic. And because there's a Serpentarium in town, the clinic has antivenin. And that's why, when you are bitten, you are going to live."

Thad was right. Wendell had been bitten. Thirteen times in nine years. And he'd lived.

The first time had been a burning, swelling, blood-blistering toxic nightmare that happened in a spinning swirl of his surprised yells (SHIT! DAMN! SNAKE! SHIT!), rushing nurses, and a doctor's quick instructions.

The second time was even less fun. The next few times were bad, too. But not as bad as the first two.

The ninth time, Wendell waited a few hours before walking to the clinic. He'd had things to do and lost track of time. Was locking up the shop that evening and suddenly remembered and said out loud, "Shit, I better get this looked at," but stopped for a chocolate ice cream cone (the poison parched his mouth with the taste of dull, dry metal) before stepping through the clinic door, where a nurse looked up and said, "Bit again?" And Wendell nodded sheepishly, then visited with her for a few minutes before walking back to the patient room to receive the antivenin.

The eleventh time, he'd taken Tylenol, eaten a bowl of chocolate ice cream to take away the metal-varnish taste coating his tongue, called the clinic to let them know he'd be in later, then laid down for a nap.

The thirteenth time, he saw the snake strike his arm. Felt the impact of the head and saw the two puncture marks as the snake pulled away. He stared at the bite, considering what to do. Then, without surprise or excitement, he knew. And said out loud, "Ice cream. I'm going to need some chocolate ice cream."

LYING IN THE PIT WALK's venom-filled darkness, he felt the cosmic spinning of the universal rotation, the eternal vibrato of karmic cogs falling into place. In that darkness, a vision engulfed him, flowing over him like a midnight tide and filling his ears with a susurration of soft forest sounds. And screams. And filling his mind with a rush of images—

—images of a tumble of tall white stones, broken and leaning, painted with blood. And two side-by-side, coffin-shaped piles of rocks. Protruding from under each pile, a pair of skeletal hands clenched and unclenched. The bone fingers scraped and clicked against the rocks, leaving small white tracks of bone dust, like chalk against a slate—

—and the image became a deck of black-and-white picture cards. The cards looked like a thick stack of old Polaroid photographs. They were white-bordered and gray-toned, with a sticky sheen of chemical developer coating them. The cards riffled in front of Wendell like a child's flip-book. He heard *tat-tat-tat* as each photo card snapped forward. As they flipped, the individual pictures ran together, creating a silent film.

Tat-tat-tat. The first photos showed Wendell from behind. They showed him standing, facing the front of the Serpentarium. Then showed him turning and staring directly at the camera. *I'm looking back at myself,* he thought from the darkness where he watched. Only now, in the vision, he was no longer only Wendell. He was now also *something* else, was now *someone* else. His features shifted and morphed, and he saw that he was now—an Indian. A large, well-muscled Indian now stared back at him.

Look, I'm an Indian, he thought. *A warrior. And I'm beautiful.*

Tat-tat-tat. More pictures flipped forward. The cards showed Indian-Wendell raising both hands. His hands were filled with loops of coiling snakes. He dropped the wriggling snakes into a large waist-high, solid-plank box. After dropping in the snakes, he set a plank-top lid onto the box, then wrapped it with a heavy iron-linked chain that appeared at his feet—

Tat-tat-tat. Indian-Wendell pulled a circus-prop sized combination padlock off the SERPENTARIUM wall where it was hanging. He threaded the padlock through the iron chain's links and pushed down. The padlock's arm went *CLACK!* in the darkness as the lock arm ratcheted down into the lock works—

Tat-tat-tat. Indian-Wendell waved his hands over the box (*Hocus Pocus!*). He looked at the heavens, then back at the camera—and he winked! Winked at Wendell in the audience. Winked as if saying, *Now watch this part, this is the good stuff, this is why you buy your ticket.* He dialed the padlock's combination, the dial so comically oversized that Wendell saw every sequenced number. He watched every spinning tock-mark as the dial moved left, right, left, right, and *POP*—

Tat-tat-tat. Off comes the lock. Then the lid opens. Indian-Wendell reaches deep into the box, his whole torso disappearing for a moment. Then he straightens, one arm still in the box, obviously holding something heavy, but he tugs mightily and lifts out (*Presto Change-o!*)—the first monkey (*Ta-Da!*). The monkey immediately walks to the padlock and STARTS DIALING THE COMBINATION!

Tat-tat-tat. A second monkey comes out of the box.

And another.

And another.

Monkey after monkey is pulled out, until finally Indian-Wendell is hidden in the pile of the animals, with only his face showing through the growing mountain of monkeys—

Tat-tat-tat. Indian-Wendell pushes his arm forward through the monkey-hill. His hand, palm forward, is stiff, fingers tight together and pointing straight up. His face, serious and intent, begins moving. Watching the flipping cards of the vision-film, Wendell sees Indian-Wendell's mouth open and watches him begin forming a word. And Wendell knows—because it's suddenly like every old shoot-'em-up Western he's ever seen—he knows the word he's going to hear. In the unformed darkness from where he's watching, he sees Wendell-Indian ask him—

"HOW?"

And stepping closer, asks again, "HOW?"

And again. "HOW?"

Except now Wendell-Indian wasn't mouthing the word anymore, now he was screaming it, screaming, "HOW? HOW? HOW?" And the darkness enveloping real-Wendell wasn't dark anymore. It was bright and blinding and burning. *My God, everything was burning!*

And nurses were now a part of his vision. Doctors, too. The doctors and nurses were all yelling, yelling, "HOW many bites does he have?" And, "HOW long was he lying in there?" And, "HOW much antivenin do we have?" And, "HOW is he still alive?"

He felt the rocking motion of the cosmos, but wondered if it was the wonderful universal rotation or maybe something else? Because he also heard the spinning squeaky-wheel *crree-crree-crree* sound of a fast-moving hospital gurney. He thought that maybe he was no longer in the vision, that maybe he was dying—

He tried to speak. A nurse noticed him staring at her, trying to talk. She leaned close to his mouth, but not too close because his gums were bleeding and his nose was bleeding and his eyes were bleeding and his skin was dewed with a sweat of blood drops. Leaning in, she could barely hear his whisper as he slowly breathed out each word: *"Eyymmm...gohn...nah...kneeed...zum...chaw... coal...lay...tice...screeem...."*

He LIVED.

The immunity in his blood was stronger than the poison. And when he left the hospital, he left with a mission.

He made the snakes disappear. (*Hocus Pocus!*) He gave them away. Gave them to the county's conservation officer to do with what he might.

And he bought monkeys (*Ta-Da!*): eight Japanese macaques. Snow monkeys.

And of course—in a way—he killed himself.

He ended old Wendell's life and began anew as an Indian (*Presto Change-o!*). At least he tried to. He tried connecting with his "hidden Indian"—the Indian soul that the vision had revealed, the spirit he now felt living inside him. He changed his name, stopped being Wendell and became Chicory Dirtfoot. He began trying to follow the old ways, after first studying them in books at the Brown County Library. He started speaking a traditional greeting, *Ya-Ta-Hey!* to all who entered his store, and never once asked anyone, "How?" He began wearing turquoise and silver squash blossom jewelry. Braided his hair and let it grow longer. He became more spiritual. Burned the sage stick every day, letting the holy smoke purify himself and his home. And he remembered to present the gift of sacred tobacco (usually a few packs of Marlboro Reds) to the leaders of the sweat lodges he began attending. And he stopped drinking. Mostly.

And every day, to fulfill the vision he'd been given, he tried teaching a monkey—the first monkey—to escape from his cage.

SETSU IS THE first monkey. The monkey troop's alpha male.

Chicory cleans the cage at dawn each day. He mops first, then puts out fresh food and bedding. In the early morning, the monkeys—all except Setsu—are usually still sleeping, their arms and legs tangled around each other like a braid of hairy ribbons.

Setsu is always awake. Always sitting alone and hunched over, arms folded, facing east, his brown eyes fixed on the rising sun. He always turns his head to watch Chicory open the door. *I've been waiting*, he seems to say. The monkey is smart, that much is obvious.

After the cleaning the cage and the filling the food dishes, Chicory checks the water in the cage's large hot tub. He makes sure the water's clean, and that it's hot enough. The monkeys like soaking in the steaming water. As they soak, the expressions on their red faces is the same one seen in hot tubs everywhere. *Damn, this feels good. I could go to sleep right now.*

Morning chores done, Chicory sits down cross-legged next to Setsu. With a sense of delicate expectation, the monkey looks at him. Chicory reaches into his pocket. Pulls out a note. Hands it to the monkey. Setsu takes the paper from him. Holds it in his black-fingernailed hands. It's the same note Chicory gives Setsu every morning. A simple diagram of illustrated instructions showing how to work the oversized, large-dial, combination padlock on the cage's door. The oversized lock on the cage is exactly the same—and set to the exact same combination—as the second padlock that Setsu carries everywhere, clearly understanding that it's his.

The drawing shows a series of four lock-dials. Above each dial is either a clockwise or counter-clockwise arrow and a large number. Each number matches the number that's also shown on the lock-dial below it: "Left-10, Right-23, Left-8, Right-1." After the lock diagrams, there's a sequence of other pictures: an open padlock, an open cage door, a monkey stepping through the door, into the freedom outside the cage.

Most mornings, Setsu stares intently at the paper. Sometimes he looks at the drawings. Other times he watches the mucous trail that drips out of his nose and onto the message. With Setsu still holding the paper, Chicory picks up the long, heavy padlock Setsu always keeps close (dragging it with him on the ground, even carrying it up into the ropes). Chicory slowly dials the lock's combination, dialing exactly like it's drawn on the paper, exactly like he'd seen in his vision. As he dials, he shows the monkey the direction he's spinning the knob, pointing to the numbers that he's turning the knob to.

Each morning—after looking at the note, after dialing the combination—they sit together for a few minutes and watch the rest of the sunrise. After the sun's properly up, Setsu shakes himself and stands. Seems to say, *Well, time to get moving. Another day, another banana and all that...* He moves off to join the rest of the waking monkey troop. Or sometimes he slips into the hot tub's steaming water, sinking down until only his head shows above the surface. He rests in the tub, eyes half-closed, a contented sigh often escaping from between his lips.

SOME EVENINGS—late in the thick, black-velvet part of night, the part that's after today but before tomorrow—Chicory awakens in his bed. Unable to sleep, he walks through town to the monkey cage. He opens the cage door. Steps inside. Relocks the door and sinks quietly down, sitting with his back pressed against the night-chilled steel bars, feeling the cool concrete floor beneath him. He can hear the murmured sleep whistles of the monkeys above him. The troop sleeps huddled aloft in the ropes and hide-away boxes. All except Setsu. Just like he's awake in the mornings, Setsu is also awake in the nights.

In the cage, they both sit motionless, watching the moon and stars.

Sometimes Setsu rises and walks over, moving like a hunched, gray ghost. The only noise Chicory hears is the steel scraping of Setsu's padlock, scraping against the cement as the monkey drags it behind him. Arriving beside Chicory, Setsu sits. He turns his head, looks at Chicory for a moment (*Nice night, isn't it?*), then looks again at the moon.

Together, they sit in silence.

A part of the night.

Friends.

A contented sigh often escaping from between Chicory's lips.

HARLEY 10

"**T**UMOR-EARS! Tumor-ears! Tumor-ears!"

He gasped the words as he shuffle-danced with the fifth stuffed-full mailbag he'd pigeon-walked to the truck this morning. His baseball cap, already pulled low, slid even lower, riding down his sweaty forehead. At the mail truck, he held the heavy bag against the rear bumper, bracing it with his hip. He rested there, hunched over, breathing fast, waiting for his cramped spine to relax. When his back finally unclenched and the muscles loosened enough that he could almost stand upright, he tried to stretch, then squatted down and grabbed the bottom of the mailbag. He took two deep breaths, getting ready for the weight, then quickly stood and dead-lifted the bag up, swinging it over the bumper and into the truck's cargo hold.

As he threw the bag, another back spasm and a wave of light-headedness hit him hard, made him dizzy. Inertia carried him forward into the truck and he fell clumsily, his knees rolling over the bumper, his arms reaching out, his outstretched hands slapping against a mailbag and pushing it over. An avalanche of stacked and stapled notices slid out. He landed badly, half in and half out of the truck, his breath hiccupping in tiny hitches and starts as he stutter-shouted, "KEE-RIST HAVE MERCY!" and felt his rippling back pain morph into yellow nausea, making him swallow and gag to stop from vomiting.

Even in his pain, he knew his cap had fallen off. He pawed for it through the spilled papers, his arms moving frantically until he found the hat and pulled it back on, snugging it down over his head while lying prone and gagging.

FOR EIGHTEEN YEARS, Harley had been delivering the mail along the same two routes. First, the morning walking route through town, then the afternoon driving route, a long, straight stretch down Highway 46, then a sharp left onto Salt Creek Road, following the big winding circle around the base of Jonah's Belly. Most days, he felt like he'd won the job lottery, like no one anywhere had a better job, a job that let him spend most days alone with his time and his thoughts. And there wasn't much better that a man could ask for than time alone—for time to think, time to open his eyes and see...to really see. *Nosiree,* he thought. *A man couldn't ask for much more than that.*

On good days, he scooted quickly through the mornings, dropping mail at the few real homes still left in town, the ones not yet turned into storefronts or sold to someone who was planning to turn them into storefronts. Then he delivered to the shops along the town's streets. The storeowners always tried to slow him down, tried to take his day from him, always asking the same questions about the tourists, always with the same anxious appraisal: *What do you think, Harley? A good crowd today? Lots of buyers walking around?* Just once before he retired he wanted to give an honest answer, wanted to say out loud, "Do I look like I give a running shit? Do I look like I care a good goddamn?" The tourists tried to slow him down too, asking their own stupid questions. *Hey, buddy, where can a guy take a piss around here?* was the usual winner, just ahead of *Where can a guy get a beer around here?*

When everything worked smoothly, he was out of town by mid-morning and onto the back roads that five million annual tourists had no idea existed—and that was dandy-fine with him.

Let them all stay in town, bumping and rubbing and sweating against each other.

He loved the empty roads. The solitude, the quiet. Loved having time to sit back. Take off his hat. Open his eyes. And being free to see…to really see.

No doubt about it, most days were good days.

Then there were the other days. Bad days. Days like today. Days when the legendary Pony Express rider fell off his trusty horse. Sprained his back. Almost projectile-vomited his morning eggs and bacon across the village mail.

He lay in the back of the mail truck, half-buried under spilled notices. Legs dangling two inches above the pavement. "Tumor-ears! Tumor-ears! Tumor-ears!" he murmured again. *Two more years* to finish his twenty years to a fully-funded retirement. *Two more years*, and then he'd be free. Free to sit and look. *No! That wasn't right. He'd be free to sit and…see. To really see.*

His right hand moved to the bill of the ball cap, then finger-walked to the top of his head, his fingers finding the spot they were searching for. He pushed down lightly, pressing his scalp through the fabric, feeling the slight, spongy depression in his head. He traced the slight concave dip of skin that stretched across the drill-hole in his skull. The flesh sagged there like a loose pool cover over his third eye—over his path to higher thought, over his way to see… to *really see.*

Stroking the soft skull-spot, he smiled. He'd made the right choice a year ago, when the relentless stabbing, twisting headaches and the cave-full of screeching brain-bats in his head had him trying to choose between the two solutions sitting right in front of him on his kitchen table. One choice was a dandy-fine, twelve-gauge, walnut stock, short-barreled shotgun that looked delicious—looked absolutely good enough to eat. The other choice was a variable-speed hand drill, its Teflon-coated, one-inch disc drill-bit appearing full of sharp promises—promises to let all the noises and pain out of his brain, and maybe even a few promises to let some sunshine in.

HE REMEMBERED it all—

—remembered looking from one choice to the other, his gaze drifting back and forth between the gun and drill before finally settling on the drill's circle of steel cutting teeth. Then, choice made, he stood and walked over to a small, knickknack shelf on the kitchen wall. The shelf was cluttered with a jumbled collection of multi-colored pill bottles. Some of the bottles were capped and others were open, some were empty and others were not, some had his name on the prescription and others had the names of people who—with a little light-fingered help from Harley—hadn't received their monthly "medicine through the mail" drug deliveries. He grabbed one of the open bottles and shook a small pile of white tablets into his hand, then grabbed another bottle and emptied its last remaining yellow tablets onto the white pills. Without looking at the pills, he palmed the whole handful into his mouth and dry-swallowed them in a single gulp. As he finished swallowing, he looked up and saw his reflection in the cheap plastic mirror hanging above the shelf. The dinner plate-sized mirror was covered with a reflective coating of rippled, silver film. Printed across the bottom in flame-blue, yellow-tipped letters were the words *LOOKING GOOD WITH NATURAL GAS!*

As a rule, Harley didn't like tourists and hated the fucking gas company, but a few weeks ago he'd met someone who was the exception to his rule. He'd been delivering the mail through town when a tall, red-haired man in a black suit had stopped Harley to ask a question, or maybe just to talk a bit—Harley couldn't remember exactly what. Interruptions normally pissed him off, but this time was different, this time it was okay…he could tell that the red-haired man was one of the good guys, was someone who actually cared. The man's bright blue eyes were so full of concern, were filled with so much kindness and understanding. Although Harley couldn't remember the details of their conversation, at the end of it the red-haired man had given him the mirror as a token of appreciation for whatever assistance or advice Harley had provided. And now, still grateful for the red-haired man's generous gift, Harley lifted the mirror off of its hook and took it over to the kitchen table, where he propped it up against a row of empty liquor bottles. Sitting back down, he stared into the mirror and re-read its message: *LOOKING GOOD WITH NATURAL GAS!*

Exactly, Harley thought. The red-haired man was right. It was time. Time to start looking. Time to start *looking good*.

Grabbing a full bottle of whiskey, he poured the alcohol down his throat, then splashed it across his tools. Then lifted the bottle and poured it over his head. Using a pair of orange-handled scissors, he cut a circle of hair off the crown of his head and shaved off the last bristles with a disposable razor and a can of Barbasol menthol shaving cream. Head freshly shaved and looking oh-so-pretty, he put a safety mask on to cover his eyes, pulling the silicone straps tight against his forehead, then slipped two terrycloth sweat bands over his forehead, pushing them down against the top of the mask to soak up the blood he knew would eventually come.

Headbands and safety glasses in place, he smeared the shaved spot with a numbing, sticky, mixture of Anbesol, Cortaid, and Benadryl, then drank more whiskey and waited for numbness— from the pills, the whiskey, or the goop on his head, it didn't matter which—to set in. And when numbness finally came, he wiped off the paste and picked up a shiny silver dollar coin and a short-bladed paring knife. Peering into the mirror, he pressed the coin down onto the shaved patch of his scalp and held it there with his left thumb while holding the knife in his right hand like a pencil, his finger pads close to the blade. He lifted the knife and set the sharp tip against the edge of the silver dollar on his head. He breathed in and breathed out and breathed in one more time, then grunted and pushed on the blade, pushing it through his head-flesh, cutting down to the bone, then cutting around the edge of the coin, jaggedly tracing the circle with the knife, and while he was cutting—

—the bats darted and swooped and screamed in the darkness, beating into each other, biting, their black parchment wings rasping and flapping in a dark, trapped frenzy. They heard the knife digging above them, heard the *scritch-scritch* of it cutting through gristle and skin, heard its sharp tip scoring the surface of his skull bone, the booming, scratching sound of it vibrating in his head like a fifty-gallon steel drum being pushed across a rusty metal floor—

—and there was blood everywhere, a warm bath of it pouring down his head, running through his hair and into his ears, down the back of his neck, streaming down his forehead, across his goggles. Watching himself in the red-haired man's mirror, he cut almost all the way around the silver dollar, then put down the knife and the coin and picked up a grapefruit spoon. He touched the edge of the spoon's serrated bowl with his finger, checking its sharpness, then reached up and wedged it between the edges of his freshly sliced head skin and pushed the spoon down until it hit his skull. He wiggled the spoon under the lip of flesh, using the serrated tip to tear through the wet suction bond of skin on bone. As the spoon cut his scalp, he heard the sound of ripping Velcro strips echoing in his brain along with the screeching bats and other screaming coming from somewhere else inside his home, and he knew—

—the other screaming was his. But it seemed so far away, so removed from him, because now he was watching from somewhere else, from nowhere near the man he saw prying on the grapefruit spoon's blood-smeared handle, popping up a round dollop of scalp that folded wetly back on a thin hinge of uncut head-meat as he let go of the spoon and reached for the drill, and—

—felt his bare skull with his other hand. Looked into the mirror again, but couldn't see much anymore, not through the blood-covered goggles. Set the drill's saw-bit against his slippery, exposed head bone. He pushed down, giving the bit's steel teeth a firm bite, setting the cutting circle properly in place. And still watching from far away, from nowhere near the man with the drill, he heard the drill's whirring spin, smelled burning bone, tasted burning flesh. And watched the man push down harder, watched the bit sink lower, a moist mist of skull grit and crimson falling all around.

He watched till the bit cut cleanly through the bone—then dropped the drill on the table and saw a disc of head bone pop out of the bit and roll away like a tossed poker chip. He watched it roll, thinking, *I'll see your bet and raise you two.*

Then more whiskey. Down his throat. Over his head.

And more screaming.

He plunged his head into the cooler full of ice-water on the table, and even underwater he could still hear the screaming. Lifting his cold, dripping head out of the cooler, he pulled a thick, folded towel down against his head to soak up the water and the blood. Then dropped the towel and grabbed the flapping scalp-hinge between his slippery fingers and flipped it down over the open head-hole, stretching the flap tight over the hole's edges as he held a bottle of Superglue over his head with his other hand and squeezed out the glue, squirting it onto the stretched, overlapped skin until the bottle was empty. He flung the bottle away. Fell to the floor. And then—

Nothing.

No screeching. No rasping whir of bat wings. No screaming. No flying waves of small, biting white teeth. No claws scratching against the walls of his brain's dark tunnels.

Nothing.

Just silence. Wonderful silence—

Except, of course, for the voice.

The good voice.

The voice that began teaching him, began telling him how to use his new "third eye." That began telling him how to see. *How to really see.*

Later, he knew he'd been right. Knew that he'd chosen correctly. He'd done exactly what he wanted done. The noises were quieted. The pain had gone away. He'd let the bad things out, and good things had come back in. There was no mash of horrible sounds in his head anymore. Now there was only the good voice—the good, warm voice he heard when he woke days later on the floor. The voice that knew so much, that knew so many secrets. The voice that whispered when he'd opened his eyes, whispering to him softly. Saying, *Looking good, Harley. Looking good...*

STILL LYING in back of the truck. His breathing starting to sound normal, his nausea finally settling down. *Well, it was time to get working.* Time to climb his ass out of the back of the truck and start moving again, like he'd done the last eighteen years, like he intended to do for two more (...*tumor-ears, tumor-ears, tumor-ears...*).

He stood, ready to once again deliver the mail to the most beautiful place on earth. Beautiful for now, at least—until whatever dirty shit the gas company was planning to do actually started getting done. The company's mailers were a damn wonder of confusing warnings. Five bags of the stapled and stacked notices were already in his truck, with eight more bags of the same shit still left to load. And all of it to let people politely and officially know that the corporate ass-screwing was about to officially begin...and you didn't need a third eye to see that storm coming.

He picked up one of the notices and read it again, the same one being sent to everyone in Brown County.

NEW WAY INDIANA GAS & NATURAL RESOURCES, INC.
FORMAL SUBMISSION AND PUBLICATION OF INTENT
PROPOSAL TO DEVELOP
BURIED HIGH-PRESSURE NATURAL GAS PIPELINE
AND REQUEST FOR LANDOWNER PERMISSION OF
PROPERTY SURVEY AND RIGHT OF EASEMENT
"Now You're Cooking With Gas!"

The multi-page notice was filled with pictures of happy people enjoying "the miracle of natural gas." With diagrams, too, renderings of the proposed pipeline. And captions under the drawings: *You'll*

Never Know We're Here! An Incredible Supply of Untapped Reserves! USA's Second Largest Gas Field! SAFE! SAFE! SAFE! LET'S DO THIS TOGETHER!

Not good, he thought. *Not good at all. Those gas-bastards are gonna ruin this beautiful place.* Staring at the pages, he started feeling angry. Angry at anyone planning to dig and drill and cut through these hills. He started thinking that he might not deliver the mail today after all, at least not this particular mail—

Then he heard the voice. The warm, good voice. The voice that knew so much. *But, Harley, wouldn't you like to be cooking with gas?* asked the voice. *Wouldn't you like turning up the heat, naturally?*

And answering the voice, Harley thought, *Maybe. Maybe I would.*

BLUE

11

THE CIRCLE'S MAGIC is transient. It is here, and then not. I'm learning the feel of it, the sense of its waves. Learning how it moves in pulses and bursts. How it ebbs and flows in spirals of unpredictable direction. Its touch is not a simple equation. There's no set pattern of "this does this, then that does that." Like music, there are lulls and rests, then trills and staccato riffs.

I've learned that one of my first thoughts about the Circle was wrong. Even on days when the thick, powerful push of its magic-infused air almost sparks against my skin, not all of my steps return me to the Circle. And not every walk to the back of the closet in the cabin carries me to the Stones.

The magic is more random than that.

On some days, the Circle seems to pause and wait. It stands quietly on those days, looking like nothing more than a simple circle of tall, leaning stones. On those days, when the Stones send no whispers or storms of augury coursing down the hill, I'm filled instead with the sense of everyday magic and wonder that is already and always here...and that is still a most powerful thing.

Everyday magic and wonder: It is waking in this place where the air is lush with possibilities. It is the friendships and love I hold dear, knowing those feelings will stay strong. And it's the music that fills this cabin. Each day, I listen to the voices of Solomon Burke, and Johnny Adams, and Toni Price, singers who find the pulse of each song, who sound *exactly right* about sorrow and sex and love and loss and kindness and anger and the small moments of life that fill every day.

Everyday magic and wonder: It is the wind that's here, the ripple of air that brushes over water and flowers and earth, that rushes between tall branches, over fallen logs, and through cool shadows. That wind is the breath of this place, the inhalation and exhalation of these hills.

Everyday magic and wonder: It is even the simple joy of good drink. The taste of strong black coffee. Tumblers full of brittle-cold water. A glass or two of rich red wine at day's close. These are the tastes of my morning, noon, and night. The tastes of thought and reflection. Of celebration and relaxation. Of conversation and contemplation.

Every day.

Magic.

And wonder.

I START EACH day with a mug of that strong black coffee.

I rise early each morning and sit at the window, staring sleepily out into the woods. Sitting there, I try to remember to give thanks for the many blessings that fill my life. And I try to remember to offer prayers for those who are in need, for those who are in pain.

I try. I do. And most mornings, it works.

But there are other mornings. Mornings when I remember other things. Mornings when I think of the lessons I've learned. Harsh, unforgettable lessons. About cause and effect. About action and reaction. And, mostly, about sticks and stones.

They are the lessons I remember every time I pass the small yellow sign posted near a wide bend in Salt Creek road. The sign is polite. Brief. Cautious.

PLEASE
WATCH FOR FALLING ROCKS

I drink my morning coffee, and I think about the yellow sign. And about the road. And about a moment in time, eleven months ago. Some people would put a small white cross at that spot near the road. The cross would be a sentimental marker of their tragedy. It would be their reminder. *Here*, the cross would tell them, *here is where my wife was wounded. Here is where my son was killed.*

But I have no need of a small white cross. I need no reminder. I will never forget.

Besides, the sign is always there.

The sign is a reflective yellow diamond, the official shape of WARNING. It is a common sign, usually seen at the edges of roads along steep hills and mountains, or posted beside low trails that cut through tall, stony ground.

The yellow signs are messengers. Foretellers of possible harm.

There is always an unkempt scatter around the signs, a fallen jumble of jagged rocks and chipped boulders that have dropped down from the high places above. These broken stones serve as validation, as geological proof that the sign is right. *Rocks Have Fallen. And More Rocks Will Fall. Watch Carefully!*

When they see these yellow signs, travelers glance nervously down at the collected tumble of fallen debris, studying the deadly mixed scree of sharp edges and blunt heavy objects. Next they fearfully look up, ready to swerve their cars or dodge aside. Staring skyward, the travelers search for descending danger. But they see nothing dropping toward them: No rocks are falling. Not then.

Because the rocks rarely fall.

Hardly ever.

And never while we're watching.

THERE'S A CHILDREN'S story, told on long road trips when interest in the passing scenery has waned or when the game of License Plate Bingo has been played too many times during too many highway hours and weary parents want a few quiet minutes. That's when, as the car approaches one of the yellow diamond-shaped warning signs, parents tell their children the story…

Many moons ago, a great Indian tribe lived in this place. Their lands were vast, stretching as far as a wild goose could fly in two suns' time. The tribe was happy. Their life was good. The warriors were strong, the hunters, skillful. The tribe enjoyed peace, and there was food for all.

The leader of the tribe was the wisest of chiefs. He was a noble man, respected by all the People, near and far. The Chief had once been both the fiercest of warriors and the most cunning of hunters. Now, as Chief, he had guided his people well for many years and was a loving father to his only child, a beautiful daughter named Forest Flower. She was beautiful indeed. Her hair was long and black, and the light in her eyes was keen and calm. And it was time for her to marry.

Two of the tribe's Braves were in love with Forest Flower. Each wanted her as his wife. The names of the two Braves were Many Bears and Falling Rocks. Both were courageous and strong. Both had been victorious in battle. Each was sincere in his love for Forest Flower. And each was angered by the other's love for her.

The wise Chief knew he must solve this problem. He had watched his daughter closely and knew that her heart was filled with love for Falling Rocks. But he also knew that he must act fairly, as each Brave was a worthy choice. The Chief decided that a contest would determine who would marry Forest Flower. He offered the two Braves this challenge: Go into the woods and hunt. Whoever returns with the most pelts, with the most beautiful and rare furs, will win Forest Flower's hand in marriage.

With that challenge, both Braves rode their mounts into the forest, each traveling in a different direction. Their bows were strong. Their quivers were full. Their knives were sharp.

Days passed. Then weeks.

Finally, Many Bears returned from the forest. His horse, piled high with soft pelts, pulled a sled hidden beneath a heaping mound of even more furs. There were skins of fox, deer, beaver, and buffalo. The tribe was amazed at the success of Many Bears' hunt. Certainly, they thought, Many Bears would win the hand of Forest Flower.

In anticipation, the tribe awaited the return of Falling Rocks.

They waited. Then waited some more.

After months had passed, the tribe beseeched their chief to declare Many Bears the winner of the contest. Knowing his daughter loved only Falling Rocks, the Chief did not want to name Many Bears the victor, not without giving Forest Flower's true love a chance. "No," he told the tribe. "We will continue to wait for the return of Falling Rocks. When Falling Rocks left," said the Chief, "his bow was strong, his quiver was full, and his knife was sharp. He will come back to us. And we will wait for him."

So wait they did.

Months went by. Then years. But still the Brave did not return.

Some believe that he is still in the forest, still hunting for the most beautiful and rarest furs, wanting to be sure he wins the hand of Forest Flower. Through all the passing years, the Chief instructed everyone to keep searching for the Brave, to keep looking until he was found. Even today, the tribe continues to look for him. And that is why, when you drive through these hills, you will see signs that say WATCH FOR FALLING ROCKS.

IN ONE MONTH it will be a year.

In one month, an anniversary will pass.

An anniversary we will endure.

Eleven months ago. When Elissa was eight months pregnant. When the dome of her belly dimpled and bumped with the rolling turns and tiny kicks of our growing son.

Eleven months ago. When we weren't watching for falling rocks.

And when, unwatched, one fell.

We were driving home along Salt Creek Road. The evening sky

was a dusky ochre ocean, with clouds that were orange and purple-tinged pillars of unraveling white fire. The colors were reflected in the salt stream beside the road, turning the water into a melting glaze of hammered copper and bronze. The sun was setting quickly, darkening the tall hill on my side of the car.

Elissa's hands were resting on her stomach, waiting for each small push of fist or foot, each press of our baby's hip or shoulder. I remember looking at her hands. They were outlined against the green and purple paisley swirls of her maternity dress.

Approaching a wide bend, I slowed down and looked across Salt Creek, looking for the clearing where, on other nights, we'd sometimes seen a family of deer grazing. My head was down, angled to see past Elissa and out her window. The deer were there again. I saw them, five twilight-blurred shapes standing in the field on the other side of the stream. One of the shapes wore an outline of antlers. I remember his head turning toward us, watching us, appraising our threat.

"There," I said, taking one hand off the steering wheel and pointing.

Elissa was looking out her window, too. I remember how she turned her head toward me, just the smallest of turns to see where I was pointing.

And above us, unwatched, a falling rock fell.

The rock hit us.

It struck the car where the roof joins the windshield. It exploded through the window. The window shattered inward in a rain of tempered glass.

And the rock still fell.

It crashed against my wife's body, crushing into the cushion of her flesh and the fluid that was our son's only safety. And then the car was careening and tilting, turning off of the road and rolling over and over, down to the stream.

And the rock still fell.

It tore between Elissa's legs, then through the fabric and

springs of her seat, slamming down against the car's steel floor then bouncing back up and out, flying through the glassless window. Elissa followed the rock through the opening, flung out of the car like a loose bundle of limbs and cloth.

The car flipped over and over and landed on its top. My head crashed down into the roof, the roof that was now somehow below me. Slumped there, at the edge of consciousness, I looked at Elissa. She was at the water's edge, lying there as if sleeping. She lay with her arms at her sides, with her waist and legs submerged in the molten flow of the bronze and copper-colored stream. The full skirt of her maternity dress was a black floating oval in the water.

Then all I saw was darkness.

GORDON FOUND US.

He was coming to visit for dinner that night. Had also slowed down to look for deer. Instead, what he saw was us. He radioed for help, then waded into the accident and into the creek and began to save us. The people he called came quickly, joined him in the stream, and tried to fix what they found.

Elissa died. That's what they told me later. That lying there in the stream, she died and was then brought back by those working to save her.

For a moment. though, she was gone.

For a moment, I'd lost everything at the water's edge.

In the hospital that night, Gordon sat by my bed, telling me the things that I needed to know. I learned that I had suffered little harm: minor head trauma, a slight concussion, cuts and bruises and bumps. I would spend a day under observation, then I could leave.

But my Elissa was broken. She was torn and cut and bleeding, her body a mash of pulped tissue and pain. Her injuries made a whole list of medical damage, a dictionary of terms meaning nothing good. All of it meaning that I might lose her again.

And our fine small boy was gone.

In the days that followed, I heard words like "uterine rupture" and "fetal skull fracture." But I didn't hear them that night. That night, Gordon only told me the "what" of things, not the "how" or the "why." That night, I heard only that I must tightly hold on to Elissa, because she was the one I still had. And I saw that Gordon, hushed and weeping, would hold us both.

THE FALLING ROCK first struck Elissa's left hand. The hand that was resting on the shelf of her belly. The hand that danced to the music of each message of warmth and motion from the life growing inside her. As the rock fell against her hand, it crushed the design of delicate bones it found there, tearing off her little finger. The other bones in her hand healed. But the little finger was gone.

Now, when we hold hands, we both feel the small thing that is missing from our clasp. And this absence feels right. It feels true. It feels like we feel inside. Like something is gone. Like something empty.

And we hold hands all the tighter.

BLUE 12

I WAS RELEASED from the hospital the day after the accident, but I did not leave. I waited for Elissa. Waited for her green eyes to open with more than a look of numb, sedated haze. Waited to know that I had her still. Waited to be the one to tell her about our son…and waited to hold her when she heard.

I slept in a chair by her bed. Brought food up from the cafeteria. Gordon spent many quiet hours with us, trying, I think, to will a portion of his vast strength into us. Trying to protect us from whatever other harm might try to visit us at our weakest time. He spent the rest of his time working and taking care of the animals at our cabin.

On the third day, Elissa opened her eyes with a look that was clear and aware. She didn't raise her head, but turned it slowly from side to side, carefully considering the scene to which she'd woken.

She looked at me first, then at the bland details of the hospital room around us. She stared for a few moments at the medical machines standing sentinel at her side. Then— her mouth beginning to tremble, her eyes beginning to fill with tears—she carefully looked down where our child had been growing in the perfect home her body had made. She saw that it was now hidden in bandages. And saw that it was empty. And again, she looked at me.

I moved closer to her, trying to touch her so very softly, trying to be so very careful of the bandages and sutures and dripping tubes that were needled into her body. I don't know which one of us was whispering, or which of us was keening, or who was holding whom. The distinctions did not matter. We were two parts of a whole. An animal that cried and comforted, that flailed and soothed, that collapsed and gave support. We stayed that way for an evening and a day, at times one of us drifting off and the other staying awake, blurring even the lines between our dreams. Our edges seemed to disappear. Each one's heart becoming the other's heart. Each one's arms the other's arms. Each one's mouth the other's mouth. Each one of us breathing for both of us when the other could not breathe. Each of us growing stronger. Together. As one.

I WENT HOME on the afternoon of the fifth day. Elissa stayed, still wrapped in bandages, still surrounded by machines. Gordon drove me from Bloomington Hospital back to the cabin. We rode in silence, tired and not talking.

Pulling up to the cabin, I stepped out of his truck. I stood there stiffly, looking at the cabin, suddenly overwhelmed with a paralyzing sense of confusion. Unable to decide what to do next. Go up the stairs—*and then what?* Go inside—*and then what?*

"Blue," I heard Gordon say behind me, "go get some rest. Go inside and sleep. Go. Sleep. Now."

Unable to form any words, I nodded. Then went inside. And I slept. But only for minutes. I opened my eyes and sat up, feeling awkward in my home, feeling like I was wearing a stranger's clothes. Things felt tight around me. Uncomfortable and airless. Without Elissa beside me, I could not breathe.

I needed to get outside. Needed to take a drive. Needed to go to the place where a family of deer sometimes grazed in the evening. To the place where a diamond-shaped yellow sign stood near the wide bend in Salt Creek Road. I needed to go there, where my wife had been crushed and torn. Where my son had been bloodied and baptized in a creek of reflected fire. To where my boy had been brutally born and had brutally died.

I drove Elissa's car because my car had been wrecked beyond repair. Her car's windows were closed, so when I opened the door, I smelled the captured scent of my wife. I sat there a few minutes, windows still up, inhaling and exhaling. Feeling Elissa beside me. Feeling able to breathe again.

I drove carefully. Tentatively.

Near the yellow sign, I pulled over, parking as close to the hillside as possible. Getting out, I looked up, watching for falling rocks. And saw nothing.

Then I crossed the road and stood there, looking down at the creek, at the quiet flow of water and afternoon sun. There was so little there to see, so little to remind me…. The few gashes of torn earth showed me where to look, but no one else would look here and be able to remark, *An accident happened here. A woman was horribly hurt. And a baby died.*

It made me wonder: How many places did I casually pass each day that held the memories of accident and tragedy? How many places did I look at and see nothing, while another person—someone watching in anguish from a distance—saw me and thought, *How can he not see? How can he not know? How can he not feel?*

The creek was beautiful. The water was a rippled, glass-green on top, with a blue-clay shadow beneath. Across the creek, the open patch of grasses and spring flowers was calm. Our car—a wreck of bent steel and broken glass—had been hauled away. And now my wife lay in a hospital bed and my boy's tiny body was buried. All hint of trauma was gone from here. Except for me. I stood as evidence, as proof of damage and grief.

One other thing was here, too, setting back from the water's edge.

A brown rock.

The rock that had fallen.

It had bounced off our car and landed in the soft soil. Where the rock struck, the ground had crumpled under its weight, forming a rolled collar of earth around the rock's base. I walked down the creek bank and over to the rock. I sat down on the grass, near enough to touch it. But I did not touch it.

I studied it, this rock that had waited an eon to fall.

It was shale stone, one of the large, thick blocks that sometimes slough off of high, crumbling outcroppings and then fall. Narrow, tinted bands of red and chocolate hues ran through the tanned-hide color of its surface. A goiter of dark brown moss grew near its bottom, just inches above the ground that cradled the rock. A drying splatter of thick mud coated the front of the rock.

I stared at it, unable to lift my eyes from its indifferent face. Was unwilling to move from its stoic company. I searched its surface for any hint of emotion—passion? remorse? love? I looked for anything that lay within its form, studying it for any clue that might explain to me: *Why?*

And I found nothing. There were no secrets it would share. No answers it would give.

How do you describe the size of the mallet that strikes and kills your child? How do you give it dimension? You don't say, "It was bigger than the earth from which it sprang. Bigger than the sky from which it fell. It was so big that, as it tumbled down, it blotted out every day he would have ever seen and shrouded every night he would have ever slept. The rock was larger than his whole life. It was a world whose gravity sucked in and swallowed all our dreams, that pulled them down and extinguished them, forever and ever, amen."

No, you don't say things like that.

Instead, you make comparisons. You say, "The rock was about the size of a large jack-o-lantern. Or a big bag of ice"—you say and think such silly things. Such stupid things. Such strange and empty and small things.

I REACHED OUT. Touched the rock. Laid my fingertips on its top. Felt its solid feel. Felt the thin, granular dust of erosion on its surface. I moved my fingers over it, along the striated color lines across its planes.

I ran my hands slowly down the rock's sides, trailing through the plastering of mud that was dry on its surface but still wet and cool beneath. My fingers left scalloped tracks in the mud, like little roads across a stone world.

My hands moved to touch the egg-sized bulb of dark brown moss growing on the rock's base. I expected to feel the spongy give of lichen, the velvety texture of short, mossy tendrils. I didn't expect what I felt instead. Didn't expect the rubbery, elastic sense of it. Or its cold adhesive touch. Or how it quickly painted my fingers with a slippery brown stain. As I pinched the bulb between my thumb and finger and pulled, I didn't expect the sticky, pinkish-brown rope that stretched free—the rope of chewing tobacco-stained bubble gum. A brown wad of Creel's "calling card" that was squashed down onto the rock.

And a shrill noise filled my head—a noise so loud that, for a moment, my eyes rolled back in their sockets and my eyelids fluttered at the frantic shock of the roaring sound, at the reverberating echo of a refrain I remembered from so long ago...*dots and plugs, dots and plugs, dots and plugs, dots and plugs....*

TWO HOURS LATER, I'd climbed the hill and found the spot, a rocky ledge that looked like every other rocky ledge on the hill. But this one's perimeter was beaded with a circle of tobacco-stained gum. Little balls of it lay everywhere, stuck on tree trunks, dropped on the ground, smashed onto other rocks.

The two Glammerys must have waited for quite a while. From here they could see down the long stretch of Salt Creek Road, the stretch where cars slowed down to make the wide turn, then slowed even more as people looked out across the creek and into a small clearing, looking for a family of deer.

Standing on the ledge where the two of them had stood, I rolled one of the sticky balls of gum, tobacco, and Creel's mouth-grease between my fingers. I looked down where they had looked and saw what they had seen: I watched my car drive into view. Watched it slow for the turn. Then saw it slow even more to see the deer. I watched Creel and Simon each pick up an end of the rock. Holding it between them, they swung it back and forth, the arc of the swing increasing with each grunted count of "One, two, three...."

I watched them throw the rock.

And I watched it fall.

And, once again, I saw my wife and son die.

My reaction was emotional. Was tinged with hysteria. It flooded my brain—igniting, searing, uncontrollable. I crumpled to the ground, knees buckling as if in prayer. Seeing—understanding— what had been done to my family scorched my eyes with a bright, fiery, all-consuming blaze. But the fire wasn't the collapsing, narrowing vision of hysterical blindness. No, it was the opposite of blindness. It was sight—hysterical sight.

In the white fire that filled my mind and my eyes, *I saw everything,* Everything was clear. Everything was available. Everything was an option. I saw it all in the bright-edged glare of hysterical sight. It was sight without boundaries or filters—sight that allowed everything and anything. Absolutely anything.

MONTHS LATER, I returned again to where the rock had fallen. To where the rock had ripped through my wife's flesh and bones.

And I found the bones.

The three bones of her finger were lying on the creek's bank. They'd been picked clean, the skin and muscle once covering them had either rotted away or been eaten. The bones were small and white, lying together like eggs in a tiny nest. They were powerful and horrible tokens, torn from my wife's hand and cast aside. I picked them up carefully, feeling anger filling me anew. I shook them in my hand, like dice about to be rolled. They bumped and knocked together, the terrible electric charge of them growing in my palm, numbing my arm with a shock of emotions.

The bones were a trinity of precious and damaged reminders, one for each of us—mother, father, and son. I vowed that I would always keep them near me. That I would never forget.

I took off the small totem bag that I wear around my neck. I opened the pouch and dropped the three tiny bones into it, one at a time. Each bone rang as it hit the folded medallion of the melted dog tag lying at the bottom of the leather bag. With the bones inside, I closed the pouch and slipped it back around my neck. Hanging from my neck, the bag was surprisingly light for all that it held—all the love and rage, all the memories and hopes and pain, all the gathered forces of lightning, gravity, evil, and dreams. It was all there inside the bag—all the hurt and perfect things, all the lives and deaths. All of it hanging by a single leather cord. And weighing almost nothing at all.

BLUE

13

I STOOD ON THE TOP of the rocky ledge and looked down at the wide bend in Salt Creek Road. Looking at the yellow sign that asked people to "Please, Watch For Falling Rocks." My thumb rolled a damp dirty marble of gum and tobacco in the cup of my hand. The marble left a trail of moist brown tracks that cut back and forth across my palm, crossing my lifeline again and again.

I stared down, no longer seeing where the rock had fallen. Seeing, instead, where the rock had been *thrown*. I thought about my wife. And about our son. And, just then, I may have gone insane—a little bit, for a little while. Maybe. Likely. Whatever it was, it was a wonderful feeling—a feeling of freedom. And clarity. I was filled with the floating lightness of an absolute absence of doubt.

I climbed back down to Salt Creek. Stood over the rock. Placed a foot on each side of it. Planted my legs like iron posts driven into the earth's core, then bent my knees and reached down. My hip and chest muscles tensed and relaxed, and I felt them fill with power. I gripped the sides of the rock, my hands driving their strength deep into it, anchoring my fingers like hammered pitons. Then I exploded upward, pulling the rock free from its earthen cradle by the creek.

I lifted the rock's dead, heavy weight and carried it to the car.

I needed the rock.

For later.

BACK AT the cabin, Grendel was half-sleeping on the porch, his body a long, slack picture of relaxation. Hoping for a tummy-rub, he rolled onto his back as I climbed the stairs. I sat beside him on the sun-soaked wood and scratched the fur on his stomach and throat until his eyes closed and he began making rumbling snore-sounds.

Then I stood. It was time to get ready. Was time to prepare. With my plan already made, I walked through the home and gathered things. For later.

I went first to my son's room. From the stacked mountain of unopened child's toys, I pulled out a red, white, and blue star-emblazoned carton. (*America's Pastime! Baseball in a Box! T-Ball Starter Kit!*) Pressing against the box's clear shrink-wrap was a toddler-sized leather baseball mitt. In its tiny pocket, held tight forever, was an even tinier white rubber baseball. (*Balls stay caught with new STAY CAUGHT GloveGrip!*) The mitt was left-handed, deliberately picked from a tower of right-handed mitts. (*"A southpaw, definitely a southpaw," Elissa had said, touching the left side of her growing belly and laughing, putting the box into our cart.*)

Before leaving the room, I also stooped and wrapped an arm around the midsection of the giant tiger standing regally in the corner with the two other members of the LAND OF OZ COLLECTOR SET. (*Collect Them All! Lions and Tigers and Bears, Oh My! ALL WITH NIGHTGLOW EYES!*)

I put the T-ball box and tiger in the car.

Back inside the cabin, I grabbed the bucket we kept near the door. The bucket was filled with veterinary supplies, all the things needed to help the injured beasts Grendel kept carrying home. I loaded the bucket and two folded plastic tarps into the trunk.

Knowing that I now needed to sleep, I went back in and stretched out on the bed. Closed my eyes. The bright white glow of hysterical sight still lit the back of my eyelids. It reached into my brain—illuminating every thought, shedding light on each possible path and action. While examining those many actions, I finally fell asleep, feeling contented and calm. Waiting for the deep, dark night.

Waiting for later.

I REMEMBERED their phone number. I don't know why, I just did. I'd only heard it once before, but somehow it stuck. "Sometimes it's just easier to call them than to call anybody else," Gordon had said. "Shit, they're faster than the County's roadkill squad. More reliable, too."

A few minutes before, we'd driven around a dead deer lying in the middle of the road, We'd stopped the truck and dragged the deer off the road. "Now what?" I'd asked, looking at the warm, still-limp carcass.

"Now we call the 'it's-fallen-and-can't-get-up' hotline," Gordy said. "Now we dial the Glammery-ghouls. We'll give them an anonymous tip about where they can find free, fresh meat on the bone. Hell, they'll be here before anybody at County's even logged the call."

He called from the Gatesville General Store, using the store's outdoor payphone. I stood beside him, listening as he said each number that he dialed. He added a hoarse rasp to his voice when the Glammerys answered. He told them where to find the deer, said how it looked like it'd just been hit. How it was still warm. "Better get over and snarf it up fast," he said, "before the turkey buzzards beat you to it." Then he hung up and grinned at me. "All aboard! Roadkill Railways is leaving the station!"

I didn't ask Gordy why he was making sure food got to the Glammerys. And didn't ask why he was helping to feed the very same people that he arrested and jailed every chance he got.

I didn't have to ask; I already knew the answer.

He wasn't helping all the Glammerys.

He was helping only one.

WAKING FROM a restful sleep, I opened my eyes. In the coarse hair of the night's longest, blackest hour—the wolf's hour—I smiled.

It was finally here.

It was later.

I drove to Gatesville. The night was empty and quiet, no other cars on the roads, no moon shining down. There was no sense of mystery or promise in the darkness. There was only a blank slate of midnight, waiting to be filled.

I parked near the payphone at the General Store, then dialed the remembered number. When I spoke, I deepened my voice and changed the cadence of my phrasing. I told them about a deer I'd found an hour or so ago, how I'd found it when I was out with my hunting dogs—

—*told them how the deer was neck-shot with an arrow, wounded by some asshole that had "nailed it, but not trailed it." And how the deer wasn't dead yet, at least not when I saw it, maybe not even now. But it sure wasn't going anywhere, not wheezing like it was. I said it was at that place off Salt Creek Road, north of where Milk Bottom Road T-bones into Salt Creek, right where that little, dirt logging trail heads into the woods.*

"The deer's just about a half-mile up the trail," I told them, " laying close to the creek in a clearing made by some timber cutters. ... Sure, it's a tight fit back there, a little overgrown, but a truck can get through, easy. ... And shit no, you keep it all; I don't want none—don't even like the taste. But I'd hate seeing it wasted, know what I mean, brother? ... Hell yes, you got that right. We all certainly do got to look out for each other, don't we? Or else what we have we got then, what have we got at all?"

Then I said goodbye.

"Okay," I told them. "Later."

HANGING UP, I realized I wasn't alone, was suddenly certain that someone was watching. That someone had heard the conversation.

Glancing at the General Store's shadowed porch, I saw an even darker shadow sitting in the row of rocking chairs. A shadow sitting perfectly still, sitting there since I'd driven up in the empty night and gone immediately to the phone.

Someone was watching. Someone had heard.

The shape moved. Put its arms on the chair. Pushed itself slowly up. The chair creaked, but the shape made no sound. It formed a large, man-shaped, black hole standing silently in the wedge of darkness under the porch roof. A shape that watched. That listened. And then walked forward, into the night where I stood.

Then, before I saw anything else, I saw the starburst of broken capillaries in his right eye. Even in the darkness, his eye flashed for a moment, as if it were reflecting the dim starlight that drifted down through the night clouds above us.

"Blue," he said.

"Lee," I said.

We stood facing each other, not moving. His eye caught another bit of light, flashed another snowflake of red fire.

Then he stepped forward. Held out one hand. "Blue, there's no way of saying how sorry Michelle and I are," he said. "How sorry we are for Elissa and you. And the baby. I want you to know, whatever we can do…well, that's what we'll do."

"Lee—"

"So." His voice was low, sounding almost far-away. "I'll tell you one thing that I think I can do for you right now. I can go back to bed and keep right on dreaming this dream I'm having—this dream where I came outside and sat on the porch to get a little rest." He shook his head. "It's a bitch, ain't it, when even in his dreams, a man has to sit and rest a while? But, Blue, that's one of the things I can do right now—I can just keep dreaming." He stepped off the porch and walked closer to me. He'd moved nimbly, but now, standing closer to him, I realized again how big he was.

"Or I can do another thing," he said, near enough for me to see the scatter of red light dancing in his eye. "I can do something else," he said. "Because in this dream tonight, I want you to know something." His voice didn't sound far-away anymore. It was edged and steady. He turned his head, first looking into the black folds of night lying over the park, then looking at the payphone. His eyes stayed on the phone. "In this interesting dream I'm having, I'd help you if you asked—with whatever business you might need help doing. Whatever it is. And since you think it needs doing—that's all I need to know." He stared at me. His eye seemed to glow brighter, like a fanned flame. "Understand?" he asked.

I understood.

He was offering an incredible gift. A violent gift that I had the feeling he'd delivered before. But it was a gift I couldn't accept.

"Lee," I answered, overwhelmed with gratitude. "I'm not asking for that. I can't ask. Not tonight. Not for this thing. This thing is... it's mine."

He nodded.

A few quiet seconds moved back and forth between us, and we watched them play at our feet like kittens.

"Well," he said, turning to go back inside. "In that case, I'm off to sleep, perchance to continue dreaming."

I watched him cross the parking lot to the small home on the other side of the road. Before he got there, he'd already blended into the black cover of the night, disappearing within it like a blurry figment of the dream he intended to rejoin.

EARLIER, BEFORE making the call, I'd driven down the logging trail and looked at some things. Arranged some others. After the call, I returned quickly, parking in the brush farther down the trail, away from the clearing. I now stood on the far side of the clearing, behind a thick oak tree, waiting for the arrival of Roadkill Railways. Waiting for the Glammery-ghouls.

It was dark. More than seeing the night, I heard it. Tree branches moved against each other, scraping and whispering. Small, clawed feet moved through the low, wiry coils of thorny greenbrier that twisted up from the ground. Something splashed in the creek, then gave a surprised sharp grunt and scrabbled up the bank and into the woods. Somewhere far above, an owl with a cry like a woman's scream called down from the whorled black sky.

I HEARD their truck coming.

The logging road was old. It had been cut and cleared long ago, and years had passed since lumber trucks drove up and down it, hauling out their heavy loads. When the road was new and busy, the trucks' large tires had pressed parallel ruts into the ground, creating a humped, center "guide rail" that ran the length of the road. Over time, grass and debris had begun filling the ruts, and erosion had leveled most of the guide rail. The ruts and guide rail were still there, but just barely—like visual echoes of a phantom road, something more sensed than seen.

The passing years had also narrowed the road, the woods inching forward to fill the open spaces. A gauntlet of tendrils and thin branches reached out from the sides of the road toward the center. I could hear them sliding and scraping along the sides of the Glammerys' truck, making the frantic scratching sound of fingernails dragging across the inside of a metal coffin.

The truck moved slowly, rumbling with a low growl of unused horsepower. As it drew nearer, its headlights speared into the trees, bouncing up and down as the road dipped and rose. There was another light, too. A spotlight. It stabbed out toward the creek, searching for the wounded shape of a neck-shot deer. When the truck reached the clearing, it stopped like an animal checking its surroundings. The engine and headlights abruptly shut off, and the sudden absence of noise and light made the silence seem somehow quieter. Made the darkness somehow darker.

The spotlight's illuminated tunnel flashed out from the truck's window again, the light playing slowly over a grassy area on the creek bank.

"Well, fuck me," said Simon. "It ain't here." His voice was the ugly sound of an accident, full of grinding gears and ripping membrane.

The spotlight snapped off.

I heard low voices. Then truck doors opening and closing. The spotlight blazed back on as they started toward the creek. I watched their silhouettes from my place behind the oak. They stopped in the trampled, tall grass by the water—grass I'd walked on earlier, pushing it down, matting it. Making it look like an animal had writhed there in pain.

Each man held a rifle, barrel down. As the spotlight swept over the area, Creel was muttering. "Shit, it was here alright. Looks like it rolled around for hours."

I pulled back behind the tree as the spotlight made a jerking pass through the clearing, searching for where the deer had gone to die.

"Gone. Fucking gone," said Simon.

The light slipped through the grass and the branches, then swung around and flashed across the creek. Their backs were turned to me as they looked where the light shone into a thicket. The spotlight's beam pierced the growth and caught a pair of reflected eyes—the eyes of a large animal. Something big. Something paralyzed by the light, staring directly back at the beam. Unable to blink or move.

"Simon!" Creel hissed. "There! Hold the light still." He raised his rifle to his shoulder, automatically tilting his head to aim, immediately lost in the rush of the hunt, in anticipation of the kill. It captured their attention, becoming their entire focus.

I stepped from behind the tree. Moved toward them. I walked silently, quickly crossing the dark clearing, getting closer as Creel was sighting down the barrel.

"Look at those eyes," he whispered to Simon. "It's big, ain't it? But what the hell is it?"

I was almost across the clearing as they went quiet, both of them waiting for the bullet. Waiting for the death moment. When Creel fired, I was standing right behind them—my hips already turned for power, my hands already gripping the T-ball bat's handle, already raising the bat over my left shoulder in a home-run stance, then I twisted back just a little more before releasing into the swing.

I swung the bat low and fast across the back of Creel's knees.

When the bat hit his legs, they made a loud, snapping sound, then were swept forward and up, both legs floating horizontally in the air for a millisecond, making it look like Creel was reclining on an invisible raft, his gun held straight out in his extended arms. Before he started falling, while he was still stretched out flat in mid-air, I lifted the bat and swung it down, chopping across his ribcage. I bent at the waist, following the bat down as it sank into his chest, driving him to the ground, the force of the blow making Creel's hands release the gun into the air, tossing it into the night—

—and Simon was right beside me now, lit in the pillar of light beaming from the spotlight he'd dropped. He raised his rifle, then realized how close we were. Seeing me bent over his brother, he kicked at my head, almost connecting, but I rolled away from his boot, letting my body collapse as I turned. His kick scraped across my cheek, his leg going past me—

—and I dropped, falling heavily onto Creel's body as I short-swung the bat, smashing it across the leg Simon was standing on when he kicked at me. The bat crashed below his knee, folding and splintering the bones. His body pitched forward, falling toward me as I lay on top of Creel. As he fell, I turned the bat upright and stabbed the round metal end at his face. It hit his mouth, shattering his teeth in a rain of beige confetti and snapping his head back before he landed on top of me.

Now fallen, he didn't move.

And beneath me, Creel was also still.

I CRAWLED out from under Simon and stood up. Looked down at him and Creel. Both of them were still breathing, but both were unconscious. Blood was running out of their mouths, streaming from the corners of Creel's mouth and bubbling frothily out from Simon's, making them look like vampires that had messily fed.

I walked through the creek and crossed it to the dense thicket on the other side, to where Creel had fired his shot at the animal now lying on the ground. Creel's aim had been deadly. His bullet had hit the stuffed tiger right between the eyes. Where the bullet exited, an anemone of soft foam hung down the back of the tiger's head.

I picked up the tiger and walked back to the Glammerys. Set the tiger down, positioning it so that its unblinking *NIGHTGLOW EYES!* were staring at Creel and Simon. "Watch 'em, boy," I whispered to the tiger. "Don't let the bastards go."

I'D HIDDEN the bucket of first aid supplies in the bushes. It was stocked and ready for whatever animal emergency Grendel brought to our door. It held the standard things: tubes of antiseptic ointments and salves, hydrogen peroxide, a skin stapler, scalpel, scissors, chemical cold packs, surgical tape, gauze, and rolls and rolls of Vet Wrap—a wrinkled, woven fabric that, when pulled and wrapped around broken limbs, sticks only to itself while holding everything else tightly in place.

THE COLD CREEK water woke them.

They awoke disoriented. And wet. And immobile. They were wrapped twins, each one a mirror of the other. Both were bound with wide, layered bands of Vet Wrap. The cloth bands were wrapped around their ankles and knees. Their arms were bound in front of them with fabric around their elbows and wrists. More bindings circled their torsos, winding behind their backs and over and around their chests and arms, holding their arms and hands immobile.

Looking down at them, their arms and legs ringed and trapped in the fabric bands, I remembered a small, white, rubber baseball held forever in the tiny, laced pocket of a child's left-handed baseball glove. Thinking about it, I began to laugh. *Glammerys stay caught with new STAY CAUGHT GloveGrip!*

I watched them. Saw them beginning to figure things out. Watched their eyes focus and clear as they began rolling their heads from side to side, both of them already assessing and calculating, plotting and scheming.

And I waited for them to see it.

They were on their backs, lying with their waists and legs on the damp creek bank. Their shoulders and heads were angled down into the water. The water was shallow, just deep enough to touch their ears and jaws, but not deep enough to cover their heads or fill their mouths. As long as they didn't roll around or edge farther into the stream, Creel and Simon could still hear and see. They certainly saw me. I was staring down at them. I was standing at their feet, the toe of my right foot pressing against the bottom of Creel's left boot, threatening pressure that would push him into deeper water.

Their eyes moved back and forth, taking in what they could.

But they still didn't see it.

They said nothing. Their eyes finally stopped moving from side to side, stopped looking at anything but me. They stared into my eyes, and I stared into theirs. I saw only anger in their eyes, only a vicious glint. I saw no fear in their eyes. No shame. No heavenly soul.

And I wondered: *What don't they see in mine?*

MY MIND was blazing. My muscles and skin were adrenaline-gorged, arcing and snapping with fire. I wondered how to begin. Wondered what to say. How to make them understand. But I didn't really need for them to understand. I was the one who needed to understand...and knew I never would.

As for Creel and Simon, I just needed for them to be done.

I needed for them to be over.

"YOU SHOT my tiger," I said. I nodded at the stuffed animal. Patting its head, I softly recited a few lines of William Blake's famous poem—

Tyger, Tyger burning bright,
In the forests of the night...
In what distant deeps or skies,
Burnt the fire of thine eyes?

"I changed it around a little, but that's a good one, don't you think?" I said conversationally. "You know, for a pretty po-em, right?" I asked.

They watched me quietly. Carefully. Not responding. They turned their heads and stared at each other, their expressions looking like they wanted to confirm they'd heard the same thing.

Then Creel spoke. "What the hell are you thinking? Are you nuts? What do you think you're doing?" His voice didn't quaver. It was strong. Disbelieving. As he talked, his body subtly shifted, moving with his vehemence. Moving just a little. But when he finished speaking, it was enough movement that the water was now higher on his ear, and a little more of his chin was covered.

I saw the look in his eyes as he realized what had happened.

Simon hadn't moved. Hadn't said anything. The few times he'd turned his head to look at Creel, the water had rinsed some of the smeared blood off his face, but new blood continued pulsing out of his mouth. His eyes were no longer locked on mine. Instead they were moving frantically, looking everywhere.

But I could tell. He still hadn't seen it.

"Creel, Creel, Creel," I said. I looked at him. Waiting. Silent.

"What?" he screamed back. "What?"

"I want you to know something. There is no deer here tonight."

"No kidding, you crazy shit." He was being careful not to move. Was intent on not shifting his position. "When this is over, I goddamn guarantee we are going to kill you. You are dead. Do you hear me?"

"Creel. Simon," I said. "Kill? Dead? Are those the words we're using tonight?" I made my voice stay steady, made it sound calm. But I wondered, how could they not see the white light still burning inside my skull? Not see the scorching, searing fire of it radiating out of my mouth and eyes, blazing like a blinding torch or a funeral pyre? "I wasn't going to mention it," I said, "but I'm glad you brought it up. Let's talk about 'kill,' let's talk about 'dead.'" I paused. Looked quietly down at them. "Let's talk about my wife. Let's talk about my son."

They said nothing. But I could see I'd answered a question—that I'd given them a piece of information which, until just then, they weren't certain I knew. Until just then, they hadn't been sure if I knew that the falling rock had been no accident. They'd been wondering if maybe this was about the other times, the earlier times in school.

Now they knew.

Now we all knew.

But they still hadn't seen it.

"So...what do you guys think?" I asked. "Do you want to talk about it? Or should I just tell you a story? Because I have a story I think you should—"

"—fuck it." Simon said. I noticed how his torn voice now seemed like the right sound to be coming out of his broken, bloody mouth. His voice fit him now. He rolled his eyes toward his brother. "I knew we were wrong. I knew it. I told Creel—"

"Simon!" said Creel. "Just shut the hell up—"

"But he didn't listen," Simon continued, his eyes boring into mine. "I knew we were wrong. I knew it! I kept telling him, over and over again—"

"—Simon! Goddammit!" Creel screamed. "Close your goddamn mouth! I'm—"

"—told him, and told him." Simon kept talking. "I told him while we were waiting for you and your family to come down the road. How I knew it was wrong. If I told him once, I told him a hundred times…" He drew in a quick breath, pausing, making sure my eyes were on him before he continued. "I told him there were three of you down there. Three living people—"

"Simon!" Creel yelled again.

Simon was still staring at me, talking without pause over Creel's screams. "That it wasn't just one person, it was three, so I told him we shouldn't throw just *one* rock, I said we should throw *three* rocks, that we should throw a rock for every single fucking one of you!" He stopped, waited to see my reaction, then rasped "There! How's that taste in your mouth, shithead?" His voice sounded like a chainsaw. "How do you like that, Little Boy Blue?"

He stopped talking. Smiled widely with his bloody, damaged mouth.

Creel was absolutely still, his eyes shifting quickly from me to Simon and back again.

The owl I'd heard earlier screamed again, its cry haunted and full of anguish. As the screech died away, there was silence all around us, like the night was holding its breath, waiting to hear my reply.

I ended the silence.

"The story," I said…and felt the night exhale a thin, tense breeze. Its breath rattled briefly through the reaching branches, moving the dangling vines from side to side, setting them swaying like a dark garden of hangman's ropes. I looked at the two of them in the stream. "Let me tell you the story," I repeated. And then I began telling them a children's story, a story that's told on long road trips when interest in the passing scenery has waned or when the game of License Plate Bingo has been played too many times during too many highway hours and weary parents want a few quiet minutes. A story that is told after the family's car has passed a certain yellow, diamond-shaped sign.

"Many moons ago," I said, "a great Indian tribe lived in this place. Their lands were vast, stretching as far as a wild goose could fly in the passage of two suns. The tribe was happy and their life was good. The warriors were strong, and the hunters skillful—"

As I tell the tale, I continue watching them. Knowing that they still haven't seen it. Knowing they still have no idea.

WHEN I FINISH the story, Simon isn't smiling. Not anymore. He doesn't know why, but he's worried now. The story made him feel uncertain. When it's over, he waits a moment then whispers, "What the fuck is—?" his voice dying at the end of his unfinished question.

Creel stayed quiet through the story. He's also been trying to loosen the Vet Wrap, trying to stretch the bands around his wrists and elbows. It hadn't worked. The Vet Wrap held. His efforts have shifted the creek gravel beneath him, though, moving him farther into the water, far enough in that his neck could no longer rest on the creek bottom without water covering his face. He has to hold his head up now, using his neck muscles to keep his mouth above the water.

I see a new look in his eyes.

"Blue," he says, "what do you—?" He's panting as he speaks, his head coming up, going down, water running into his mouth. He coughs it out. "What do you want?"

"I just wanted you to know."

He lifts his head up as far as he can. Wanting away from the water. Trying to sound reasonable now. "Know *what*? What do you want us to know, Blue?"

"That when you get there, you can tell them to stop," I reply. "You can tell them it's over."

He misunderstands. Gets excited. Screams. "Okay!" and spits

out another mouthful of creek water. "Okay, I'll tell them! We're done! It's stopped! It's over! Just get us out—"

"Creel, no," I say, cutting him short. "Don't tell me. You need to tell *them*. Tell *them* it's over. That they can stop watching now. Tell them you found him."

As I talk, I walk a few feet to one side and then stop. I stand beside it. Waiting for them to see.

Creel keeps screaming, "FOUND WHO? WHO'D I FIND? WHO'S 'THEM'? WHO DO I TELL?" while trying to keep his head above water, and then Simon starts screaming, too—

—and I know that, finally, Simon has seen it. That, finally, he understands.

"WHO?" Creel yells again. "BLUE, JUST TELL ME, TELL ME, WHAT DO I SAY?"

I bend down. Pick up the big rock that's been resting on the creek bank. The rock with the brown lump of tobacco and gum stuck to it. I carry the rock into the creek. Hold it above Creel's head. He pushes his head back, instinctively wanting to get away, but instead only dunks his face under the water.

I can see his open eyes beneath the water. "Falling Rocks," I reply. "Tell them that you found Falling Rocks."

I let go of the rock.

"You can tell them to stop watching for him," I say, reaching down into the stream, into the sudden bloom of darkening water. I lift the rock and drop it again. "Tell them that his bow was strong." I lift the rock again. It falls again. "Tell them his quiver was full." Again, I reach into the dark water that, even in the night, I can see is staining my hands, gloving them in Creel's blood.

"Tell them his knife was sharp."

The rock falls again.

Each time it falls, it settles deeper into the water.

SIMON IS TRYING to escape. Fear moves and strengthens him. He lifts his bound legs up off the bank and throws them backward over his head, their momentum rolling him deeper into the creek in a sort of reverse somersault...and it works. His knees come down planted in the creek, leaving his face buried in the water, pressing against the creek bottom. But he pushes his shoulder blades against the bottom and bends up at the hips, lifting his head out of the water.

He sways there, then tries to stand. But his body remembers that his leg is destroyed, that the T-ball bat has ruined the bony mechanics of his hoped-for flight. He collapses back into the water, landing again on his knees.

Facing me, he works hard to catch his breath. The noises coming from his throat sound awful, like a shaken pail of glass and nails.

"Simon," I tell him, "when you think about it, you were right."

His mouth drips blood into the creek, the blood flowing so freely it sounds like light rain falling on the water.

"When you think about it," I repeat, "your brother should have done exactly what 'Simon says.'"

I reach into the creek. Lift the rock out of the sunken pocket of Creel's head. Holding it, I walk over a few steps and look down at Simon. I think again about the toy baseball mitt. And about my wife. And my son.

"Simon," I say, "you know what? For once, you were the smart one. You were absolutely right. You should have thrown three rocks, not just one."

Then I whisper, "Catch."

And the falling rock falls.

THE GLAMMERY brothers became a local mystery. A disappearing act. People kept a running conversation about how they had crawled out of their black, stinking hole one night but never crawled back in. They were "missing persons" of a different sort—the sort that everyone hopes *stays missing,* but also worries that they might eventually return, meaner and angrier than ever.

People didn't need to worry.

Their truck was at the bottom of the county's deepest, private-property lake. And the brothers were still inside a hole, but a smaller, hidden one this time—one filled with a huge nest of rattlesnakes. I dragged what was left of them out of the creek and put them in a cave I'd found, a low rocky-mouthed doorway slanting down into the earth. I left them there to turn to dust, left them for the snakes to curl through their bones.

When I dragged the bodies into the cave, the snakes struck again and again against the thick, high boots I wore. I smiled then, imagining that even the rattlesnakes were upset at the thought of enduring the Glammerys' eternal company.

14
OLD KING COLE. NANNY TINKENS. THE ROCKMAN

COLE OPENED HIS EYES and saw that the room was dark. But it was the very best kind of dark—the just-before-light kind of dark, with nothing bad hiding inside, with no monsters or riffraff lurking. The kind of dark that was full of good things: good things like his plans for today—a day he'd see any minute now pressing its nose against the small window above his featherbed, the morning light calling to him, yelling *LET'S GO! COME ON!*

Except he wasn't waiting for daylight. Not today. Not with just two days left before his parents came to take him home. Not with so many Things Still Left For Him To Do. But before getting out of bed, he stopped—stopped and made himself try to see, made himself try to hear...like Nanny T. was teaching him to see and hear.

He took a big breath. Filled his chest.

Let the air out slowly.

Cleared his thoughts.

Calmed his mind.

But then he heard it: the little, yipping voice inside his brain, the voice saying, *Si! Si! Si!* The voice sounded like Speedy Gonzales, the sombrero-wearing Saturday morning cartoon mouse. Hearing it, Cole couldn't stop himself from giggling. Then giggled even more when a second voice answered—this one sounding like Pepe Le Pew, the love-starved, cartoon skunk—Pepe's voice saying, *No!*

No! No! And, of course, Speedy's voice machine-gun blasted back another hyper-fast, *Si! Si! Si!* Followed by another of Pepe's drooling *No! No! No's!*

And now he wasn't just giggling. Now he was full-throttle, bust-a-gut laughing out loud. Laughing so hard his stomach felt sore. Unable to stop, he rolled over and buried his face in his feather pillow, muffling the sounds so he wouldn't wake Nanny T., still sleeping and snoring in the room next door.

Si! Si! Si! and *No! No! No!*

It was their secret, inside joke. It started last year, during his first episode with Nanny T. That's what she called them. "Episodes." Not lessons. "Oh, my," she'd say, waving an age-speckled hand in front of her face, acting like a silly girl about to faint. "I do believe I feel another episode coming on!"

Then she'd teach him: How to see. How to hear.

LAST YEAR was the first time he'd come to stay with Nanny Tinkens. For two weeks and three days. Long enough for his parents to go on a *grown-ups' vacation.*

"You understand, don't you, honey?" his mom had asked him. "Your dad and I are going on a different kind of vacation, one you wouldn't enjoy. Besides, you'll have fun with Nanny Tinkens, won't you?"

She'd reached out then, almost touching his hair, but then drew her hand back and brushed her own instead. "You will. Won't you, Cole?" she asked again, her voice hesitant and nervous, unsure how he felt, not knowing if he'd agree, not knowing that—

—he was thrilled! Two weeks with Nanny T.! Two weeks in a cabin in the woods! Two weeks of hiking and exploring and gold panning and fun!

But he'd been careful answering.

No matter what Mom said, she didn't like Nanny T. ("She's your mother and you know I love her. You know I do," his mom always told his dad.) Cole knew she wouldn't like him feeling excited about visiting Nanny T. And she'd *really* not like it if she realized that Cole knew exactly why his parents weren't taking him on their vacation. Or if she discovered how happy he was that they were finally trying to fix whatever was going wrong between them.

"You guys go," he wanted to tell her. "Go and try not yelling." Or—sounding weirdly opposite of "try not yelling"—he also wanted to say "try being not so quiet."

At least with yelling, things were obvious. With yelling, conversations were clear and understood. His parents' silences were worse. Their silence was dangerous—it was the quiet sound of chess players and generals determining their next move, developing a strategy for how to vanquish their opponent—each one intent on destroying the other.

"I'll be fine," he answered his mom. "Really, I will. You guys go ahead. Just don't forget me." His dad had pulled him close then, hugging him hard, saying, "Forget my old King Cole? Never. Not a chance."

Being held like that, Cole pressed his head against the side of his father's neck and inhaled the wonderful smell of Royall Lyme aftershave. It was the scent of bear hugs and laughing and stories and good-night kisses. His dad's smell.

ROYALL LYME All Purpose Lotion. Even the bottle was neat. A small, narrow-necked, translucent-green bottle capped with a gray pewter, screw-on crown. The pewter crown was small, but it had heft and weight, affirming that the bottle's contents were indeed Something Special.

Molded into the glass in the center of the back of the bottle was a raised cluster of limes hanging from a leafy lime tree branch. Above the limes was the word ROYALL with a raised-glass king's crown. Below the branch was the word LYME. And on the front was a square of treasure-map parchment, printed in flowing green script:

Royall Lyme

All Purpose Lotion

A delightful essence scented with the oil of nature limes, to be used as an

AFTER SHAVE LOTION

and as a BODY COLOGNE

Royall Lime (Bermuda) Limited

Hamilton, Bermuda

Made in Bermuda

Reading the label, Cole always imagined a glistening island, dense with lime trees. An island surrounded by deep blue Caribbean water. A lush, exotic realm filled with swashbuckling pirates, dangerous riffraff, buried treasure, and—more recently—beautiful island girls.

The girls surprised him.

They'd just recently started showing up. They hadn't been there last year. More surprising, some even reminded him of the girls from his fourth grade class at Ethel P. Neder Elementary School. He told no one—not even his best friend, Dean the Bean—that there were girls on his island now. It wouldn't be any good at all if his friends knew about the girls.

AT COLE'S LAST birthday party, after he'd opened all his presents, his father handed him one more gift. Tearing off the wrapping paper, he looked down at the wooden treasure chest on his lap. The chest was the size of a big cigar box, with hammered brass straps and ridged rows of round brass nail heads. He'd looked up at his dad. Smiled his thanks. The box was great. A perfect place for special things. For secret things. Not knowing what to expect, he'd opened it. Inside was a surprise—the box's first treasure: his very own bottle of Royall Lyme.

"TRY THIS," his father said, tucking Cole into bed that night. "Sprinkle a little on your pillow and sheets." As he talked, Dad lightly shook a small rain of drops out from the bottle. "There," he said. "Now close your eyes and imagine you're swaying in an island hammock, dozing between two lime trees. Surrounded by tropical blue waters." Leaning down, he kissed Cole's forehead. Said, "Go to sleep, son. And dream dreams of pirates and treasure…."

HE HOARDED his bottle of Royall Lyme. Was careful with every drop. Miserly. Kept the bottle safe in his treasure chest, and kept the treasure chest safe under his bed. At night he'd reach under his bed and pull out the chest. Taking out the bottle, he'd unscrew the pewter crown and carefully tilt the bottle, letting exactly three drops splash onto his pillow. Then he'd hold the open bottle under his nose, letting the scent hang his hammock in a grove of lime trees, letting it point his dreams to blue water. Then, as real as real could be, he'd feel his father leaning down and kissing his forehead. Heard him whispering, "Good night, sleep tight, my little King Cole."

LAST YEAR, after they returned from their grown-ups' vacation, Cole noticed that his parents seemed better. A little. For a while. If nothing else, at least things stopped getting worse…and that was better than before.

His parents noticed something, too. Noticed that the eleven-year-old boy they took home seemed older than the boy they'd dropped off. Stronger, too. His skinny frame was now lightly etched with muscles. And his skin was a red-gold bronze of sun and wind.

"Did you have a good time, Cole?" his mother asked on the way home. "Did you and Nanny get along? What did the two of you do?" Mom was turned in her seat, watching him as she asked her questions. She waited for his answers, looking for signs of a problem, for hints or reasons to decide: *See, I knew it. He's not staying there again.*

He'd been careful. Like he always was.

"It was okay," he said in a carefully bored voice. "We took walks. Looked at stuff. Listened to stuff." Then he'd allowed his voice to be a little sad, a little low. "It was fun," he said, "but probably not as much fun as you had...."

Mom was immediately buoyed up by his hurt tone, was immensely comforted by the slight injury she heard there. Instantly, she stopped wondering if he'd had too much fun at Nanny T.'s, was no longer worried that he might have adopted any of Nanny's hillbilly-common ways. Mom also stopped fretting that—worst of all—he might have become friendly with the common riffraff. She now felt certain that all was well. No balance had shifted, no control had been lost. With that settled, she could then give Cole her bad news. "Now, honey," she said, "you know we missed you, too. And the three of us are still going to take a vacation together. But sometimes it's good for moms and dads to spend time alone together."

Reaching back over the seat, she patted his knee. "Thank you for letting us do that. It's a special kind of wonderful gift you gave us. And...," she said, looking at his dad, then back at Cole, "and we were hoping you might think about giving the same gift to us again next year, that maybe you'd visit Nanny Tinkens next summer, too." Pause. "Would you think about that, honey? Would you?"

She looked at him intently, making sure he saw that The Decision Was His. Making sure he saw how much she appreciated the sacrifice she felt she was asking of him—to spend another two weeks in the place she held in such quiet disdain. Feeling sure in her heart that, deep down, he must certainly share her opinion. And entirely unaware that, again—

He was thrilled.

Careful, he told himself. *Be careful. Be very careful.* He lowered his eyes, kept them downcast, studied the floor behind Mom's seat. "Oh," he said, letting the word draw slowly out. Then, still looking down, he said, "Sure, I'll think about it, Mom."

He paused, aware she was watching.

After a moment, he raised his eyes and looked directly at her, knowing she'd think he was trying to be brave. Knowing she'd see that he wanted to make her happy. "But I think it would be okay," he said. Then he nodded twice, as if making himself believe. "You guys should go again. Definitely."

He'd smiled at her then. The look his mom was now wearing made him happy. Happy for the way she quickly reached out and touched his dad's shoulder. And happy for himself too—already looking forward to another two weeks of Nanny's "episodes." Already eager to continue playing their game of Opposites.

AT THE BEGINNING of the first episode, Nanny T. had paused, looking closely at him. Making sure she had his full attention. "Just remember," she said, pronouncing each word gravely, with deliberate enunciation. "*Si! Si! Si!*" Her gray-haired head bobbed with each clear-spoken syllable, adding emphasis to the message. She repeated it. "*Si! Si! Si!*"

He'd cracked up—immediately picturing Speedy Gonzalez racing around the house like a mouse full of caffeine and Pop Rocks. He'd automatically answered. "Oh, *No! No! No!*" trying to make his voice sound like Pepe Le Pew's, making his French accent drip and roll as he waggled his eyes at her.

Nanny had stared at him, confused by his response. Then shook her head and repeated herself, now saying each word even more slowly than before, with even greater deliberation. "No—*Si! Si! Si!*"

Feeling caught in some sort of alien conversational loop, he'd answered again, this time matching her same slow emphasis. "Yes," he said carefully, his cartoon-inspired French accent enveloping each letter and sound. "*No! No! No!*"

So began their game of Opposites.

It was an easy game, one that made them laugh.

After their famous *Si! Si! Si!* and *No! No! No!* conversation, they started saying the opposites of things to each other. The first one up in the morning would say, "Good night! How about some supper?" when the other one awoke. Or at supper, she'd call out, "Breakfast's ready," and he'd answer, salivating at the wonderful food smells and absolutely starving after a day exploring the hills, "No, thanks, I'm not really hungry." Then, after eating everything on his plate, he'd say, "That wasn't any good at all. I wouldn't eat any more of anything," and she'd know he wanted another plate heaped full of everything.

At night, before going into his room and collapsing into the plush heaven of his feather bed, he'd lean down and hug her, saying "Good morning." And she'd say, "Good morning," back, and then, holding him tightly, she'd tell him, "My, my, I can't wait for you to leave."

"And I can't wait to go," he'd answer, wanting to stay forever.

THE EPISODES began in a single quiet moment. A moment hidden in other moments, a moment in which something changed. *Something important.* And something else started—something exciting and powerful and strange. In that moment something inside him knew, something telling him, *This. This is what you've always wanted to know.*

She'd begun teaching him on the second day.

She fixed a big lunch that they ate in the cool cave of her kitchen. Drinking down a last big swallow of Coca-Cola, she looked at him and burped a long, rumbling freight-train of a burp. Then, burp finished, she cocked an eyebrow at him, giving him a self-satisfied challenging look, waiting for his response.

He answered the challenge, using the secret technique he and Dean the Bean had perfected over the years. The secret wasn't to take bigger drinks—the secret was taking lots and lots of small swallows, drinking as fast as possible and holding your mouth open when you drank, making sure you swallowed air with every tiny quick sip of liquid. Then you held the fizz in your stomach, letting the pressure of all the little exploding bursts build to one giant, cresting belch-bomb before you threw the bomb bay doors wide open.

He worked fast, taking sips and swallows until one whole glass of Coke was gone. Then he refilled the glass and drank it down, too. Let it churn a moment, letting it roll and bubble. Then he launched his bomb belch—aiming the blast right at Nanny T. He threw his arms out. Closed his eyes. Opened his mouth as wide as he could. Unleashed a rumbling torrent of throat-thunder straight at her, a rolling conveyor belt of buzzes and croaks. When the burp-buster pit was emptied, he closed his mouth and opened his eyes—

And was horrified.

Nanny T. was stunned. Was staring at him, unable to make a sound, her face a shocked expression of terrible surprise. He immediately realized his incredible, embarrassing mistake. Was suddenly, absolutely, and positively sure of his insult. He'd misread her expression as a challenge and, grinning like a loon, burped directly into her face. He was so quickly sorry and so ashamed, so ready to apologize. "Sorry, I'm so sorry, it was a mistake, I am so sorry, I thought—"

But Nanny T. just shook her head. "That...was...most... excellent." She extended her arms to him. "You truly are," she intoned, "The King."

And what else could he say back to her? There was only one thing he could say. Only one thing that he had to say. *Had to.* He humbly bowed his head and raised his upper lip just a little bit, curling it into a hint of a snarl. "The King thanks you, Baby," he murmured, his voice smooth with a sweet, Southern drawl. "The King thanks you very much."

Laughing, Nanny had stood. "Let's go outside and get some fresh air," she'd said. "The air in here seems a little stale, don't you think?"

OUTSIDE, NANNY T. settled into the big, white, wicker chair that she kept right in the middle of her front yard—

—*"It looks cheap, that's all I'm saying. Cheap and low class," he remembered his mom saying to his dad while they were riding in the car. "I know she's your mother, and I love her, I do, but it seems so… so hillbilly-common. Like the whole little house." Mom always gave a little laugh to emphasize how ridiculous the whole notion was. "I mean really, dear. A chair? In the yard?"*

His dad had looked in the rearview mirror, looking at Cole in the back seat and giving him a fast, faint smile, like he was asking, "Hey, what are you gonna do?" Then he'd lowered his eyes and looked straight ahead. "She likes being outside," he said aloud. "She likes looking at the trees." His dad's voice had gotten softer, but the softer part was covering another thing. Was hiding something. Something hurt and angry and growling. "By the way," he'd said, "that 'whole little house' was my home. I grew up loving that big white chair. And I still love sitting outside in a chair in the yard."

Cole hadn't looked away from the mirror. He was staring at it, hoping his dad would look into it again and grin again. That he'd give him a smile that would tell him things would be okay. But his dad's eyes had stayed pointed straight ahead.

"And so, my dear," his dad said, "I'd say there's a mighty large chance that I might be a little 'hillbilly-common' myself. I'd say there's a very large chance indeed."—

—Cole loved that white wicker chair. And loved it even more when Nanny T. told him, "Grab yourself a chair and bring it outside."

So he did. He picked up a big kitchen chair, hobble-walked

it outside and across the lawn, and set it down next to Nanny's chair. Then he plopped down and grinned over at Nanny, feeling a surge of silly joy as he looked at the fat dollops of yellow dandelions dotting the lawn. He couldn't stop from laughing out loud at the sense of goofy fun he felt sweeping through him, all from just sitting outside. *Maybe me, too,* he thought happily. *Maybe I'm a little "hillbilly-common" myself.*

Sitting outside in the tall kitchen chair, swinging his legs back and forth over the top of the carpet of dandelions, he painted the bottoms of his dangling feet with soft flower brushes of yellow and green. The flowers tickled, making him smile even wider, making him reach over and hug Nanny in his happiness.

THEY SAT together on their chairs, enjoying the day. After a while, Nanny looked at him softly—her softness wasn't covering anything, wasn't hiding something hurt or angry or growling. "Tell me," she said. "What do you see? What do you hear?" Then she closed her eyes and leaned back in her chair. Wisps of her gray hair moved in the warm wind blowing across the open yard.

He looked at her blankly. He didn't know what she meant. But knew exactly what she didn't mean. He could say, "I see the trees. I see the yard. I see the cabin." He could say, "I hear the breeze in the leaves. I hear the birds in the trees. And yesterday—I know I'm wrong, I know it sounds silly—but I think I heard a lion roaring in the woods."

He knew he could say these things, but he also knew—deep inside—those weren't the answers she wanted. In that moment, one moment hidden in other moments, he knew that she was asking... something else.

"No, it doesn't," she said quietly, eyes still closed. "Not to me."

Confused, he asked, "Doesn't what?"

"Doesn't sound silly." She'd opened her eyes. Looked at him. "You're right. I heard the roaring, too. It did sound like a lion."

Cole had looked at her, his eyes widening, his mouth dropping open. *She heard me! She heard my thoughts!* And Nanny T., looking at him with the same challenging look she'd given him in the cabin, asked again, "Now your turn. Tell me, what do you see? What do you hear?"

He'd stared at her in awe. Felt astounded and happy. Immediately and absolutely accepting what she'd just done. His mind was a bright blank of astonishment, unable to think of a single thing to say. But then he knew. Knew the best response of all. Because, like before, what else could he say? There was only the one thing that could be said, only one thing that *had to* be said. So he smiled at her. And answered, "That...was...most... excellent." He extended his arms toward her, raising and lowering them in an exaggerated pantomime of supplication. "And you, Nanny T.," he said, "truly are...The King." He bowed his head down low, pausing a beat before saying, "All hail The King, Baby—"

Then he jumped out of his chair. Threw his arms around her neck in wonder and excitement, laughing and saying, "Nanny, how? How? I want to know! Can you tell me how?" as Nanny T. hugged him back, folding the thin twigs of her arms around his neck, squeezing him close, laughing with him and crying. Both happy. Each excited for the other. Nanny T. telling him, "Of course, you'll learn. Sure you will. Learn to see. Learn to hear. Maybe, sometime, even learn to sing."

"WHAT ELSE?" he'd asked. "What else can you see? What else can you hear?"

She leaned her head back in the chair. Closed her eyes again. Was quiet. Then said, "I see...a blue butterfly at the edge of the woods behind us. Sitting on a thistle. Pale orange spots on her wings. Her wings hardly moving at all, fanning up and down. Her long curly tongue dipping in the thistle-top...and now her wings beat down and she's flying. And I hear...the small wind that she's pushing with her blue wings."

Cole turned and looked over the back of his chair, staring toward the woods. Saw nothing. Thought, *No, there's not*—but then saw a dime-sized flutter of blue. A floating dot of powder and wings.

"And a coyote," Nanny said. Her voice was the voice of someone retelling a wondrous dream. "Scraggly 'n' brown. But his muzzle's black and his chest is thick. I'd say Mr. Coyote has a Labrador retriever hiding somewhere in his family kennel. He's watching us from over in the scrub pile...but now he feels me watching him. And now he's moving, wanting to hide—"

Cole looked into the trees past the farthest edge of the yard, staring at the high Tinkertoy pile of broken branches and scrub that had been tossed there over the years. He saw movement in the hollow depths. Saw the narrow black line of a coyote's nose. Caught a curving sense of dirt-colored hair as the coyote turned and faded away, moving deeper into the brush pile, then disappearing into the woods.

"He's leaving. Slinking away." Nanny T.'s voice was still soft, her eyes were still closed. But now she was wearing a little grin on her face. "I hear his paws padding over the ground. And the little whine he just made—he's wondering what's following him, what it is that he can't see." Her grin grew larger. "Why, it's just me, Mr. Coyote! Watching you back. Wondering why you're watching me and Cole?" She blinked her eyes open and looked at Cole. "Ready?" she asked.

He nodded yes, thinking, *Please, please, please.*

She nodded back. "I believe you can do it," she said. "Just remember—*Si! Si! Si!*"

Si! Si! Si!

It wasn't Mexican. It wasn't even words. It was an abbreviation. A quick way of remembering the steps she wanted him to learn: C.C.C. *Clear. Conjure. Connect.*

Clear: Calm his mind. Concentrate on "nothing." Clear his thoughts for the next step. "You've got to empty it out before you can fill it up," she always said.

Conjure: Fill his mind with the place he wanted to see and hear. "Where is it that you want to see and hear things? It has to be somewhere close. Somewhere you've already been. Now think, when you were walking and standing there, you were blinking all day long—meaning that all day long, you were closing your eyes. And in all those blinks, you couldn't see where you were. But you knew you were there. Because even with your eyes closed, you still saw it. Your mind was so full of the place that you couldn't even tell when it disappeared a million blinking times."

He looked at her. Felt himself blink.

"Act like you're there," she said. "Act like your eyes have just blinked closed. Fill your mind full with the place again." She pointed a finger at the yard. "It doesn't go on forever. At the start, it works better in close places, like here in the yard. Later, you can go farther."

Connect: After he "cleared and conjured," after his mind was filled full, he had to just *be there*. Had to pay specific, exact attention—had to look at the details of what there was to see. Had to walk into the bushes. Go inside the buildings. Look behind the trees. Stop and watch things. Listen to them.

"I showed off a little, earlier," she said. "You'll be able to hear sounds, but you won't be able to hear my thoughts. Not right away. That takes longer. And even then, it needs to be *really loud* thinking. And you, King Cole, well, you were practically yelling about your lion."

It wasn't all lessons. She didn't let him sit all day. "Into the woods," she'd say, waving him toward the trees. "Go play. Go exploring. Then tell me what you find."

There was plenty to find.

Mostly, he hiked through the woods and spent his time near Salt Creek, walking alongside it, wandering upstream one day, downstream the next. Wading in it, too, looking for gray-green crawdads and quick underwater clouds of minnow-fish. Surprising the little frogs. Sometimes even seeing small water snakes swimming by, their little heads sticking up, moving back and forth, carving endless S's into the water.

Best of all, though, was his favorite thing: gold panning. Nanny T. gave him a small, folding camp shovel and a wide green pan. "The gold shows best against the green," she said the first day, standing with him in the stream, showing him how to fill the pan with dirt and gravel dug from the bottom. "When you're digging, just try figuring out where you'd go if you were a bunch of heavy little marbles." As she talked, she dug into the outside edge of a bend in the creek. "Try figuring out where you'd roll in the water, where you'd pile up 'n' stay."

She showed him how to swirl water in the pan and shake the heavy stuff down to the bottom. "Not the big stuff," she said. "The heavy stuff. Like gold." How to use the back of his hand to sweep the gravel and dirt out of the pan. How to trap pockets of fine black sand in the terraced angles of a ramp of little steps molded into the pan's edge. And, last, using a little water in the tilted bottom of the pan, she showed him how to spread the trapped black sand into a thinning fan across the pan's bottom, revealing beneath it—*gold!*

Small, thin flakes of gold—some no bigger than grains of sand—glowed bright against the pan. "Stick 'em with a toothpick," she said, poking at one of the flakes. "See how it sticks? Now put it in your collection." She reached into her pocket and pulled out a glass vial about the size of his thumb. Unscrewing the top, she dipped the toothpick's point into the bottle. They both stared as the gold flake dropped off the toothpick and floated slowly to the bottom. "Glycerin," she said, watching the gold sink. "Thicker than water. Slows the gold down, makes it easier to see. More fun to look at, too."

She screwed the cap back on, handed him the vial, and pointed to the creek. "Now go find yourself some treasure," she said. "Try filling this bottle with gold before you go home." Then she sat down on the stream bank to watch him pan. After a while, though, he looked up and saw that she was gone, leaving him alone to his adventure. Looking where she'd been sitting, he saw that her light old bones had hardly pressed into the sand at all.

AT FIRST he was afraid. Afraid of being alone. Afraid of being in the woods—

—*"You have to be careful, Cole," his mother always said. "There's riffraff everywhere. They're always watching. Always lurking. They get you when you aren't looking, when you aren't paying attention. And when they get you, it doesn't matter how good or how smart you are. Once they've got you, the riffraff will do all sorts of bad things. Unspeakable things. Horrible things." She'd stopped and looked out through the window curtains. "Promise me," she always said, and he was always sure she'd seen something evil outside, something watching, lurking for him. "Promise me you'll always pay attention, that you'll always be looking. And promise me not to go near the riffraff."*

"I promise," he always answered, looking out the window, too, feeling afraid because he couldn't see what she saw. And even more afraid that one day he might—

—so he'd worried about the riffraff that might be lurking in the woods. Worried about unspeakable, horrible things. But nothing bad happened. Not then, and—as days went by—not later, either. Without knowing when it happened, he stopped worrying and started thinking of the stream as *his*. He even stopped worrying as he hiked through the woods. And wasn't frightened at all until the day he looked up from his gold pan and saw THE ROCKMAN—

A hunched, shaggy-haired creature. Standing in the water beside him. Staring down at him, holding two large rocks in his hands. The instant Cole saw him, his thoughts screamed, *I WASN'T PAYING ATTENTION! I WASN'T LOOKING! I WASN'T BEING CAREFUL—*

He'd been digging in the same hole all morning. Had found gold everywhere and was thinking, *Maybe. Maybe I can fill this vial.* He'd been concentrating, too, thinking only about the water and the pan and the black sand and the gold and the hole. Before he knew it, it was lunchtime. He felt hungry, but thought, *Holy cow! Look at all the gold!* and decided he couldn't leave now. Decided to swirl through a few more pans before he left, to see if there was more gold deeper down. Then he'd turned with the shovel, ready to dig again, and saw STANDING RIGHT BESIDE HIM—

THE ROCKMAN.

He was tall, but his shoulders curled forward, bending his body into a thick comma. His face was old, with lips that folded back over toothless gums. But looking at the Rockman's arms, Cole saw that they weren't an old man's weak arms—they were strong, with planks of heavy old-growth muscle. The muscles bunched out from the torn armholes of a mud-stained T-shirt and cascaded down the man's arms, ending at two brutal stubs of wrists and hands. Each hand held a large, round rock in a clamp of thick, calloused fingers.

Staring back at Cole, the Rockman gently swung his arms backward. The rocks swung back with the arms. Then the Rockman swung his arms forward. *He's going to throw the rocks at me! Going to hit me with the rocks!* thought Cole, paralyzed in the moment, standing transfixed in the creek. Then the Rockman turned slightly and tossed the first rock at the creek bank, then lobbed the other one immediately after it, the second rock exactly following the first one's arc. *He's strong,* thought Cole. *He could hurt me, could kill—*

—the first rock landed on the bank. And just after, the second one fell onto the first. Slammed together, the two rocks shattered, bursting apart in a glittering spray, the explosion of rock fragments catching and turning the sunlight as they fell. *What the—?* thought Cole, watching the bright reflections.

The Rockman smiled at Cole, then walked to the creek bank. Knelt down near the shattered rocks and began sorting through the shining pieces, pushing a thick finger through the fragments. Working quickly, he filled a cupped hand with broken stones, then stood and walked back to Cole. He held his hand out, showing Cole a handful of sparkling bright pieces.

Diamonds? Cole thought. *Diamonds in the rocks?*

They weren't diamonds. They were crystals. And they were beautiful. The captured light bounced back and forth in the small mound, reflecting from crystal to crystal, revealing their clear and misty colors. Whispers of rose, gray, brown, and yellow filled the Rockman's hand.

Cole looked at them, entranced. *Treasure,* he thought. *A pirate's treasure.*

"These," the Rockman said, offering the crystals. "Take these."

Cole stepped back and shook his head and stepped back again. "No," he said politely. "They're yours."

Still holding the crystals out to Cole, the Rockman reached up with his free hand and pulled at a leather cord hanging around his neck. He lifted the cord over his head, pulling out something hidden under his muddy T-shirt. He held it out to Cole. "This," he said. "I have this," showing Cole a wire-wrapped, palm-sized cluster of sparkling geode crystals, bound together in the shape of a hanging arrowhead. The crystals were multi-hued shades of cloud, and drizzle, and shadow.

After a moment, the Rockman slipped the pendant back on and let it drop back down under his shirt. He nodded at the crystal pieces in his hand. "Here," he said again. "These, take these, I don't keep them. Now I just find them. Now I just look," he said. "It's enough."

He poured the crystals into Cole's hand. With his hands now full, Cole looked up at the Rockman again. "Thank you," he said, not sure what else to say. After a moment he added, "I'm Cole. Cole Tinkens."

A confused expression crossed the Rockman's face. As if recalling a lost memory, he slowly answered. "Thad. I'm Thad."

"Geodes," Nanny T. said later, looking at the handful of crystals spread out across the bottom of Cole's treasure chest. "They're hollow, bumpy round stones—like globes. The name even means 'little earth.' Just look," she said, picking up one of the pieces. "All dirty and dull on the outside. But split them open and look what's hiding inside. Beautiful, just beautiful—aren't they?" She set the crystal down and stepped closer to Cole. "And, honey," she said, reaching out and cupping her fingers against his cheeks, cradling his face like an open hymnbook. "You don't need to worry about the Rockman. He's fine. He's like…" Her voice trailed off as her hands left his face and pointed delicately to the glittering stones, to the treasures held hidden in bumpy dull shells.

During his first visit with Nanny T., he saw the Rockman six more times. Always somewhere along the stream, digging buried geodes out of the earth with his fingers. Hunched over, he carried loads of them out of the water and built small piles of them along the creek. Sometimes he'd break the rocks open and study what was inside. Picking out a few of the most colorful crystals, he'd hand them to Cole, saying, "These. Take these."

A few times, they spent an entire day in view of each other at the stream. Each enjoying the water. Each enjoying the other's silent company. Nodding "hello" to one another as they worked. Cole filling his gold pan. The Rockman picking up geodes.

One afternoon, Cole sat down beside the stack of geodes the

Rockman was building and reached into the lunch sack Nanny T. had packed that morning. Pulling an apple from the bag, he offered it to the Rockman. "This," he said. "Take this."

The Rockman paused. Stopped building his rock pile. Stared at the apple in Cole's hand. Stayed silent, looking at it.

"For you," Cole said again, waiting for him to take it, but now sensing something else happening. Maybe something wrong.

The Rockman just stared at the apple. All at once—horribly, embarrassingly—Cole thought, *He doesn't have any teeth! He can't eat it! I was stupid—*

Then Thad reached out and gently took the apple from Cole's hand and held it up, letting the sun touch its skin. He held it like a crystal to the light. Said nothing, just stared. Then he said slowly, as if digging up a long-lost memory, "The Gala apple. A thin skin of pale pinkish-orange stripes over a bright yellow-red background. Crisp, creamy yellow flesh with a mild, sweet flavor. Of New Zealand origin. Developed as a cross of Cox's Orange Pippin and the Golden Delicious varieties. A harvest time beginning in mid-August and lasting through early September."

He stopped talking, but kept looking at the apple. Then looked down at Cole and smiled. "One of my favorites," he said. Then, gently, being careful not to bruise it, he set the apple on top of the rock pile he was building. Still smiling, he said, "Thank you, Cole. It is beautiful. And later...I will gum it to its core."

Then, for the first time, Cole heard the good sound of the Rockman's laughter. And Cole joined in. Laughing with his friend by the stream.

COLE STRETCHED again.

Time to get moving.

Time to start doing some of the Things Still Left For Him to Do.

Sliding out of bed, he moved slowly, trying not to bump into anything. He felt around for his clothes. Found them and pulled on his jeans and the T-shirt he'd bought in town (*SURF BROWN COUNTY! The Ocean Was Here Just a Minute Ago!*). Getting ready to walk through the woods, he double-knotted his tennis shoes.

Nanny T. was still sleeping. Her low snores from the next room guided him in the dark like a lighthouse horn, signaling him to the door and down the stairs. She'd sleep another hour or two, long enough for him to get to the stream and shake out a few more pans of gravel. The small vial she'd given him last year still wasn't full. And he wanted it to be full. Wanted it full before he went back home.

He planned to gold pan all morning, then be back at the cabin for lunch. After lunch, he'd practice with Nanny T. She was happy with what he could see and hear. He was getting better at *Si! Si! Si!* It was easy to see the yard now. Easy to see what was hiding in the grass. To see what was moving through the tree line. Like the coyote. It was back. He'd seen it, the same one that Nanny T. saw last year. Its black muzzle was now crisscrossed with a scattering of white-haired scars.

He could hear things, too. Could hear the breathing of the animals he watched. Could hear the tiny clicking of a mother bird's beak touching against her babies' beaks.

Walking past the open door of Nanny's bedroom, he whispered into her room, speaking softly so she wouldn't wake up. "Good-night," he said. "Sleep tight. I can't wait to leave and go home soon."

Then he stepped carefully down the stairs, avoiding the squeak-spots. In the kitchen, he filled his canteen and slipped some apples into his pack. He'd give them to the Rockman today, as a kind of going-away present. If he didn't see him, he'd stack the apples on top of a rock pile. The Rockman would like that.

Slipping out the back door, he saw that the just-before-light kind of dark was now touched with pale gray, making it light enough for him to see his way to the trees.

SHE'D HEARD him laughing in his room. Had heard him rustling around, trying to be quiet. She kept on snoring, acting like she was still asleep, wanting him to have his private morning time. Wanting him to have a chance to enjoy the dawn-lit woods.

But she almost gave herself away by chuckle-snorting when she heard his whispered greeting at her door. She'd acted like it was a sleep-cough, though, and he hadn't caught her playing possum.

She waited till she heard him on the stairs (there was no way to walk down the steps without the squeaks following you all the way to the kitchen) before she whispered her own "opposite" back to him. "Good-night to you, also, King Cole. And, my, my—I can't wait for you to leave."

When she heard the backdoor close, she rose from her bed and pulled on a pair of shorts and the T-shirt Cole had given her, with ¡ARRIBA! printed on it in flaming red and yellow letters across the front and a picture of Speedy Gonzales racing across her belly.

She went downstairs, wanting her morning kiss from Granddaddy Longlegs. In the kitchen she set the teakettle on the stove and lit it, then put two slices of bread into the toaster. Wondering the whole time, *Why are you watching me, Mr. Coyote? And who are you telling what you see?*

The coyote worried her. She'd seen him a few times over the past year, but now he'd been here every day for the past month, hiding just inside the tree line of the woods. Hiding and watching.

Sitting in her chair, she watched him right back. Even followed him when he left, trying to figure out where he went, what he did. She'd been surprised five days ago when she'd followed him through the woods and saw him lie down in the concealment of some heavy brush. Looking around then, she saw what he was studying.

He was watching Cole. Was watching him pan gold in the stream. Then, with enough worry boiling through her to make it possible, she'd screamed in her mind, *SCAT! SCAT! SCAT!*

Someone watching her sitting there in the chair might have seen her lips move, might have seen the slight puckering of her white eyebrows—

—and the coyote had jumped in surprise. Had snapped his head around, bit his own haunches, and then raced off. But he could still feel her following him, could hear her still screaming, *SCAT! SCAT! SCAT!* until she grew tired and stopped. Opening her eyes, she slumped in the chair and calmed herself down, but she needed the rest of the morning to get her strength back.

Since then, she'd checked in on Cole a few times every day.

She was sure about the boy. He was like her, a *see'r*. (*"Not 'seer'* she'd once told her fine young husband. *'See'r.' Mostly, I just see the things going on.")* No, see'rs couldn't tell the future, she'd added, but they could certainly keep a watch on things.

The boy had the gift. She knew that for certain. He could see *and* hear. Maybe could even sing one day. Maybe. He was still having fun with it, too. Soon, though, she'd start teaching him that it wasn't just fun. Would teach him that he was a part of *something*, something she wished her own boy was a part of—but he didn't have it in him. No matter how many times she'd sat with him in the yard, asking him, "Tell me, what do you see? Tell me, what do you hear?" he'd never been able to answer. Not *the answer*. No. Instead, he was just a good boy. A good, kind boy who grew up to be a good, kind man. A good, kind man who'd married very poorly—

— *"Now, Nanny," she could still hear her long-leggity man telling her, "when did you start sitting on a throne instead of a chair? When did you 'hear something' that told you to go right ahead and start judging others?" And, of course, he was right. "Sure, I'm right," he'd told her. "Don't forget," he'd said, pausing and grinning at her. "There wouldn't be a Cole here today if our son hadn't married that hateful, horrible woman." And Nanny always grinned back. "She's his wife and I love her, I do," her voice perfectly mirroring her daughter-in-law's cadence and tone. He'd laughed then and walked over to her on his long-leggity legs and bent down and kissed her and she'd tasted the cinnamon of his mouth—the taste of those little red-wrapped candies he always kept in his pocket, eating them all day long. And he'd tell her, "Oh, I do so love you and your 'hillbilly-common' ways."*

HE HAD EATEN the red candies every day, right up until two weeks before he died. He ate them from the time he woke till the time he brushed his teeth at night. Had eaten so many of them that, candy or not, his breath was always the flavor of warm cinnamon spice. At night, lying beside him, their bodies under the tent of blankets held up on the bent knees of his long legs, she'd breathe in the cinnamon scent of him, then drift into dreams of bakeries and apple pie.

Eating the candies had killed him.

Actually, *not eating* the candies is what killed him.

She'd looked at him one day, surprised to see a toothpick in his mouth. "Candy's gone," he explained. "Thought this'd do till we have a chance to pick up some more." Taking the toothpick out of his mouth, he leaned down to kiss her and she smelled the cinnamon oil he'd soaked the toothpick in. She remembered thinking, *Probably better for him than candy,* and then kissed him back, tasting the warm spice of him. Thinking thoughts of cinnamon toast.

Days went by, and they didn't go into town. He kept a toothpick in his mouth, chewing through a bundle of them every day, carrying them around in a plastic sandwich bag in his pocket. He made fresh ones every night, pouring oil over them in a little glass dish on the kitchen counter.

He'd died on his way to the store, while making the long-delayed trip to pick up groceries ("And one hundred pounds of my candy!" he'd shouted as he left). He'd slowed down to navigate the big bend in the road when his car was bumped from behind by another driver. Both cars had been moving slowly, so slowly that there wasn't any damage from the impact, but the jolt had been strong enough to trigger the airbag in her long-leggity man's car. And the inflating airbag had moved fast enough to drive the toothpick in his mouth right through the back of his throat, deep into the headrest in back of him, just like a tornado throwing a piece of straw though a telephone pole.

After the accident, when he was in his coffin—not the extra-long-sized coffin that the funeral home had suggested, but the regular-sized one she told them to use, telling them to just lift his knees and tent his legs a bit, that that was how he was most comfortable sleeping—she filled one of his front pockets with the red-wrapped candies and the other pocket with a bag of his flavored toothpicks. "There," she'd whispered in his ear. "Now please wait for me. I've got a little more seeing to do, but I'll be along in a bit. Wait for me"

THIS MORNING, she stood in the kitchen, cradling a teacup in her hands. *It showed how silly this world was,* she thought. A man spends his life as a warrior—preparing to fight, getting ready for when she needed him, waiting for whenever she saw what she was looking for—and then he's killed by an itty-bitty toothpick. *It was simply stranger than silly.*

She closed her eyes. Lifted the cup to her lips, whispered, "Good morning, my long-leggity man," and drank the hot cinnamon tea. She held it in her mouth a moment, enjoying his morning kiss, thinking thoughts of apple pie and cinnamon toast. And of lying beside him under a tent of sheets and blankets.

Then she opened her eyes again and looked out through the back door. Her chair was in the yard, as usual. The white wicker seat looked like it was floating on top of the curling low mist that was rising from the ground. *My flying chair,* she thought. *Flying me here and there.* And she whispered again into her tea, her voice cracking a bit with worry, telling him, "I believe it's almost here. But without you here, I don't know who to tell. And don't know who will fight. And I won't know when to sing. But I do know that

I hope you've waited." She swallowed the last of the cinnamon-flavored brew. "Because I believe it's almost time. And I believe I'll be along in a bit."

THE BLACK CARS. THE NORTH CAR

L ATER, WHEN HE WAS DYING—when his heels were drumming their final spastic riffs on the porch and his palms were slapping up and down in flopping, convulsive counterpoint—right then he thought again, *Every time. Every goddamned time.* He also noticed that his life wasn't flashing in front of his eyes. Of course, given his immediate circumstances, even if his life was going to flash, none of it was going to happen in front of his left eye. Nothing could ever again flash or flicker in front of that eye, not anymore—not with the long, blue and yellow, flame-shaped pen stuck so deeply and so blindingly inside of it.

His head seemed curiously uninvolved with his body's awkward quivering dance toward death. His head—face-up, tilted to the right—was unmoved by the jumping vibrations that gripped and lifted his limbs. His right eye stared past the bridge of his nose at the protruding pen. The pen quivered and bobbed in response to the blood and brains that were pressing and stirring against the ballpoint end embedded deep inside his left eye's bony socket. His right eye—wide-open, its emptying black pupil now so large that it almost completely obscured his walnut-brown iris—looked up the length of the flame-shaped pen, watching the floating, tiny red-plastic match flame that was sinking slowly toward his face.

The red-plastic match flame in the ballpoint pen was riding atop a descending miniature silver rocket ship. The match flame had a small, painted face, with black-dot eyes, a happy comma of a smile, and also had a painted stick-arm raised and waving *Hello—* or maybe, in this case, *Goodbye*. Bright yellow, plastic fire shot out from the rocket's bottom.

His eye watched the rocket ship float down. The ship slid through a clear liquid-filled tube in the center of the long plastic pen. The tube looked like a thermometer, with its temperature degrees marked by small horizontal red lines along its length. Words were printed along the pen. And although he could no longer read them, he knew what they said, because he'd read them just seconds ago, before what happened next had happened. Only a moment ago, before it happened, he'd read *TURNING UP THE HEAT, NATURALLY!* and thought, *Hmm, how clever.*

At the very end of things, he would have liked to see his life one more time. It had been a good life. Good enough that he'd enjoy seeing it again in his last few seconds. But all he saw was the pen. As the rocket ship landed in the ruined crater of his left eye, the only thought he could think was the very same one he'd been thinking since he fell: *Every time. Every goddamned time...*

THE FIRST TIME it happened was in the second grade, on the school playground's merry-go-round spinner. It was his favorite thing. Facing the ride's center, he'd sit on the spinner's steel braces, sitting like he was riding a horse. He'd hold the center bar as someone started spinning the ride. As the ride spun faster and faster, its speed became so strong that he could feel the centrifugal force pulling at him, tugging at him, trying to throw him off...until finally—and this was the best part, the incredible part, the greatest part—

—he'd let go. Would open his hands and throw back his head, releasing the bar and feeling his body lifted off the ride, arms flying out, filled with the chaotic sense of flying backward. Of being pulled off the edge. Of hurtling, crashing freedom. But in the instant before disaster, he'd suddenly stop falling, saved from hurt by keeping his legs wrapped around the steel brace, his ankles locked together behind it. It was wonderful, being able to thrill in the free spinning danger of it all, but at the same time staying safe, staying entirely unhurt—

Except for the time he was hurt.

He'd been riding with his arms thrown out, his head thrown back, and then felt one of his arms grabbed, yanked hard and back, pulling him off of the brace. His legs unlocked as he fell backward and landed half-on and half-off the ride. The ride kept spinning, dragging him around and around with it, dragging his face and arms through the pea gravel and splintery bark mulch until the merry-go-round finally started slowing down.

He heard laughing, heard someone saying something as—bleeding, scraped, and, yes, crying—he rolled off the now-stopped ride. His arm was throbbing. (*"It really hurts,"* he told the doctor later. *"It should,"* the doctor said. *"That's how broken arms feel."*) He tried to stand up so he could *Go Get Help.* Then felt a moment of confusion as he realized he couldn't stand up, couldn't even lift his face off the ground. Then felt the shoe that was pushing on his back, pressing him down. And he heard talking again, this time hearing the words—hearing "Superman, Pooperman, fell down and went bang!" as the shoe pushed him down harder into the gravel, pressing each small stone into his skin.

There was more laughing as he rolled over and looked up at the small group of kids that had gathered around him. The group now repeating, "Superman, Pooperman! Superman, Pooperman!" Then he saw the kid who'd hurt him. The kid whose shoe was now pressing on his chest, pinning him in the dirt like a bug.

The kid's name: Greg Clint.

That was the beginning. That was the first time. He didn't know it then, but that was the start of the rule.

THE SECOND TIME it happened was years later.

He had a job. Not a perfect job, not by a long shot. But a start, something that might lead somewhere. That could maybe turn into something. It didn't seem like something at first, didn't seem like anything at all, but he didn't have a college degree and didn't have any experience, either. So, shit, with credentials like his, who was he trying to fool: It was a GREAT job.

Every day he tried to do two things.

First thing: He tried to remember to be grateful. Tried to remember to be grateful even when a swell of embarrassment swept through him as he pinned his big round badge on his bright red vest. No name on the badge, just a title and a slogan going around the perimeter of the badge in big red letters: *ASST. MGR., LOW-LOW TOYS. Low-Low Prices! Big-Big Smiles!* He tried to remember to be grateful for having this job—a job that was a chance, that was a possibility. That was maybe a way to something better.

Second thing: He tried to learn something new every day. *Anything new.* Like reworking the employee schedule to save a few payroll hours. Or learning the names of the 247 mini-action figures in the MOBILIZE! role-playing game (*aisle 6, second shelf*). Or trying—and this one caused the problem, this was the one that cost him his bright red vest—to find ways to improve the toy store's displays.

Every toy shipment came with photos from headquarters. The photos showed ways to display the merchandise, the *official ways* to stack and pile and hang each toy. *Good suggestions*, he thought. *Good ideas, unless you had even better ideas.* And he always had better ideas. Could always think of something different to do with the toys. Could always figure out a better way to get the customer's attention—

—which was why he was building a huge, giant-ass soccer ball in the middle of the store, building it with the truckload of soccer balls delivered that morning. Each ball was packaged in a square, black-and-white cardboard box. He'd looked at the display picture that came with the balls and seen nothing special, just a photo of the balls lined up along a shelf. So he'd thought of something better—

—figured out he could stack the balls to show either the black or the white part of each box. Figured out how to stack the boxes so they locked together. By using the black or white side when appropriate and by locking them together so the display wouldn't collapse, he was using the boxes to build a big, eye-catching soccer ball. *He'd already sold twelve balls before he was even done!*

The display had been almost done. He was standing on a ladder. Was finishing the top of the ball when someone started kicking the bottom of the display. Kicking and yelling, "NO! NO! NO!"

The display began falling. And the person kept kicking. Kept scattering the boxes and yelling, "DO IT LIKE IT SHOWS IN THE PICTURE! PUT IT ON THE SHELF LIKE IN THE PICTURE! I'M SICK OF THIS INSUBORDINATE, CREATIVE BULLSHIT!"—

—and he was going to climb down from the ladder. Was going to stop the screaming person. But through the flying boxes and kicking legs and swinging arms, he saw that the screaming person was wearing a *blue* vest—not a red one. And he knew that a blue vest came with a rectangular badge—not a round one—a badge with a title *and* a name.

That's when he thought about the idea. About the possibility of an actual rule. A solid "Rules Are Rules" sort of thing. *Maybe, just maybe*, he thought, watching the man below him. The man still kicking the display and still screaming. But now screaming, "FIRED! YOU'RE FIRED! YOU'RE FIRED!"

As he watched, he contemplated the badge on the blue vest…

LOW-LOW TOYS
DISTRICT MANAGER, ALLEN MARK
Low-Low Prices
Big-Big Smiles!

The third and fourth time it happened, he'd been in his first apartment. He was living on the middle floor of an old, three-story house, each floor a separate rental. The house was perfect, with wood floors, graceful curving arches between the rooms, built-in bookshelves.

And it was cheap.

It was in an aging section of the city, on a shabby street lined by houses with no yards, each house separated from the street only by narrow, uneven sidewalks, and separated from its neighboring houses only by crumbling shoulder-wide walkways. The landlord was an active churchgoer and felt he was pleasing the Lord by putting a roof over his fellow man's head at a reasonable cost.

For two years, things had been good. Everybody had been happy: the landlord, the Lord, and the house's three renters. Until the blind man next door complained.

The blind man: An ancient, nicotine-stained man who advertised his business in the bulletin of a local church. On Sunday mornings, discarded copies of the bulletin flew along the uneven sidewalks in a holy litter-cloud of Good News!

PIANO TUNING
Bradley George, Sole Proprietor
—*A Fellow Parishioner*—
Blinded By The Light, But In Tune With The Times!

The same blind man who picked up his phone and dialed the landlord, a man who was *A Fellow Parishioner.* The blind man who complained about an unacceptable situation. An immoral situation. A situation occurring in the home next to his, the same home owned by the landlord…

A problem with sin.

A problem with the renter in the house's basement.

The basement tenant was an average guy, but he was an average guy with a very above-average, beautiful fiancée—a fiancée who wore jasmine perfume and moaned wonderfully during sex. Her perfume followed lightly behind her, a hint of it always finding its way into his middle-floor open window whenever she walked by. And her throaty, encouraging screams rose through the old house's shared ductwork and found him at all times of the day, her energy and appetite making him glad for everyone in the world, and also, he thought, making everyone glad.

Everyone except the blind neighbor.

The blind neighbor who sat all day at his window, facing the walkway between the houses. Who whispered, "Come 'ere, girlie, come 'ere," whenever he smelled jasmine in the air. The blind man who sat so very still at the window when the fiancée's love cries floated through the air, sitting so still as though to feel the vibrations of her sex, as though to somehow hear her quiet murmured gasps and moans—

—"*Maybe it's because his other senses, you know—his nose and ears and sense of touch—maybe they're all super-finely-tuned and, you know, maybe they're overcompensating for his eyes,*" the basement tenant once said. Then he laughed, saying, "*But whatcha gonna do, man? I mean, after all, the poor bastard's blind!*"—

—the same blind man who, one day, as the fiancée walked by, pressed his face against the window screen and rasped, "Gimme a fuck, girlie, gimme a suck," but didn't have such super-finely-tuned, overcompensating senses that he could avoid the thick jet of pepper spray the fiancée sent streaming through the screen and into his mouth—

—soon after which the blind neighbor made his call. The call complaining about the sinful situation. The call complaining about "continual fornication."

And suddenly not everybody was happy anymore. Not the landlord. Not (according to the landlord) the Lord. And not—after being told to move—the basement tenant.

Only the blind neighbor was happy.

That was the third time—it was the time that made him remember the other two times and made him put them all together and think, *It is a rule. An absolute rule. An absolutely "Rules Are Rules" sort of rule.* But then he thought, *Yeah, right*, and probably would have quickly forgotten it, never thinking about it again, except, only two days later, the new renter moved into the newly-vacated basement apartment and ruined the house.

The new renter played loud scratching music, discordant noise that floated up the same ductwork that had once been filled with soft, wet cooings and welcoming moans and sharp inhalations. And the new renter burned incense that smelled of rotting meat and piss, its black and yellow odor crawling through floors and walls and sticking to everything in the old house with small, suckered feet. He also somehow blocked the ductwork from below, trapping the cool air-conditioning in the basement during the summer and keeping the warm furnace heat for himself during the winter. And as a final bit of dickhead fun, the basement renter would take the bizarre mail (*Fetish Fun!* and *Death Now!* and *Fatal Photos!*) delivered to his own mailbox and would place it into the other two renters' mailboxes, leaving an unwanted daily deposit of lurid, frightening mail with no theme or pattern to it other than all being sent to the same addressee: Tommy Kevin.

That was the fourth time.

It was the final straw.

The deciding vote.

The rule maker.

It was the reason that, later in life, he made decisions not to hire certain people and decisions to fire certain others. It was the reason he told his daughter to be careful around an early boyfriend, and (thank God) she eventually broke up with him, because only two years later the slippery prick was arrested for rape. The rule was the reason he'd sold off parts of some businesses, and the reason he refused to buy parts of others.

All because of the rule. A damn good "Rules Are Rules" rule.

Proven time and time again. One that he'd learned over and over and over.

The rule: *A man with two first names will fuck you. He'll fuck you every time. Every goddamned time.*

EARLIER IN THE DAY, before the visitor with the pen arrived, he'd been sitting in the front room of his Brown County cabin. Was already bored with every minute of early retirement. Was wishing that his ex-wife would call him less often and that his daughter would call him more. Was trying to think of possible ways to fill the long afternoon in front of him. And was glad to hear car wheels out on the driveway. He'd perked up, interested in who might be coming to visit. He'd been curious enough to stand by the open door and look out. Had been even more curious when an unfamiliar black car turned into view. The car's hood was decorated with blue and yellow lettering across the hood. *TURNING UP THE HEAT, NATURALLY!*

Happy for the distraction of a visitor, he'd thought, *Here is my afternoon. Here is a little conversation.* He watched the car stop and park. Then watched a smiling man step out of the car and wave at him. In the man's waving hand was a sheaf of papers. In his other hand was a blue and yellow flame.

The man walked toward him. He was short and his cheeks were fleshy, hinting that he might be a little heavy, but the heaviness was hidden in his nicely tailored, dark gray suit. His hair was short, its salt-and-pepper color showing some age, some maturity. The man's blue eyes were clear and bright and full of confidence and pleasure that perfectly matched his welcoming smile. All in all, the man appeared to be a professional. Someone interesting. Someone worth talking to on an empty afternoon.

He stepped outside the cabin, stood on the porch, and nodded to the man. At the bottom of the porch steps, the man nodded back, saying up the stairs, "I was hoping for a little bit of your time."

"How lucky for both of us, then," he answered with a laugh. "I happen to have a little bit of time. I happen to have all the little bits of time that you might need."

"No matter what, at the very least," the blue-eyed man said, "you get this great gift." He held up the plastic pen, then shook it to make it look more like a real flame and showed the floating match's flame-face that was spinning in the center tube. He turned the pen so that the words along the side could be read. Still shaking the cheap pen, the man stared at it, then raised his eyebrows disdainfully. "And as you can see," he said, his tone self-mocking, half apologetic, "I do mean at the absolute *very least*. The *very, very* least."

Standing at the top of the steps, looking first at the pen and then at the blue-eyed man, he laughed again and gestured for the man to come join him on the porch. He was already looking forward to the company. Was enjoying the idea of having a conversation with someone who knew when to make a joke about himself. "I have to be honest," he said to his visitor. "That pen looks like it's better than all of the other free, plastic, flame-thermometer pens I have."

The man laughed with him. "In that case," he said, "you can have two. Really, pleeeease take two! Pleeeease!"

They were both smiling by then, both of them enjoying the easy back-and-forth rapport. Tucking the papers under his arm, the blue-eyed man walked up the steps. "Sean Jake," he said, sticking out his hand. "Good to meet you."

He shook Sean Jake's hand, still smiling but now thinking, *Sonofabitch, even in the middle of nowhere. A man with two fucking first names.* Already knowing he wasn't going to agree to anything they discussed, that he wasn't going to do anything with anyone named Sean Jake. But he didn't want to be rude. Didn't see any reason to tell the man that anything had changed—

"Something just changed," said the man, looking at him. "Didn't it?"

And, hey, that was a little spooky, but he had to give the man credit. Had to concede that Sean Jake could sure read the signals. So he decided not to insult him, not to waste anyone's time.

"Something did. A little," he answered, then pointed at the papers in his visitor's hand. "But if you want, you can leave the information here," he said, knowing he wouldn't read anything. Knowing he'd just throw it all away—

"You'll just throw them away," the man said.

And that was even spookier, but…

"Oh, well. Fuck it. If we're done, we're done," the man said, stepping closer, not moving like he was heavy or old at all. Still holding the sheaf of papers in one hand, but now sweeping his other hand forward in a low arc, stabbing up and out. Saying, "Here, you can keep the pen."

LATER, THE BLUE-EYED man in the gray suit stood over the body. He reached down. Grabbed the pen. Twisted it in small, tight circles to work it free. As it came loose, things inside the body's head made little breaking noises. "Actually," the man said, looking into the body's single, staring, open eye, "I'm taking this back. I know I said you could have it, but…you know…Rules Are Rules."

BLUE

16

GORDY AND I are walking in the woods. We started mid-morning, leaving from the cabin. Gordy's in the lead. This is his trip; he's the one who invited me. We're on one of the deep earthen rolls of the hill, but not walking toward the Circle. I don't know what I'd tell him if we walked in that direction, don't know what I'd say if we approached the Stones. I've only told Elissa about the Circle, and even her I haven't told everything—I still haven't told her about the child that I hear crying there. The child I've still not found. The child still lost on Jonah's Belly.

HE'D CALLED earlier and said he wanted to show me something. Said he wanted my opinion.

"About what?" I asked.

"You'll see," was all he said, making this truly high mystery for him, and Gordy is not a mysterious guy. He is a "who, what, when, where, how, and why" kind of guy. That's why I haven't told him about the Circle. Not yet, at least, not until I can answer more than "where"—and even that, I think, is more of a "*where* does this all lead?" kind of question. Which, of course, is something else that I can't answer.

Not yet.

GRENDEL PADS alongside us, his pace graceful, sleek, silent. He disappears and reappears like a tufted-eared ghost as his huge paws smoothly miss the same low briars that snag at Gordy and me. At times he walks beside me, walking so close that his body presses against my leg and I feel the coiled power of him, the tight spring of his muscles. When Gordy and I stop to rest, Grendel rests, too. He leans lazily against me, his head level with my thigh.

Gordy reaches down to scratch Grendel's ears. "You know," he says, "your lynx thinks he's a lion." Grendel pushes his head against Gordy's hand, cat-speak for *scratch harder*. Gordy obliges and Grendel closes his eyes in pleasure, lifts his chin, offers his throat—cat-speak again. *Here, too.*

Gordy squats down and gives Grendel's neck a work-out. "Do you have any idea how many calls we've taken about him over the last few weeks?" he asks, now scratching Grendel's shoulders. "I'm talking about calls from everyone, from old-timers and new-timers, everybody reporting the same thing—all of them scared shitless, saying things like, 'Send the police, I heard a lion,' and 'Send the police, I saw lion tracks,' and 'A lion's loose, send the police.'"

Gordy puts his hands around Grendel's face and slowly pushes the cat's head from side to side, saying, "Oh, Grendel, Grendel, Grendel. You are one bad, bad cat." Bending forward, he touches their noses together. "And you are scaring the hell out of people. So listen to me, cat, you'd better keep it down for a while. Keep quiet. Stay hidden, too. You've got the villagers frightened. They're lighting torches and forming lines, getting ready to start beating the bushes." As Gordy talks, Grendel's eyes open and stare at him. The cat's yellow eyes are calm and his chest rumbles in a low purr.

We start walking again. Now we're not far from where, years ago, I found a small cave. The same one that I pass when I walk home from the Circle.

The cave where the Glammerys lie rotting.

The cave isn't far from the stub of an old, forgotten fire trail, a narrow road started long ago and never finished. A big nest of timber rattlers call the cave home. The snakes are beautiful—a reptilian rainbow of black, brown, yellow, and pinkish-gray. At the bottom of the cave's down-sloped entrance, the snakes are now curled together and sleeping in a scatter of bones. Like the snakes, the bones are colorful, too, with white-gray centers and green moss smears on their knobs and edges. The larger ones are spotted with brown bits of decay.

"Rattlesnakes," Gordy says suddenly, surprising me, making me think he's somehow reading my mind.

He stops and looks around. "About three years ago, I relocated a bunch of them here from the town's Serpentarium, when the guy there decided he wanted monkeys instead of snakes. I put them somewhere right around here. Inside a nifty little cave."

"Wonderful," I answer. "Poisonous snakes in a cave. Right around here. That's real good to know." I keep walking, moving away, thinking, *No, no, no.* "You should show them to me sometime," I say over my shoulder.

He looks around again. In the direction of the cave—the direction of the snakes, the direction of the bones. "Maybe next time," he says, then starts walking again, following me away from the cave, away from the snakes, away from the colorful bones.

"Next time," I agree, hoping that he doesn't ask where I think I'm going as I lead him away…after all, this is his trip.

We hike another hour.

Grendel leaves us, going off again to scare the villagers.

"Almost there," Gordy tells me. "But right here," he says, stopping again. "Right where we are now?"

"Yes?"

"Something interesting. Last week I killed a coyote. Shot 'im right here by this tree."

"Why'd you shoot it?" I ask him. "What happened?"

"He jumped me. Scared me so silly I almost pissed myself." He laughs a little. "The thing scratched and bit the hell out of my back and neck before I could shoot him." As he's talking, he pulls down the back of his collar and shows me a crosshatch of nasty black scabs and stitches.

"Gordy, Christ! A coyote? How the hell did he do that? How'd—? Did he attack you from behind? Did you trip? Were you sitting down? Were you drunk?"

"I wish!" He's not laughing anymore. "No, I didn't trip. And I wasn't drunk. He jumped me. Jumped out of the tree like he'd been waiting for me to come along." Then Gordy abruptly stops talking. He looks at me while I think about what he's said.

And what he just said would be (I think) entirely understandable, would be absolutely normal, just simply another crazy episode of *When Good Coyotes Go Bad*, except he knows that I know—and I know that he knows—that coyotes can't climb trees. "But…," I say. "But…"

He lets me sputter for a second, lets me be confused, then says, "Exactly." He turns and walks away without saying another word. I follow him, now truly wondering what it is that my friend has found.

"Okay," he finally says. "We're here."

Where's "here"? I look around, not seeing anything different. Gordy looks at me expectantly—waiting for me to see "it," whatever "it" is. I decide I won't ask him. I look carefully around some more, slowly turning to see it all. I look where we're standing—down at the ground, thinking maybe something's buried there, maybe protruding from the forest floor, something—

"Cold," he says, watching me, watching my eyes. "Absolutely freezing."

I look at the bushes, peering into their thick depths, wondering *maybe in there?* I don't see anything, though, so I look at the other things in front of me. I look at the trees, studying each one, thinking that maybe somebody carved something into their bark.

"Warmer," he says. "Not hot. But getting closer."

I look up, snapping my eyes up quickly with the memory flash of Gordy's torn and stitched neck, suddenly certain I'll see a coyote leaping down, hurtling toward me, jaws open—

Then I see it.

Or rather, I see *them*. Not coyotes. Squirrels. Flying squirrels. But not real flying squirrels, more like squirrels—flying.

"On raging, burning fire," Gordy says, his voice a disbelieving whisper.

Real flying squirrels don't fly. They glide. They launch off of trees and throw out their legs, stretching out the thin folds of skin between their forelegs and hind legs, turning themselves into furry, square Frisbees with tails. But the squirrels I'm looking at aren't gliding. They're hovering. And darting. And rising and dipping and chitter-laughing their asses off. Flying—*really flying*—from one tree to the next. Floating from one branch to another.

"But…" I say, shaking my head, waving my hands at what I see. "But…"

"Exactly," Gordy answers. "Exactly…"

Standing silent and staring upward, we both watch the little aerial ballet.

Gordy finally turns away from the squirrels and looks at me, his expression one of wonder and confusion. "What's going on, Blue?" he asks. "You're the magic man. And this," he points up with his hand, not lifting his eyes, "this is surely some kind of mind-messing magic. Shit. I mean. Look. So tell me. Tell me what the hell is going on here?"

It's then that I hear a falling squirrel scream, sounding like the high-pitched squeal of a pinched balloon. Instantly following the scream, we're caught in a rainfall of dropping squirrels. Squirrels that were lighter than air only moments ago are now crashing to earth. Holding our hands over our heads, we start running, trying to dodge this sudden deluge of rodents. When it stops, we turn and look back at the squirrels. None of them seem hurt from the fall, but some are clearly pissed off. They stay where they've fallen, looking longingly up at the trees, no longer interested in doing the actual work of climbing there. What they want now is for their bodies to float weightlessly upward. And when wishing doesn't work, they start biting at the squirrels around them, blaming the others for the loss of their wings.

"Blue?" Gordy is still waiting for an answer.

What can I say? "Okay," I say, trying to think of where to begin, of how to tell him about the Stones. "Okay," I say again, looking at the confused, earthbound squirrels. Some are limping, others are still trying to *jump up*—they want to do again, whatever it was they were doing before.

I start talking. "The Circle's magic is transient, it is here…and then it's not—" but then I think, *No, that's not the beginning. That's not how it really starts.* And I stop.

Gordy sits patiently. He's willing to wait.

I start again. At the beginning. The true beginning.

"There is another Stonehenge," I tell him. "A tall, staggered Circle of weathered, white limestone pillars—"

And I tell him everything.

Well, almost everything.

I tell him what I've learned. And tell him what I think.

I even tell him about the child that I hear crying there.

But I don't tell him about the snakes.

Or the cave.

And I certainly don't tell him about the bones.

When I finish, I wait for his response. I'm interested in what he'll think, in what he'll say.

"But…," he says, shaking his head, waving his hands, unable to finish his thought. Unable to find the words. "But…"

"Exactly," I answer. "Exactly…"

BLUE 17

HE STRANGE DREAMS continue, filling the nights with stories I watch from afar. They are not my stories, they're someone else's. I watch them, each night seeing a little more, each morning remembering a little more. I wonder about what I am being told. Wonder if what I'm seeing is something that I am supposed to stop from happening, or if it's something I'm supposed to stop from happening *again*.

I dream....

IT IS NIGHT.

A circle of tall fires surrounds a group of old men who stand in a ring. Their clothes are gone. Naked, they are a circle of wrinkled flesh. The men are quiet, their eyes are closed. A white rock, tied with leather cord, hangs down from each neck. The cords are pierced with sharp thorns that scratch the men and make them bleed. The dripping blood flows freely down the cords and over the white rocks, over the men's shoulders and down their ribs and spines, down asses and thighs, calves and ankles, finally dampening the earth where the old men stand. The weight of the rocks bends the old men forward, bowing their heads. More white rocks are lashed to the palms of the men's hands, tied there with more tight cords. These cords, too, are thorned.

Each old man stands in front of a deep hole. The holes are black, long passages into more darkness, ultimately dropping into deep, cold waters. One by one, the men open their old eyes and stare into the hole in front of them. They feel the stone's weight around their neck, feel their fingers wrapped around stones they cannot drop.

Then they begin screaming.

WHEN I WAKE from the dream, there is a moment when I still hear their screaming, a moment when my own throat feels caught in a tight cord and my hands bend and cramp, feeling bound around heavy rocks. Then I realize where I am, that it was only a dream, that I'm in bed with my Elissa. Even then, knowing I've been dreaming and the dream is over, even then, I sometimes still feel myself teetering on the edge of a black hole, trying to keep my balance, about to fall into dark waters that will swallow and cover me.

THE DREAM persists. It grows stronger. Comes more quickly.

Each night Elissa and I kiss and I fill my hands with the smooth skin of her, fill my mouth with the sweet orange taste of her. But no matter how close I hold her beside me, no matter how near I keep the thought of her in my mind, I still drift to sleep.

And I dream.

I SEE THE OLD MEN. I feel my hands cramping with the same cords that bind their hands, feel my head bowing forward under the weight of a white rock hanging from my neck....

The fires burn tall and bright, creating small bowls of light at the black edges of my dream. Where there should be a sky above or a forest around us, instead there is only absolute darkness. But one thing I know in the dream (I simply know it, in the way one knows things in dreams) is that there is a force in the darkness beyond the trees.

Something just outside of the firelight. A black force that's waiting and watching...

The old men's spines are red from both the fires and the blood running down from where the cords cut into their necks. Their hands are the same flickering flame-and-blood red as their backs. Their arms hang heavily at their sides. The stones tied to their fingers are blood-slick and dripping.

The old men have been standing in silence, in acceptance and surrender, but now, staring into the deep holes before them, they are screaming again, their quavering old voices sending pleas out toward the reaching branches of the dark trees, into the empty black sky. I suddenly see what I haven't seen before—there are other figures standing behind the old men, standing between the old men and the circle of fires. The others are also men—men who say nothing, who are unmoved by the old men's trembling voices. They let the old men cry, let them yell until their voices are hoarse and weak. Then, done listening and tired of the pleas, tired of the cries, the others begin shouting. Their strong, loud voices drown out the old men. Frightened by the shouting, the old men shuffle forward, moving slowly toward the holes.

Stumbling under the weight of the rocks hanging from their necks, wet with blood, the old men look down into the holes in front of them. The men behind them step forward, edging the old men closer to the dark pits. The movements make a play of wild shadows on the ground. The shadows form a creature of twisting black lines and shapes that spreads and grows, its limbs first falling across the holes, then seeming to tumble into the depths, into the deep cold waters below.

The ones behind the old men keep shouting, and soon the old men feel powerful arms reaching around their tired, wrinkled bodies, feel their feet being lifted from the ground...then feel their bodies held out, suspended over the dark holes beneath them. The old men are slowly lowered into the holes, the strong arms holding them tight now loosening, now letting go. The old men begin sliding down, slipping deeper into the holes. It looks like they are being swallowed by the earth.

I WAKE UP, but still feel like I'm being pulled down by the weight of a white rock hanging around my neck, like I am sinking toward deep waters. I can still feel the rocks bound to my hands. I have no hold, no ground beneath me. I slide into the earth, into the darkness—a darkness where something is waiting at the edges, watching in the night. I try to scream, but my voice is silent, my cry unheard. Then someone's arms encircle me, stopping my fall, drawing me back from the void and holding me close. Someone whispers to me, telling me my cries are heard, telling me I am safe. I smell the scent of oranges as she breathes on me, feel the smooth skin of her against me, the feel of it anchoring and saving me—freeing my throat from the bloody, leather cord, freeing my hands from the heavy stones.

And, again, I'm amazed by her magic. Again, I am wholly captured and held by her love.

THE END of the dream—or, more correctly, where the dream stops—is always at the same point: in battle. A battle that I've never seen the end of. An endless, unfinished battle meaning—what?

I do not know the answer.

I know only one thing about the dream—

Always, blood is spilled.

DREAMING AGAIN.

Something is watching from the black ring of trees. Something waiting beyond the fires. It is untouched by the light, moving in the darkness. I can't see it—it is part of the night, part of the black shawl that enwraps everything—but I feel its gaze. I feel its power. I know it is listening to the shouting, that it is watching the old men being slowly lowered into the holes.

The old men are covered with the blood from their wounds. The rocks they wear—the ones hanging against their chests, the others tied into their hands—are no longer white. They are now dark, red weights that look like slaughtered hearts wrapped with butcher's twine. The old men's blood drips into the deep holes…and then the old men begin to follow their blood, sliding deeper into the holes as the arms around them loosen and the shouts, now almost songlike, become louder—

—which is when the huge owl flies down from the sky. The owl falls silently from the black clouds, landing between one of the old men and the other man lowering him into the hole. The owl's powerful wings begin beating against the younger man. Its wings crash into him, pushing him back from the hole. The owl's talons rip at the bloody cord around the old man's neck. The bird's shrieking interrupts the younger man's shouts. Its beating wings begin loosening the man's hold on the old man—

—and it is now that I see the dark force waiting in the woods, the powerful something that has been watching in silence and darkness. At first, I only see its golden eyes, eyes brighter than the firelight they catch and reflect. Then one part of the black night separates from another part and I see the cat—a finely-muscled panther—bounding over the fires, springing at the owl and the old man. The cat's mouth is open as it leaps, its teeth a white curve of knives. Its extended claws reflect the firelight not already trapped in its eyes.

THE DREAM stops there. On some nights I wake with a dream-carried fear that makes me look quickly into the bedroom's dark corners, searching for a huge cat readying to leap and bite, to slice and kill. I anxiously peer into the shadows, searching for those firelight-filled golden eyes and claws. Thankfully, on those nights I often hear a sound that calms me, a sound telling me there's no panther crouched in the dark corners—I hear Grendel's loud rumbling snore. And I feel his slumbering weight stretched across my legs. The sound and weight of his presence are soothing and reassuring. Then, like Grendel, I purr and turn and drift back to sleep—

—*sometimes drifting back to the cries of old men bound with thorns and rocks, to dreams where I'm tumbling down narrow holes, my body again falling into a deeper pool of darkness, my ears again filling with the sounds of chanting as bloodied old men are dropped into the earth.*

THE WARRIOR, ALWAYS ONE MORE ARROW

NIGHTTIME AGAIN.
Again he sits in darkness.
Again he listens to the songs.

THE CIRCLE is singing.

Its song is a lament, a farewell to one leaving...a song for the eighth pillar. The eighth Stone is gray, a rock of dark ashen pallor. The Stone is pocked and pitted, more worn by time than the other Stones are worn, less strong than the other Stones are strong.

The eighth Stone is fading. It is thinning, its width now much narrower than the hole it fills. And being smaller, the Stone tilts, leaning low toward the Circle's center. At the eighth Stone's base, its tilted angle opens a gap between rock and earth—and pulsing out from the gap is a breath of air, a breeze scented of cool and deep salt-seas.

While the other Stone pillars are straight and still, the eighth Stone trembles. Barely. Invisibly. Like an invalid old man turning slowly in his bed, his movements so small that they're indiscernible as his body creeps through an unconscious rotation, trying to move away from his pain, trying to find relief. Seeking ease. Seeking peace.

The other Stones sing songs of that peace. They sing to give the eighth Stone that relief. To give that ease. And to comfort him as he dies.

SETTLING BACK, the warrior closes his eyes. Draws into himself. He ignores his surroundings. Ignores the empty street and the few shops where lights still burn. Ignores the man slumbering on the floor beside him.

He clears his thoughts. Calms his mind. Then looks outward—
Seeing.
Through the streets.
Over the hills.
To the Circle of twelve Stones.

THERE ARE twelve Stones. And long before twelve Stones, there were twelve holes—twelve passages falling straight and deep into the hill. Twelve holes falling into the old waters beneath Jonah's Belly. Before the holes were closed—before the twelve Stones filled and covered them—air would sweep across the green hill and rush down the deep holes. The sweet breezes blew far down into the earth and flowed over the great dark pool that lay below. As the air swept across the hidden sea, it mixed with the vapors of ancient waters and legends and powers. Then, having inhaled, Jonah exhaled, pushing the charged air back up through the holes and out over the ground, the breeze now a salt-touched elixir full of magic and gifts, bringing bounty and good health to all it touched.

But no breezes rush across the ground and sweep down into the holes now. No air blows deep down into the earth and sweeps across a hidden sea. No wind, ripened with magic and miracles, is breathed back out over the hills. The Stones have closed all of the holes but one—the one with a small, tilted gap at its base. A gap that widens and then narrows with the turns and trembling of a fading, shrinking Stone.

A Stone that shakes with an old man's pain. That moves with the palsy of dying.

LISTENING to the song, he watches the Circle. His back cramps again, the muscles knotting and pulling, his body curling with spasms. But his thoughts are elsewhere, remembering another time, remembering another night, a night so long ago....

A night when blood built a path, and when blood opened the way.

A night when there were circles within circles on Jonah's Belly.

ON THE CIRCLE of the hill was a circle of twelve holes. Behind the circle of holes stood a circle of twelve elders—each one able to take on other shapes. Behind the circle of shapeshifters stood a circle of twelve Singers—Singers of the final songs (songs of stone, songs of bone). Behind the Singers lay a circle of tall fires. And beyond the circle of fires, just beyond the firelight, that's where he had circled... waiting.

THE ELDERS shed their clothing. Removing the coarse blankets of this life, they discarded the coverings of their old bodies and stood as naked and wrinkled as babies. Ready for new beginnings, ready for new lives—

Ready for new shapes.

Around each elder's neck hung a cord, and from each cord hung a limestone rock, a fragment of the hard white bones of an ancient sea. More limestone was tied into each elder's hand, making each hand a pattern of cords wrapped around fingers wrapped around rocks.

Small hooked thorns pierced the cords. The thorns cut the elders' skin, making the men bleed. Blood ran freely from the cuts—flowing down their bodies, running over cords and flesh and rocks, dripping from their hands and running down their legs and over their feet, finally flowing into the earth. The blood bound them all, joining men and rocks and hill together into a single being. Making them one.

Each elder bowed his head, giving thanks for days gone by and for days still coming. Then each old man opened his eyes and stared down, unblinking, into the hole before him. The fires' smoke circled them, making their eyes water. As the tears slipped down the elders' faces, they shone with moonlight and firelight.

Now the elders began singing the final songs, songs of stone and songs of bone. Their voices were the sounds of rushing wind—of sweet breezes flowing over the hills, of breath dropping down into the holes. The songs also held the infant cry of new life, vibrating with an echoed wail of thankful blessings, filled with whispers of strength and stone.

From the dark trees where he circled, he heard the songs. He heard them, but he did not pause to listen. He continued moving in the darkness that wrapped itself around it all—around the fires, the singers, the elders, and the holes. Waiting and ready, he stared into the black night.

The Singers had stood silent, listening to the elders. Now their voices also lifted to the moon, their song joining the elders' song and becoming the same plea, whispering the same messages of strength and stone. As they sang, they watched the elders and waited, waited till they saw the old men begin moving toward the holes.

The Singers stepped close behind the elders. Each circled an elder in his arms, cradling and holding the old man, gently lifting him and stepping forward until each elder was suspended safely over a hole—held safe from tumbling down, held safe in the Singers' strong arms.

The Singers continued singing. Their song was now the only one filling the night. The elders' voices had been lost to the spirits of the new shapes they'd called, their voices were now lost to the Stone.

The Singers carefully lowered the silent old men into the holes till their knees disappeared into the hill. Still singing, they held the elders in place, held them with love and reverence, held them as gently as they dared. They held the elders who were men, men who were becoming…more.

The Singers felt the shifting begin. Felt the weight in their arms increasing. Felt the elders start to change—

Which is when the night fell down on them.

Which is when the attack began.

HE HEARD the song change, heard the screaming begin. He turned in the darkness, spun toward the circle and began to run, knowing he might have already failed, that he might already be too late. But still running, still moving. His four powerful legs took him out of the darkness and into the firelight. In the light, his black-furred shape separated from the dark where he'd waited—and the leaping panther was suddenly revealed. His golden eyes glowed with reflected firelight as he sprang into the circle, his massive paws outstretched, claws reaching for an elder's throat—

—the same throat now held in the razor-sharp talons of the owl that punctured and tore at the elder's neck while its giant wings beat back and forth, smashing into the Singer who held the elder tightly, but whose hold was beginning to loosen, who felt the elder begin slipping down.

THE GREAT HORNED OWL had been waiting. Perched hidden in the tall trees at the circle's edge, it listened and watched—listening with ears that could hear a beetle crawling through the dried leaves at the base of the tree, watching with large golden eyes that saw, by moonlight alone, a rabbit two hills away peering out from the depths of its hole. The owl waited, grasping a branch with powerful, knife-edged talons—talons built to slice through warm flesh and lock tight, crushing whatever they held. It waited with wings that were edged by a small fringe of soft barbed feathers that allowed the night air to slip easily through, keeping the owl's flight silent, a soundless rush of death.

The owl listened to the song begin and to the panther's steps. It watched the circle of men standing in firelight and saw the cat moving in the darkness. It waited for the instant just before the shapes changed, when the men's thoughts were on only the song and the shift was about to happen.

Then the owl flew down.

It dropped noiselessly from the night sky, a vise of blades extended on each foot. It smashed between an elder and a Singer, talons snagging and slicing and crushing. As its wings beat back into the Singer, pounding and crashing against the Singer's arms and chest, cutting his face and eyes, the owl began screeching. The Singer tried to continue singing. Tried to hold the elder.

But his grip loosened.

And his song faltered.

THE PANTHER leapt. Becoming a sleek battering ram of black fur and muscle, he hurtled himself at the frenzy of feathers, beak, and talons. His teeth and claws reached forward, but he was unable to use these weapons because the danger to the Singer and elder was too great. The panther crashed into the owl, knocking it loose, and both beasts burst through the space between the Singer and elder, the panther landing on top the owl, the owl's locked talons filled with glistening pieces of the elder's neck. Both were suddenly covered in a spraying, slippery rain of blood that spurted out of the back of the elder's neck and sprayed everywhere—onto the panther, the owl, the ground, then suddenly—

It stopped.

Suddenly, no more spraying blood.
Suddenly, no more songs.
Suddenly—
Silence.

THE SINGER felt the shifting begin. Felt it as the owl's wings slashed at his eyes, beating and blinding him. He felt his song falter, but found it again and sang the last words. As he felt the change deepening, a growling wall of black fur tore the owl away from him and the elder he held, and a torrent of blood immediately shrouded him. The blood made his grip on the elder less sure. As the elder began to slip from his grip, the Singer finished his song, and then— song finished—threw open his arms and stepped back. But his feet slipped on the blood-wet ground, his legs flying backward out from under him. He felt himself tumbling forward, falling toward the elder, falling toward the hole—but there was no hole.

Instead, he landed at the base of a tall white pillar.

The eighth pillar in a Circle of twelve new Stones.

THE PANTHER and the owl were gone. They had shifted, and now they fought as men, sliding in the blood-soaked grass. They broke their holds on each other and rolled apart, then pulled themselves up, stood facing each other, naked and blood-covered. Shadows of tall Stones and trees fell across both men, painting them with dark stripes that rippled and bent.

The warrior, his eyes still filled with the gold of the panther's eyes, looked quickly at the Stones, then back to the one he battled. "Brother," he said, breathing heavily, tired from the change, tired from the fight. He pointed at the Circle of tall pillars behind him. "This is over. The song is sung. Stone is Stone." He dropped his hands, held them out, palms upturned. "Brother, let this end."

The other, his muscles still feeling the sense of wings growing from his back and talons for his hands, stopped moving. He looked at the newly formed Circle of Stones, his gaze lingering on the eighth pillar. "Stone is Stone," he said. "But even Stone dies. He looked down at the slick ground and smiled. "Especially Stone that bleeds so much." He took a deep breath and abruptly straightened. "Bone dies, brother. Stone, too. And blood always builds a path, blood always opens a way—"

—and the owl again filled the man's space, its quiver of talons and wings flying toward the warrior, who raised one arm in front of his face, ducking under the attack as the wings beat silently down at him. And the owl soared into the night.

THE WARRIOR SITS. Brings his thoughts back from the past. And brings his sight back from the Circle. Brings it back over hills, back through streets. He opens his eyes and sees the moonlight still upon him, sees the man still slumbering beside him. The shop lights which burned earlier are dark now, and the street is no longer empty—he sees again what he's seen for the past three nights: a black car driving out of the darkness.

The car approaches. It begins passing him, but slows almost to a stop as it draws near. The moonlight somehow falls only on him, not on the car. The car's windows remain black and opaque, hiding whatever's behind them. The car seems to pause and consider him. They watch each other, warrior and car, and then the car drives on, melting back into the darkness. He watches it go. Thinks, *The path is built. The way is open.*

He stares after the black car, absentmindedly scratching the rash of flea bites covering his ankles. Then he stands up and stretches, groaning as his backbone pops and cracks into place. He steps closer to the street, looking where the car had disappeared. *Almost time*, he thinks. He looks at the man sleeping on the floor, then walks back and sits down beside the snoring form. He pats the man's back. *Good idea, my friend*, he thinks. *Stay low. Stay very, very low.*

THE BLACK CARS. THE EAST CAR

THE BLACK CAR surprised her. Not just that there was a car, but also how it looked, how it felt. There it was, parked at the end of her drive, just behind her home, looking like it had been there for hours—hell, looking like it had been there for weeks. *Looking like it belonged there.*

The car gave off a hinky-dinky vibe, a weird feeling that made her quit pedaling and squeeze the handbrakes hard enough to skid the bike's back tire around as she stopped. Standing with both feet planted on the gravel drive, she straddled the bike and stared up at her little white bungalow with its purple-painted porch and dark green trim. For a surreal, tilted second she thought, *My house, right?—*

—which is when the man in a black suit stepped around the back corner of the bungalow. The man didn't seem like much of a threat, didn't act like he'd been hiding or look like he was thinking, *Shit, I'm caught*, or *Great, the bitch is finally here for me to rape.* Instead, wearing an embarrassed sort of "hope-you-don't-mind" expression, he waved to her. Already forgetting her earlier flutter of uncertainty, her brain then answered her earlier question: *"Damn straight, my house!"* She started pedaling again, noticing as she got closer that whoever he was, he was holding a yellow and blue flame-shaped something in one hand and a bunch of papers in his other. When she was almost to him she had three quick thoughts: First,

Be nice to the trespasser. Second, *Breakfast done?* And third, looking around, *Where are my dwarfs?*

SHE'D TAKEN a short morning ride, just up and down a few quick hills. Stretching her legs. Enjoying the smooth shift of gears, the *click-click* of the bike chain moving over the gear teeth, the feel of her legs muscles pumping on autopilot. Enjoying the simple *Good air in, bad air out, one-two, one-two* mantra of her thoughts.

But especially enjoying feeling strong again. Finally.

It had been a while since she'd felt so good. And, hey, all it had taken for her to get to this point and feel this good had been to go through two long divorces in four short years, the first divorce, friendly, the second, not friendly at all. And, truthfully, yes, she'd been just as "not friendly" as him (maybe even more so), though by that time she was feeling so pissed, so angry that it was happening again that she hadn't given two shits about civility.

Sometime near the end of her second marriage, she had made a new commitment—a different sort of commitment than the ones she'd embarrassingly made (and then failed miserably at) twice before to two different "lifelong loves" (committing publicly both times, in front of the same group of friends both times). This time, though, she made the commitment to herself, in private this time—a commitment to the absolute destruction of all her remaining relationships. Friends, family, acquaintances. All of them. She wanted them gone. Wanted their sympathy, their snickering, even their strong shoulders of sisterhood and support to just go the hell away.

Looking back, it seemed that she'd finally made a commitment she could actually keep. As it turned out, she was quite good at absolute destruction. The only difference was that her friends, family, and acquaintances didn't disappear...she did.

First, she liquidated her accounts. Sold her stocks. Quit her job. Took her 401k nest egg—a big, big egg—as a single direct payment after telling a very helpful, very insistent investment advisor, "Screw the tax consequences. Give me the money."

Then she left. And left nothing behind. Gave no forwarding address. Sent no *I'm Moving!* cards with a cute little butterfly looping across the card. She just got in her car and drove away, looking for a place to hide.

She ended up in Brown County, Indiana, where she intentionally drove deeper and deeper into the hills, following the road left and right with no plan or reason until she was finally absolutely and intentionally lost. And there, lost in the hills, she'd absolutely and accidentally found a perfectly hidden home at the end of a long, perfectly hidden drive. The **Home For Sale** sign at the side of the road was the only reason she'd even spotted the driveway. She paid cash for the house that day, telling a very helpful, very insistent realtor who also owned a mortgage company, "Screw the tax consequences. Take the money."

Then she hid herself away. Threw away her watch. Ripped up her calendar. Decided to...*just live.* Alone. On her own time. By her own schedule. She started staying awake late at night, relaxed and calm, staring into the small campfire she built every evening. Always throwing a few shovelfuls of dirt over the flames when she went to bed.

And she started waking up early, long before sunrise and cooking breakfast in the embers of the night-before campfire. She'd rake back the fire's dirt blanket, stir up the still-glowing bed of coals underneath, then would lay foil-wrapped packets of food on top of the coals. The packets were filled with big chunks of potatoes and onions, tomatoes and peppers, all of it sprinkled with salt and butter.

And she started taking bike rides while breakfast cooked. Her legs and lungs worked hard for the first few weeks, almost crippling her with pain as she made her way up and down the hills. But then the rides got easier, her breath came more smoothly, and her legs grew thinner and muscled.

Everything became a part of an easy flow. Every good day blending into another day, each day beginning to seem better than the last. Except *(goddammit)* for one thing—

She was lonely.

She ignored it for a while. Then acknowledged it. Then said to herself, *Okay, I need some company.* She spent time considering the problem from all angles. Sorted through option after option, searching for the right answer.

When the answer came, it was so correct, was so perfectly and exactly right. It was really just a decision to leapfrog ahead a few years and realize that she was already happily on her way to becoming a cliché. That she was becoming the perfect crazy lady in the woods, and there was only one thing missing.

Cats.

She needed cats.

Lots and lots of cats.

PEDALING TOWARD the man, she saw writing—a light blue flame, each letter tipped with yellow—across the hood and door of the black car: *SOMETHING'S BURNING! NATURAL GAS!*

She stopped a few feet from him. He held the blue and yellow flame-shaped thing out to her. Laughing a little as he talked, the man said, "Behold, I give you fire!" and clicked a trigger on the flame-shaped thing. Sure enough, a tiny flame ignited on the end pointing at her. Standing there, the man let out another can-you-believe-this-shit sort of laugh, the kind of laugh that showed he was in on the joke, that told her he knew it was just a cheap trinket of plastic crap. She saw lettering on the lighter that spelled out the same *Something's Burning! Natural Gas!* message painted on the car.

"But hey!" the man said, looking over at her campfire—her silver foil breakfast packets still cooking on top of the coals—"it looks like you might actually be able to use this thing. And that," he said, turning the lighter around and handing it to her, "makes you a winner!"

Reaching out to take it, she noticed that his hands were dirty, his fingers streaked with black and red. "Little accident, city boy?" she asked, looking up at his face, then back at his hands.

"Little one," he answered. He put his hands behind his back. "Sorry about the mess."

"Your mess, not mine," she said, guessing he'd fallen somewhere. Or maybe tripped in a thorny patch of greenbrier and scratched himself. He was lucky he hadn't torn his suit. "Here's what," she told him. "First, go wash up over there at the hose. Then come back and tell me why you're here—why you're intruding on my perfect day, why you're trespassing on my perfect land (*letting herself laugh a little right then, letting him know that she could joke, too*). And then, Oh-Great-Giver-of-Fire, maybe you could even join me for a little breakfast (*letting him know she was a nice person, that she was willing to hear what he had to say*)."

"Lovely," he said. He dropped the papers he was holding and stepped closer. "Just one thing first," he said, his hands reaching for her face.

SHE'D GOTTEN CATS. Seven kittens. Looked at them and had no idea what to name them. Tried for hours to figure it out. Then decided, *Enough. Names'll come. In their own time. On their own schedule.*

She cut a hole in the bottom of her front door and installed a swinging pet door in the hole so the cats could come and go as they liked. What they liked, it turned out, was sleeping curled up on her bed all night. And eating breakfast with her outside every morning. Then napping a few hours on the purple porch. Then disappearing to hunt or play all day before coming back at night to sleep on her bed. The seven cats got with the groove of things immediately, living exactly like she did—on their own time, on their own schedule.

But doing their living with her. Together.

The cats made her laugh as they slipped through the pet door every morning and slipped back out through it every night, all seven entering and exiting in single file. One day after breakfast, as she watched them disappear into the woods, walking in a line, tails held high over their asses, she started whistling *Hi-Ho, Hi-Ho,* then burst out laughing. She'd figured out what to call them. *That's perfect,* she thought. *My seven dwarfs. Taking care of me in our little hidden home.* Which made her, of course, Snow White. Which was also perfect. Snow White, the princess hiding away in the woods.

Safe from harm.

Protected from evil.

"JUST ONE thing first," he said as he stepped close to her, dropping the papers he was holding, and reaching for her face. Startled, she looked directly into his eyes. She knew she should step back from him, that she should run away or kick him with her strong legs. But at the same time she saw how blue his eyes were, how bright and clear and deep, and how they drew her in. And she felt herself falling into his eyes, falling into a bright blue flame. Then—from far away, somewhere with blue fire all around—she felt his thumbs pushing into her eyes. His thumbs worked deeper into her skull, digging under her eyes. She felt his breath against her ear as she heard him whisper, "I'll take those."

And she felt fine, felt safer than ever. More than anything else, she wanted to stay in the blue fire at the bottom of his eyes, wanted to do whatever it was that she heard his voice whisper. Wanted to do whatever it was at all.

LATER, CROUCHING by the campfire, she reached into the flames, the same dancing flames now reflected in her new, bright blue eyes. Her other eyes, the eyes she'd woken with this morning—eyes the color of a light brown egg—those eyes were gone. Her new eyes let her see from somewhere else, from the warm blue fire. She heard him talking from far away, saying, "Breakfast. You need to eat. Eat up and then we'll go."

He watched her grab the seven foil packets out of the fire. Her hands became black with ash as she tore open one of the packets. A little curl of calico tail dropped out from the foil.

She ate until the foil was empty. "One more," he said, and she grabbed another packet. Ripped it open and ate again. He reached over as she ate, gently wiping the corner of her mouth and her chin, brushing off the bits of ear and whiskers sticking there. He smiled at her, his smile making her happy.

He watched her grind a small paw between her teeth. Waited until she finished. "You are the fairest of them all," he whispered. Then he pointed at the spilled pieces of foil and fur on the ground. "Your mess, not mine," he said, nudging a tiny triangle of pink nose with his shoe.

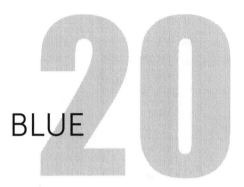

BLUE

I AM AGAIN physically transported again by my dreams.

Brought here while sleeping, I awaken at the Circle's center and hear a song. Although it's not a song I've heard before, I recognize it at once. I understand its mournful, low sounds. It is the universal music of farewell and sorrow: I am at a funeral. I am hearing the music of grieving.

Listening to the song, I stand and turn slowly in the night. I am surrounded by the ring of pillars. I see that the Circle is broken, that the single tilted Stone is now gone. There is no remaining sign of it. No broken base, no fallen section lying on the ground. Not even a speck of white dust of any sign of erosion. The pillar has done what Stones cannot do. It has evaporated and drifted away.

Where the Stone had stood, there is now a dark hole. A rush of sharp air escapes this newly uncovered hole and brushes against me. Its touch tingles on my skin, its scent fills my mind. It is the scent of early harvest and the small of a woman's back. It is the heady bouquet of a wine that tastes of eucalyptus and pepper and pine and earth.

Standing near the hole, I bow my head. I listen to the song and offer my prayers, honoring the one who has gone. And I hope— hope that I soon understand why I am here, and that I am worthy of this Circle. And I hope I am ready for whatever is coming. Because, clearly, whatever it is—its time is almost here.

CLETE. BILLY G. THE MATCHMAN

*T*HE BILLY GOAT *was peeking at him. It poked its head out from behind the tree to look at him, but kept the rest of its body hidden. Its short curved horns tilted out from the tree, looking more slender and smooth than the branches around them. But from even this far away, from all the way down the hill, he could see the goat's eyes. Could see them looking down the hill and into his window.*

CLETE GLAMMERY stayed in his trailer—

—"A suggestion," the red-haired man had told him. "Stay small. Don't stir. Stay tucked tight away. Although," he offered, "you and your family are always welcome to join us. After all, there's plenty of room, always plenty of room for everyone." He laughed when Clete said nothing, when Clete only looked down and turned away. "And so, and so…" the red-haired man said, letting the sentence drift off, his blue eyes staring at Clete, his laugh still in the air—

—so Clete stayed small. Didn't stir. Stayed tucked tight away.

He shut his boys and the women inside their places. Told them *Stay the hell down* and only let them come out in the daytime, when the black cars were gone. He began watching the black cars—watched them drive out of the hole each morning, watched them return each night.

Nights were the worst. During the nights, he sat alone in the dark, watching outside without a single light on in the trailer. He sat, thinking and worrying. Worrying about the pain in his stomach, the queasy burning that was there all the time now, like something chewing on him, biting and grinding and eating at his guts. And he thought about the way things had gotten changed around on him, about how for most of his life his brain had been crammed full of thoughts about things he wanted but did not have. But now, sitting still and quiet and alone in the dark, he could only think about all the things that he *didn't* want—he didn't want to be seen, didn't want to catch the black cars' drivers' attention, didn't want their blue eyes turning toward him, didn't want to join the other people who'd started following the black cars home.

And after last night, not only did he not want to be seen, he also didn't want to be heard. Didn't want to make any kind of noisy *trip-trap, trip-trap* sounds across anybody's bridge. Because of all the things he didn't want, he really, really didn't want to join Billy G. up on the hill.

THE GOAT was looking straight at him. It stared down the hill, looking directly into his window. Its head wasn't moving, but the mass of flies surrounding it gave it a sense of movement. The flies were feasting—even in the twilight, he could see their shimmering wings as they flew back and forth from the goat's tongue to its eyes. Another black cloud of flies was balled around the goat's nose, nibbling the mucous and flesh. From his window he could see the black ball moving, expanding out and then contracting in, as if the goat were filling the ball with breath from its lungs.

HE WORRIED about his stomach pain, knowing sure as shit that some green cancer was eating him from inside out while another part of him howled, *You WISH it was cancer! It AIN'T cancer, IT'S WORSE! You know EXACTLY what it is!*

Every night, he sat motionless by the window, holding a folded-back corner of curtain and looking through the smallest slit he could make and hoping his shaking hands didn't ripple the curtain. *Trying not to stir, trying to stay small, trying to stay tucked tight away.* At dusk, the cars wound back down the hill. The black ones, and now the other ones too. The black cars flowed like a single thing, crept like a long drop of nighttime mercury. The other cars moved more slowly, more haltingly.

The cars always stopped at the bottom, the black cars parking in one group, the other cars parking farther back with the rest of the collection that was growing near the two black trucks. After parking their cars, the four blue-eyed drivers went inside their dark trailer where they…*did what?* The drivers always disappeared until the next morning, when they returned to the cars as quietly as they'd left them the night before.

The other drivers—the ones that followed the black cars home—also left their cars. When he saw them step out of their cars, Clete's hands trembled, sometimes so fiercely he had to let the curtain go so it blocked out what he was seeing. He recognized some of their faces, but he didn't recognize their eyes—their bright blue eyes weren't anything he'd ever seen before. Over the years, he'd seen some of the people in town and knew others from his trash route. Only they were different now. They were *his* now, the red-haired man's. They weren't who they used to be. Maybe weren't even *what* they used to be.

Now they were something else.

DEATH HAD MADE a giant of the billy goat. Its head peered around the tree at a height where a horse's head would be. It looked like the biggest Billy Goat Gruff of all time. Only this time, the big Billy G. had certainly gone over the wrong damn bridge and messed with the wrong damn troll.

Clete almost giggled, thinking how the *Three Billy Goats Gruff* fairy tale had been rewritten last night. Now the last line of the story would read, *Trip-trap, trip-trap, holy-shit!*

He remembered last night's sounds. The sounds of the goat's head being ripped from its body, the sounds of its skin being shredded, and tearing muscles, and popping bones. The squelching thick sound as the head was speared onto a high, short branch. The thing that pushed the head onto the branch had patiently twisted and turned the torn head around so it was looking down the hill at Clete, letting him know: *I seeee youuuu....* Then the thing had crouched down and begun feeding on the body. It started making other sounds. Sounds Clete would never forget.

Tonight, through the slit between the curtain and the window frame, Clete looked up the hill. Blood and other juices had spilled out from the goat's head and dried on the tree. The flies were eating there, too. They flowed down from the head, covering the tree bark like a fuzzy black bib. He stared at the goat and shook his head. Thought, *You shoulda stayed small. Shoulda not stirred. Shoulda stayed tucked tight away.*

WHEN THE OTHER cars followed the black cars down into the hole, they drove slowly past the trailers and buses and parked farther back in the mixed pod of vehicles that had been collected over the past week, close to the two semi trucks that had arrived a month ago. The two trucks were black, oversized machines. Like the black cars, they were painted with blue-flame slogans across their hoods: *HEATING UP THE HOUSE!* and *A NATURAL WINNER!* The letters C.N.G. were painted on the trucks' sides, with *Clean, Nice,* and *Good* printed neatly beneath the abbreviation.

How the big trucks got up the road and then down the hole was a trick Clete still hadn't figured out. But he knew the answer to another trick: the trick of the disappearing truck drivers. He'd been watching from behind his magic curtain and seen the drivers arrive and park the two trucks. Saw them swing down from the tall cabs. Both drivers were husky and fond of tattoos and piercings. They looked like pirates, each one wearing three gold hoops in both ears and a wide gold hoop through his nose.

Then they'd pulled the rear loading ramp out from one of the trucks and walked up the ramp. One pushed the rear door open and rolled it up the track. As he opened the door, the other driver straightened and turned, looking around like he'd heard something that pissed him off. As he slowly turned his head, searching for the sound, Clete saw the light blue, burning holes of the pirate's eyes, eyes that were lit from somewhere else, eyes that saw from somewhere else...

That's when Clete's cancer twisted inside his guts for the first time, twisting and sawing through him as it melted his intestines. *WRONG! NOT THE FIRST TIME!* the voice inside him howled. *AND NOT CANCER!*

Once the rear door was up, the two drivers walked into the black hole and pulled the heavy door down behind them. They'd closed themselves in over a month ago. Nothing coming out, and nothing else going in—not once. Until last week, when the other cars began following the black cars home. The other drivers—all of them with the same burning, empty blue eyes—parked their cars near the semi trucks, walked up the loading ramps, and rolled open the doors. As Clete watched, they'd stepped into the darkness of the trailers and disappeared down some kind of rabbit hole, the doors falling shut behind them, slamming down with the sound of a metal jaw snapping shut. Stopping Clete from seeing any more—

Except for what he saw three days ago.

He'd been watching a new group enter the semi. One of them had reached up and pulled down the open door. Then, just when the falling door had almost banged shut after them, someone inside had foot-scuffed five shining golden rings out of the truck. Four of the shining gold circles bounced down the metal ramp, kicked out from the dark hole like bright round bones. The fifth ring had stayed at the top of the ramp, not bouncing or rolling. Instead, it stayed anchored to the ramp. Weighed down by a fleshy lump of pirate nose.

HE SHOULDN'T have seen it. It should have been too dark to see. Moonlight didn't fall here, and the night never got lighter. Except for last night. When moonlight fell, and when the night had lightened.

Then he'd seen it.

Then he'd known.

He'd seen it in the moonlight, had watched it eating the goat's body, making noises in the night. Spilling, dripping noises that slurped and crunched. He watched its huge arms and curved claws holding the carcass above its head, squeezing the goat meat over its jaws so the gush of blood rained down its throat. Then it lowered the goat to its mouth. And he saw its teeth begin to tear.

At some point, the thing's bright blue eyes looked up from its shredded meal and stared down the hill. That was when Clete heard it talking to him, talking in a voice that was wet and slurred. Its words slipped roughly out of its mouth and echoed down the hill, calling to him, *Alwaays plennny of roooom. Rooomm for youuu and yourrr familleee. Plennny of roooommm…*

And then the voice paused. He knew that the blue eyes were watching him. The same eyes he knew he'd looked into before. So he sat still—staying small, not stirring, staying tucked tight away. And heard it once more. Laughing like it had laughed before, dismissing him like it had dismissed him before. *Annndd sooo, annnnnddd ssooooo….*

That's when the words ended.

And the other sounds began again.

IT WASN'T CANCER.

It was worse.

It was fear.

Fear was eating him up. Was chewing on him from the inside. He was afraid. And that was something he thought he'd never feel. He was the one who *caused* fear, the one who *made* fear—he wasn't the one who *felt* it. He never felt it.

He was a bad man. A bad man who did bad things, and he enjoyed it all. He'd always known that he'd end up in hell, always knew that one day he'd call hell home, but he'd also always figured that he'd die first *and then* figure out how to deal with hell's bullshit. That *after* he died was when he'd figure out how to cheat the devil.

But he'd figured wrong. He hadn't died and gone to hell—

Instead, hell had come to him.

MONTHS AGO.

Months ago, the red-haired man had driven into the hole and stopped and stood beside his black car, waiting patiently till Clete walked out to him. He'd looked at Clete, then looked around the hole—at the bent trailers and rusting buses, at the garbage and the goats and the shit spilling down the hillside. Then he'd looked at Clete again, looked with his bright blue eyes. Had smirked and said, "Love what you've done with the place," he said conversationally—

—and that was enough for Clete. He'd thought, *Screw you, Blue Eyes*, and was already pulling his knife out of the sheath against the small of his back, already planning to cut this mocking shithead to pieces and feed him to the goats, when the man had said, "Wait"—

—and Clete had waited. Had surprised himself and put the knife away. He'd looked into the man's bright blue eyes and thought, *Yes, yes, I'll wait*. He was suddenly, unaccountably eager to hear what the man said. Didn't even feel his own backflesh slice open as he missed the sheath and pushed the knife blade down hard against his spine. And didn't feel the blood pouring down his legs, staining his pants. Entranced, he'd listened as the man said, "Tell me about the two boys. How are Creel and Simon?"

And looking into the man's eyes, Clete could tell that the man honestly cared about Creel and Simon, that he really, really wanted to know about the boys. It wasn't just some bullshit, insincere pleasantry, not just some casual question.

Knowing this, Clete had been filled full of sadness for what he knew he had to tell the red-haired man. He'd felt so sad he'd started crying, his breath breaking into hiccups as he spoke. "Gone. My boys are gone. They're both gone, and I don't know where...." His tears had poured out, knowing how the news would make the red-haired man sad, knowing how upset he'd feel, and with all his heart, Clete didn't want the man feeling sad, didn't want him feeling hurt. But then the man made Clete feel suddenly better, made Clete's tears stop for a moment, then start again because now he was so very happy.

The man had looked at him—his eyes were so blue, so blue and warm. "I have an idea about the boys," he said.

LATER, THEY'D talked some more after making their arrangement.

"And so, and so," the red-haired man had said. "You help me, I help you. Each one helping the other. Of our own decision. Of our own free will and desire. It's all so pure that way, yes? All so very fulfilling."

"My boys?" Clete had asked, hardly believing what he'd heard. "You'll help me find my boys?"

"And more," the man had answered. "After my...business." He'd stared straight into Clete, staring so hard that Clete felt the blue warmth again, felt himself circling a place that would take him in, a place he knew he could go in an instant. Part of him wanted to go, wanted so much to go.

But the red-haired man interrupted his thoughts. "You won't be troubled? About the...?" then he let the question hang, letting

Clete recall the arrangement to which he'd agreed. And Clete, dancing at the edge of someplace warm and blue, knew that the man was really and truly asking the question, that he was really and truly concerned.

"Fuck 'em," Clete had answered. "Fuck them all."

"Exactly," the red-haired man agreed. "Fuck 'em all."

"But why?" Clete had asked a minute later. "Why help me? Why help my boys?"

"Love, of course," the red-haired man had answered. "Only love." His blue eyes turned away from Clete and he looked up the trash-littered walls of the hole, focusing on something he saw there. He stared a moment, then whispered, *Nice goats*, and called softly up the hill, "*Hey, Billeeeee-Geeeee...Hey, Billeeee-Geeeee...I seeeee youuuuu...*"

22

BLUE

O UR MAILBOX sits on Salt Creek Road, at the bottom of a driveway that curls slowly up to the cabin. I walk to the mailbox each morning, taking time to notice the small day-to-day changes that occur in the short distance I go through the woods—the new pattern-plays of sun and shadow along the path and the different ways the overhead leaves let light pour down onto the ground. The new tracks of claws and paws captured in the soil, their impressions suggesting the wood's hidden travelers. Even the new scent of each day, the bright and dark notes of bark and earth, of green and blue, of breeze and calm.

My daily walk is a simple thing. An interlude. A chance to appreciate things that are literally lying on the path to my door. The walk is usually a few quiet minutes of "there and back again."

Except for today.

My walk *there* was usual. My walk *back* is not.

As I walk back, my hands shake, making the packet of mail I'm holding feel alive in my fingers. My eyes are unable to move from the message on top of the stack. The words transfix me, scrambling my thoughts. I'm suddenly oblivious to the small changes along the path: the leaves, the light, the shadows, the scents—they've all disappeared, swept aside by the rushing wall of change, hidden and obscured by the approaching tornado that I'm holding in my hands. When I opened the mailbox there should have been a thunderclap, an explosion accompanied by the lightning pyrotechnics of an upended world. At the very least, there should have been some booming crash or bellow giving sound and form to the world I felt shifting and folding as I read the message.

But there was no thunderclap. No rattled skies. There was just me standing by the mailbox—my heart tight, my eyes blurring, my attention singly focused on the piece of paper in my hands. I'm suddenly standing in a world far different than the one I left at the top of the path. Walking back to the cabin, I'm a different animal than I was only minutes before. I should leave different footprints now, new prints that are unrecognizable from the first.

I hold the mail carefully, bearing it forward like a fragile gift.

AT SOME WARM moment four years ago, I realized that Elissa was living with me at the cabin. I remember the math I performed while trying to confirm this blessing, all the calculations that I quietly figured again and again until finally I believed. My observations were numerous: She spent more time at the cabin than away. We touched hands or shoulders or lips each day, sometimes seeking each other out for that very reason. There were more rooms that had some hint of her in them than rooms that didn't—her books in this room, her bra in that one, canisters of her favorite teas in the cupboards. The clues were all there for me to piece the answer together. She had accepted my invitation. She had made this cabin her home.

I was thrilled by the daily proof of her, joyous with the daily evidence of her in my life. I noted each change in the rooms, each place that she had wrapped herself in. I watched the small rituals that made *this* her favorite chair, *that* her favorite corner, *this* the couch where she naps. I listened to each new sound she brought, the music of her presence that was now part of *our home*: her footsteps, her voice calling from the porch, the in-and-out of her breathing at night.

I gathered in the details of her and carried them with me, wanting to take nothing for granted. Wanting to understand everything about her. What I didn't know, what I learned later, was that she too was looking for clues, that she too was studying the hints of me that she found—she was watching the patterns I walked, listening to the sound of my footsteps, memorizing the rhythms of my breathing.

I remember walking into my writing room one day and finding Elissa sitting at the desk. She'd found the postcard collection I kept stacked on the bookshelf. She'd spread the postcards across the desk, covering the entire surface with rows of pictures. Even from the doorway, I could read the large block lettering on most of the cards and see the colorful details of their bizarre photos. Elissa stared down, transfixed by the pictures, her attention snagged by the surreal world they described, her mind stepping across the thresholds of the strange homes they welcomed her into: *THE FROG MUMMY CIRCUS! SEE SIX ROOMS AND 7,000 FROG MUMMIES OF LOVINGLY DETAILED CIRCUS FUN! VISIT SWAMPERS, IL! and THE UNIVERSE'S LARGEST DISPLAY OF SEEPING GOITERS! VISIT LANCIT, OR! and THE VAULT OF FRONTIER HORRORS! EXPLORE THE UNEARTHED CHAMBER OF A PIONEER MADMAN! VISIT SOLONELY, KS!*

Elissa raised her gaze from the postcards and waved her hands over the desk. "What are these? Who sent these to you?" Then she started laughing. "Are you planning a trip?" She picked up one of the cards and held it out to me, her laughter making the picture quiver. "Really, Blue," she said, her giggles growing louder. "We really need to go here, don't you think?" I looked at the postcard. *NOAH'S ARK OF LOVE! AN ORGY OF LIFELIKE TAXIDERMY EXHIBITS! MATING ANIMALS FROM AROUND THE WORLD! VISIT STUPHT, PA!*

As I looked at the front of the card, I knew what she was seeing on the back. Or, rather, I knew what she *wasn't* seeing. Other than my name and address—always printed in an elegant, careful hand—nothing was ever written on the cards: no return address, no message, no signature. *No clues. No hints. Nothing.*

"I don't know who sends them," I told her. "I don't know why they come."

MY POSTCARD COLLECTION.

I've received them over the past twelve years. A new card arrives every few weeks, sometimes more often, sometimes less. I now have 274 cards. As a collection, it isn't big, not from a perspective of simple volume, not when the gift stores in town carry over 500 different postcards, each one printed with the same slogan: THE BEAUTY OF BROWN COUNTY, INDIANA. But the *number* of cards in my collection doesn't matter. The *places* shown on the cards do.

THE BEAUTY OF BROWN COUNTY cards feature scenery that is rarely actually seen by the town-tied tourists who mill around in the stores. The cards are photographs of rolling hills and autumn-washed trees, of untrodden fields covered in bittersweet and rosehips, of small streams running like shining silver zippers between quilted patches of wildflowers. The Brown County cards are beautiful and filled with local color.

The postcards that someone keeps sending me are certainly not beautiful, but they are bursting at the seams with local color— of a most peculiar sort. They're a celebration of odd attractions and eccentricities, of small things made large by individual obsessions. They are the small towns' siren songs to the passing highway drivers. They're colorful, civic seductions, advertised on billboards standing by remote exit ramps, their messages offering reasons to leave the long, unremarkable highway and drive into town to see a local, very remarkable, one-of-a-kind attraction…and to spend your money in the local restaurants, gas stations, and hotels.

The towns understand what they're selling. And they know they need to sell fast, that they need to entice the motorist traveling at 70 mph. So to make the quick sale, the towns show a little skin. *SEE THE TATTOO HALL OF FAME! HOME OF THE TATTOOED FAMILY AND THEIR COLORFUL DOG "INK"! VISIT NEEDLES, OH! EXIT NOW, THEN LEFT 4 MILES!* Or they give a quick peek at the crazy uncle who's been kept locked in the attic. *VISIT LARRY'S MUSEUM! WORLD'S LARGEST COLLECTION OF TURTLE HEADS AND SPACECHILD EVIDENCE! VISIT COMPULSION, MS! NEXT EXIT, THEN LEFT 7 MILES!* Or they offer a look up their skirts, and maybe even a titillating roll in their dirty laundry. *TOUR THE BIRTH HOME OF THE BED-AND-BREAKFAST, TAG-TEAM SERIAL KILLERS! VISIT WELCOME-IN, LA! THIS EXIT, THEN RIGHT ONLY 12 MILES!*

A UNITED STATES road map hangs on the wall of my writing room. It's a large map, covering half the wall, with a pushpin stuck in each place from where I've received a postcard. The pushpins are small, and each pin is topped with a tiny round glow-in-the-dark bead. The swirl of 274 pins flows back and forth across the map, each one piercing the name of a small town that sits "just up this exit, then Left or Right Only 4 to 17 Miles!" The map is a record of constant travel, of someone's quest through the smallest pieces of the big picture, with stops made only in the farthest-flung off-the-road places, on the map's littlest black dots, at the small furry edges of notice.

ELISSA CAN'T stop laughing. She gasps for breath and holds her sides. "Noah's Ark of...of...of..." she tries again, "...Ark of Love!"

"The cards just come," I tell her. "A new one every two or three weeks. Always from a different place. Never anything but my address written on the card." I point to the map. "I track where they come from on this."

The map takes away her laughter. The map is serious, a clear attempt to find function within form. It is a literal connect-the-dots of information and invites study. Without a word, we both stare at it.

After a few minutes, I turn off the lights. "Watch this." The room is instantly black, the map lost from view. "Keep looking," I say. "Let your eyes adjust."

The seconds tick by, the darkness seeming to lengthen the time. Then I hear her breathing change, hear her soft *Oh!* and know that she sees it now. The glowing pinpoints seem to emerge from beneath the night, rising to the surface. Each bead is a point of light. They float in front of us, a pushpin Milky Way in the black tide of space. They spill across the darkness, forming a constellation of travel. Then she solves the mystery—in only a few seconds, she deduces what I should have figured out long ago.

As she whispers it, I know it is true. "They're from your brother," she says. "They're from the King of the Gypsies."

Holding hands, we stand together in the darkness, staring into the galaxy of stars my brother has sent me.

Now, walking back from the mailbox, I reach the cabin at last and stand still in the driveway, studying the bundle of mail again. Except for a single piece of mail, I hold the usual things: a few letters, a catalog, magazines, a thick mailer from a gas company with the words *VISITING SOON!* printed across the front. And one very different thing—

A small rectangle of cardboard.

Another postcard.

The picture on it is of an old barn. The barn's front eaves are buckled and collapsed forward, giving it the appearance of kneeling. The face of the barn is painted black and white with a faded advertisement to Chew Mail Pouch Tobacco. The rest of the barn is red and green. The red is a soft, sun-weathered and peeling wash of paint that was first brushed on decades ago, and the green is vine-green—young leafy ropes of wild grapevines spill down one corner of the barn, like a green arm draped over the barn's shoulder. The barn is on the top of a hill, and the hill is covered with daisies and dandelions.

The barn on the postcard is beautiful.

And, more importantly, it is familiar.

I drive by that same barn every time I go into town. Elissa and I have sat in the shade of that barn, and I have picked her bouquets of those same flowers. I agree with the words printed across the photograph. They proclaim that the barn is indeed one of the many sites that reflect *THE BEAUTY OF BROWN COUNTY, INDIANA!*

The picture isn't the only thing that's familiar. So is the elegant careful writing on the back of the postcard. The fountain ink is brilliant blue, the color of bright melted sapphires. The same hand that has always written my name and address on the other postcards has done it again—and then done more. This time there's a message, a quick flourish of words that entice and lure me, that give me a reason to drive into town.

GYPSY MOON ATTRACTIONS!
Madam C Sees!
All You Want to Know. And More You Don't.

The words capture and invite me.

And I can't wait to go.

Elissa sees me standing in the middle of the drive, staring at the postcard. "Blue?" She calls. "What is it?"

I answer her with words I've never said before. Words I never thought I'd say. "My brother," I say. "He's here. With my mother."

As I speak I feel the glowing pushpin-stars whirling around me. I feel their light shining on my face and on my hands. The light is warm. I know to navigate by it, that it will guide me to the lost pieces of my family. To my brother, Alassadir, and to my mother,

Callista Marie. And when we meet, I wonder what my mother, Madam C, will see. I wonder what Madam C will tell me that I do want to know, and what she'll tell me that I don't.

AFTER WE DRIVE down the driveway and turn onto Salt Creek Road, heading to town to find my mother and brother, Elissa looks back over her shoulder. "Did you see that?" she asks.

"See what?" I look up at the rearview mirror and realize I hadn't been watching the road. I've been lost in my own thoughts— thinking about my long-lost family, wondering what might happen when we meet again, watching the possibilities play out in my mind...and not paying attention. I see nothing in the mirror. "What'd you see?"

She's frowning, staring at the road behind us. "A black car. I think the driver was staring at us. That maybe he was slowing down to turn into our drive."

"So?" I reach over, grabbing her knee and doing my best Foghorn Leghorn imitation. "I-say, I-say, I-say, I don't know nobody in no black cars. And anyways—I-say, I-say, I-say—I'm taking my girl to the carnival." But she still frowns, still looks like something's bothering her. I shake her knee. "Don't worry about it," I say. "Whoever it is, they'll come back." But I slow down the car, preparing to turn around.

She looks back again, then shrugs it off, putting away whatever's worrying her. She smiles. Laughs. Then tries out her own version of good ol' Foghorn. "I-say, I-say, I-say. No sir, we don't know nobody in no black cars. No way, no how, no shit!" She laughs again and points straight ahead. "Onward ho! Let's go carnival! Let's go say 'Hi' to Mom!"

"Besides," she adds, "You're right. Whoever it is, they'll come back."

BEFORE GOING to town, I make one quick stop. I pull over at the base of a small hill, parking and getting out of the car before Elissa can guess what I'm doing. I run up the hill, toward the black and white **Chew Mail Pouch Tobacco** barn kneeling at the top. I reach down as I run, filling each hand with a bouquet of daisies— picking only the flowers with the brightest buttons in their center, gathering them until I'm carrying two universes of brilliant yellow suns, each sun circled in a frame of perfect white petals, each petal the shape of the smallest feather from the smallest dove.

My hands full, I run back to the car. Bowing deeply, I hand Elissa one of the bouquets. She takes the flowers. Then grins, saying, "He loves me."

As we drive, she pulls a single daisy from the bunch. She touches a finger to a petal. "He loves me," she says, then lightly touches the petal next to the first, again saying, "He loves me." She works around the entire flower, touching each white petal, repeating each time, "He loves me. He loves me. He loves me." Looking at the flower and then at me, she touches the last petal. "He loves me," she says, completing the circle. She points at the daisy. Shrugs and says, "It's unanimous."

I nod, absolutely agreeing, conceding the wisdom of daisies.

23
THE BLACK CARS. THE SOUTH CAR

HEAD DOWN, eyes closed...she listened.

She could hear the two of them running, trying to get away as fast as they could. She listened carefully, tracking the sound. Wherever they went, she knew she'd find them. Like all the other times, there'd be something that gave them away, something she'd notice—a small cough, an exposed heel of shoe, the rustle of straw in the barn.

Then she'd have them. Then they'd be hers.

(*One-Mississippi, two-Mississippi, three-Mississippi.*)

The last time they'd stayed together, making it harder by giving her only one target instead of two. When she found them, they'd been tightly hugging each other, making themselves as small as possible, their heads on each other's shoulder, their eyes scrunched closed, hoping she'd walk by, hoping she wouldn't see...then screaming and running when she did.

(*Four-Mississippi, five-Mississippi, six-Mississippi.*)

One set of footsteps—long, quick strides, probably Jillian's—was running toward the weeping willow tree, seeking safety in its cocoon of hanging branches. She'd lost track of the other one—probably Jackson, being quiet. Then she heard a sound, the sliding scuffle of sneakers across the woodchips by the wood splitter—definitely Jackson, thinking he'd be safe from her there, crouched down in the stacked maze of firewood.

(*Seven-Mississippi, eight-Mississippi, nine-Mississippi.*)

Maybe she'd let him think that for a while. Maybe toy with him a few minutes, letting him think he was in a safe place. Let Jillian think that, too. Let them see her looking for them, acting like she couldn't find them, let them hear her talking to herself, hear her wondering if she should give up, if she should stop hunting.

(*Ten-Mississippi....*)

The slow ten-count she'd been keeping in her head ended. She stepped back from the porch post she was pressing her forehead against—"home base" if the kids could reach it, which they wouldn't, not this time, she promised herself. Because right now Momma was going to kick a little hide-and-seek ass! She raised her face from the crook of her arm, then yelled out—calling slowly, giving them a few more seconds to hide—"Ready or not! Here I come!"

She spun around fast, putting on a show for the kids, knowing they were probably watching—

—and almost spun into the man in the black suit STANDING RIGHT THERE. Standing right in front of her. Standing so close that his black suit and blue eyes filled her sight—

—then, mid-spin, she heard him say, "Boo!" Saw him smiling. And saw that his hand (holding something large, holding something heavy) was rising toward her, and—

—almost pissing herself with the surprise of him, her body slammed back hard, straight into the post, the back of her head making a hollow little *thunk* sound as skull met wood, knocking her breath out in a frightened wheeze. *What the hell?* she thought. *I was listening hard and didn't hear him! I didn't hear him!* and her arms instinctively went above her head, shielding her from his coming hand, and—

—in the same millisecond of her surprise and fright, he said, "Whoa! Whoa! Whoa! Careful there!" and quickly stepped quickly away. His face full of concern, his hands pulling back. Immediately becoming the picture of a man not wanting to scare her. Of a man just as surprised as she was.

She felt an instant wash of relief, and her fear immediately began dissipating as she saw what he was holding in his hand: a blue and yellow basketball painted with an exclamation of red letters: *WE'VE GOT GAME! SCORE WITH NATURAL GAS!*

The fright of the moment now gone, she smiled as the man tentatively held the basketball out again. "Or, footballs," he murmured tentatively. "I have footballs,too." His eyes still looked concerned. "Would you rather have a football?" He tossed her the ball, saying, "I am so sorry." As she caught the ball, he smiled at her and asked, "Friends?"

She smiled back. Then noticed the black car parked in the drive. *How did I not hear THAT? How did I not hear a big black car?* she thought. Then she looked back at him, looked into his face and saw again how blue his eyes were, how warm they were. And when he stepped closer—closer than he'd been before, so close she couldn't see the black of his suit, so close she could only see the blue fire in his eyes—she now felt no fear. Felt no surprise or shock or need to back away. Instead, she leaned in. Leaned in and fell into the blue fire. As she fell, she listened to the wonderful voice she could hear calling her. The voice in the warm blue fire.

JILLIAN WAS WATCHING. She was balanced on the balls of her super-fast, SuperStar green sneakers that were laced up with bright new white laces. Her shoes felt ready to fly like bright green rockets, ready to run *right now*. She felt the shoes' power thrumming through her ankles, charged and ready to GO.

But she didn't run, not yet. Instead she stayed hidden in her favorite spot, deep in the willow cave. It was a perfect hiding place. She could see out, but no one could see in. That way, if someone was about to find her—if she saw they were going to stick their head through the thick green drape of willow branches—she could scoot out the back of the cave before they saw her. Then she'd either try making it safe to home base or would run behind the pump house.

Or maybe run to Jackson and hide next to him in the firewood. Both places were great hiding spots. No matter how many times they used them, Mom never remembered to check, at least not at the beginning of the games.

So far this morning the score was Kids, 5, Mom, 1. And Jillian—*always Jillian, thank-you-very-much, never Silly-Jilly, never Just-Jill*—was feeling pretty good about game number 7. Until she saw the black car pull up. Until the man in the black suit walked over to Mom.

Not knowing if she should do something, not knowing what else to do, she stayed in her cave. Hidden and safe. Saw Mom walk over to her car. Watched the man in the black suit follow.

JACKSON CROUCHED low, making himself as small as he could, wanting to make sure of his win. Mom had only found him once so far, and he couldn't wait to tell Dad. He already knew what his dad would say and do—he'd grab Jackson and toss him straight up in the air, throwing him so high that Jackson's belly would flippity-flop when he started dropping back down. Then Dad would catch him and hug him tight, saying, "Mom only found you one time! That's *speck-tack-you-lar!* That's my son! That's Jack's son!" Then Dad would laugh and say, "Jack-son! Jack-son! Jack-son!" and throw him in the air again and again.

It was gonna be the greatest when his dad got home in two more weeks. It was gonna be SPEK-TACK-YOU-LAR. That was his dad's favorite word. And Jackson's favorite word, too. Jackson used it every day, as often as possible. He'd even used it this morning when he told Mom that her pancakes were really, really SPEK-TACK-YOU-LAR!

When he first saw the black car, though, he'd almost run out of his hiding place. He'd thought Dad was home early, that maybe he'd landed at the airport, rented a car, and come straight home. But then the stranger in the black suit got out of the car, not Dad, and Jackson had watched the man walk over to Mom and seen him talking to her. Watched him give her a big blue and yellow ball.

Then, with the man in the black suit walking right behind her, Mom walked to her car. She pulled her keys out her pocket and opened the car door LIKE SHE WAS LEAVING! WAS MOM LEAVING—

—and he didn't know what to do. Didn't know if they were done playing the game. Didn't know if he should stay where he was, or if maybe he should yell something to Mom. He was about to stand up and yell, but then he remembered he didn't *have* to do anything because he was only five. He was the baby. Silly-Jilly—she went crazy when he called her that—was six. She was the oldest. The big sister. She'd know what to do. Then he'd do what she did.

It was a great idea. It was, he thought, *SPEK-TACK-YOU-LAR!*

Peeking through a hole in the wall of stacked wood, he watched his mom about to get into her car. Then saw the man in the black suit put a hand on Mom's shoulder and stop her. Jackson looked over toward the big willow tree and tried to see through the green wall of branches around his big sister. He wondered what Jillian was going to do. And wondered when she'd do it. And wondered why he was feeling so afraid. And why he was being so careful to make no noise.

SHE WAS at the car. Was ready to go. Was *ready to go right now.* Was thinking of nothing else but staying close to the blue fire, staying close to the voice. She'd heard the message. Knew what she was supposed to do, where she was supposed to go. And was GOING RIGHT NOW when she felt the man's hand on her shoulder. "Forgetting something?" he asked, bending to whisper in her ear.

She listened. Nodded. Thought, *Of course! Of course! Of course!*

Understanding what he wanted, she turned back to the house.

"Ollie Ollie Oxen Free! Ollie Ollie Oxen Free!" she called, bending down to roll the blue and yellow ball toward the wood pile.

She straightened up and leaned back against the man in the black suit. They stood together, watching the rolling ball, waiting and listening, until they saw the curtain of weeping willow branches begin to part and heard the scuffle of sneakers on wood chips. And she heard the man behind her whisper again.

"Spectacular," he said. "Spectacular."

HARLEY

HE WAS NEVER ALONE.

The eye was always looking. The voice was always there.

The voice was warm. Caring. Curious. As he delivered the mail, it kept asking him questions. Asking, *And who lives here? And when are they home?* The voice always asked sincerely, always asked honestly, truly wanting the answer. It wanted to know about the people they saw, asking him (always sincerely, always honestly), *What do you think, Harley? Are they KEEPERS or SLEEPERS? Are they NEAT or are they MEAT?*

And the eye—unseen, but bright blue, he knew it was bright blue—saw everything. He could feel it looking out from behind his own eyes, could feel it staring out from the hole in his skull. It read each envelope he delivered. And studied each house he passed.

As he drove his route, the voice sometimes spoke. Telling him, *Stop. Stop here a moment. Stop here and see.* After he stopped, the eye began moving, gathering in details, looking closer, letting its gaze linger on a bike leaning against a tree, on toys in the yard, on the flowers in a garden.

The eye moved slowly, missing nothing. It was teaching him how to see. How to really see. As the eye stared at the houses, studying the painted porches and the open gates and the small green yards, sometimes he heard the voice start singing. It sang the same children's rhyme every time. *Ten little, nine little, eight little*

Indians. Seven little, six little, five little Indians. Four little, three little, two little Indians. ONE LITTLE INDIAN BOY!

Later, when whoever the eye was looking for still had not been found, the voice started asking, *Where is he, Harley? Oh where, oh where, can ONE LITTLE INDIAN BOY be?*

Harley always answered, "Maybe at the next house, maybe one more down the road." Then he drove to the next house (hurrying there, wanting so badly to help, wanting to help all that he could), asking hopefully when they arrived, "Maybe here? Is he here?"

We shall see, we shall see, the voice answered. Then he felt the eye begin searching again, feeling the slide and pull of it in his brain as it focused on the gaps between the house's parted curtains, staring into the rooms.

As he sat in front of the houses, people sometimes looked out the windows and doors and waved, happy to see his mail truck, even happier when he waved back. (*The eye always watched them waving, he felt it moving from face to face.*) As he waved, he always heard the voice counting the faces at the windows or door, heard it singing its counting rhyme. *One little, two little, three little Indians, four little, five little, six little Indians, seven little, eight little, nine little Indians, TEN LITTLE INDIAN BOYS!*

His days were wonderful. Harley enjoyed every one. He enjoyed listening to the voice. Enjoyed waving to the people. Enjoyed feeling the eye moving in his head. Observing all. Seeing everything. *Really* seeing.

Watching the people at the windows who were waving to him, he always gave serious thought to the questions the voice asked. He wanted to answer sincerely, to answer every single question honestly and thoughtfully. Ultimately, though, no matter which house he was staring into, his answer was always the same: There were a lot more SLEEPERS than KEEPERS. There was a lot more MEAT than NEAT.

CHICORY

25

A DAY OF PRAYER and pinwheels.

All day long, he'd been thinking his prayer. All day long he'd felt the silent hum of it in his brain, the rise and fall of its single word, repeated again and again: *Please. Please. Please.* His prayer was constant, forming a long, linked chain of cries. *Please. Please. Please.* Thinking his prayer, he wept—wept at his helplessness, wept at his fear. And wept at last night's memory.

All day long, he saw pinwheels of colors—whirling spirals of blue, white, and green, the three colors that filled his mind. The colors were short-lived, there, then gone, then back again. They were brilliant, searing, and fast—blinding flashes of painted pain that flashed blue-white-green, blue-white-green, blue-white-green. The colors of his helplessness. The colors of his fear—

The colors of last night's memory.

REMEMBERING last night. Thinking maybe he'd imagined it all. Hoping that maybe it was just him finally taking this whole "Indian vision-quest" thing too far. Or maybe the whole "Great-Spirit's-oneness-of-all-things" bullshit had gotten all confused and turned around in a really bad nightmare. Or—at the end of all other reasons—maybe the simple truth was that he'd finally baked his ex-druggie brain at too high of a heat during one too many sweat lodges. Like last night's lodge.

But he knew the truth. *No, I didn't imagine it. Something is coming. Something bad.*

And he prayed again, *Please. Please. Please.* And he wept again, his tears spilling from a night-river of memory. A river filled with flashing waters of blue, white, and green.

LAST NIGHT'S sweat lodge had begun at midnight, the instant marking both an end and beginning of each day. They'd begun building the lodge yesterday morning, him and the same three guys he always took a sweat with. The four of them had called themselves different things through the years: "Band of Smothers," "Hot Airs," "The Steam Team"—goofy shit like that. His friend Hans Irons had even printed up T-shirts with *Wanna See My Lodge Pole?* printed on the front and *I've Got Hot Rocks* on the back. But not a single one of them ever had the balls to actually wear the shirt in public. Instead, they just put them on after their sweats, to wear on the drive back home.

The T-shirts were one of their private jokes, one of the ways they laughed at themselves and had a good time. But laughs or not, each guy was careful-serious about the sweat ritual and the ceremony. There was no laughing about that. They were grateful for the lodge, each one of them, grateful for the cleansing gift of the "Creator's Breath" and the peace it gave them, grateful for the sense of rebirth they received from it.

When they'd started building that morning, each had first offered praise to the Creator and to Mother Earth, each guy feeling thankful to share in the day's lodge-building. They'd all been quiet and calm as they worked at their tasks: as they cut, bent, and tied the supple willow saplings ("As we are taught by our forefathers, the saplings form the small domed shell of our sweat lodge.") and covered the domed willow shell with blankets and furs and gathered sweat stones ("the stones that are the bones of Mother Earth") for the fire. They were quiet and prayerful as they dug a shallow rock

236

pit in the lodge's center, using earth dug from the hole to build a small, mounded altar outside the entrance. They were quiet as they collected dry fallen wood for the fire and built a large firebox beside the lodge. ("As we are taught by our forefathers, we stack the heavy logs across each other, sprinkle cedar shavings and sage on the layers, place sacred tobacco at the center, and lay the stones on the pile.") They were prayerful as they brought buckets of water from the nearby lake to splash on the fire-heated stones, the water which would give form to the Creator's Breath and make the holy steam.

CLOSING TIME. The day finally over. He'd finished the cleaning chores. Was now sitting in the monkey cage for a few minutes, trying to calm down, trying to stop crying, trying to stop worrying. But was unable to calm or stop because he knew—*he knew*— Something was coming. Something bad. Something that pressed down on your forehead with the heel of its hand (*or with its claws, last night it had claws*) and kept pressing—

—*pressing till your skull buckled inward and your eyes bulged out. Until you heard the cracking noise of splintered bone and felt your head-juices sloshing against the wet sides of your brain-bowl and you felt the liquids spilling out, mixing with the blood already dripping from your ears—*

—that was the Something on its way: *If. If* he believed what he saw last night. *If* he couldn't make himself forget. *If* he couldn't turn it into only a bad dream, into nothing more than a twisted vision of something that wasn't real.

But it was real.

He knew it was.

SITTING IN the monkey cage, he remembered where he'd found his one-word prayer of "Please," remembered where he'd first heard it. It was something from long ago, from his carnival days, when he'd operated one of the big whirly-rides, one of the real vomit-rockets. The ride operators always gathered at the end of the day and laughed as they swapped stories about the kiddy screams they'd heard once the machines got really cranked and turning, when everything was spinning and tumbling and the kids were falling back and forth in the twisting metal cars, hanging loosely against the web of strap-in belts, their little bodies slamming again and again into the barely padded restraint bars pushing into their guts.

The ride operator standing on the control platform always heard the children's frightened screaming, all the *please stop, please stop, please stop* screams and the *please no, please no, please no* cries. (All the children screaming so politely in their terror, so trusting that someone would listen and help them if only they just said, "Please. Please.") When the terrified screaming started, the operator always nudged the ride's speed up, making it tumble even faster, like he thought the kids' cries were just from their excitement because this was, after all, a thrill ride. Acting like he didn't hear the real fear in their voices. Like he couldn't understand the words.

Now, tonight, sitting in the monkey cage, his eyes closed and his head nodding slowly back and forth so that it lightly bumped again and again against the bars, Chicory felt himself spinning and tumbling, felt himself dangling and falling against a loose web of strap-in belts, his belly suddenly nauseous, tight with the pressure of a crushing restraint bar pressing into him. He heard himself whispering his prayer, heard his voice crying softly, *Please, please, please* (politely trusting that someone would listen, politely hoping that someone would hear him and help), repeating again and again, *Please, please, please.* Then waiting and wondering. Waiting to see if he'd soon feel the nudge of the ride's increasing speed. Wondering if he'd soon feel the cage begin to tumble even faster.

THEY'D BUILT the sweat lodge in a good place near a hummingbird's nest—always a good sign. They'd built it by a lake where beaver swam, which was another good sign. To purify themselves, they fasted for the day, the hunger sharpening and attuning their senses, bringing body and spirit closer.

At midnight the woods were beautiful—the moon was a brilliant night jewel, a circle of polished white fire. The flames and coals in the firebox gave the glow of a dawning sun, half-risen from the earth. The fire-heated rocks were red and orange with heat, filled with the fire's life. The scents of the sage and cedar filled the air, drawing the ancient ancestors close. Before entering the lodge, they'd used a burning sage stick to cleanse themselves, cupping the fragrant smoke against their skin, brushing it over their heads.

Then, drawing back the soft leather hide hanging over the lodge's low doorway, they'd stooped down and entered.

Hans had been was the leader of last night's sweat. He'd brought a leather drawstring bag to the sweat. The bag was filled with tokens of honor and bits of memory. He'd taken the items out, placed them on the altar: a pouch filled with ashes from the fires of past sweats; a handful of small, tied bundles of cotton cloth filled with tobacco, the bundles to be burned later in the fire; and a collection of souvenirs found in the places where they'd built their other lodges…a fox's skull, a sprig of bittersweet, a pinecone, a handful of colored feathers.

As leader, Hans also brought the heated rocks into the lodge. He lifted the stones from the fire with a pitchfork, carried them into the lodge, set them carefully in the pit. Then he'd dipped a small willow branch into the bucket and splashed the first sprays of water onto the stones. As the first steam rose, he spoke, honoring the four directions—invoking the North's courage, the East's wisdom, the South's harmony, the West's love. After honoring the four directions, he splashed more water on the stones and began singing, his song calling to the ancestors for guidance, asking their blessings.

And there, sitting in the steam and listening to the song, his lungs filling with heat and his mind seeking calm, Chicory was given a vision—

A vision lit with blue fire...

THE VISION.

...the lodge filled with heat. Each shallow breath he took burned his lungs. His head pounded with the beat of his blood, with the rhythm of the song. He stared into the fire pit, first seeing the pale red glow of the rocks, then seeing the glow changing, the red becoming almost white.

The lodge felt hotter then, the steam thicker. The whitish stones grew even brighter and then turned blue. Then the blue light grew brighter still. The blue light filled the dark womb of the lodge and coiled around them like the steam, touching their skin, flowing into their lungs. The light pushed open the animal hide doorway and spilled out from the lodge, its blue glow leading them into the night.

Chicory followed the others as they followed the blue fire. They bent low beneath the doorway, then stood up outside and looked where the blue fire led. To the altar. And to the feet of what stood there at the altar—a huge, scaled beast with hands of wrinkled leather and clustered black claws, its mouth an abomination of curving jagged teeth and a thick black tongue. Two bright blue eyes stared from the folds of its face, watching them approach. Chicory heard the slide of wet skin and scales as it lifted its arms to greet them. The four men flinched and bunched together as the thing lowered its head, bringing its jaws full of teeth near their heads, its tongue flicking and looping as it slipped out and in between its teeth, its mouth so near their faces that they felt its breath. It inhaled sharply then, pulling their scent deep into its snout, into its mouth so it could taste their smell.

It reached forward, a claw touching one of the four men. Chicory watched and saw the man nudged gently to the side. Then the claw touched another, and another, then the claw reached for him. The beast in the vision pulled Chicory forward. Its mouth hovered near his face, and he was staring up into the blue eyes that were staring back down into his eyes. He heard his scent drawn in and held and savored—then saw the blue eyes narrow. The black claw went around his neck, pulling him even closer, the beast's red-rimmed nostrils breathing him in even more deeply, and then…it laughed. A rasping laugh, full of bloody metal and knives. Then the beast began singing to him in a grotesque singsong voice, a voice that was a broken crash of splintered bones and rotted marrow, singing to him. *Do you know the monkeyman? The monkeyman? The monkeyman?*

He looked into those blue eyes. Felt the mouth still poised over his face.

Then it spoke again, its voice now flat, *Yes, you know the monkeyman.* Then said, *Later, 'gator,* and the claw pushed him aside, separating him from the other guys, setting him in a different part of the blue fire, a darker flame, a darker place from where he watched the others through a blur, seeing them draw closer to the altar, closing tight around the beast.

The beast turned, reached down behind itself, then stood tall again, now holding something out to the others, a form lankly draped across its scaled arms. Watching from the blur, Chicory saw something that made his heart cry out, something that— at first—his mind denied. At first all he saw was only small back and forth flashes of white and green through the clustered group of three men, his attention caught by the swaying tick-tock, tick-tock pattern of green and white colors in the vision's flickering blue flame. For a moment, he saw only the colors: white-and-green, white-and-green, white-and-green. Then his mind allowed in the gruesome reality of what he saw, allowed him to see its true shape. The shape of two tiny, bright green sneakers on two tiny girl feet on two tiny girl legs. The green sneakers were crisscrossed with bright white laces. The long white laces were untied and dangled back-and-forth, back-and-forth, back-and-forth in the bright blue fire.

The beast laughed and spoke. Chicory heard its gargled words as it lifted its arms, offering the small body to the three gathered men, saying, *Good bread, good meat, good gosh, let's eat!*

And Chicory's three buddies moved closer…

Then the vision faded.

Then the blue fire died.

Later, when Chicory opened his eyes, he saw the red glowing stones and heard the lodge song still being sung. He felt the burning steam in his lungs, the heat in the air. But instead of feeling hot, he was shivering and chilled, feeling something new—

Feeling the cold cramp of fear in his heart.

Feeling the phantom touch of claws on his skin.

IN THE MONKEY CAGE. Sitting still. Feeling terrified. And alone. Even Setsu didn't want his company tonight, the monkey giving him an *I'll just take my lock and go over there* look, then dragging his oversized padlock to the other side of the cage, evidently preferring to sit with his monkey-back to Chicory and stare out at the street.

Et tu, Setsu? Chicory thought. Then had another thought— one he'd been almost-hearing for weeks now, one that he'd felt knocking hard against his brain, requesting permission to enter. It was a thought he'd been trying not to hear, but one he now allowed himself to think. *Maybe I should get drunk. Maybe really, really drunk. And I do mean "really, really."*

He stood up. Brushed his hands together, then wiped them on his jeans, his palms suddenly itchy with his craving for cold beer. Lots and lots and lots of cold beer. He waited a minute, then decided—decided to completely drown everything he remembered about last night. To drown what he already knew: that Something Bad wasn't coming soon—

No.

Something Bad was already here.

HE'D TRIED to forget what he'd seen when the vision faded, what had happened when the blue fire was finally gone. He tried not thinking about it. Tried, but couldn't stop remembering that as they left the lodge, he'd gone first, stooping and exiting, then turning to wait for the others, watching them crawl out of the low doorway, watching each guy stand up. And as they stood and looked at him, he'd seen their new bright blue eyes...blue eyes that flashed like fire in the night.

As they left the woods, he'd walked behind Hans, following as they went in single-file to where they'd parked their cars. As they walked, the white moon shone down, lighting their path. It also lit what he saw poking up over the top of Hans' back pocket, something not quite completely covered by the bottom of the *I've Got Hot Rocks* T-shirt. It was the new thing that Hans had picked up and tucked away for his collection of souvenirs, a small reminder of this night's lodge: a tiny green sneaker, its bright white laces untied and dangling down, swaying back-and-forth and back-and-forth and back-and-forth—

—and seeing that small, empty, little girl's shoe, Chicory began whispering his prayer, his soul crying out, trusting that someone would listen, hoping that someone would hear. *Please. Please. Please.*

BLUE. ELISSA. ALASSADIR. CALLISTA

26

ODAY I MET the King of the Gypsies.
Today I met Madam C.
Today I found my family.

Elissa and I drove to the fairground. It's only one mile from town, but it could be twenty. Or two hundred. The two places—the town and "the ground"—never meet. Much like the town is for tourists, the fairground is for locals. In town, the attractions never change. It's always the same small stores, the same art displays, the same dried flower and grapevine wreath-decorated streets. The only changes are the seasonal rotation of streetlight banners and different flowers in the curbside planters. The town's predictability is part of its charm, one of the reasons that people come back.

Unlike the town, the fairground has no charm.

It is not predictable.

And it never stays the same.

The fairground is five acres of a flat, grassy stage for a year-long play, a place where the costumes and audiences are always changing. Fast shuffles of vinyl block-lettered signs announce the play's ever-shifting acts as banners for the morning's *Gun and Knife Show* are quickly switched for the afternoon's *Pacifists' Resource Fair*. The sign changes are so swift and efficient that the different audiences often mingle between acts, creating crowds of unlikely community—allowing a rush of anxious amateur geologists (excited to see the new *Advances in Mining* displays) to chat amiably with misty-eyed, elbow-linked chains of people leaving the *Earth First! Vintage Collectibles Showcase.* Or an inflow of *Wiccans Hearing A Message (WHAM)* meets an outflowing tide of *Baptists Against Magic (BAM)*. As they intermingle, the groups smile and nod politely to the other, everyone's souls filled with their particular spirit of choice.

Few of the events appeal to everyone, with most of them targeting specific interests or audiences. But as Elissa and I drive near to the fairground, I hear one of the rare sounds that can summon the largest crowd, creating a community of all groups—

I hear the carnival's song.

We follow the sound of the music, then turn into the parking lot and stop suddenly, amazed by what we see.

The fairground is transformed.

An ornate, tall wooden gate arches across the event ground's entrance. A cascade of delicately carved moons and stars flow down the gate's side panels. The moons and stars gleam against a painted background of blue-black night. Gold letters flow across the top of the arch: GYPSY MOON ATTRACTIONS. The letters seem to dance to the caravan music of a tambourine and violin somewhere in the distance. To the left of the letters on the arch is another painted carving—a Gypsy wagon camped for the night on a curve of hilltop. A lantern glows behind the wagon's closed shutters. The glow slips between the shutters' slats and softly lights the hill. The spill of lamplight gives a hinted, dim outline to things standing at the edge of the darkness, to things hiding in the blue-black night.

Transfixed, I stare into that painted night, realizing that I recognize what is hiding there, that I know the outline of what is standing just beyond the lantern's glow. I have seen those exact shapes before. I'm looking at the shapes of twelve tall Stones.

It is the Circle.

And as I stand there, unmoving, looking at the carnival's

painted gate, I feel the powers of accident and omen again stirring in my world.

ENTERING THE CARNIVAL, we see a checkerboard of walkways between the rows of rides and games of chance. The big crowds aren't here yet. At this time of morning, only small dots of people are wandering up and down the wide aisles: new parents with infants in swaddling-cloth backpacks, young couples holding hands and strolling, senior citizens moving slowest of all, supported by the polished metal scaffoldings of canes, walkers, and wheelchairs.

The air is a heavy banquet of smells: powdered sugar and cinnamon, hot fried dough, popcorn, pink cotton candy, grilled hot dogs and sausages, and the sharp citrus perfume of lemon shake-ups.

"My God, I'm hungry," Elissa says, grabbing my arm and pulling me over to the food booths. We're ravenous. I buy two of everything, filling a cardboard tray with waxed paper-wrapped treats. We gorge ourselves as we walk, getting sugar on our fingers and cinnamon on our chins, slurping icy-sweet drinks…and it's wonderful. Everywhere we walk we hear the carnival's music: the whir and spin of rides, the call of the midway barkers, bubbles of laughter.

Then I see it.

As we turn from one row to the next, I see it tucked in between two game trailers and looking like a lost stray from a mysterious caravan—the Gypsy wagon. The one in the sign.

The home of Madam C.

Then I see something else, and suddenly I cannot move. Even knowing that my mother waits inside, I'm wholly transfixed by two things. First, I see the words engraved above the door. Words I already know. Words befitting a fortune-teller: *Some free, some caught. Some see, some not.* The second thing: I stand in awe of what I see on top the wagon, gracefully growing on the roof—

—standing there, staring up, I hear a new sound in the music, a voice (a mixture of memory and spirit) that's talking only to me. The voice grabs me in an engulfing bear hug and almost lifts me into the air. Hearing it, I think, *All here. We are all here.* And what else can I do but stand ever-so-still and smile, staring at the wagon's roof, caught in a spell of time and memory....listening to the voice of my father.

AS A CHILD I always asked my father questions. And he always answered with poems and pictures. I once asked him something—asked "Why do...?" or "Why don't...?" about whatever was concerning me right then. I've long since forgotten my question, but I've always remembered his answer.

He raised his eyes heavenward, searching for what he needed. For minutes, he stared quietly upward, but he found no words waiting there. His gaze slowly lowered, drifting down from the clouds until it finally settled on our roof. While I stood there beside him, watching him, I saw him find what soon became his favorite answer to almost all my questions concerning origins and destiny and purposes and control. To all those questions and more, his oft-repeated answer was the poem of a single, simple image, a picture of maple trees growing in rain gutters.

"Each spring," he always said, "a thousand, thousand flocks of maple-leaf whirlybirds fly free from the branches of a thousand, thousand maple trees. And, now free, each whirlybird twirls on its own insubstantial path of air, turning and lifting on the breezes that it finds. Certainly, each one's singular physical peculiarities—its individual ridges and bumps—influence its flight, turning it this way or that. But, largely, their journeys are a matter of the air that they ride. It's a simple question of the currents in which they travel.

"Their biggest decision—the little true control they have of their flight—is whether they enjoy the ride, whether they find joy in the trip's unexpected turns. And soon, as eventually happens to all of them. their flight is done and they land.

"Most of them fall where the ground is good. It's ground where they can take strong root and grow. Where they'll eventually become another tree in a forest of trees, where they'll live lives without mention, undistinguished and unnoticed, but on good safe ground, on common ground."

He always paused here and looked at me meaningfully, letting the moment sink in before he repeated, "On *very* common ground."

Then he said, "However, there are other paths. Wonderfully uncommon paths taken by a different sort. By those who decide to enjoy the journey. Those seeking the updraft rather than the downdraft. The ones who dance in the air currents, rejoicing in the river of invisible atoms ferrying them to and fro.

"They're the whirlies who've sailed over the safe ground. The ones who fly above the crowd, landing where most of their brother and sister maple whirlies have never been and will never see. The ones not aiming for common ground. Ones whose souls are filled with the journey, with the joy of travel and discovery.

"When they land, it's with the light green step of adventure. Of course, some die." He always gave a little head-shake here. "That's the price sometimes paid. Some die, but not all." And here he smiled. "The ones who live find a life in the small margins of survival that they wrest from their surroundings. They sink roots into the barest of soils and stone, then drink deeply, enjoying the fine edge upon which they balance. They live as long as they can, experiencing each moment, knowing and feeling things that no common maple knows or feels." He held up one finger, then two. "The sounds of the city, heard from a jagged crack in a concrete sidewalk. The smell of geraniums and marigolds and snapdragons, all growing together in a window-box garden. And, of course, for some," he finished, looking up at our steep roof's edges, smiling at the perimeter of maple seedlings standing watch on the top of our home, "for some, there is the rare view of the entire forest's treetops...seen from the deep trough of a third-story rain gutter."

And as he and I watched, the line of small trees growing like slender green jewelry in our guttering seemed to bend down toward us, as if bowing in acknowledgement of the admiration in my father's eyes. As if swaying in gentle return of the affection in his voice.

Each time he told this story, he also told me a poem. He never wrote the poem down, and it was never printed in his books. He gave it to me and I kept it safe in my heart. As a child, I thought that the poem was about his "whirlies." As I grew up, however, I realized that it was more—it was about our lives. He never told me the title. In that way it was left unfinished, a work in progress (which, again, was like our lives).

> *Some free, some caught.*
> *Some see, some not.*
> *Some fall, some fly.*
> *Some called, some die.*
>
> *In time to earth.*
> *Like flesh and bone.*
> *Drink deep in birth.*
> *Find root in stone.*

And now, staring at the top of the Gypsy wagon, I can hear my father's voice as I read the words engraved above the wagon's door. And I hear him as I look at the line of maple seedlings growing tall in a long row of rooftop planters. The young trees wave softly in a carnival wind, each of them a poem, each of them a picture. And each one reminds me to rejoice in the journey, to seek uncommon ground, to enjoy the unexpected turns.

SOMEONE HAS quietly joined us. A man stands beside me, also looking up at the maples. After a moment never taking his eyes from the wagon, he speaks. "Years ago," he says, "I learned that Dad was dying. I decided to go see him—but only to *see* him, not to visit. At the close of one of our shows, I sent the carnival on to the next stop, then drove straight through for three days back to Brown County. I drove up the hill to his home and stopped near enough to see, but far enough away not to disturb you or him.

"Even though he was sick, it looked like it must have been a good day for him. You were both outside—him in a wheelchair, you beside him, sitting at the picnic table. It was sunny, and both of you were sitting in the shade. Dad was writing—I like to think it was a poem. You were reading. Both of you were quiet, neither of you said more than a few words the entire time I watched. You were just enjoying the afternoon sun, relaxing in the quiet company of family.

"Using binoculars, I watched you and Dad for hours, laying stretched across the hood of my car like some sort of sniper. I focused on everything, every little detail, trying to memorize it all. I was trying to see myself in the picture—a picture that was quiet and still, that wasn't always moving. I was trying to imagine what life must be like when it's lived in a home that is solid and strong and built on the side of a deep green hill."

I feel his smile in his voice as he goes on. "Then I saw the row of maples in the guttering. Somehow they made the home seem even stronger, like it was actually part of the hill—a part so sure and certain that even the trees took root and grew there. Before I left, I took a box out of my trunk and walked into the woods. I filled it full of earth and handfuls of whirlybirds. I brought them home and planted them in the exact same planters you're looking at now."

He stops speaking. We continue staring at the maples for a few seconds more, staring at them until, at the same moment, he and I turn and look at each other.

"Brother Blue," he says. Then he nods to Elissa. "Sister Elissa."

"Alassadir," I answer. "King of the Gypsies." Then I add the word I've always wanted to say to him. "Brother."

We stand there together, quiet, smiling at each other, uncertain what to do next, but feeling happy and overwhelmed by the wonderful company of family found. Finally, not knowing what else to say, I smile at him. "I got your card," I say. "Actually, I got all of them."

Laughing, he grabs Elissa and me in the same encircling embrace. "Come inside," he says. "Say hello to Mom."

WHEN WE MEET my mother, she is dressed in the wings of a luna moth. Layers of translucent, pale green shawls drape her shoulders. The shawls are edged with purple and yellow and lie folded across her back, hanging down almost to the floor. They shimmer as she moves, as if they've captured moonlight in the fine moth dust of their surface. Wrapping my arms around her, holding her for the very first time, I expect the silver-green dust of wing powder to rub off of her and onto my arms—and for a quick, silly moment I don't squeeze her because I don't want to hurt her by brushing the dust from her wings. But then I feel the sure, fierce strength of her hug, so I hug her back, knowing that I am holding a most rare and beautiful creature of flight in my arms: Callista Marie, my mother.

I'm surprised how much taller I am than my mother. When she raises her arms to pull me close, I have to bend low to meet her hug. She's small in my arms, smaller than in all of the times that I've imagined her.

That's when I offer her the second bouquet of daisies. I've carried the flowers all morning and they're drooping now, but she takes them in her small hands and smiles up at me. After a minute, she looks at Elissa and walks over to her. Without speaking, the two of them put their arms around each other and hug. I hear my mother say, "He loves us."

"It's unanimous," Elissa answers.

I FEEL SOMETHING heavy pressing against my leg. A bulbous gray circle is bumping against my ankle. This big gray ball makes a squeaking coughing sound, and I see the smaller round circle of its head looking up at me with two blind, milky eyes. It makes another coughing sound, again pushing against my leg.

"Blue," Callista says, "he's purring. He remembers you."

That's when I feel a tear slipping down my cheek. I fold to the floor and gather Ebeneezer into my arms. As I bring him close, the fat, blind cat reaches out with his paws until he touches my hair and his feet begin pushing and kneading. I press my face into his neck and feel the rumbling purr inside him.

It is the feeling of welcome.

The feeling of home.

WE SIT TOGETHER in the Gypsy wagon.

As the hours pass, we share our lives. We tell our stories.

At one point Alassadir says, "I used to ask Mom, 'Why my brother? Why this brother I never knew? Why was he chosen to live in one place? Why did he live in a home on a hill, green with trees? Why him?' I'd ask. 'Why him and not me?'"

I stare at him, dumbfounded. "I always asked Dad the same question about you," I reply. "'Why him and not me?'"

Alassadir looks at Callista. They share a small smile. "What was Dad's answer?" he asks.

I decide to tell him the silly truth, no matter how strange it sounds. "That it wasn't because you were first-born. That he kept me because of the color inside my mouth, because it's…well…blue."

Alassadir is quiet as he considers my answer. After a moment he nods. "Well," he says. "That's *one* reason."

He looks at Callista, and she stands up and walks over to the daisies. She's arranged them in a dark ruby vase. Against the odds, the flowers are refreshed, their yellow centers again pointing upward. Callista delicately pulls one of the stems from the vase and studies it, bringing the flower to her lips. "Tell him another reason," she says softly into the petals, whispering to the flower like she is telling it secrets. "Tell him another reason about why he lives on a hill and why you don't. Tell him why you couldn't embrace your dying father on that day, why you could only watch your brother and father from afar."

Although her head is bowed over the flower, Callista's eyes move to Elissa, and I see that my mother is crying, her tears falling into the center of the small golden sun she's holding in her hands.

"And tell them both," she says, "why they can't go home right now...not yet."

So Alassadir tells us a story. And when he finishes—after he's given me "another answer"—I sit stunned, wondering, *How? How could I believe this? How could I ever know that this was true?*

But even then I knew.

The story was true.

Its truth was there in my heart. And maybe that was the only way to understand it.

Because some things you just already have to know.

When Alassadir's story is done, we all talk some more. Callista and Alassadir answer our questions, wanting to be sure we know and believe the truth of what he's just said, wanting to be sure we understood it all. All of the long truths. And all of the short, bloody ones.

The long truths are treasures, hidden in the unwritten, untitled poem. They're a legend of family and pledges and magic and love. My father's poem was a gift within a gift, a present waiting to be opened and understood.

But the short truths were not treasures. They were warnings about things that were sharp, about things that chewed—

About things still to come. But things coming soon.

When he feels we understand, when he believes *we believe*, Alassadir looks at Callista and she nods, then he says, "It's safe now. Safe for you to go home."

I ask them what we will find when we go home.

"Something bad," Callista says. "Something red. And something black."

"You don't *know*?" Elissa asks her.

"Not with my near-sight," Callista answers. "With far-sight, yes. Far-sight sees exactly 'what' and exactly 'where.' It goes someplace and looks around. But not near-sight. Near-sight gives a sense of things—of good things and bad things, of when something's happening or when something's going to happen soon, and what it will feel like...like something red, and something black."

"Far-sight?" I ask her. "That, too? You have it?"

Callista walks over and raises her arms toward me, and I bend down again into the small strong circle of her embrace. "Not me," she says into my ear, then draws back and looks up into my eyes. "I don't. But my sister does. Your aunt...Nanny Tinkens."

She smiles at my surprise. "We'll go see her tomorrow."

As we leave, Callista pulls me close again. "Son, it is safe tonight. The bad things are already done. So sleep tonight if you can. But remember, there are more bad things tomorrow. Tomorrow is a red, red day."

BLUE

I WILL NOT SLEEP TONIGHT.

It is only fair.

I am the one usually woken by nightmares, the one whose memories tear me from sleep—and it is always Elissa who comforts me, always Elissa who calms me and leads me back to safe dreams.

But not tonight.

Tonight, I am the one who will stay awake. Tonight, I will comfort her. I will talk to her until she drifts to sleep. I will hold her until her cries quiet, until her tears dry. And then I will hold her more.

I will not sleep tonight.

It is only fair.

Feeling her shaking, knowing she hurts, I raise my hand to her face. My fingertips stroke her forehead, touch her cheek, brush her closed eyes. And I almost murmur the same words that I've heard her murmur so many times before, almost say to her what she's always said to all of the small, hurt animals that she's cradled in her arms—her fingertips stroking their foreheads, touching their cheeks, brushing their closed eyes as she whispers her soothing, familiar song. "Sleepy eyes," I almost say. "You've got such sleepy eyes"—but I stop before I speak, realizing how those words—tonight, at this moment—would hurt her even more than she is already hurt, would wound her even worse than she is already wounded. So I do not say those words.

Instead, I whisper other words: "I love you. I love you. I love you."

And I try thinking only of the woman I hold.

And not the blood outside our door.

LYING HERE, holding her, I can still smell the carnival scent of cinnamon on her skin. Her jeans, draped over a chair, are still marked with faint white stripes of the powdered sugar she brushed from her hands. I can almost imagine that the day was perfect. Almost. But then another cry escapes her mouth and she curls closer to me, trying to disappear into my arms. Trying to hide from what has hurt her.

I think about today, about the Gypsy wagon carved on the archway, and wonder what I might have seen if I'd looked a little longer at the carving, if I'd stared a little deeper into its painted night, past the moons and stars and Stones. I learned something today. I learned that it isn't just the Stones that are waiting on top the hill. It isn't just the Circle. Other things are there, too, waiting in the darkness, watching from just beyond the lantern's glow... other things with teeth.

THE BLOOD.

It isn't just on the other side of our bedroom door. It's also in here, inside our room. Dried on my hands. Smeared on her jeans, over the streaks of powdered sugar. And on the floor, where our shoes have left their drying, red-smeared tracks.

Outside our home, blood is everywhere. In shallow puddles. In dripping trails swabbed across the cabin's back wall, painted there with brushes made from torn rabbit limbs and ripped swatches of fur—the same fragile limbs that Elissa once straightened and fixed, the same fur she once bandaged. The blood has been drained and flung from animals Elissa once held in her arms and made feel

256

safe, the same animals she touched with her fingertips—stroking their foreheads, touching their cheeks, brushing their closed eyes—helping them to heal as she whispered, "Sleepy eyes. You've got such sleepy eyes."

The rabbits' bodies are gone. Other than their blood and a few clumped, wet bits on the ground, they're gone...except for their ears. Their ears were left behind, each ear stuck into the hutch's wire-screened doors. Stuck there, the ears look like furred darts, thrown in some macabre game.

"Did you see that?" she'd asked early this morning, when we left for the carnival.

"See what?" I'd answered, busy focusing on my driving.

"The black car," she said. "The driver was staring at us. Maybe slowing down to turn into our driveway."

"Don't worry," I'd told her. "Whoever it is, they'll come back."

Those are the words that stay in my mind: "They'll come back."

Lying here now, I am filled with hope—hope that they do come back. But it doesn't matter now whether they come back or not, because I know something they don't know. Something they don't know yet, but will soon. I know that it doesn't matter whether they come back or not...because wherever they are, I know that I am going to find them.

I left her side only once, just long enough to make a single call. Long enough to tell Gordy what had happened. And tell him about the black car. He wanted to drive over immediately, but I told him not to come tonight. "Be here early tomorrow morning," I asked him. And I asked that when he came, that he came ready to hunt.

I UNDRESSED HER and held her, and, in time, the in-and-out of her breathing told me she was sleeping. But her body still trembles. Even asleep, she moves deeper into the circle of my arms, backing away from whatever is creeping toward her in her dreams.

Holding her, I remember the maple whirlybirds growing on the wagon's roof. I remember their lessons: Rejoice in the journey. Seek uncommon ground. Enjoy the unexpected turns. But now, I add another lesson from the list, one that seems truer tonight than all of the others. *Of course, some die. That is the price sometimes paid.* And as I think about it—about tonight, about what has been done—I know one more thing: The dying is not yet done, the price is not yet paid...I'll make certain of that.

THERE IS MORE than the blood.

There's something else, too. Something Elissa didn't see.

The blood painted on the outside wall moves in loops and swirls across the wood in a dark design of curves and lines. The design was drawn with rabbit paw-brushes torn from Troll's legs— his blood-soaked feet were lying on the ground by the wall, dropped there like broken tools.

But what was painted isn't just a swirled design. There are words there, too. A phrase that's hidden in the blood in the loops and curls. *Peek-A-Boo.*

It reminds me of a baby's game. And of the child crying at the Circle. And of our own lost son. It also reminds me of the words that finish the blood-painted phrase, the same words that also finish the baby game. *Peek-A-Boo...I See You.*

"I See You." That is the message delivered by whatever is standing just beyond the lantern's glow. By whatever is watching us from there.

Lying in our bed, holding Elissa as she sleeps, I can see the almost-full moon shining through the window. The light is brilliant, so bright that I almost worry it will wake her. But then

I imagine the frightening darkness of her sleep, the black corners of her nightmares, and I think *Brighter! Brighter!* wishing I could give her a white torch of moon for her dreams, its fire blazing and conquering all shadows.

STREAKED IN dried blood, my hands look black, as if stained with ink and shadow. Blood looks black in moonlight. It shouldn't. It should look red. The color is there, of course, but we don't see it, and there's no real reason we don't—no reason we shouldn't see the range of blood's red hues at night, no reason we shouldn't admire its maroon and scarlet rainbows. After all, the bright moon is simply a mirror, shone on by the sun and lit with her light. The moon's light is a reflection of the sun's spectrum of colors, including red. But we don't see the colors in the moonlight.

Our own eyes hide them from us.

Our eyes resist the colors and narrow our perception. They dim the night's colors and refuse to let us see clearly. It is our eyes that see only shades of gray and black—because our eyes know. They know that there are things we should not see, not in the night. And they know there are things that we should hope do not see us, not in the night. So our eyes protect us. They keep us safe from the bad things waiting in the dark, the things that would lead us deeper into the moonlit woods. The bad things that would lure us nearer to them along night trails baited with pretty-colored bits and bright-colored pieces, all of the colors ever-so-lovely and inviting in the moonlight...if only our eyes would see.

ALASSADIR'S STORY

WHEN ELISSA and I were sitting in the Gypsy wagon and listening as Alassadir told us his story, all other sounds around us grew small and distant. All other things became blurred—until finally there were only my brother's voice and the stillness of the wagon. And in that stillness there was only the world that he created, only the storyteller and his tale.

He began…

THERE ARE sacred places—some above, some below, others here on earth. Jonah's Belly—the Circle—is one of those sacred places. And there are keepers of those places, guardians of what is there.

We are those keepers.

We are those guardians.

The sacred places on earth…there are more of them than you can imagine. They take all shapes and forms: mounds of earth, tall stands of ancient trees, springs that feed into cold ponds, sandy arroyos in deep canyons. But for all their different forms, these sacred sites are always in the same kinds of places. They're always where no one goes. Always away from crowds and noise. Always hidden far away, yet somehow near beside us. Always close, but unrevealed.

LISTENING TO Alassadir, I thought of the postcards he'd sent from places where no one goes. From hidden faraway places that are nearby but unrevealed. Thinking about this, I suddenly understood the seemingly random path of his Gypsy carnival. And I knew that I could now better read the map on my wall. Each glowing map pin is the bead of a secret rosary, each stop, a murmured Station of the Cross along a pilgrimage. Yes, my brother's life has been a pilgrimage, a trek away from crowds and noise, a path that follows narrow roads to tiny towns. It is a journey that stops at each place only long enough to do two things: to provide a carnival of fun to those who do not travel, and to attend to the hidden churches along the way.

LONG AGO, the hill was an open blessing, a fountain of old magic, powerful and good. Magic flowed from the hill with every breath of the earth, with every mist of the ancient sea that blew out into the air.

The People were grateful for the Circle, but they were careful, too, always careful to honor the hill's spirit. Careful, most of all, to keep the magic in balance. They understood the truths taught in the oldest stories. The truth that a battle is always raging, that the world is always at war as chaos battles order, death battles life, evil battles good. In small battles and great ones, all sides fight all other sides.

The great fights hurt everyone. They disrupt harmony and break the lives of the People. That's why balance must be kept, why equilibrium must be maintained. It is better that small victories be piled in both pans of the universal scale than for one side to win everything. When one pan grows heavy with the bloat of total triumph, the balance tips and the pan heavier with total victory falls quickest. And when the victory-heavy side swings down as fast as an ax, the other side thrusts up like a knife, just as fast, just as sharp. And as the scales swing up and down like knives and axes, the world and the People are cut to pieces and their blood flows in rivers into the world.

So it is best to keep balance.
And best when both sides bleed a little.

AS ALASSADIR spoke, his voice sometimes became stronger and filled the room with the power of pounding drums, their rhythm seizing our hearts and calling our pulses to follow where it led. Other times, though, his voice seemed to come from far away, making us strain to hear it, making us lean in to catch the hint of words that sounded like faint birdsong on the wind. Or the distant cry of a long lost child.

HARMONY was enjoyed. Balance was kept. All was well—
Until the treaties were signed. Until official government papers gave new strangers possession of old ground, and the new owners of an ancient land told those already living there to get out. Then a new battle began, this one, alas, among the People. Among those blessed by the hill. Among those who had always honored the Circle.

Most of the People knew it was time to leave. They also knew that leaving was only one part of a longer story, a story that had been told long ago. Most wanted to follow the story as it had been foretold because they knew that later, in a distant time, they would return. Because that, too, was part of the story.

Most knew. Most agreed. Except one.

One of the People wanted to use the Circle to change the story, wanted to wield the Circle's magic and make it a weapon...a weapon to tilt the balance of the great scale.

At first, maybe he believed what he was doing was right, maybe felt that what he wanted to do was good. But once he decided to pervert the Circle's purpose, it wasn't long before he also decided to use the magic only for himself, to make the force of it his alone. With that decision made, it took even less time for him to decide that once the power was his, then he had to make certain no one could ever take it from him. So he made his plan. First he would glut himself on the Circle's magic. And then he would destroy the hill.

ALASSADIR PAUSED and fell silent. It was a pause of reflection, of remembering what is lost and wondering what might have been. Callista walked to where he sat and stood silently behind her son. Still silent, she wrapped her arms around his shoulders, laid her cheek on the top of his head. Soon, with the shimmering green and purple wings of her shawl folded protectively over him, he continued.

IDENTICAL TWINS. Brothers at war. It is the same in all the old stories, isn't it? It is always twin brothers who battle one another, always twin brothers who are the bloodiest of all. They are the opposing sides of the eternal battle. The stories make sense, though. Twins make a perfect picture of the fight—their hands strangling each other's neck, their eyes glaring into each other's eyes. They're joined forever in struggle, and forever by blood...the blood in their veins, and the blood on their hands.

Yes, it's the same in all of the old stories, and it is the same in this one, too. There's a good twin, and there's a bad twin. The good twin honored the Circle. The bad twin sought its power. He darkened the Circle, staining it twice with innocent blood, draining the lifeblood of two children into the ancient salt waters. With one child's blood, he built a dark path to the magic. With the other child's blood, he opened a dark way to call upon the Circle's power. When the way was open, he called out to other things to come. Things which would tip the scales, things that would change the Circle. Things that would also change him.

It was then—with the magic begun, with the dark twin's soul changed but the Circle not yet destroyed—it was then that a battle was fought. A mighty battle, like those of old. A battle between brothers. Between the good twin and the bad.

ALASSADIR STOPPED and looked at me, his twin. We sat in the quiet wagon, each brother considering the other, looking at the other's face and seeing the obvious physical differences—our different shades of hair and different eye colors, our different heights and weights—but also seeing something familiar, something the same in the other's eyes. Something the same in the other's look. We both felt like we were staring into a mirror that did not cast back a true reflection, but instead showed someone "almost alike."

He broke the silence. "Twins, Blue. Like us. Always a good twin and always a bad twin. And always one about to kill the other. But never fraternal twins, always identical—at least in the stories." He gave a small smile and shrugged his shoulders. "And so, my brother, I think you and I should be just fine. Although, of course, we can never forget: You and I are the world's first 'identical-fraternal twins.'"

Hearing him, I realized that Alassadir had heard the same story of our birth that I'd been told, how our father's initial confusion and awe had made his newborn fraternal twin babies appear identical to his eyes. And I wondered…when Alassadir was young and first heard the ancient stories that he was now telling, when he'd imagined the battles between a good twin and a bad twin, had he pictured the battling twins as the two of us? In his childhood imaginings, had one of us always been "the good twin"? Had one of us always been "the bad one"? And, if so, who was which? Which one of us had triumphed? When he'd lain dreaming in his childhood bed, a bed that was forever traveling, had he dreamt of a war where our hands were locked tight around each other's throats? Where we glared into each other's eyes and were drenched in each other's blood?

And as I wonder these things, I realize that I have another question: *Who is this brother of mine?*

WHEN ALASSADIR began the story again, his voice led us back to the top of Jonah's Belly, back to the Circle. Taking us to where life and death and magic and family all folded together under the brilliant light of a full moon—

It wasn't one battle, it was two. The twins fought two battles at the Circle. Both times, the good twin won. But at the end, a price was paid. A price that's been paid through the ages. In the first battle, which he fought after he'd been changed forever in his soul, the bad twin was hurt. And, hurt, he fled. With his leaving, the dark way he'd opened closed behind him and the dark path he'd built was erased. Because each time the path to the magic is built, that path can be walked only once. And each time the way to the magic is opened, it is open only once.

Although he'd fled, the People knew the dark twin still lived, and that he would return again. They also knew they had to leave their land. But before they left, they had to protect the Circle, and so they chose to protect it with blood and stone. To fill the Circle's deep wells with the stone that had once swum in the ancient sea. And they had to make the stone stronger with their flesh, with the blood pumping in their hearts.

Under the full white moon—the moon that called strongest to the sea beneath the hill, the moon that drew up the deepest magic— they built another path and opened another way. They gathered in ceremony, the "shifting ceremony," where the elders sang out to the spirits of the stone, asking the spirits to guide them into their final skins. Into skins of stone.

Yes, the spirits heard the song and came. The elders had lashed pieces of stone to their bodies, cutting the skin where the stones were tied, giving the spirits entry into their rent and bleeding flesh. As they sang, the elders' good blood spilled down into the holes and fell into the waters below the Belly.

Then the elders began shifting, began becoming the Stones that would fill the holes that fell to the sea. It was then that the second battle was waged. The dark twin had healed quickly from the first fight. Whatever had changed him had also made him stronger and more powerful. And so, with his dark path now gone and his dark way closed, he fought only to disrupt the ceremony. Knowing that he could return at another time to build a second path and open a second way, he battled to leave at least one well open, to prevent one hole from being closed. Intent on this, he flew down from the sky. Sweeping down, his eyes were golden with hate, his talons were outstretched before him.

The dark twin attacked and the second fight began. This time, the two brothers fought first in different skins, in shifted forms. The dark twin fought as an owl, the good twin as a panther, each shape powerful and deadly. One struck silently from above. The other was a streak of night across the ground. And after they had fought as beasts, striking and clawing and biting, they shifted again and fought as men.

Again, at the battle's end, the good twin won. And again, both sides bled. An elder was mortally hurt as he shifted, and, in dying as a man, he continued dying as a Stone—a Stone dying through the ages.

The battles were fought. The ceremony was done. The Circle was protected. A ring of Stones, quiet and tall, now stood on the hill. But one Stone was dying. And the dark twin still lived. And so began another story. The story of our family.

As ALASSADIR spoke, Callista walked to a small stove in the wagon's corner. She placed a kettle on a burner, heated water, then poured the rolling water into a purple teapot. The purple glaze was crackled with a fine lace of age lines, telling of long use and care. She took a canister from a shelf above the stove and used a long silver spoon to drop loose tea leaves into the hot water. She stirred the leaves into the water with the spoon, murmuring words into the steam that rose from the pot, then poured the tea into four wide, shallow cups. The cups were thin and milky white. The soft sunlight that slatted between the wagon's shutters shone through the cups, making them glow as though filled with some bright potion.

Callista handed us each a cup and kept one for herself. As we listened to the story, we sipped our tea. I looked down at the loose tea leaves swirling in circles in my cup, entranced by how the leaves almost touched my hand, by how the two—the leaves and my hand—were separated by only the thinnest wall of glowing glass.

Alassadir tilted his cup up once and then again, taking two quick swallows, then continued his story.

WHEN THE GREAT SPIRIT *made the People, he gave them many gifts. Some gifts were for use each day. The gifts that fed the People. The gifts that kept them warm and healthy. The gifts of knowing when to plant and where the wild herds have moved. Gifts of knowing where the fish were hiding, and which herbs to feed to the sick.*

There were also other, less ordinary gifts. These were the wild gifts that kept the People safe, that protected them and gave them power. There are gifts that let them see what others cannot see, the gifts of long-sight and near-sight. And the gift of taking the shape of those that live around them, the gift of shifting skins, which gives the People the bear's strength and the deer's speed. And there also is the gift of the Singers who sing the songs that speak to the Great Spirit, the songs which call the spirits to us.

And of course there was another rare gift: the gift of the warrior soul.

"MY GIFT is stories," said Alassadir, smiling first at Elissa, then at me. "I keep the old tales so the People will never forget. It's a quiet gift, but one that joins us together. The stories bind us to our history." He smiled again. "They remind us of that which is yet to come."

AFTER THE SECOND *battle, the People made a new plan. They knew they had to leave the land and abandon the Circle. But before leaving, they chose a family that was rich with blood that carried the powerful gifts, a family blessed for generations with those who could see, and shift, and sing...and who were filled with warriors' souls.*

The family was made the Circle's stewards. For forever would they watch the Stones and protect them. And just as they would watch over the Stones, they would also watch for the return of the twins. Because it was their own sons, the good twin and the bad, who had battled. Just as the dark twin had hidden himself somewhere to wait for the Stone to die, so, too, was the good twin also hidden and gone. He'd risen on the final breeze that was breathed from the Circle and disappeared in a wave of magic that caught his soul and carried him upward, wrapping him in the blanket of fog that so often covers the top of the hill.

The family knew that, in time, their two sons would return. One son was coming back to destroy the Circle, the other to defend it. It was no longer only an old story. Now it was the family's story—it was their twins locked in eternal struggle, their sons whose hands were held around each other's throats, joined together forever by blood...by the blood in their veins, by the blood already spilled onto the ground.

The family's plan was simple. Some would stay, others would go. Those who stayed would live near the hill. They would keep watch each day, waiting and preparing. In time, those living near the hill would forget the others who lived away, would stop recognizing them as family. And their ignorance would help hide them from the dark twin as he looked for them, would help keep them safe as he hunted for them.

Those who left the hill would keep watch from afar, but they would also return from time to time to honor the elders and be near the old magic so they could sing songs of courage to the Stones. But they would not stay. They would always move on. Their endless movement would hide them from the dark twin and keep them safe as he hunted.

Those staying and those leaving would always live apart. They would never see each the other. But all would use their gifts for the same purpose: To watch. To protect. And to battle.

Through the years, not all of the family's children received the sacred gifts. The blood blesses some, but not all. Of the gifted ones, some learned the story early on, whereas others learned it much later. But when the time finally came, all those gifted ones would join together on the hill.

They would gather when the Stone died and the twins returned. And they would all fight again at the Circle.

So those who left became a wandering tribe that traveled unnoticed, crossing back and forth across the country, always returning to pray and pay heed. When they drew too much attention as Indians, they traveled as a band of magicians and entertainers, working the country roads until finally they became a Gypsy carnival. Now they moved from town to town, hiding in the glow of neon lights and flashing bulbs.

This is how I became King of the Gypsies, and why I live in a home that never stops moving. And it's why you grew up in a home built upon a beautiful green hill, a place set firmly on the ground, where it's the world that travels past.

You know...except for death and the passage of time, the plan was a good one. At one point, however, almost everyone traveling and almost everyone living on the hill had died. To keep strong, another plan was made. A plan to buy time. Children were separated from each other, dividing their wild gifts between the two groups. Parents were also separated, parting so that each could be with a child. But— whether this was a good plan or not—time continued to pass, and people continued to die. Until finally, again, it is just us. Until, now, we are all that remain.

ALASSADIR LIFTED his cup again and swallowed, then lifted it higher and swallowed again. In my mind, the double-sip habit became one of the things I'll always think of when I think of him. He set his cup down.

"The dark twin," he said. "He's here now. He's returned because the Stone has died. He's back because now he can draw the magic up from the earth. He's going to destroy the hill. His path has again been built. His way has been opened again."

My brother looked at his almost-empty cup and shrugged. He looked at me. "The bad twin is here, Blue. We're here. And you're here. But at this point, our team captain is still missing—the good twin has yet to show up. And that is *truly* not good news for the home team. Because the big game is scheduled for tomorrow night—the night of the full moon."

He shook his head. "Brother," he said, "things are certainly getting interesting."

We sat in silence for the longest time until he began speaking again. "Our family has a poem," he said. "It's a piece of our story, passed from parent to child."

He began reciting it then, and as he spoke, I began speaking it, too, already knowing what he would say, already knowing the words by heart—but somehow, now hearing them for the first time. Hearing a story of a divided family. Of some staying and some going. Of those with wild gifts and those without gifts. Of separation and reunion, and earth and stone and battle.

> Some free, some caught.
> Some see, some not.
> Some fall, some fly.
> Some called, some die.
>
> In time to earth,
> Like flesh and bone.
> Drink deep in birth,
> Find root in stone.

He finished his tea, tipping his cup up twice and draining it. Callista held her hand out to him and took his empty cup, then took ours. Setting the cups on the wooden tray, she sat with it balanced on her lap and stared down into the cups. Soon she picked one up and cradled it in her hands, looking closely into its white bowl. She closed her eyes, but still seemed to be studying whatever it was that she saw.

After a while, she wordlessly set the cup back on the tray, lifted the tray from her lap, and carefully placed it on a table beside her. She sat with her head bowed, as if still studying the cups. After a moment, she looked at Alassadir, staring at him the same way she'd stared into the cups. She nodded.

After her nod, Alassadir turned to me. "It's time, brother," he said. "Time to free your warrior soul."

ELISSA. CALLISTA

IN THE SCUFFLE of leaving the Gypsy trailer and saying goodbye, after Alassadir finished his story and they'd all hugged each other, after Alassadir had grabbed Elissa and kissed her cheeks, shouting, "My sister, I have a sister!" there was a moment when she and Callista were alone together while the two men were turned away and talking.

That was when Callista picked Elissa's empty teacup from the tray and looked again at the wet leaves still stuck to the cup's bottom and sides. Pressing the cup into Elissa's hands, Callista stood on her tiptoes and whispered into Elissa's ear. "He doesn't know, does he?"

Elissa said nothing. Just shook her head and smiled as she stared at the leaves, searching there for the baby Callista had seen hiding in the cup. Then she and her newly-met mother-in-law wrapped their arms around each other and stood unnoticed by Blue and Alassadir, rocking from side to side in their embrace, filling the air with a soft flutter of small croonings and murmurs, weaving a hopeful song that spun and spilled around them.

THE BLACK CARS. THE WEST CAR

HE WAS WATCHING her through the big front window of their home. She was sitting in the black foam seat of the John Deere backhoe she'd rented yesterday. Last night was the first time she'd operated the thing, and now look at her— only a few hours of practice, and she'd already been digging like a mole all morning, scooping out metal-toothed buckets of earth and dumping them near the garden. He could tell she thought he was watching her because sometimes she lifted her straw sunhat and waved it in the air like a rodeo cowboy, yelling "Yee-haw!" and smiling at the window, hoping he was looking out at her but not sure, unable to see him through the reflection of mirrored glass....

Years ago, she'd covered the window with sheets of silver film. *Reduces Glare! Stops Fading!* had been printed on the silver film's package. Now, after years of sitting motionless in front of the living room window and gazing out, he sometimes wondered how much of him might have faded to nothingness without the silver film's protection—thinking that by now he probably would have become invisible, that by now he might have become a man made of clear glass, with the only thing left of him being the hollow hiss of his labored, mechanical breathing.

But that hadn't happened. She'd covered the window with the protective silver film and kept him here. As she always did, she had once again saved him: She'd stopped him from disappearing.

Watching through the window, he couldn't hear her "Yee-haw!" over the sound of the big digging machine. But he didn't have to hear it. After all these years, he knew his sweet Mary, knew the things she yelled when she was doing all sorts of things—*and, oh, happy days, didn't those thoughts make a man wish he could stand again, just long enough to walk outside and pick her up again in his arms. Pick her up so he could lie down with her just one more time.*

Every time she waved her hat and yelled, he yelled, too, taking three deep breaths of oxygen, then lifting the rubber mask off his face and shouting, "Yee-haw!" right along with her, cheering on his pretty cowgirl...then collapsing, wheezing and spent, glad she couldn't see him behind the reflective window as he fumbled to get the damn mask back on as fast as his weak arms would allow. Also glad she couldn't see him slumping forward in his wheelchair, his thoughts singularly focused on pulling in as much air as fast as he could through the little breathing tube. Every time it happened, he thought that he might just as well wheel over to the oxygen tank and start sucking directly on the tank's metal nozzle, sucking like a hungry fifty-four-year-old baby nursing on a tit full of canned air.

WHEN HIS BREATH returned he looked around the room and thought, *At least I'm surrounded by friends.* He'd been told that a man could never have too many friends, which made him, he supposed, about the luckiest man alive. After all, just look at the friendly, helpful crowd around him. Standing over in the corner was his "Little Buddy Breather" oxygen system. Next to that was his "Sleep Chum" hospital bed. And his closest friend ever, his "Pee-Potty Pal," was strapped tight to his wasted thigh and extended its own flexible "tube-of-friendship" straight up the flaccid middle of his pink, wasted appendage. *I was misinformed,* he thought. *It appears that a man certainly can have too many goddamned friends.*

Every day he asked himself why he bothered. Why he kept swallowing pills out of bottles and breathing air out of cans and leaking urine into bags and shitting into elastic-waist diapers. *Not that I'm complaining*, he told himself, *Not that I don't enjoy the amusement park fun of having one tube in my nose and another one in my dick. But still, really, why?*

He asked the same question every day.

And every day he answered with the exact same answer, which was the only answer: Mary. Because of Mary. Because thirty-four years of marriage later, she still smiled into windows she hoped he was watching her through. Because she still yelled "Yee-haw" like a bronco-riding outlaw when, really, she was just saving them a few needed bucks by digging the new septic tank hole herself. And, most of all, because he was still absolutely crazy about his wife. Because he still absolutely adored every minute he spent talking and laughing and living with her. And also because—wonder-of-unbelievable-wonders—she was still crazy for him.

He had no idea how he could be so lucky. He felt amazed every single day, as he ate his pills and drank canned air and pissed into bags and shit into diapers, to find that at the same time he was doing all of this he was also so obviously one of God's very fortunate few...because Mary loved him still. He knew it was true. He knew it every time he looked outside.

"Just look at the garden," she'd told him once as she wheeled him to the window. "If you ever start thinking 'Does she really?' or 'Does she still?' just look at the flowers and remember this: *I am yours forever.*" Then she'd lifted his hand to her breast and bent her face to his lips and kissed him slowly, her mouth so open and warm.

THE GARDEN was her gift to him. It was beautiful. Was something filled with color and life for him to see. Something to fill his day. And something for them to talk about, too, something for them to do together—"together," he knew, in the loosest sense of the word, but still...*together*. Together, talking about the choice and placement of flowers. Together, handing seed catalogues back and forth. Together, passing scraps of penciled diagrams to each other, trading ideas and comments, asking each other, "The roses here, maybe? The tiger-lilies behind the tall grasses?"

During the day she worked outside on the plans they'd made. She turned the soil, shifted things from here to there, and planted the seeds and fragile starts. Then, weeding and watering it all, she worked to make it bloom in front of the window like they'd already seen it in their minds.

She always came in at noon to escape the heat and poured herself a glass of iced tea, then sat for a few minutes beside him, relaxing and looking out the window. Then she'd go back out and came in again at the end of the day. After her hours outside, she wore a perfume of the sun and earth and flowers and mulch and sweat, gifting him with the heady scents of her day.

She would kiss him then, always. She'd kiss each of his fingers, one at a time. Then she'd lift his oxygen mask, and he'd feel the close heat of her face. In that heat, he felt the same sunshine she'd felt, and he'd bask in the warmth that was captured in her skin and lips, the same warmth now radiating to him. And always, after her kiss, he asked her, speaking softly, "Mary, Mary, quite contrary, how does your garden grow?"

"Why, with love of course," was her answer. "With lots and lots of love." And she always kissed him again. Always.

IT WAS ALMOST noon now. She'd be taking her break soon and would come in for a glass of something cold. She'd be thirsty now, and would visit with him while she rested. She'd started digging early, but the day had heated up fast. Still, she was making good progress. The hole was already at least six feet deep and just as long across. *Not bad for a tenderfoot backhoe-riding cowgirl,* he thought. *Not bad at all. In fact, it was absolutely amazing.*

He waited for her to come in, excited about talking with her. He'd had an idea for the garden while looking at the dirt she was dumping. Thought maybe they could build some terraces, maybe tie it all together with some sort of waterfall or fountain. But then he realized that, as excited as he was about the idea, he'd have to wait a little longer before sharing it with her. Because even though Mary couldn't see it (her back was to the road) and couldn't hear it (the backhoe was too loud), a black car was making its way up the drive to their house.

Wonderful, he thought. *New friends.*

BEHIND THE mirrored glass, he watched the car come closer. It was black, but also more than black. Looking at it, he felt a "feeling of black," a sense of emptiness. He tried to see it a little better. Something was written across the car's hood in bright blue and yellow letters. When the car stopped, he read the words: *BURIED TREASURE, DEEP AND CHEAP! NATURAL GAS!*

The driver got out of the car. He was wearing a dark gray suit. But the suit didn't fit the "feel" of the man, didn't match the way he moved or acted. Mary still didn't see the car, didn't know about the man behind her. She didn't see his face when he looked around— but he wasn't just "looking around." It was more like someone checking for something, making certain of something (*making certain Mary was alone?*). She didn't see what else the man did, how he lifted his head and sniffed the air, his head bobbing slightly up and down, sniffing like an animal trying to catch a scent. And she didn't see that the man was now walking toward her back, one hand disappearing into his jacket, reaching for something hidden there.

SOMETHING GRABBED her ankle. She felt it and almost screamed. She'd been intent on digging, was thinking about getting a few more bucketfuls out of the hole before she went inside...and suddenly she felt the surprise of a hand on her leg, pulling at her. Startled, she yanked her leg away and looked down. She saw the man in the dark gray suit. A man with the bluest eyes she'd ever seen. *A rainbow of blue*, she thought. *Every blue I've ever seen.* He was saying something, but she couldn't hear him, not over the noise of the backhoe.

Then he stopped talking and held something out to her.

She turned the machine off and listened to the sound of the big diesel motor dying. Then she looked down at what was in his hand. It was a long, flat box of seeds, the box's entire front covered with pictures of colorful flowers. Bright blue and yellow letters bloomed across the box's top: *BEAUTIFUL AND BOUNTIFUL! NATURAL GAS!*

"They're beautiful," she said, looking at the pictures.

"And bountiful, too. Don't forget bountiful," he said, smiling at her. "It says so right there on the package."

Looking into his eyes again, she smiled back. *Every blue I've ever seen.*

She climbed down off the backhoe and turned to face him.

"Beautiful garden," he said. "Lovely. Truly."

"And that—?" she asked, nodding at the box.

"Yours," he said, stepping closer and offering it to her. "Lovely. Truly," he repeated, stepping so close to her that she saw she'd been wrong—so very, very wrong. There was more in his eyes than every blue she'd ever seen. There was also fire, a fire of blues she'd never seen before, of every blue she'd never imagined. And from inside the bright fire she heard a voice calling, calling her into the blue.

She heard the voice and went to it. Went to find the source of the fire. Went wanting to find its deep blue heart, wanting to find it *now*, to go to it *now*. But then, from somewhere far away, she heard the man's voice again. Heard him say, "Planting time?" and heard him shake the box of *BEAUTIFUL AND BOUNTIFUL* seeds. Then he bent close to her ear and spoke again. And his words were so perfect, were so very lovely that she thought she might cry.

When he was done speaking, she looked at him, unable to think of better words than the ones he'd just given her.

"Lovely," she answered. "Truly."

Then she turned and walked to the house. She looked up at the reflective silver window as she walked, hoping he was there. Hoping he was watching.

LATER, AFTER she'd finished—after she'd poured the backhoe's last bucketful of dirt back into the hole and sprinkled the last handful of seeds onto the earth—she knew that the man in the dark gray suit had been exactly right: The garden was perfect now...now that the hole was filled in, now that the new seeds were planted. Looking at it, she relaxed into the dark gray clasp of the man's arms, basking in the blue warmth filling her heart, and in the blue light spilling from her eyes. The blue fire inside of her made everything seem bright and strong—

It even made the garden grow.

Looking down, she saw five tiny, white seedlings already pushing weakly up through the newly planted ground. She knelt down to them, and they curled and stretched, looking for the sun. She brushed the tiny clods of wet, clinging soil away from their delicate waving stems and daubed the blood from their scratched skins and plucked two torn fingernails from their stalks. Then, as she always did, she bent and kissed each one of them softly. Kneeling near them like this, with her mouth so near their tips, she could hear a small sound from beneath the earth—the muffled hiss of air, the hollow mechanical rush of breath being pulled through a tube.

She smiled then, knowing how much he enjoyed the garden.

Remembering how much he always loved the new flowers.

Imagining how very beautiful he would grow to be.

CLETE. THE MATCHMAN

31

CLETE HAD BEEN following the rules. He'd been staying small, hadn't stirred, was keeping tucked tight away. But he'd been peeking. Taking little looks through the curtains. Watching the black cars drive out each morning. Watching them return each night. More of the "other drivers" were arriving every day. He'd been watching them, too, as they followed the black cars down the hill and parked, then disappeared into the depths of the black trucks.

All that was fine. Like he'd said before: "Fuck 'em."

But this morning things had begun happening.

Bad things.

Today the "other drivers" weren't disappearing into the trucks.

Today they were coming out.

He could see they weren't people. Not anymore. Not the things walking down the truck ramps with wide smears of bloody grease on their mouths and hands. The things with eyes that glowed bright blue.

Peeking outside, Clete watched one of the blue-eyed things pull a handful of something out of his pocket and stuff it into his mouth, pushing it in open-palmed and greedily, like a child with a treat, filling his mouth so full that he had to poke at the snack with his fingers to push the food all the way in. Then he chewed, slowly grinding his teeth down onto whatever was filling his overfull jaws, his mouth opening and closing with the effort. Then the thing's mouth opened so wide that something popped back out and lay balanced for a minute on his lower lip—

It was a toe. A pinkish-gray, cheese-doodle curve of a middle toe.

The toe lay curled on the man's lip, then fell to the ground.

Watching it fall, Clete thought, *This little piggy had roast beef, and this little piggy had none.* Then whispered aloud, "And this little piggy cried 'wee, wee, wee' all the way home," his whisper rising in volume as the thing chewed once more and swallowed, then reached into its pocket again, grabbing for more little treats.

Clete tried to stop shaking. Let the curtain fall and tried not to move. He wanted to stay small, to not stir, to stay tucked tight away. He didn't hear his own shrill whispers. Didn't hear the *wee, wee, wee* he kept repeating again and again in the solitary darkness of his trailer.

He hadn't seen the exact moment the trucks' back doors rolled open.

One minute he peeked outside, and the doors were down; the next time he looked, the doors were up. With their doors open, the two trucks stood black and empty, like the square mouths of two abandoned mine shafts leading straight into hell itself, tunnels the red-haired man could follow right back home in his shiny black car.

Staring out the window, Clete tried to see into the darkness of those trucks. He began to make out details he hadn't seen before, shapes arranged along one of the inside walls. He squinted and looked again. Thought, *Bunk beds?* Yes, the shapes looked like stacked bunks now—three levels of them, from floor to ceiling. As his eyes adjusted to the darkness, he could see other forms emerging—subtle, almost hidden forms that looked like short upright columns. They looked like they were growing out of the trailer walls and standing on the bunks.

He blinked several times and leaned forward. Then he saw: it wasn't bunk beds; it was built-in shelving—three rows of shelving running the length of the wall and into the darkness toward the front of truck. Each shelf was filled with short columns of cylinders, rows of them, lined up side by side on the shelves. The cylinders stood still and silent, like squat nozzle-topped soldiers. Looking closer, he saw something else: a design of curved lines printed on each cylinder. When the lines finally came into focus, he saw that it wasn't a design. It was letters. The same letters as on the outside of the trucks: C.N.G. *Clean. Natural. Good,* thought Clete, remembering the words painted on the sides of the trucks.

"Sure," he murmured. "You fuckin' betcha."

AFTER THE DOORS opened, the blue-eyed things hadn't come out right away. Nothing had happened for most of the morning. Clete had seen the open doors, then spent the next few hours peering out his window, trying to see deeper inside the trucks. Then one of the things had stepped into view. When it stepped out of the dark and onto the ramp, it surprised Clete and he'd jumped straight back, tripping over his chair and falling hard on his ass. He slammed the floor with his hands, almost screaming with rage, but then slapped his hands over his mouth and screamed nothing at all—

Hoping he hadn't already made too loud a sound.

Hoping he was still being small.

Hoping they hadn't heard him stir.

MORE BLUE-EYEDS appeared throughout the morning, most of them coming out one at a time, others in groups of two or three. Maybe the groups were families, Clete thought, maybe still acting out of habit, their bodies still filled with the muscle memory of doing things "together." They moved slowly, as if listening to someone who was telling them how to walk, how to put one foot in front of the other and take a step. They shuffled to the roll-up door, then waited at the top of the ramp, not a single one of them blinking in the sunlight.

No wonder, thought Clete. *Not with their own bright little blue-fire eyes.*

They walked down the ramps the same way they'd walked to the door, in a slow, shuffling gait. Most of them were walking alone, but a few stayed in their groups, all of them leaning awkwardly forward as they made their way down the sloping ramps. Large gaps of time separated the descending groups because as one group started down, the next waited until the ramp was empty. When they were all finally down at the bottom, they waited there, grouping back together in a crowd. They stood in silence, as if waiting for instructions. Wanting to hear again from whatever they'd been listening to before.

Then they heard it.

Clete saw the reaction to the message he couldn't hear moving through the crowd. But, after seeing what they began doing, he could guess what they'd all heard inside their blue-eyed zombie heads. *Hey, everybody! Let's go driving!*

THE BLUE-EYEDS were walking faster now, were becoming more comfortable with movement. Clete saw the one he'd watched earlier reach deep into his pocket again, grabbing another grimy handful of tippy-toe crunchy-munch. *Hot damn!* Clete thought. *Look at that one. Walking and chewing at the same time.*

It didn't take long for them to get to their cars and sit down inside. Then, once seated, they just sat still, staring emptily ahead through their blue eyes. The ones who'd walked alone, sat alone. The ones who'd walked together, sat together. They all looked like they were enjoying a long drive in the country.

The cars' trunk lids all popped open at once—

What in holy shit? Clete jumped backward again, almost screaming again, but at least not falling on his ass this time.

Somebody was knocking at his door, had maybe been knocking for quite a while. He'd been staring out the window, concentrating on the trucks and the cars. He hadn't seen anyone walk to his door. *Anyone or anything*, he thought. *There're a lot of "anythings" out there, too.*

The knocking was light and fast, the sound of one finger tapping against the doorframe, like maybe one of the blue-eyed bastards had suddenly remembered how to knock on a door. Like maybe one of them wanted him to open the door so they could croak, "Trick or treat," and grab themself a big handful of Clete's own gobble-toes.

Clete reached for the pistol on the table, planning to make sure that whatever was out there got a full 9mm. load of "trick" before it got anything else from him. Then he heard something that stopped his hand, freezing him where he stood, making him now wish that it was only some hungry blue-eyed asshole at his door.

"I cannn hearr youuuu," he heard the red-haired man saying. "I cannn hear youuu in there." Then—the finger still light-tapping on the door—he heard, "Clete. Clete. Clete. Clete. Clete." The red-haired man was calling his name, saying it fast and sharp, making it into less than a word, turning it into nothing but a sound. Into a single point of repeated noise.

Hearing the red-haired man calling him, Clete shuffled in the dark to his door. Unable not to answer. Moving slowly. Walking alone. Wondering what instructions he would hear.

He opened the door.

"Hey, Clete...trick or treat!" said the red-haired man, stepping into the room.

Did you know, the red-haired man had asked him, that there are places in the world where from the moment you're born, your life's role is already known? Places where you can only become whatever your family already is, where your life can only be that which came before you. Imagine all the types of babies, their lives already decided, their professions already established: plumber-babies, shopkeeper-babies, doctor-babies, grocer-babies, and even, at the very last, beggar-babies...and how wonderful it is to be a beggar-baby.

When a beggar-baby is born, the family passes it back and forth among them. As each person holds the baby, they happily break one of its bones. With each broken bone, the family smiles and kisses the baby's little forehead, maybe even dabs a drop of celebratory wine into its shrieking, gasping mouth. The baby is handed around and around, until it is time to break the final bone...the backbone.

When its back is finally broken, when the baby is now a gruesome, screaming deformity of a child, and everyone cheers and is happy—because they've done the best they could do for the child. They have given it the best chance it could ever have of being a successful beggar. They've broken its back for love.

Only for love.

All for love.

STANDING IN his trailer, looking into the man's blue eyes, Clete knew in his heart that the man understood *so much*, that he knew Clete would do anything for his missing sons.

"Your sons are so near," the red-haired man said. "So very near. But first...first, something small."

Clete looked deeper into the red-haired man's blue eyes. He felt the love for his sons in the man's voice, and he answered with the words he knew were right: "Anything. Everything."

"I need the help of one of your boys," said the red-haired man. "Do you think that one of them might help? Do you think one of them might—" but he was speaking to an empty room, because Clete had already gone to get a son, to get his boy Renny to help however he could.

To help for love.

Only for love.

285

All for love.

Returning with Renny, Clete saw the red-haired man standing by the window. He was peering through a small gap in the curtains, standing to one side, the same way Clete stood when he was peeking outside. The red-haired man didn't look up when they came into the room but just went on staring out through the curtains. Then, as Clete watched, the red-haired man pulled the gap closed, then flipped it open again. He did this a few times—open, closed, open, closed—did it enough times for Clete to know the man was playing a game. Then Clete realized the game was for his benefit, that the red-haired man was playing with him, was doing an imitation of Clete spying out his window.

The red-haired man—still standing to the side of the window, still opening and closing the gap in the curtains—turned and whispered. "Peek-a-boo, Clete. Peek-a-boo-boo," he said, laughing as he spoke, letting Clete know it was all in good fun, that they were still great friends.

Then the red-haired man abruptly turned to Renny. Stared into his eyes. Said, "Renny, I'm serious when I ask you this—

"Renny, do you know the monkeyman?"

LATER, AFTER hearing what the red-haired man wanted, Renny and Clete stood close together, grinning and happy, Clete feeling so happy for his boy—happy that Renny was going to help the red-haired man, and happy for himself, too. For being so close to finding his two missing sons.

"Soon," the red-haired man told him again. "So very soon."

Renny was happy, too. "Like shooting fish in a barrel," he said. "Only monkeys, instead. A big barrelful of monkeys." He pointed his finger like a gun and made ricocheting bullet noises, going *ksshew, ksshew*, and then making noises like the squeals of a little dying monkey, doing it again and again until all three of them were laughing so hard that Clete could barely catch his breath.

RENNY

32

HOURS LATER, after talking with his father and the red-haired man, Renny was still smiling, was still feeling happy about being able to help. Was thinking, *This sounds great! This is gonna be fun!* Maybe not as much fun as some of the other shit he and his brothers had pulled over the years, but still damn good. At least this thing was something new, something not even Simon or Creel had done before—and he couldn't think of a single reason why not. No, he could only smile and wonder, *How had they missed this?* And how lucky could he be, that he got to be the first? This thing seemed like a given, like something they would have already done years ago as a prank just to kill some time. Because by now, when his list of All-Time Favorite Things To Do included shit like rape, robbery, assault, rape—

—*laughing out loud when he listed rape twice, remembering what Creel had said the first time Renny helped his brothers grab a woman. Creel'd said it when Renny was crawling off the crying bitch and Simon was crawling on. "Don't buckle up yet, little brother. Just get back in line. After all, go once or go twice, it's all the same price"*—

—because with a list of hobbies like those fun little ways to pass the time, Renny couldn't help but wonder to himself: Why hadn't he already enjoyed a little monkey-murder?

AFTER THE THREE of them had finished talking, he walked back to his trailer. Floated, really, feeling thrilled, feeling really, really good. Maybe feeling so good, he told himself, because now he had the chance to get out of the hole and do something different. Or maybe because he was getting away, even for a little while, from all the weird shit going on. Or maybe he felt so happy because—after looking into the red-haired man's eyes, after looking down deep into the man's blue-fire soul—he wanted to make the red-haired man proud of him. And also, in the end, he was doing it for his dad: He was doing it out of love. *But, hey, whatever the reason, a man can still enjoy himself, too, right?*

As he walked into the trailer, the fresh excitement had his dick rocked up like blue steel, ready to poke holes in concrete. Or, even better, to poke a few holes in a pretty piece of ice—a strawberry-blond piece of ass and ice. *Yeah, a poke at the Princess sounded perfect.*

It wasn't like she'd be hard to find.

She'd still be in bed. Still curled up in the same voiceless ball he'd left her in this morning, just like every morning, her arms folded tight over herself, not letting him have a little squeeze-and-pinch like he liked. Giving him nothing. Acting exactly the same as she'd been acting for the last few years. At least when Simon and Creel had been here, it'd been easier to push some cooperation between her legs. Hell, anymore, with all the shit she made him put up with—all her little "please, please" cries, all her little tears and screams—well, it was just plain embarrassing.

Not only was it embarrassing, it also pissed him off. Who the hell did she think she was? More importantly, *whose* did she think she was? Because no matter what she thought, he had a newsflash for her: *She was his now.* She was in *his* trailer, in *his* bed, between *his* sheets. But even with all of that being a total hundred percent true, the bitch somehow still seemed to think that she got to make the rules.

Well, tonight he had another newsflash for the Princess: It was time for some New Fucking Rules. He smiled, then, thinking how correctly he'd phrased that: "Time for some New *Fucking Rules.*" Indeed it was. Time. For *his* New Fucking Rules.

With his cock in full lock-and-load position, he went to the back room. Unable to keep from laughing in his excitement. Eager to teach her some manners. "Rise and shine, lil' love of mine," he called out. "Wakey-wakey!" And sure-as-shit, there she was, just like he thought. Still in bed. Arms still folded tight. Body all balled-up in a little bump, just like he knew he'd find her. It was all so predictable with her, so unsurprising. At the heart of things, that was her real problem: She had no new ideas. Had no imagination. Lucky for her, though, he could help with that—because tonight he had enough ideas for everybody.

LATER, WHEN he was resting—after he'd wrapped his hands in her hair and pulled her head up to where he could whisper in her ear and tell her, "School's out," then slap her scratched ass—that's when he started considering what tools to take with him tonight. And then hot damn if he didn't get the happy-giggles again, because that was when he got a mental picture of himself sneaking up to the monkey cage and whispering in his best Elmer Fudd voice to an off-stage audience, "Beee vew-wwy quiet. I'm monkey-huunnntting." *And that was the difference between him and the bitch. He was the one with a sense of humor.*

Once he started laughing, he couldn't stop. The joke was just too good, was absolutely hilarious. He said it out loud to the Princess while poking her with his dick, holding it in front of him like Elmer's blunderbuss, thinking that even she'd enjoy the laugh. "Beee vewwwy quiet," he'd said. "I'mm monkey-hunnnting." *Poke. Poke.* But, no, even funny shit like that didn't register in her brain. *Proving again,* he thought, *how seriously messed up in the head she was. It was a shame, really, how she couldn't enjoy the simple things.*

GETTING READY wasn't hard. The hard part was the waiting— waiting for dark, waiting for the town to fall back into its nighttime coma, waiting to get going. He didn't need to take much, just bolt cutters and his mini-crossbow. That was all he actually needed...the sheath knife was something extra, something for a little fun...for when he scalped the little fucker.

He waited till midnight, then drove carefully into town. He paid attention to everything: the clouds covering the moon, the dark shop fronts, the empty sidewalks and streets. Even paid attention to the silence filling the air.

He started getting excited again. Excited about the fun he was going to have. And about the idea that he might even have a little more fun later, after he got home. Thinking that maybe he'd play with the Princess again—that maybe this time they'd play with some of the things he was planning on using tonight. Things like the knife.

He parked his truck in a spill of darkness under an overhanging maple on the far south side of town, along one of the outer streets. Then pulled on a long overcoat and slipped the cutters and the crossbow into the coat's big pouch-pockets. Crossing the street, he threaded his way through the shadows along the edges of the sidewalks and alleys.

It was amazing how quiet the night was, how dead the place felt. Hell, if he wanted to, he could walk down the middle of the street whistling "Yankee Doodle Dandy" and he'd bet no one'd even notice. It was like walking in a ghost town, with everyone all tucked up tight in their little beddy-byes, their ears plugged full of sugar plums or whatever other crap they dreamed about.

It felt like he was invisible. Like he was some dark angel of death.

It felt perfect.

HE SAW the cage across the street. Looking at it, he couldn't believe his luck. Felt like falling on his knees and shouting, "Thank you, Jesus!" because this was just about too fuckin' easy. It was a fuckin' *gift*, like getting the keys to a bank and being told, *Have a good time. Take all you need.*

It was un-damn-believable. The cage door was standing wide open. But compared to what else he saw, the open door was nothing. He could have cut through the padlock with his bolt cutters in no time at all, so the unlocked door was good, sure, it was a bonus that made life easier, but it wasn't even close to the whacko-world hot-shit *jackpot* that was *in* the cage—

The pretend-Indian asshole was fucking *sleeping* in there.

From here, not only did the pretend Indian look asleep, he also looked naked. Naked and undefended. "Say 'Hello,' Big Chief," Renny whispered as he started across the street. "Say 'Hello' to the Happy Hunting Grounds."

THE UNLOCKED padlock was hanging on the open door. No need for the bolt cutters tonight. Just the crossbow and knife. He set the cutters down outside the cage. Pushed the door open a little wider and stepped lightly through. The door swung easily on its hinges, making the soft gliding sound of well-oiled steel.

Well, well, well, maybe the Indian wasn't just sleeping after all. Up close, he looked passed-out drunk, lying slumped over just to the left of the door, his back pressed against the cage bars, like he'd fallen asleep while watching the monkeys. His long hair hung over his face, moving in time with his heavy, rattling breaths.

It wasn't hard figuring out what had happened. First, the fake Indian had gotten tanked up on actual firewater. Then he'd decided—with a drunk's perfect logic—to sleep it off in the cage with all of his monkey buddies. Maybe he'd wandered through town, naked and unnoticed, all the way from his house to here. Or maybe he'd taken off his clothes as he walked, dropping them along the way. However it'd happened, he'd arrived at the cage wearing only his birthday suit, because there wasn't a single piece of clothing anywhere. Once he got here, he'd unlocked the door, stepped inside, and sat down. Then the dumb prick had forgotten to lock up after himself.

Renny looked down at the unconscious, prone drunk. *You poor, stupid asshole,* he thought. *Don't you know yet? Don't you know that it's a big old, bad old world out here? Don't you know you should always lock your doors?*

BUSINESS FIRST, then fun.

First: Shoot the monkey.

For whatever reason, the red-haired man wanted that big ol' monkey dead, so that was the first job. Put an arrow through the monkey's chest and watch it die. Then he might cut the cap of skin and fur off its skull as a souvenir. Maybe later he'd sew the monkey scalp over his truck's shifter knob. And since he was already planning to do some cutting, maybe he'd also snip the monkey's paws off with the bolt cutter and give them to the red-haired man as a present.

Then, after the monkey was dead, he could have some fun with Ol' Imitation Injun Joe. Maybe even snip something off him, too—and maybe give it to the Princess as a present.

He reached into his coat and pulled out the mini-crossbow. It was a beautiful thing, its black steel blending into the night, almost disappearing in front of his eyes. It fit his hand like a pistol, the sweet machinery making no noise at all as he cocked it back and fit a six-inch steel arrow into the groove. Unlike the bow, the arrow didn't blend into the night. It gleamed like a small silver sword. He had a full quiver of them—forty-five silent slivers of moonlight.

Looking at the loaded crossbow, damned if he didn't almost get another case of the giggles, thinking *Beee vewwy quiet* again.

He walked across the cage floor and looked up at the ropes and monkey-box hanging above. The ropes were empty, without a single monkey shape slumbering in the netting. They must all be in the wooden box, sleeping in a cuddly monkey ball, feeling safe and hidden.

Well, the hidden monkeys weren't a problem. From this close, the arrows would fly straight through the wall of the box and bury themselves deep inside the soft, dozing monkey bodies. He might kill quite a few before the rest of them figured out it was wakey-wakey time. Once they started running out of the box to get away from the surprise of steel and the blood all around them, well, that was when things would get really fun, because that was when he could really share the love. He'd brought forty-five silver treats…enough for the whole class.

He aimed at the floor of the monkeys' sleeping box. Was squeezing the bow's trigger when he heard something…the soft gliding sound of well-oiled steel. Then heard the smallest *snick* of noise. Swiveling around, pumped with a sudden surge of adrenaline and anger, he leveled the crossbow in front of him, ready to shoot the drunken Indian *right now*. Ready to shoot the freak right in the back as he tried to get away. But, instead, was surprised by what he saw. And didn't understand how things could have changed so quickly—

The cage door was shut.

And the padlock (*snick*) was locked.

The lock was swaying, like someone holding it had just let go. Except no one was there. The drunk was gone. Then Renny saw a shadow move, saw it rushing toward him, the shadow was running fast, coming at him on all fours. "Monkey!" he said out loud, recognizing the charging shape as it crossed the floor in an instant, almost making it to him before he could aim the crossbow low enough to shoot the monkey before it got past him. But the monkey didn't swerve around him. Instead, it ran straight at him, and he saw its arm swing up, saw the quick flash of something in its hand, arcing toward his face…and in the moment between recognition and impact, he thought, *Padlock?* then the lock hit his temple and his finger reflexively pulled the crossbow trigger and the arrow flew right straight into the wall of the hot tub along the wall of the cage, and he thought, *What the—?* as he sank to his knees and swayed there a moment, stunned and confused, his body wanting to stand again, wanting to GET UP! but he saw the heavy padlock swinging at him again like a metal fist, and then heard the hollow *tunk* of the steel lock hitting his forehead, the sound echoing deep inside his skull. And he heard the crossbow clatter on the ground, but didn't know when he'd dropped it, and then felt himself crumpling, folding slackly to the floor of the cage, hitting the concrete hard. He heard the slap of his cheek as he hit the floor, but he was still conscious, still thinking, still seeing what was going on.

Lying on the floor, he could feel the cool concrete against his cheek, could smell the disinfectant lemon soap that the floor had been scrubbed with, could even feel the prickle of a single piece of straw pushing into his chin. He felt all of these things…which meant he wasn't dead, but he also knew that he must be hurt pretty bad, that his head must be messed up big-time—because he was seeing some really crazy-assed things, things that made no sense at all, that had to be some sort of fucked-up hallucination. Because he was looking at the monkey and it looked to him like the monkey was…*fading*—

—no, not fading. Fading was wrong—

—the monkey was *drifting*. Drifting in and out. And flickering. Flickering and changing in front of his eyes. Becoming something else. Something taller. Something different. And then it wasn't a monkey at all—

It was an Indian. A goddamn Indian, standing naked in the center of the cage, still holding the padlock in one hand. Now, though, seeing the man's face, Renny could see that it wasn't "Chicory-the-Imitation-Injun." No. It was someone else. Someone not drunk, not even a little bit. Someone standing steady and quiet. Someone looking down at Renny, studying him. Renny watched as the Indian took a step toward him, walking soundlessly past the crossbow on the floor. And Renny immediately felt so happy that the Indian didn't stoop and pick it up. Felt so happy the Indian wasn't going to shoot him. Began hoping that maybe the Indian was going to leave him alone.

But then the Indian knelt beside him.

And Renny felt the tug of his knife when it was pulled out of the sheath on his belt. And could feel his hair being grabbed and pulled, felt his head being lifted off the floor—

—and just before he felt the blade against his throat, before he could think of something to say, of something to beg, he heard the Indian whisper in his ear. Heard him say, *Be very quiet.*

Then felt the knife slide through his neck.

Felt the knife's edge biting deep.

And then felt nothing at all.

THE INDIAN stood by the body. He stretched his arms to the sky, reaching as high as he could. *Battle—it felt good.*

And it felt good to be standing straight again. Good to be tall again, to move as a man. Setsu had been a good skin, but it felt good to move and bend in his first skin again, to slip it on after waiting so long. He said his name aloud to the night, feeling the name in his mouth, hearing it in his ears. "Always One More Arrow." The name was good to say. Was good to hear. A warrior's name.

Yes, this skin felt good to wear.

A warrior's skin.

A skin for battle.

Now it was time to leave, time to find the man at the Circle, the man who also heard the child's cries. But, first, before he left, he would answer the message he'd been sent. He picked up the crossbow and the spilled quiver of silver arrows. He studied the bow a minute, figuring out its workings, then fit an arrow into the bow's grooved slot and cocked back the lever, pulling the string taut.

And began stitching his reply.

LATER, STEPPING into the darkness, the warrior shifted again, putting on another skin that he'd worn so long ago. His limbs and muscles remembered the shape, his body blending into it with sinewy grace. He would wear the warrior again, but now he needed speed, needed to move through the night.

The panther came to him. He felt the change as its skin slipped over him, forming itself to him, shifting, letting him see through golden eyes that captured details other eyes would miss. Letting him hear with ears that caught the faintest, most faraway sounds.

His massive padded paws made no sound along the empty streets as he ran through the town. His black, furred body disappeared into the darkness like a forgotten dream, like a movement barely glanced at. Something elusive. Almost unseen—

Then gone.

33
COLE. NANNY TINKENS. THE ROCKMAN

"**O**NE MORE DAY."
The words described everything to King Cole—
One more day to pan gold.
One more day to walk in the woods.
One more day with the Rockman.
One more day with Nanny T.

And only one more day before his parents came to take him home.

Like he'd done yesterday, Cole woke before dawn and went out to the woods. He hiked quickly, hurrying to get to the stream. The branches he pushed away from his path were slick with dew. Each day, as the morning warmed, the dew performed a brief magic just for him. As the sun rose, the woods became loud with the sound of dewdrops falling—it was the sound of a hidden rainstorm, an unseen mystical downpour, haunting and far away in the early quiet. The invisible storm came and went quickly. In one moment, its pattering sound echoed through the trees, in the next, it disappeared and left only memory. As the dew-rain fell, it never touched him, the drops always seeming to fall somewhere around him, leaving him dry in the eye of a storm he could not see.

He took the path he always took, his body remembering the way, moving instinctively, automatically bending low beneath hanging brambles and vines, his feet smoothly stepping over a hopscotch tangle of bushes and fallen branches. Like a forest animal, he watched the woods around him, looking into the velvet green-brown shadows. Today, out of the corner of his eye, he saw one of the shadows pause, then saw it start to follow him. And he knew he wasn't alone.

It was the big coyote, the one with the scarred black muzzle. It slunk alongside him, keeping to the farthest edge of his sight, blending into the underbrush, making no sound while keeping pace with him. Now, looking again, Cole saw that he'd been wrong. It wasn't only one coyote. There were more—a lot more, all moving together like a single gliding beast. Then the beast split apart, its solitary shape dividing as it flowed around four close-growing trees. The single animal split into five silent pieces of the same dark cloak, then it knit itself back together when it moved past the trees.

It was a pack.

Following him.

Watching him.

He'd been followed before. The big one had been around for days. But today was different. This was the closest it had ever come. And, before, it had always been alone.

Maybe it was his imagination, but he sensed the coyotes knew he'd seen them. And, now seen, they seemed to move closer to him. And they weren't as silent as they had been earlier—he could hear their footfalls now, their paws scuffing across the ground. At lighter places in the shadows he could see their faces turning toward him, returning his stare. Their eyes locked with his, their mouths drooping open in wild canine grins that mocked him and told him they knew how frightened he was. That told him they knew he wanted to turn around and run back to the cabin. That they knew what he really was—just a little cry-baby, ready to run home and surrender his last day in the woods, hiding under the covers of his little-boy bed.

The coyotes were right: he was terrified. Even as he continued forward, he felt the burn of fear growing in him, felt his legs tensing to sprint away. He could feel the push of hot tears behind his eyes as he saw that the pack was slinking even closer, on both sides of him now. Worse, his path ahead was blocked. The trunk of a huge fallen oak lay across his path, its dead branches sticking up like the slats of a forest fence. On other days, he'd climbed onto the trunk by grabbing one of the thick branches and pulling himself up, then made his way across the tree by threading his body between the dead and brittle branches. But today the branches looked like they were set closer together than before, like there was no space for him to slip between them.

He stopped and turned around, then walked slowly backward toward the fallen tree. The coyotes were on both sides of him, grinning big smiles of teeth and tongues. Stalking through the underbrush, they came closer. He stopped walking backward when he felt his shoulders press against the fallen oak.

Trapped and scared, he watched the beasts come nearer.

He stood still and waited. Thinking. Trying to decide.

Trying to decide what *not* to do.

"PEOPLE ALWAYS get it wrong," his dad had said two years ago, holding him close, letting him cry against his chest. "Usually, the best thing to decide—the first thing to decide—is what you are *not* going to do."

Two years ago. He and his best friend Dean had been enjoying a summer Saturday. Like always, they were doing their favorite thing—riding their bikes. They rode everywhere. Even their nicknames were about bikes: *Dean the Bean and His Pedaling Machine* and *Let's Roll Cole.*

Like always, they were racing. That day they'd raced down the big hill on Tulip Tree Road and made the sharp right turn at the bottom onto Magnolia Lane. They'd practically flown down the hill and were leaning into the turn, trying to keep up their speed for the final straightaway. Coming out of the turn, they rose off their seats and pumped their legs, trying to regain lost speed and be the first to cross the finish line on Bayberry Street, each boy pedaling hard, both of them looking down for an instant, then both looking up at the same time and seeing the rope that was stretched tight across the street. The rope was at handlebar level, exactly the right height to cut into them and throw them off their bikes. Even now, two years later, he could remember what it looked like: a multi-colored taut line of tied-together jump ropes, big clumsy knots joining three different lengths of fluorescent pink, green, and yellow ropes.

Pulling hard on both ends were the Hugo boys. All four of them. The Hugos had big kernels of yellow teeth filling their mouths, giving them field-corn wedges for smiles. The yellow smiles were what Cole saw first—wide yellow smiles on dumb red faces, looking stupidly happy, waiting for Dean and Cole to crash straight into the line.

It didn't happen. Instead of hitting the rope, *Dean the Bean and His Pedaling Machine* and *Let's Roll Cole* dumped their bikes, both of them braking hard and leaning backward, falling onto the road and sliding, their momentum carrying them under the line. As they slid, the skin on their legs and arms peeled off, rolling up in ragged tendrils, leaving bright wet scrapes of pink flesh, peppered with gritty bits of asphalt shrapnel.

As Dean and Cole shakily stood, the Hugos doubled over laughing. Andy Hugo, the oldest, a year older than Cole, had always tormented him, was always pushing and tripping him, always throwing rocks or dirt clods. Was always making fun of his name: "Colin? COLON? Isn't a COLON just about a complete asshole? So doesn't that make you a walking, talking rectum? Huh, COLON?" Then would always yell, "Something sure smells brown!"

Wounded and stunned, Dean and Cole began hobbling home, a trail of little red blood-buttons marking their path. Cole heard Andy calling behind him. "Now that's what I call an ass-wiping! Huh, COLON? That's what I call a real shit-smear!"

COLE'S DAD, washing his car in the driveway, saw them first. Saw their scraped and bleeding skin, saw the bits of the road embedded in their flesh, heard their pain-filled breathing and cries. He immediately knelt down. Put his arms around both boys. Held them until their explosions of sobs died down. Then he led them inside to the bathroom, sat them down on the edge of the bathtub and began cleaning their wounds. With Cole's dad crouched beside them, lightly dabbing a sterilizing sting of hydrogen peroxide on their skin, they told him what happened.

Behind his father, his mom screamed as Cole talked. "Riffraff! Vermin! Hillbilly trash!"

When he finished with the bandaging, his dad stood and looked at Cole's mom. "I'm going to go talk with a few people," he said. "You stay with the boys. Maybe get everyone some ice cream." Then he walked out the door and turned in the direction of the big curve at the bottom of Tulip Tree Road.

HIS DAD was gone for quite a while. Long enough for everyone to finish their ice cream. Long enough for Dean's mom to come and take him home. Gone so long that Cole began worrying…what if all four Hugos jumped his dad? And what if their dad did, too? Their dad was a big guy who had a weight bench in his garage. The garage walls were lined with hallway mirrors so that the Hugos' dad could see his muscles growing. He rolled the garage door up every night to make sure everybody in the neighborhood could see him exercising, and as he worked out he had his boys add more weights to the bar he was lifting, having them call out the count each time he pressed the bar above his chest, wanting the neighbors to hear how strong he was.

Cole was worried. What if a guy like that got into a fight with his dad?

Then he saw his dad walking home.

And his dad looked fine.

301

WEEKS LATER, *after Cole had had fourteen fights with Andy Hugo, after he'd begun pushing and tripping and kicking and fighting Andy whenever he saw him, after all the other kids on the street had deserted Andy (at first because they'd become afraid of Cole's sudden and unhesitant ferocity, afraid he might decide to fight them too, then later because they no longer feared Andy, because they no longer felt his power), that was when David Steaters—the crippled kid living across the street from the Hugos—told Cole that he'd seen Cole's dad walking to the Hugos' house on the Saturday Cole and The Bean were hurt. David said the Hugos' dad was lifting weights in his garage when Cole's dad walked in, that the Hugos' dad had thrown the weights on the floor after Cole's dad had said something. Then Cole's dad had turned around. It looked like he was leaving, but then he reached up and grabbed the garage door and pulled it down hard, making it bang and bounce against the concrete floor when it hit, closing the two men inside the garage.*

"That's all I actually saw," David said, squinting as he tried to remember more. "But even with the door closed, I could still hear something. It sounded like glass breaking—a lot of glass breaking." And Cole had remembered the mirrors, then realized that the Hugos' garage door was no longer opened at night. That, for weeks now, the neighborhood's nights had been silent, with no one hearing the clang of heavy weights sliding onto a bar, with no one braying out the count of the lifted metal.

WHEN HE RETURNED from the Hugos, Cole's dad walked into the house without a word. He held his hand out to Cole, and Cole took it. His dad led him back into the bathroom and closed the door, leaving his mom alone in the living room. Cole sat down on the edge of the bathtub again, and his dad sat across from him, on the closed toilet lid.

"Well, King Cole," his dad said, "the Hugo kids say it was an accident. They say they were just playing tug-of-war, and that you and The Bean came around the corner too fast for them to do anything. Andy Hugo says he's worried sick about the two of you. He says that he hopes you're both okay."

Cole felt his heart breaking. He knew it was a lie, but didn't know how to prove it. Didn't know the words to tell his dad. Then his dad spoke again. "Of course," he said, "they are completely fucking lying."

Cole couldn't help it. He started crying again, only this time with relief, with the surprise of hearing his dad so bluntly say what Cole knew was true. And even though he was crying, he was laughing, too, unsure how to react, wondering if he could say, "Fuck, yes!" or if that would still be against the rules.

Then his dad reached over. Pulled him to his chest. Told him, "People always get it wrong. Usually the best thing to decide—the *first* thing to decide—is what you're *not* going to do."

COLE WAS QUIET. All he could do was look up at his dad's face.

"Let me tell you how things stand," his dad said. "Mr. Hugo and I talked. And now he's going to talk with Andy and his brothers. He's going to tell them that from now on, only Andy and you are involved in this. And no one else in the Hugo family is going to get between you two—not the brothers, not Mr. Hugo, not even Mrs. Hugo. What all this means, King Cole, is that now it's just Andy and you—and I am giving you full permission to win. But first you need to decide: What *aren't* you going to do?"

While he talked, his father pulled paper from the toilet roll, gathering a pad of it into his hand. He dabbed the wad of toilet paper on Cole's face, wiping away the tears. "Son, these are the last tears you'll ever cry about Andy Hugo. Decide right now not to do it again. Decide right now not to give that asshole any more tears."

When Cole's face was dry, his dad shifted Cole back to the edge of the tub. "The truth is, you can't decide not to be afraid. Everybody feels afraid. But you can decide not to run away. And you can decide not to wait for the next fight to start, and not to let Andy be the one who starts it. And you can decide not to be surprised if you get hurt when you're fighting, and not to stop fighting when it happens. Most of all, you can decide not to ever let another Andy Hugo make you lose a single moment's joy—or, at the very least, not to let them have it for free. Because you can decide that the price of messing with you or your family will never be worth the hell that you'll make them pay. And then, King Cole, after you've decided all the things that you're *not* going to do... well, the rest is really simple."

THE COYOTES were grinning more widely, their lips pulled back, showing jagged clamps of teeth and black gums. They were closer now, standing behind a thin lacework of brush, their mud-smeared muzzles poking through the wall of weeds. Their open mouths glistening with hanging strings of drool.

Cole could hear their panting, could feel the warm cloud of it wafting over him, moist and heavy with the decayed, meaty scent of carrion. They were watching him. Smelling his fear.

And he *was* afraid.

But he was also pissed—pissed that they were stealing his "one more day." Pissed that he was scared. Pissed that they were enjoying this. And pissed that he was trapped, his exit blocked by a wall of branches.

So he decided—

Decided what not to do.

Decided not to wait.

Decided not to run.

Decided not to let them win for free.

Moving quickly, he spun around and grabbed hold of the branch that was pressing into his spine and wrenched it backward. The branch was long and solid and thick, but the quick force of his pull snapped it off at the trunk, giving him a weapon. Raising his staff over his shoulder, he turned and ran straight at the big coyote. Screaming a war song, he swung at the animal's head.

The coyote ducked easily, dancing back from the attack. As it moved, Cole was already running left, swinging the stick low in a sweeping arc at the two coyotes standing there. The one nearest him jerked sideways and pivot-jumped, rising on its hind legs and turning. But the coyote beside it crouched down instead of jumping away, and the first one tripped over the second one. The two of them got tangled up together, then they both landed awkwardly on the ground, scrambling for a moment in a tangled ball of fur.

Still charging, Cole let his sideways swing carry through and up, lifting the staff over his head, then slashing it back down, hammering the branch across the middle of the two coyotes and hearing a sharp bark of pain. Then he immediately swiveled right, holding the staff in front of him, ready to fight—

—but the other coyotes were gone. The area was clear. Only the big coyote remained, staring directly into Cole's eyes. The two of them stood there, considering one another.

Cole stepped forward, holding the branch out in front of him, ready to stab and parry. The top of the branch tapered to a sharp, natural point. As Cole advanced, the coyote retreated, taking one step back. Cole took another slow step forward, and the coyote took another step back. It was still grinning, still staring into Cole's eyes, acting unafraid, but also keeping a specific distance between itself and the boy, as if it wasn't allowed to come any closer, as if listening to something that commanded, *Not yet, not yet...*

Sensing this hesitation, Cole sprang forward, a fast launch of boy and stick aimed at smashing the smile off the coyote's face, wanting to blind the eyes that were looking at him so hungrily. But again the animal evaded him, running from Cole's charge. This time though, the coyote didn't turn again to face him. Instead, it melted into the underbrush, disappearing so quickly that Cole almost wondered if had been there at all.

HE TURNED, again heading toward the stream.

He kept the stick in his hand, liking the strong, straight feel of it and deciding to use it as a walking staff. At the fallen oak tree, the branches along the trunk no longer seemed to barricade his way. He climbed up onto the trunk, pushing himself up with the help of his stick, then wove his way between the branches and jumped down on the other side. That's when he heard the first sounds of the morning's invisible dew-rain begin rattling down through the canopy of leaves. The drops fell softly at first, then built to a torrent. The rain sounded closer than usual, as if it was coming toward him. As the storm approached, the boy paused, expecting the chilling shock of it to finally drench him. He felt his skin dimpling with goose bumps, anticipating the cool touch of rain. But before it reached him, the dew-rain ended, quieting somewhere very near, but still somewhere that he could not see.

HE SAW the Rockman's body.

Arriving at the stream, he looked down the bank and saw the body lying face up near the water. Although no tree branches stretched across the creek where the body rested, the Rockman's clothes were wet with night dew. His bare arms and face were hard and unmoving beneath the lace of drops that covered them.

Cole jumped down the steep bank and ran toward the still body of his friend. As he ran, his shoes threw plumes of fine creek sand into the air behind him. He yelled, filling the woods with his cry of surprise and grief. And at the sound of Cole's yell, the body stirred. The eyes blinked. And the massive arms flexed, their braided muscles lifting the thick hands up off the ground. The hands wiped the dew off the sun-browned and wrinkled face, then the arms fell to the body's sides and pressed against the sand, pushing the torso upright with the sound of a waking groan.

With his eyes still half-closed, the Rockman stretched

and turned to Cole. Shocked silent by his friend's miraculous resurrection, Cole stood, rooted in place beside the water.

The Rockman blinked again.

"Morning, Cole," he said. "Everything okay?"

THE ROCKMAN had slept all night at the creek, wanting to see Cole before he went back home. Wanting to give the boy a present. Today, he waited until this last day ended, after Cole had spent the day gold panning while the Rockman worked nearby. As always, the Rockman had dug up geodes, cracking the bigger stones into glittering crystal sprays, then stacking the smaller rocks into pyramid piles along the stream. He waited until his friend was ready to leave, until the two of them were shaking hands and beginning to say good-bye.

That's when the Rockman pulled at the leather cord hanging around his neck and lifted it over his head, pulling the gift from beneath his shirt. Holding the pendant in his hand for the last time, he gazed at the crystalline colors of storm and light wrapped in the shine of gold and copper wire. Then slipped the cord over Cole's head and let the pendant hang down from his friend's neck.

"This," he said. "Take this."

RETURNING to the cabin, Cole spotted Nanny Tinkens sitting outside in her chair. The early evening sun wrapped her in the warm orange and red blanket of dusklight. As the sun continued to set, the light became heavy and liquid and slow, settling contentedly to the earth and becoming still, preserving everything—for a moment—in twilight amber.

Nanny looked at her grandson's walking stick, then at the pendant hanging outside his shirt, the arrowhead shape of it resting over his heart. Smiling, she reached out and lightly laid the palm of her hand over the stones. She pressed gently—as a priest cups an infant's forehead, asking a blessing on the child —and Cole felt the pendant's uneven, pointed back pushing through his shirt. With her hand still softly against the pendant, Nanny looked into Cole's eyes.

"A good day?" she asked.

"The best," he answered. Then felt surprised when she said, "And still more things to do, still more places to go."

HE SCOOTED his chair close enough to hers that he could hold her hand, and they sat side by side, watching night come. They unwrapped round cinnamon candies and sucked on them, melting the treats into thin discs of clear hot sugar with an edge sharp enough to cut his tongue.

When the moon was above them, she released his hand. "Time to go," she said. "Time for you to see the Circle."

THEY'D NEVER "gone seeing" together. Had never "seen" anything at the same time. He hadn't known it was possible. Had never imagined they could. But they did. Holding his hand again, she whispered "*Si! Si! Si!*" as they settled back in their chairs, both of them beginning to "clear" and "conjure" and "connect."

She spoke in her mind and he heard her in his. His thoughts were filled with her words. "Stay close," she told him. "See with my eyes. Stay in my thoughts. Follow me to the Circle."

He did what she said.

His sight moved outward. He felt his vision open to what she was seeing, felt himself traveling beside her. He saw their flight between the trees. Saw the night animals in their path. Then felt the course of their journey turn upward, to the top of a hill.

And he heard sounds—crickets, the scuttle of night feet. And, again, he heard the lion's roar, far away and filled with strength and challenge. He felt the power and courage of the lion's declaration, the daring sense of its announcement to the darkness. *Here. I am here.*

Nanny spoke to him as they traveled, saying, "Look there," and "See this?" He looked where she pointed and saw the things she gave him to remember, lodged memories of them in his mind to mark the trail.

Then he heard the song.

It seized his heart, drawing him closer and closer. He felt the sad music of it carrying him, felt his spirit swelling with sorrow, making him want to give comfort and join in the singing...join in the sounds of love and age, of long travel and journey's end. The song filled his young heart with loss and grief until it was almost too much for him to bear. The song pulled him to the hilltop, with Nanny racing beside him. He knew she was feeling the same draw, that she was caught in the same song and also rushing upward.

There, at the top of the hill, he saw the Circle of Stone pillars, and, seeing them, he heard the song anew, suddenly realizing that it came from within the Stones, realizing the living hearts that they must hold. In the moonlight he saw the Stones glowing white and then even whiter with the pulse of the song. Then saw them grow dark with long, sad pauses.

As he watched and listened, he realized that Nanny's voice had joined the song. In his mind's eye he saw her glowing white and then even whiter, then saw her grow dark with the song's long, sad pauses. Without knowing how, he knew that miles away—sitting in a white wicker chair in the middle of a field of flowers and night— he knew that tears were now falling down her face, falling in a soft rain that he could not see.

He felt his heart beating. Beating so strongly in his chest that it seemed to bump against the pendant hanging on the cord around his neck. And he knew that in the darkness where his body was sitting, in a chair in a field near an old house, the pendant was moving in concert with his pounding pulse, moving as if it held its own crystal heart...a heart that glowed white and then even whiter, and then became dark with long, sad pauses.

34

NANNY TINKENS.
THE MATCHMAN. COLE

S HE KNEW...
Knew it when she heard the car in the drive.
Knew it when she heard the footsteps on her porch.
Knew it when the knock fell on her door and she went to answer.

Thinking about it, she'd known all morning. Had known when she'd heard Cole's footsteps slipping past her door, going for one last quick walk in the woods. Deep down, she'd thought, *Good. Stay far away. Stay hidden and safe.* And she'd known as she stood sipping her kiss of cinnamon tea and staring outside at the two chairs still pulled close together in the yard, remembering the night before, when they'd gone seeing together. *At least he saw the Circle, at least he heard the songs.* And she'd known as she sat at her table and looked out the back windows at the dawn drifting down through the trees. The light poured and billowed on the ground as she watched and thought, *It has all been so beautiful. It has all been so true.*

For months she'd felt it coming, had sensed its approach. And this morning, the moment she'd opened her eyes, she'd known it would be today. The only question she couldn't answer was *How? How will it come?* But now, glancing out the front window as she went to open her door, she knew that answer too: her death had come in a black car. A black car painted with blue letters.

As she opened the door, the first thing she saw was the haystack of his bright red hair. Then his blue eyes. And in those eyes, she saw that he knew, too.

THE MORNING sun's rising light was still so faint and creamy that his eyes were brighter than the sky behind him. They were twin blue fires burning in the pale white oval of his face. Looking at him, she saw that his skin was quivering on his bones. It twitched and pinched as if it was alive and eager, readying to spring.

Looking deeper, she saw something else moving beneath his skin. It was another skin, inside, lower down, a second skin made of scales and membrane and teeth, writhing under the white top-skin wrapping he was working so hard to keep in place. The second skin's long teeth were tapered shadows inside the same mouth that now opened and smiled, saying, "I am just so happy."

As she watched, a fan of black spines split through his cheek skin momentarily, then slipped back inside. "Oops," he said, still smiling at her and reaching up to smooth the cheek-flesh back down, pushing at the torn edges until the ripped seams knit themselves together before her eyes and again covered whatever was sliding and moving below.

He pointed at the two chairs in the field. "Let's wait together for the boy," he said. And then, as she walked ahead of him, she heard him singing, "I see the moon and the moon sees me. The moon sees the somebody I want to see."

When they sat in the chairs, he took her hand in his, and she saw the shape of his fingers closing around hers. But it wasn't the touch of fingers she felt clasping her hand. It was the rough burr of leathery hide, and the hard, curved edges of claws.

SITTING WITH HIM, she tried to keep her sight inside her, not letting it fly beyond. With him holding her hand, she knew that he could follow her sight. Knew he would find Cole if he saw where she flew. So she sat very, very still in her chair and tried to fill her thoughts with jangled verses and nonsense songs—making certain that her mind didn't "clear," making sure she didn't "conjure." And most of all she tried to forget what she'd seen while walking to the chairs, tried to erase it from her thoughts and pay no attention to what she'd spotted moving in the bushes near the woods. Tried to entirely forget the picture her mind had taken of Cole's walking stick, the top of it moving slowly back and forth in the tall weeds.

COLE WAS watching. He was kneeling in the weeds, staring out from where the big coyote sometimes hid itself. He'd walked back from the stream, moving fast, trying to get home, thinking he might still be early enough to make Nanny a cup of her tea before she woke up.

He'd almost stepped into the clearing, was already at the edge of the brush when he saw her walking out of the cabin. Then he saw the man in the black suit following her. The man was smiling and singing children's rhymes, but even from clear across the field, the man seemed....wrong. His eyes were too bright. His hair too red. And his so-white skin was moving, rippling like moles were burrowing beneath it. Or like snakes were crawling through his veins.

Without thinking about it, Cole had dropped silently to one knee. He felt unnoticed and safe here until he realized, seconds later, that his walking stick was still in his hand, that he was steadying himself with its upright length...and that it was sticking straight up, taller than the scrub around him. It looked like a pushpin marking the spot where he was hiding, telling everyone, *Here! He's over here!*

Through the brush, he saw that the red-haired man and Nanny were sitting in the chairs. They were looking directly at the woods, staring exactly where he knelt.

THIS MORNING, he'd woken early, remembering what he'd forgotten the day before. After the Rockman had given him the precious gift, Cole had left the stream immediately, thinking only of the pendant, excited about showing it to Nanny. In his hurry, he'd left all his tools behind—his pan, his shovel, even his vial of gold (almost full!). Everything was still at the stream.

Wanting to retrieve his things, he'd known he had to be quick, that he had to get to the stream and hustle back. Getting dressed in the dark had been easy—he'd slept with the pendant on (he thought he might never take it off) and his clothes were all in the suitcase on the dresser, packed to go home. Nanny had folded them into sharp cloth squares, putting his jeans on one side and his shirts on the other. He'd dressed and then—holding his shoes in his hand—had tiptoed past Nanny's door.

It was early when he left, darker outside than the "just before light" kind of dark he usually walked in. But he'd grabbed his stick and gone, wanting to be back before Nanny woke. Wanting to be ready when his parents came.

NOW, LOOKING out from his hiding place, he saw that there was something good. And also something very bad.

Good thing: There was a handful of thin, solitary trees growing scattered in the scrub. His stick, held as steady as he could hold it, resembled one of those skinny trees.

Very bad thing: While his Nanny watched—saying nothing, not even screaming—the man was changing. Was becoming something else. His skin was stretching thin, being pushed out from inside, and as it stretched, it became translucent, revealing something darker beneath. Cole saw something burst up for a moment, slicing through the man's face and hands before sinking back down like it was hiding between the folds of a torn blanket.

Not knowing what to do, Cole waited, trembling, making the stick he was holding shake more than the saplings around him

313

were shaking. He waited, looking for a sign from Nanny. Waiting for some signal or some way to help her. And while he knelt there waiting, Cole saw something that was worst of all—

His parents pulled into the drive, honking their car horn in "hello."

"LOOK, NANNY, happy times," the red-haired man said, turning his head at the sound of the horn, "Company has come calling." Then added, "Awww, look, he loves her so..." as her son waved from across the field, then walked around the car and opened the door for his wife.

The red-haired man stood up quickly. As he dropped Nanny's hand, his fingers split and melted into a dark yellow and black claw that surged out of the skin. He looked down and she saw that his face was tearing, too, that something bigger and sharper was rising in its place. But whatever it was becoming, it still regarded her with the same bright blue eyes, and somehow that was most frightening of all.

"Back soon," its mouth said to her. As it spoke, the mouth pushed out and filled with teeth. It looked away then, turning toward the car.

"Please, please," she screamed, hoping it would stop, wanting it to wait.

And hearing her scream, it stopped and turned enough so that she could see the lid of one blue eye drop slowly down, winking at her from inside the ridged folds of the yellow leather and scales into which the red-haired man's face had melted. Laughing, it sang again. "I see the moon and the moon sees me." Then it swung away from her and started walking toward the car.

IT KILLED his mom first.

It wasn't hard to kill her, not really. Neither his mom nor dad hardly moved as they watched it coming at them. He saw it wave one clawed hand in the air, like it was greeting them. His mom's hand began rising, automatically returning the wave—

Then it pushed a claw through his mom. Pushed it right through her stomach and out her back. She died fast, but not right away. He could hear her sounds—her cries, her screams—for a few moments while it was shaking her up and down on its arm, making her body dance like a mom-puppet.

His dad jumped on it, beating it with his fists, attacking in a fury.

It sliced his dad's throat.

Cole saw its claw reach out slowly to his father, saw the claw flick back and forth in the air, as if conducting a single musical note. Then blood sprayed out from his dad's neck. But at least there were no sounds this time, no screams and cries. At least none he could hear from across the field.

Then it turned away from his parents. Began walking back to Nanny. That's when Cole realized he was screaming. And running. And charging with his spear pointed right at the monster. But he wasn't running fast enough. He could tell he wouldn't get to Nanny before the thing did. Then he felt his arm lift the spear as he ran, felt himself hurl it forward, launching it into the air, sending it streaking across the field. He kept running the whole time, charging toward the monster, moving faster than before.

Then he heard Nanny begin to scream.

SHE HEARD Cole screaming. Could hear the blood anger in his cry. She turned away from the horror of what had been done to her son and daughter-in-law, turned away from the horror now lurching toward her across the field. She looked where Cole had been hiding. Saw him running at them, attacking with his stick— coming to save her. She watched him throw his spear. Saw it flying in an arc across the field, its point hurtling near to where she stood.

And she remembered again what she'd known this morning. So she screamed at him, "Cole! Run! Go!" then turned back to the beast and began walking at it, still calling, screaming again and again, "Cole! Run! Go!"—

She saw the shadow of the spear cross the ground beside her, the flying black needle of it slipping over her own shadow and flying ahead. Looking up, she saw the spear slicing down from the sky, aimed straight at the heart of the beast.

The spear point struck against the beast's chest and—

—shattered in an explosion of splinters, like a glass arrow smashing into iron. Still screaming, "Cole! Run! Go!" Nanny stepped in front of the beast and threw both of her arms up against its shoulders, pushing it back with all her strength. Above her screams she heard it still singing "I see the moon and the moon sees me" as it pierced her arms with its claws and held her out, lifting her feet off the ground.

Now she saw it look over her head, looking where Cole now stood. Its blue eyes returned to her. It winked, then whispered in her ear, "Try singing your song now, old woman."

She wanted to yell to Cole again. "Cole! Run! Go!" But she was suddenly so tired. And the light was suddenly so bright. And the smell of the beast's breath filled her nostrils as its mouth came closer to her face. Then she felt the touch of its teeth and heard the sound of things breaking, and thought, *Me. That's me. I'm breaking. Into tiny, little pieces.* She could feel them, could feel each of the tiny little pieces of herself breaking off and falling away. As the pieces fell, she felt a heaviness lifting from her bones, and then felt all the tiny bits of her rising on an unseen breeze. And now felt herself wrapped all around in the touch of a warm wind. And, just as she'd thought this morning, she thought again at the very last. *It has all been so beautiful. It has all been so true.*

WITH HER EYES closed, she felt the wind carrying her higher, felt the touch of sun and sky on her face. Then felt warm lips pressing against her lips, and she smiled at the taste of cinnamon that filled her mouth. Eyes still closed, she raised her hands and held his face against her face, kissing him again. Then he touched her eyes with his lips, kissing them, too. She opened her eyes and saw that he was standing in the same bright sun that she was, and then he reached out and took her hand, and they began walking away together. Walking somewhere warm. Walking somewhere green. And she felt like she could walk forever, walking beside her long-leggity man.

COLE HADN'T run away.

He saw the spear explode. Saw the thing grab Nanny and hold her. Saw it looking at him with its bright blue eyes. He'd seen its head dip down, and he'd looked away just long enough that when he looked again, it had thrown Nanny to the ground and was walking toward him now. Getting closer and closer. As he watched, he felt himself grow still, like his feet were turning into roots that went far underground, roots that stopped him from moving or running away.

It raised its claw, waving to him, and he felt his own arm lifting. He was almost waving back when he heard Nanny's voice in his head, her cry filling his brain. "Cole! Run! Go, Cole! Run! Go!" and he stumbled back at the shock of her yell. His feet became his own again, his legs began working again. And now, free to run, he ran straight at the thing walking toward him. He ran three steps forward and stopped, facing it fully, already knowing what he would *not* do. "NOT LIVE," he yelled. "I will NOT let you live," he screamed, then turned around and flew, running into the woods.

As he ran, he heard it crashing behind him, throwing the trees out of its path.

Cole ran with an animal's grace, a communion of mind and movement. He saw deadfalls that needed to be jumped and his feet were already jumping. He saw clear paths between the trees and his body was already running to where he looked. He never slowed down, never stopped, but heard it still following him, getting closer and closer. So he ran faster, running without thought, instinct guiding him. Guiding him to the stream.

And still it followed, even closer than before.

He saw the stream. Saw it through a break in the trees and down the steep bank. Thought he might make it, thought maybe he was going to slip away, and in an instant, he was through the break in the trees and jumping over the edge of the bank, and when his feet hit the ground, he was already running again—

—but he tripped, his right foot landing on an uneven mound of sand that made him stumble, awkwardly falling forward in his speed, unable to right himself before his legs tangled, sending him crashing and tumbling down the bank, rolling into the shallow stream, his head snapping forward and down—

—and in that heartbeat of time, he saw that he was going to hit the stacked pyramid of small geodes that filled his vision. In the stretched-out slow-motion moment of his fall, he had time to see the smallest details of the pile of pretty stones, time to see the glittering rainbow spray of water that surrounded him, just before—

His forehead smashed into the rocks.

First he saw a brilliant flash of light.

Then saw a dark cloud engulf the light.

And then he saw nothing at all.

HE WOKE once more, but only for an instant. For the space of twenty heartbeats, he became aware of where he lay. In those twenty heartbeats, his eyes opened long enough for him to see the claws. And as his eyes closed again, he felt teeth closing on the back of his neck. And as the twenty heartbeats ended, he saw no bright flash of light this time. This time there was only darkness. And, after the darkness, again there was nothing at all.

GORDY. SHERIFF MATSON

A FTER BLUE called him, he stayed awake for hours, unable to sleep. He lay in the darkness, thinking about what Blue had said—about torn animals and words written in blood and black cars traveling the roads. He remembered the sound of Elissa crying in the background and the hard sound of Blue's voice on the phone. Thinking about these things, Gordy knew that Blue was already planning the hunt, was already considering the pursuit of his prey....

HE FINALLY drifted to sleep. Was deep asleep when the phone rang for the second time that night. Was still asleep when it rang again and he slapped at the receiver, knocking it onto the floor. From somewhere under the bed, the phone kept ringing. He could feel himself coming awake, a cloud of foggy thoughts now starting to sift through his brain. He groped for the phone, pawing in the darkness, wondering who was calling. *Blue again?*

His fingers finally found the handset and he pressed it to his ear. He only had time for a raspy "Hello?" when an excited voice began streaming out of the phone, a flood of words pouring out without pause. He listened, trying to understand, but after a few seconds, he decided that maybe he was wrong—maybe he wasn't awake yet. The longer the voice talked, the surer he became that he must still be asleep, that he was probably still curled up in his bed and right smack-dab in the middle of some loony-ass dream. And when this dream ended, well, maybe then he'd dream another even crazier dream, full of crazier shit than the crazy shit he was hearing right now.

The glowing red numbers on the clock on the nightstand flipped from 3:59 to 4:00. He still had one more hour before the alarm would buzz. Then he realized that the voice on the phone had stopped talking. It was his turn to speak. He answered automatically, filling the pause with what he always said on emergency calls like these. "Okay, I'll be right there."

He dressed in a hurry. All that he remembered of the phone call were strange words that somehow still blurred the lines between dreaming and being awake. The words that were like the refrain of some freakish, long-forgotten children's poem: *Murder, monkeys, arrows, knife. Padlock, pincushion, crossbow, life.*

And there was one more thing he remembered. A possible piece of very good news. Something for him to hang onto and hope it was real. The possibility of it made him run to his car. He wasn't completely sure, wasn't exactly certain what he'd heard, but it sounded like there was the chance that one of the Glammery boys might be dead. And, dreaming or not, that sort of good news was always worth rushing to see.

IT WOULD BE dark for at least another hour, maybe a little longer. He'd finish with the business in town, then drive straight over to Blue's. It would still be early, but he'd sit in their driveway and wait for them to wake up. While he waited, he'd watch the cars that passed their drive, watching for a black car that might return.

Speeding toward town, his headlights dug two narrow round tunnels into the deep night in front of him. Staring ahead, he felt like he was plunging through the center of a black column. Or driving into a bottomless hole.

In town, everything was muted and shadowed. It looked like a landscape of dreams and made him wonder, *Is this real?* But he only wondered until he arrived at the Monkeyhouse and saw the sheriff's car and the town ambulance already there. *Real as real can be,* he thought. The parked vehicles' flashing strobes painted everything blue-red-blue-red-blue-red, making it look like a carnival funhouse. But this funhouse was a little different from most. This one had a body on the floor.

THE SHERIFF, Tim Matson, met him at the cage door. "Good," he said. "Dispatch find you?"

"A few minutes ago. At home. Truthfully, though, I'm not sure what's going on here. The message was a little confusing. Dispatch was...excited."

Tim nodded. "Sounds about right. Shirley's always been a little excitable. And this—" he gestured inside the cage, then stepped through the door. "This is definitely a little confusing."

The ambulance crew stayed near their vehicle, waiting for Tim's signal before coming in, so for now, he and Tim were alone in the cage, looking at the body. It was Renny Glammery. Or it had been "before"—before he was beaten in the head with a padlock, before his throat was sliced open with a knife, before he'd been shot in the back with forty-four tiny little arrows. Before all of that.

An arrow had also been shot through the hot tub. Water had leaked out, soaking Renny and washing his blood across the floor to the drain in the center of the cage.

"What do you think?" Tim asked.

"What's to think? This one's easy," Gordy answered. "Looks like a clear case of serial suicide to me."

"RENNY WAS padlocked inside," Tim said. "Whoever did it knew the combination."

Gordy didn't even have to think about it. "Well, to someone

without the benefit of your keen legal insight, that would seem to narrow your list of suspects considerably. Sounds like you'll be having a little conversation with the owner—and then, case closed. But I want you to know, I already support every alibi he gives you—even the ones including flying saucers and Bigfoot. I promise you that I'll testify whatever he says is God's honest truth. Unless he says something stupid—like he feels sorry. Or that Renny didn't deserve it."

The sheriff nodded. "Normally, sure, I'd talk to Chicory. Normally. But tonight's not exactly normal."

"I know at least one person who agrees with you," Gordy answered. "Show of hands: Everyone who thinks that tonight's not a normal night? All in agreement?" He used the toe of his boot to lift Renny's right arm off the floor so the hand dangled limply. The wet arm made a crisp tearing sound as it came up from the cement, like duct tape pulling off a roll. "Why not talk to Chicory?"

"It turns out that Chicory doesn't need your generous offer of an alibi," Tim said. "Not tonight, anyway. He was already in jail, sleeping off a monumental drunk. He's been in a county bunk all night. Wandered in earlier, drunk as a skunk. Said he'd been seeing monsters." Tim looked over at Gordy. Shrugged. "Anyway, I let him stay over. Rent free." The sheriff tilted his head at the street. "He's in the car now. He's the one who unlocked the cage door for us."

Looking at the car, Gordy saw the silhouette of a man in the back seat. As he watched, blue and red stripes rippled across the man's face.

Tim squatted and wrapped a hand around one of the arrows in Renny's back. He pulled on it evenly, moving it back and forth, trying to work it free. Eventually he stood up and wiped his hands on his pants. "Shit," he said, "that ain't going anywhere."

Gordy nodded. "I asked Chicory to stay till you got here," Tim said. "Figured you'd want to talk with him."

"Me? Why me? All this fun is entirely yours, O-Great-Protector-Of-The-Town."

"Yeah, yeah, O-Worshipful-One-Of-Nature." Both men grinned. "You're right, this part of the Glammery fun is mine. They're next on my list to talk with. But in case you didn't notice, Mighty-Forest-Ranger-Man, we're missing some monkeys. And every single, hairy one of those furry, banana-eating escapees is *your* problem."

CHICORY DIDN'T look at him as Gordy slid into the front seat of the cruiser. Instead, he looked out the window, staring at the cage. "He did it," he said, his voice like a small child's, filled with amazement and wonder. "He got out. Like the vision. He got out."

"Who, Chicory? Who got out?"

"Setsu. The real Indian. Setsu. The first monkey." The words were a whisper. "He read the notes. He read them and he got out."

Gordy kept his voice low and steady. "It looks like they all got out. That's what we need to talk about. We need to figure out how to get them back."

"No," Chicory said, "Not good. Not now. Not until...." His voice trailed off, getting smaller and smaller until it disappeared completely, following his thoughts to some other place.

"Until what?" Gordy asked gently, trying not to push too hard. Sensing something worth waiting for. After a few seconds he asked again. "Until what, Chicory?"

Chicory kept staring, saying nothing. The red and blue lights were still flashing, filling the inside of the car in strobing washes of color.

Gordy saw Tim step out of the cage and wave to the ambulance crew. The crew moved fast, entering the cage and efficiently lifting Renny—face down—onto the collapsible gurney they placed beside him. One of them snapped open a gleaming-clean sheet above the body. The white square of cloth floated down slowly, changing from a sheet to a shroud as it wafted lower. It drifted onto the arrows and settled over the body. The arrow shafts under the sheet, made it look like the sheet was covering a sleeping hedgehog. Or a circus tent filled with tiny tent poles.

The flashing lights created moving shadows and the distance gave Gordy a different perspective than he'd had staring directly down at the body. It allowed him to see something he hadn't noticed before. Something that had been there all along.

There was a shape on Renny's back under the sheet, an outline created by the arrangement of the little arrows. Rather than being hidden by the sheet, the shape was revealed by the covering. It was the shape of a single arrow. An arrow with a broad, sharp point and a narrow, feathered shaft. It was a simple picture, made with sticks, but it had a certain power.

Gordy stared from the car, entranced by his discovery. Was so focused on the arrow shape that he almost didn't hear when Chicory began speaking again.

Chicory could see the arrow, too. When he spoke, he spoke to it rather than to Gordy, and as he talked, his voice was filled with whispered awe, the voice of someone realizing something wondrous and terrible at the same time, of someone who's solved a secret puzzle. "Not a good idea at all," he breathed. "Don't catch him. Not yet. Not until…." He shook his head slowly.

"Not until what, Chicory?"

"Until he kills the beast. The beast in the black car. The beast walking on the hill." Now started, Chicory didn't stop. He kept talking, telling Gordy about the things he'd seen—about things that drove past the cage at night, about things that flashed blue-white-green, blue-white-green, blue-white-green.

As he listened, Gordy saw that the sun was beginning to rise, its light beginning to slant across the street and creep up the side of the car. He saw the dawning light, but didn't feel its heat. Instead, he felt only the cold that filled Chicory's story—the cold void of cars painted like black mirrors, the cold touch of moonlight on a lost child's sneaker, the cold flame of eyes filled with ice-blue fire. And the cold certainty in his heart that what he heard was true. As

Chicory spoke, Gordy remembered flying squirrels and climbing coyotes and the stories Blue had told of a Stone Circle on the hill, with wild magic flowing all around.

He listened, knowing that he needed to see Blue *now.* That he needed to go to him immediately and tell him what he'd learned. Needed to tell him about the hill and whatever was walking there now. And he needed to tell him about the black cars that were coursing slowly through town. And he'd tell Blue about the monkey, too. About Setsu. The monkey that read notes. And picked locks. And turned into an Indian. And then killed Renny Glammery.

CHICORY SAT with his head down, slumped against the window, exhausted and near sleep. Trying not to disturb him, Gordy carefully opened the car door. He was almost out when Chicory spoke again, asking a single question, a question that only Gordy could answer. The question surprised Gordy, but he thought about it for a moment and then answered. Hearing the answer, Chicory smiled and nodded, then settled back into the seat again, already falling asleep as Gordy quietly closed the door.

Now alone in the car, Chicory murmured in his sleep, repeating the same words again and again. "Thank you," he said softly. "Thank you."

DRIVING TO Blue's cabin, Gordy decided that there were two kinds of magic: the magic you notice, and the magic that you hope never notices you. And, thinking this, he saw something he almost wished he hadn't. Not yet, anyway, not before he'd talked with Blue. Passing a mailbox, he automatically glanced up the drive and saw a car parked near the road, and farther up the drive, nearer the house, another car. A black car. All the way from the road, he could see blue lettering across the black car's trunk: *NOW YOU'RE COOKING WITH GAS!*

Without understanding how everything could have changed so quickly, he understood though that it had. The hunt Blue talked about last night had already begun. Here. Now.

He parked just up the drive, not far from the mailbox. The name TINKENS was painted on the box, but he didn't recognize the name. Couldn't think of the family. He started walking toward the black car. As he walked, he couldn't stop from wondering: Had he noticed magic? Or had magic noticed him?

He drew his weapon, walked holding it pointed at the ground, ready to aim at any sound.

But there was no sound.

He found two bodies in the tall grass near the first car. The bodies were torn and flayed. Walking quietly toward the house, he listened intently, but only heard his own footsteps. Past the black car and the house was a small field. In the field he came to another broken body, this one sprawled by a red-spattered chair. Walking through the field, he still heard only the sounds of his own passage. There were no other noises. No crickets or bees. No birds or animal calls. Not even the brush of leaves in the breeze. Then, faraway—for only a moment, then for a moment again—he heard a single faint sound, a murmur so distant and light that at first he thought he was imagining it. Then he heard the sound again and recognized what it was. Screaming. Coming from somewhere in the woods.

HE STARTED walking faster, a lot faster, and found a trail in the field, a path of broken sticks and bushes. The path was a record of running and following, filled with signs of the hunter and the hunted. He followed it into the woods, walking slowly again, carefully, looking ahead. Then heard screaming again, closer this time. And like whoever had first fled down the path, he began running too—running toward whoever was hurt, running to whoever needed his help.

The path was clearer now, easier to follow, and he could see where both prey and predator had grown less cautious. Then he came to where the prey began stumbling, and where the predator had grown excited—where it started taking longer steps, hurrying to the kill.

The path led to a break in the trees up ahead. He ran, bursting through the opening—

And saw it…whatever it was.

Saw it sitting hunched in the stream.

Saw that it was eating.

And in that instant, two things happened. He heard a new, but familiar sound. Something close and loud, cracking in his ears. At the same time, he saw everything that had happened. Saw tracks in the sand where the beast had run to capture its meal. And saw the body that was being consumed...he saw the person it once was, the person it would never be again.

Now he recognized the new sound, that loud, cracking in his ears. It was his gun. He was holding it steady in both hands, firing again and again at what he saw. As he fired, part of him stood like an instructor to one side—judging his reactions, advising him on his technique, counting his rounds, counting "...14, 15, 16," then watching him eject the empty magazine and grab another one and slam it home, leaving only a breath of air between the shots. Then it started counting again, "17, 18, 19." As it watched him, his instructor told him that his stance was good. That his arms were locked. That his aim was true. And that the beast would fall. That the beast would most certainly die—

But it didn't fall. And didn't die.

The bullets kept going into it, but the thing didn't flinch or move. Didn't even look up.

Until now.

Its snout rose out of the basket of broken ribs it was nuzzling.

Gordy saw its bright blue eyes staring at him. Crazily, dreamily, he thought, *Noticed. I've been noticed,* then he watched as the thing stood and started changing. Its yellow and black hide began to pale and whiten. Its wrinkled leather skin began smoothing and drawing tight. He saw another shape begin forming. The thing that had been hunched over a red-splintered corpse now straightened and became a man-shape, a red-haired man now waving one hand at him, waving and walking toward him.

The instructor in his head ran through his options, then gave him one last piece of advice, advice it had never given Gordy before—or, if the advice ever had been given, Gordy had never taken it—until now. Because now there was no other option.

Run!

He ran.

Ran back through the woods. Back to his truck. Away from whatever was following him, away from whatever was calling to him as he ran. Away from whatever was calling, "Run, run! Run as fast as you can!"

So he did.

He ran as fast as he could.

And, looking back over his shoulder, he wondered, *Am I running fast enough?*

BLUE 36

MORNING LIGHT reaches through the window and touches our bed. As soft as the light is, the touch begins to awaken Elissa. She stirs in my arms, her eyes fluttering open and then closed again, her head nestling against my chest. Holding her, looking at the clean gold light across her legs, I simply breathe for a moment as we are held in the warm folds of the morning. There are times each day that are gifts, moments of grace. In those moments, it is important to find peace, to find a sort of holy stillness. Most of my moments include Elissa. She is where I find grace, where I find peace. She is a planet of two suns—one sun above that warms her and holds her and lights her way, and another sun glows from within her flesh and heart. Her second sun is the one that warms me, the one that holds me and lights my way. She is my dawn.

I SLIP FROM BED and go to make coffee, leaving Elissa stretching and turning in her slow dance of rising. In the morning's circle of light and waking and coffee, some things are easily forgotten and other things are even harder to imagine. It is easy to forget my mother's words, the warning she gave last night. *But there are more bad things tomorrow. Tomorrow is a red, red day.* Inside our cabin, it is also easy to forget the painted swirls of blood and gore that are smeared on the outside walls.

In the calm quiet of the day's beginning, it is hard to imagine what might happen today, but it is harder to imagine that something won't. Then suddenly I don't have to imagine anything, because with the smallest of sounds, it begins.

I hear the soft tread of footsteps on my porch.

The sound is faint, so slight, that it tells me more than a loud step would. It is the sound of someone being careful to hide their presence, of someone waiting outside my door to surprise me. Hearing it, I am overjoyed—because whatever it is that I'd planned to hunt and kill today, instead, that thing may have come for me. It might now be within my grasp.

As it takes another step, I reach into the closet by the door. By the time it takes its next step, I'm already holding the shotgun I keep in the closet—a shell always racked in the chamber, the safety always off.

I stand to the side of the door and aim the gun where I hope the thing's heart is. I stare at the doorknob, waiting for whatever is intent on surprise. I wait to hear one more quiet step, the step that will bring it to my door. I hear the step, and then—a heartbeat later—find that I'm the one who is most surprised of all. There's a soft knock on the door, then, hushed and hesitant, my brother's voice whispers, "Blue? Blue?"

CALLISTA is outside, too, sitting in one of our rockers. They've been waiting on the porch, waiting for the sense of someone stirring inside the cabin, for the feel of movement within. They'd parked down the driveway, far enough away that I didn't hear them arrive. But they've been doing more than simply waiting. They've also been standing guard—each one carries a large, chromed pistol. Alassadir is holding his gun at his side. Callista's gun rests on her lap, floating in the field of bright yellow stars that shine across the silky blue sweep of her skirt.

As I was watching over Elissa, they were watching over us.

The three of us stand on the porch. Grinning at each other. Sheepishly acknowledging our weapons. Then the door opens behind me and, dressed in pajama bottoms and an *I Got Mine at Noah's Ark of Love* T-shirt, Elissa steps outside. She walks to Alassadir, seeming not to notice the guns, and reaches her arms around him, hugging him and telling him good morning. Seeing her T-shirt, he laughs. "You should see their calendar," he says and kisses the top of her head. Then Elissa crouches down beside Callista. Saying nothing, she lays her head on Callista's shoulder. I have the sense that they already talk without talking, that there are already secrets that they share.

"Coffee?" I ask, gesturing inside with the shotgun.

"Cream in mine," Callista answers, rising from her chair. As she stands, a ripple moves across the starry universe of her skirt, making it look as though she's walking in the middle of a small night sky, or as though the heavens are supporting her tiny weight.

"Nice hand cannon, Mom," I tell her as she walks by.

She makes a show of dropping the pistol into the deep handbag she's carrying. "Never forget," she says, "I travel with a carnival." And before I can answer her, before we can even step inside—

I am surprised again.

And again.

And again.

There are three surprises.

The first and second surprises happen almost immediately.

The third surprise happens later, but not much later—when the third surprise happens, it is while we are still standing outside on the porch...while we're all talking with the naked Indian who had quietly stepped out of the deep green woods.

GORDY

37

H E RAN, knowing it was following him, knowing it was reaching for him. He ran without looking back. Made it to his truck. Knew to focus only on one step at a time, on each single movement and action. He didn't look behind him. Opened the truck door. Jumped inside. Closed the door. Didn't look up. Inserted the key. Turned the key. Heard the engine roar. Slammed the lever into DRIVE. Didn't look outside. Didn't look at the woods. Knew better than to look at the woods—

He looked at the woods.

He saw the red-haired man. Saw him still in the field, standing by the overturned chair and spilled body lying there. And he saw that the red-haired man was still waving to him, inviting him over. Over to share in what it now knelt down beside. Inviting him to share in what was unspeakable.

He again heard the instructor in his head, heard him yelling, *Go! Go! Go!* And he pressed his foot down. Turned the wheel. Drove fast down the drive. Drove without looking back. Raced onto the road and toward Blue's house, thinking only one thought the whole time. *Guns. We need more guns.*

HE FOUND more guns. A lot of them. Found them after he'd sped up Blue's drive and came skidding to a stop in the not-long-after-dawn light of things and then saw that on Blue's porch there were plenty of guns: Blue was holding a gun. And the two strangers standing on the porch were also holding guns.

At first he thought that Elissa, held tight by one of the strangers, was the only one without a gun. But then he saw that he was wrong. As he stepped out of his truck—holding his own gun—he saw there was one more person without a gun: the naked Indian stepping out from the woods. He didn't have a gun, either.

BLUE

THE FIRST of the morning's three surprises: Gordy arrives. Fast.

After he and I talked last night, I knew he'd come early. But this is earlier than I expected. His truck speeds toward us, sliding to a sideways stop in front of the porch. The circular DEPARTMENT OF NATURAL RESOURCES emblem on his door is facing us. Gordy's expression is a grim smile, like someone already at war. Then I see what he is seeing, seeing it the way he sees it: I see the guns, and the strangers, and Elissa being held by Callista while Cally is holding a gun, too. The minute she heard the truck coming, Cally had pulled it out of her bag.

When Gordy steps out of the truck, I'm not surprised that he's holding his own gun. He points it straight at Alassadir's chest, holding it there as I'm calmly speaking, telling him, "Our side, Gordy. They're on our side." Hearing me, he shifts his gun from Alassadir, moving it only a little, now aiming it past the corner of the porch, toward the back of the house.

"And what about that one, Blue?" he asks. "Is that one on our side too?"

His question makes us all turn our heads to see what he's looking at.

The second surprise of the morning: It isn't a "what" behind us. It's a "who."

Standing at the edge of the woods, an Indian is staring at our group.

Callista and Alassadir draw in sharp breaths. Keeping his eyes on the Indian, Alassadir turns his head halfway back to Gordy. "Hey, Boss," he says in a quiet voice, "don't shoot him, either, okay? That's our team captain over there. It would be great if you didn't kill him."

Hearing Alassadir's words, I know who's watching us: It's the good twin, the twin from the battles of long ago—and also, from the looks of him, from battles not so long ago. There's blood all over his chest, and more blood on his arms. Seeing it, I remember Alassadir's story—a battle always rages, the world is always at war.

Gordy keeps his gun pointed at the Indian. "I need you to be real sure, Blue," he says. His gun is steady, perfectly aimed—I'm certain—where a bullet would pulp the man's heart. "I mean real, real sure," Gordy says again. His voice doesn't quiver, his eyes never leave their target. "Because I've got a really neat story to tell you later about blood-covered things that come out of the woods."

"Gordy, I'm sure," I say. "He's one of the good guys. He's with us."

The Indian steps out of the tree line and walks toward us. His steps are filled with quiet power. He is magnificent. His black hair hangs down his back; its only other color is a thick rope of silver-gray that begins above his left temple. Except for the dried blood on his skin (I see now that it's someone else's blood, that there are no fresh cuts or wounds on his body), his skin is the red of annealed iron, of hot metal cooling after being made strong with fire and hammers. Pale, shiny weals of scar tissue mark his skin, dividing his naked body into crisscrossed chapters of old and bloody stories.

As he approaches, we all stand silent, uncertain of what to do or say. But looking into his eyes, seeing the fierce strength there, I am certain of this: We are going to battle. We are going to war.

So I am surprised by his first words.

Looking at me, he stops at the foot of the stairs. When he speaks, he speaks softly, in the voice of a friend.

"I hear the child crying, too," he says. "I hear the child on Jonah's Belly."

BLUE 39

THE INDIAN'S words shake me. He's heard the child? He's heard the same crying that I've heard? We stare into each other's eyes, and I feel a slow, building shock of recognition—the same feeling I'd felt only yesterday in Callista's wagon, the feeling I'd had when I looked at Alassadir. I see something familiar, something "almost alike" in the Indian's eyes, in his look. Then I remember the rest of Alassadir's story and a sweep of understanding rushes through me—the man in front of me is not just "the good twin." He's more than that.

We share the same blood.

I am part of his line.

He is family.

CALLISTA BREAKS the silence. She pulls off the dark blue shawl she's wearing and holds it out to the Indian. He takes it, nods to her, then quickly ties the shawl into a breechcloth. Clothed, he looks slowly at us, one at a time.

"I am Setsu," he says.

"Setsu?" Gordy's voice is filled with sudden surprise and recognition. "The monkeyman?" There's pleasure in his voice, and his quick, warm tone confuses us all. He holsters his gun and steps forward, holding out his hand. "Why didn't you say so?" he asks, shaking the Indian's hand. He turns back to me. "Blue, you're right. He's definitely one of the good guys."

I'm confused, not understanding how Gordy suddenly knows this man, not knowing what he means by "monkeyman." And I'm even more confused by Gordy's next sentence, when he tells the man, "I've gotta say, I love your work."

WE ALL MOVE toward Setsu, wanting to introduce ourselves, wanting to get closer to the magic we know he holds. But as I step forward, Elissa's fingers circle my wrist, pulling me to her.

"What child?" she whispers urgently. "What crying child?"

And I want to answer her. Want to say all of the right words. The words that will dry the tears I now see floating in the green sea of her eyes. I don't know what the words will sound like, though. Don't know what they should or shouldn't contain. But she needs to hear them. I decide to tell her everything, to make certain she's heard it all, no matter how much of it I myself don't yet understand. I look into her eyes. "There is a child—" I begin—

But I'm interrupted.

By the morning's third surprise.

By something else that steps out from the woods.

LATER, WHEN there was time to remember it all, I'd think about the early part of that morning, when we were all there together on the porch. I'd remember how it felt like so very much had changed in so very short a time. But looking back, I now see how much was still yet to change. And how there was no possible way that everyone could be there at the very end of things.

Later, I'd try again to feel the same sense of awe that I felt in that moment. The sense of being surrounded by the miracles and the magic of the people who were with me that morning. I like thinking that, even then, even in the middle of it all, I recognized and treasured how precious it was—how it was an instant of perfect balance, when we were all together for that moment.

And, remembering that moment, I remember the third surprise... the incredible surprise.

It was the best part of that early morning's magic.

BLUE

THE THIRD SURPRISE.

We hear it behind us. First, as a low growl in the woods, a rising and falling rumble of a call. Then we hear twigs and sticks breaking as something heavy and slow pushes through the undergrowth, moving the vines and tall grasses. We all turn and look where the noise is coming from. We see leaves quivering on the smaller trees, marking the passage of whatever is brushing against them.

Elissa and I recognize the sounds. We remain silent, trying to remember to breathe. Elissa's hand folds into mine, the bump of her missing little finger pressing against the side of my palm. I can feel her pulse in my hand, its beat is so strong that I feel like I am holding her heart.

The growl rises again, full and calling.

"Blue," Gordy whispers. "I think it's—"

"I know," I whisper back.

Just before Grendel's wide, thick-furred head pushes through the scrub, I see his golden eyes in the thicket. His eyes are filled with the same warm love that I see in the eyes of the people standing with me on the porch.

He lowers his head and strengthens the grip of his jaws around whatever he's carrying. He drags it with him through the final curtain of vines, and I finally see what he has brought home. Like everything else he brings us, it is small. And hurt. And bleeding—

—when I first found Grendel in the woods, he was small. And hurt. And bleeding. I brought him home, and we cared for him. And he made us his. After that, he began bringing home all of the others that he found in the woods, all the ones that also needed our help and caring. Usually, it is an injured animal. But this time is different. This time it isn't an animal—

This time he has brought us a boy.

BLUE

ELISSA IS THE FIRST to reach them, the first to tell Grendel, "Good boy, Gren'. Good cat." As she reaches out and gently scratches the cat's black tufted ears, Grendel slowly lowers his head to the ground. He eases the boy down, then releases his hold.

The boy is alive, but unconscious. His forehead is scraped and bleeding and bruised—maybe from running into a low tree limb, maybe from a fall. His shirt is a shredded rag of teeth holes and jagged tears. Where the shirt's pulled up, the boy's exposed skin is scratched and dirty from being dragged through the woods.

Gordy runs into the house and comes back with our bucket of first aid supplies. Elissa's hands move over the boy's limbs, feeling for injuries, and I know that somehow she is already starting to heal him, that something within her is already flowing into him, is already giving him her strength.

With the scissors from the bucket, she cuts the boy's shirt off, revealing his small ribcage. He looks fragile and vulnerable, but his breathing is steady and strong. I see that he's wearing a pendant—a simple arrowhead made of wire-wrapped crystals. It hangs from his neck on a wet leather cord.

Callista kneels beside Elissa at the boy's side. Her eyes, filled with concern, watch the boy's face, then her gaze moves to the purple and gray crystal pendant and she reaches for it. Her age-spotted hand looks ancient as it floats over the boy's smooth, white skin. Her fingers stretch out above the pendant, just above the stones, as if she's afraid to touch them.

"Back again," she murmurs. "Back home to me." She begins crying, her tears rolling down the beautiful lace of her wrinkled face. Her fingers touch the pendant as softly as petals touching skin, and she closes her eyes and whispers, "Oh, my. Oh, my. Oh, my." She continues weeping, crying without sobs or hitching breaths, her tears falling silently.

I don't know why she is crying. I want to comfort her, but wonder if I should allow her time alone for whatever sorrow she is feeling. Then Grendel stands. He's been lying beside us, watching intently as he always does when we help the things he's brought to us. Now, looking at Callista with his golden eyes, he tilts his head and slowly reaches out a massive furred paw.

We all stare, transfixed by him, suddenly aware that we are fortunate spectators at a rare event. Even Elissa, bandaging the boy's forehead, pauses to watch the cat. With his claws carefully retracted, Grendel places his paw on Callista's hand. He touches her as lightly as she's touching the amulet on the boy's chest. The long thick fur on his paw completely covers his foot, flowing down over the pads. His paw is broader across than her hand, and her fingers disappear beneath it. As he touches her, I know that she's feeling the surprise of deep, lush velvet fur on her skin.

At his touch, Callista opens her eyes. She sees Grendel watching her. When she smiles, he leans forward and licks the tears from her cheeks, making a rumbling purr in his throat. After a moment he sits back, still watching her closely.

Callista lifts her hand from the pendant and reaches over to stroke the drooping fur mustache that hangs from the corners of the big cat's mouth. "Thank you," she tells him. "I'm okay now. And I love you, too."

Still petting him, she looks at all of us and draws in a half-breath. "My sister is dead," she says. She looks down at the boy's still body. "And this boy," she whispers, laying a hand on the boy's forehead, touching his bandage with her fingertips. "This boy belongs right here. With us. With his family." She raises her eyes. "He is my great-nephew. And I—I am his great-aunt."

THE BOY—my second cousin—is sleeping on the couch now, covered with blankets, our softest pillow beneath his head. Right or wrong, we are keeping him with us, at least until this day is done. After that, we'll keep him for as long as he wants to stay, until he tells us that he wants to go.

Elissa and Gordy checked him over. Setsu also knelt beside him and felt the boy's bones, looked into his eyes, then laid his own hand over the boy's pendant. Whatever he felt or saw, he did not cry, but he did reach out for Callista. He cupped her chin and looked into her eyes, then leaned over and whispered into her ear. And held her for a moment when Callista whispered back to him, "I know."

After checking the boy, we all agree on two things. First: He will live. He's been hurt, but what he needs now is rest. Second: We will not take him to a hospital. We aren't taking him anywhere. He's staying with us. With his family.

AS MORNING begins fully forming outside, we move to the kitchen. Not much earlier, I'd given Setsu some clothes. My shirt fits him. The jeans are a little long, but with the cuffs folded up, they're fine. It is then—when we are all sitting around the kitchen table, elbow-to-elbow in the company of an ancient Indian dressed in a torn pair of my softest jeans and my FROG MUMMY CIRCUS! T-shirt, when we all are still looking over every few seconds at the sleeping and bandaged boy—it is then that Gordy asks, "Can anybody tell me what the hell is going on? I mean *other* than the dead Glammery, and the shape-shifting monkey, and the 'monster-in-the-woods-that-will-not-die,' and the amazing, life-saving lynx that drags home a hurt boy…I mean, other than all of that, can somebody please tell me what the hell is going on?"

I stare at him. "What do you mean, 'the dead Glammery'?"

Alassadir also has a question. "What do you mean, 'the monster-in-the-woods-that-will-not-die'?"

Gordy takes a slow drink of coffee. Leans back in his chair.

"Hey," he says. "I asked you first."

BLUE

GRENDEL IS STRETCHED out under the table, somehow finding enough floor space among our feet to lie down. He is sleeping, using my foot as a pillow for his heavy head. His long legs are threaded through the puzzle of our chairs and legs. At times we hear the peculiar wheeze of his cat-snore or the scratching of his big feet sleep-paddling in place on the wood plank floor. His paws move as he pounces in his dreams, leaping from hill to hill.

I look around the table, suddenly realizing the simple, necessary thing that has not yet been done. "Gordy," I say, "first, some introductions."

Nodding at each person, I introduce them to him. "My mother, Callista. My brother, Alassadir. And Setsu," I say, "'the good twin'— the one here to stop the bad guys. The one we are going to help."

"Actually," Gordy says, looking at Setsu, "I believe he already clocked in on the job a few hours ago."

"What do you mean?" I ask.

Gordy doesn't answer at first. Just takes another sip of coffee— I've put three full carafes of the hot, fresh brew on the table, offering everyone caffeine to complement the adrenaline already humming in our veins. Nerves or not, the coffee is appreciated—someone is always reaching out and grabbing a refill, then topping off the cups of those beside them.

Gordy puts down his cup. "Like I said before," he says, "I asked you first: What the hell is going on?"

Alassadir answers. "The Circle," he says. "It's about the Circle and the Stones." He pauses then and looks at Setsu—waiting for approval? For permission?

The Indian sits quietly, relaxed and motionless, saying nothing. After a minute, he gives a small smile and a nod. "Yes," he says to Alassadir. "Talk of the Circle. Tell us your story of the Stones."

SO ALASSADIR tells the story again, the same one I first heard between the walls of a Gypsy wagon. He talks again of magic and harmony and battles and sacrifice. When he recounts the two fights between the twins, I examine the rough calligraphy of scars on Setsu's skin. And when my brother speaks of the dying Stone, I see sadness in all our eyes. It is the same story he told before, only this time he tells it with the slight differences that each new telling of a tale always brings. The changes are small, barely there. But they turn the story, shifting it by tiny degrees.

He tells some parts faster, other parts slower. From some parts he takes things slightly away, while slightly adding to other parts. Although I heard the story just yesterday, these small changes make it new. Hearing it this time, told this way, I think different thoughts than I thought before, and different questions occur. I've learned that stories and history are like that—their truths are revealed slowly, often changing with each telling, with each rereading of the page.

GORDY INTERRUPTS the story only once. He turns to Setsu. "But where have you been?" he asks. "All of this time, where have you been?"

Setsu answers simply, "Here. Always here."

"And the other one? Where was he?"

"Somewhere else."

At the story's end, I'm not the only one with new questions. As Alassadir finishes, I look at Gordy, expecting him to speak again.

Instead, it's Elissa who has the questions. "What does it mean," she asks. "A path is built, a way is opened? Path? Built where? A way? Opened to what?" She asked Alassadir the questions, but it is Setsu who answers—

—I'm not yet over the miracle of his presence. I stared at the Indian as Alassadir told his tale. The man sitting beside me, the man listening to the story—his story—is the same person who once fought in a panther's skin. The same one who'd prowled through a long-ago night, walking in silent rings around a circle of old men and fire.

Of all the magic and mystery that have gathered us here, perhaps the most wondrous magic of all is the sense of ease he gives us now, the sense that he is exactly where he belongs—and that we are also exactly where we belong. Yet, as comforting as this sense of things is, as sure as this sense of ordainment feels, when I hear Elissa's questions, and when Setsu begins answering, it isn't comfort that I feel, not certainty or courage. What I feel is a tremor of foreboding, a black contraction in my stomach that draws all my worry to it and churns hot acid across the bile-filled knot. It warms and fans my fear, making it seem about to bloom—

—"What the Circle gives, it gives," Setsu is saying. "But other things—the things we take from the Circle, the things we seek—for those, a path needs to be built. For those things, a way needs to be opened. And for each of those things, a price needs to be paid—a price that's poured into the stream that circles the hill, a price that must be spilled into the ring of salty waters."

As he speaks, he looks at Elissa. I see that his eyes are filled with warmth—and with something else. After a second, I recognize what it is: Sorrow. A deep, ragged pain, pouring from his soul. I know the look, I've seen it before—reflected at me from a mirror, hiding in the hollow caverns of my eyes.

"A path. And a way," he says. "A path that needs built across the stream's ancient waters. And a way that needs opened to the magic."

He looks from Elissa to me. "Each one requiring blood. Each one requiring sacrifice. Each one requiring...a life."

His stare holds me. Something sour blossoms in my gut as I begin to realize something about his sorrow. It isn't only his sadness that he feels—it is ours, too, Elissa's and mine. He's known something that he's carried for us, as his burden alone...until now. Knowing this, I sense that he is now standing with us on a razor's edge, pointing down into the darkness below. I'm certain that he already knows what we will see, that he truly dreads what we must look upon.

Setsu leans forward, closer to Elissa and me. "Two lives," he says. "The price each side pays with the other's blood. The price my brother first paid long ago by darkening the stream, draining the lives from two innocent children. And the price he has now paid again. With two more lives."

Setsu stares into Elissa's eyes. For a brief moment—although I still feel balanced on a horrible precipice—I feel that he is the one who will give us his strength, that he is the one who will help us to heal. "He built the path with your son," he tells Elissa. "He opened the way with your blood."

Hearing Setsu's words, my mind ignites in a dizzying storm of bright flashes. I hear those words over and over again. ... *With your son, with your son, with your son.* I clutch the table's edge with both hands, trying to unhear his words, resisting the screaming vortex that is pulling me away—

—and suddenly I know exactly what razor's edge we are balanced on. My head spinning, I recognize the rocky ledge where we stand, about to tumble down. The ledge is like every other rocky ledge. Except this one is surrounded by small, brown balls of tobacco and gum. This one looks down on a wide, turning bend in the road.

If I look over this ledge, I know what I will see. I know what torn and broken thing is lying at the bottom—my family, our bodies strewn along the stream bank, with the blood of my wife and my son swirling away like red smoke into the water.

Only two things hold me from the drop. Two things keep me at the table, stopping my mind from teetering crazily and then disappearing again along the downward course of a falling brown rock—a rock that crashes through metal and flesh and bone. One thing holding me back from the fall is the comforting anchor of Grendel's head on my foot. I feel his solid weight, and it pins me fast, keeping me here in the kitchen, making me see the solid reality of our table and the coffee and the wood plank floor.

The other thing holding me here is Elissa. Her anguished cry pierces the storm in my head, her shocked expression makes me reach out as she crumples forward. And again—as always happens—by holding her, I, too, am saved. By keeping her from falling, I, too, am held at the top of the abyss, also saved from the fall. Wrapping her in my arms, I feel my balance return, feel the storm in my head subside.

I hold her tight.

Saying nothing.

Knowing there are no words.

WHEN WILL I know her so deeply that I can no longer be surprised? When will I finally be absolutely sure that *this*—*this* is all she can endure? When will I be certain that *now*—*now* is the time to carry her, knowing for certain that her strength is entirely gone? And when will I realize that I will never know, that I will always be surprised? When will I finally understand that there is no wound she cannot endure, and that her heart makes her stronger than anyone else I know?

She lifts her head from my shoulder, her eyes cold and clear, the color of jade wrapped in ice.

"What are you saying?" she asks Setsu. "Are you saying it wasn't an accident that killed my son? Are you saying that God aimed a rock at our car?"

BLUE

"ARE YOU SAYING it wasn't an accident that killed my son? Are you saying that God aimed a rock at our car?"

Elissa's questions hang above us, caught on the barbed silence filling the room.

No one moves or makes a sound. For an eternity of seconds, it seems that only Elissa and Setsu are at the table, that the rest of us have faded into ghosts. Eyes locked together, aware of nothing else, Elissa and Setsu see only each other.

"Not God," Setsu finally answers. "And, no accident."

As he answers, I know that, once again, I am wrong.

Before our son was killed, before my wife was maimed, I held her many times every day. Each time I held her, I spoke the words that filled my heart, always "I love you," and then, "Forever." I knew that I would never have secrets I would keep from her, and was certain that I'd filled each day with all of the "I love you's" that could be said—sometimes I even worried that I'd said it too often.

I was wrong.

Then, after our son was killed, after my wife was maimed, as I held Elissa in my arms and told her "I love you" and "forever" with every look and breath and word, I was certain there were now other words and truths I could *never* say to her, that I now had secrets I could never tell her.

And, again, I was wrong.

Hearing Setsu answer her question so honestly, I know that there are other things she must now hear. And that I must be the one who says them, that I must tell her the secrets I thought I'd never tell. As I start to speak, my words are whispers, spoken so softly I'm not even sure they are mine. "He's right," I say. "It was no accident. And certainly wasn't God."

Elissa and Setsu look at me, bringing me into their world. And now I tell her the thing that I never meant to tell. "Not God— Glammerys. Creel and Simon Glammery threw the rock that hurt you. They threw the rock that killed our boy."

Elissa becomes quiet. Trying to understand. Trying to make sense of my words. The rest of us become quiet, too, giving her time to think. Time to breathe. We drink our coffee. Then look over at the sleeping boy. We settle back into our chairs and stare into the whorls in the wooden tabletop. Then look back at the boy.

My mother is standing behind Elissa. I hadn't seen her get up from her chair and walk around the table, but now she is standing behind Elissa, resting a hand on each of Elissa's shoulders, pressing her cheek to Elissa's hair.

Gordy wants to ask me a question. I already know what his question is, and he already knows the answer I'll give. But he waits, his eyes boring into mine. His throat is pulled taut, as if he's strangling himself to make certain no sound escapes.

Alassadir stares down at the table, also waiting. I have the sense that he's not surprised by what I said. I'm sure that if he didn't already exactly *know,* he at least already exactly *felt.*

Our silent waiting ends.

Elissa looks from me to Setsu. "Something is missing," she says. "You said two lives were needed. But our son is the only one who died—one tiny, little life. Not two. Who else? Who else was killed?"

Setsu had answered her question earlier. Had told her that his brother "built the path with your blood." But she hadn't understood. Couldn't have understood. Not without knowing everything that had happened at the accident. So I share another secret. A secret that Gordy has also kept. Another thing I've never told her—maybe because I couldn't bear the thought of it—the secret that I'd lost her, too, that day. The secret that, for a moment, she was gone forever. "It was you," I tell her. "They killed you, too. You died there in the stream. You died there with our boy."

WHAT MUST it feel like, I wonder, to learn that you died with your child, to discover that the two of you had stood together in front of the heavens, you holding your baby cradled in your arms, gently rocking back and forth in that wondrous eternal doorway, with him cooing as you whispered secrets into his baby ears, with you seeing his baby eyes blinking as he looked at the bright glow of love shining from your face?

And what must it feel like to learn that you were pulled away from your child, to learn that you left him there alone for all eternity with his small hands outstretched, seeking your touch? That you left him alone and crying, his voice crying out for you, wanting to hear your comforting whispers in the sudden nothingness that he saw all around, wanting to see your face again, wanting to see the only light he'd ever seen in the deep and endless night?

I wonder: What must that feel like?

I'd kept the secret. I never wanted her to know. Never wanted her to wonder.

And now I'll do as I've always done, praying that it is enough. I will hold her and speak "I love you" and "forever" to her with every look and breath and word. And I will tell her what I believe, hoping that she will believe it, too—that I believe our son still feels the warm cradle of her arms around him, that he still feels the press of her kisses upon his cheeks and forehead, and that her whispers are the sweet music he still hears. That I believe the light of her smile still surrounds him. I'll tell her that I believe she walked with him to the door of heaven and she gave him these gifts. And that, with her gifts, his heaven is made more beautiful. With her gifts, his cries are only of joy.

GORDY'S PATIENCE has run out. When he's angry, his anger erases every other expression from his face, giving him a frozen mask. His anger makes his intentions unable to be seen, makes his actions unable to be predicted—and it makes my friend a dangerous man. As he's been listening, his face has stiffened and become unlined, the creases of his easy smile disappearing from the sides of his mouth. The face now looking at me is a smooth blank canvas, devoid of all emotion—and I know it is the face of his rage.

He spits the names. "Creel. And Simon. Right!"

I nod.

"And...and you?" These are the only words he says, but they are enough. I know exactly what he's asking. Elissa knows, too. She watches me—waiting for my final secret, waiting for another thing that I never wanted to tell her, that I never wanted her to know.

I nod again, finding my answer—my confession?—in a sentence that I remember from Alassadir's story. "Blood flows out like rivers," I say. "Both sides bled. First my family. Then theirs."

I don't know how Elissa feels about what I've just said. And I fear her despair about what I've done. I look down at the table. Then feel her hand over mine. She holds it tightly and nods.

"Good," she says. Then, "Thank you." And I bow my head, understanding that I've received her absolution. Whatever forgiveness I needed, she has given me. And I am grateful that she asks me nothing more.

With my head still bowed, I hear Gordy offering what I know I could have asked for. "I would have helped you," he says. "I would have *liked* to help." And I know that he would have, too, without question or remorse. He isn't only my friend, he is also—as much as Alassadir, and in some ways more—my brother. If I'd told him the truth about the accident, if I'd asked for his help, I know he would have delivered Creel and Simon to my door, wrapped up and packaged in as many dripping boxes as I wanted. I could tell him that I hadn't asked for his help because I wanted to protect him from the guilt of what I was going to do, or that I'd worried about what he might say—but I'd be lying. I know why I didn't tell him. Not because I wanted to keep him out of the fight, but because I wanted the fight for myself. Wanted my name to be the only one they screamed at the end. And if they could still scream in hell, I wanted them screaming my name there, too. Screaming it for all eternity, loud enough to lead me to them when I died.

But without any more explanation, Gordy understands—after all, he is my brother. "Well, then…guess I'll stop looking for them now," he deadpans. "Let me guess, though—somewhere in the same stream?" He glances at Setsu. "Blood spilled somewhere in the same salty 'circling waters'?" He knows me, so he knows the answer to his question. Before I finish my "Yes," he's already turned to Alassadir and Setsu. His face is polished stone, a surface with no history—meaning that he is still a dangerous man. "I have one more guess for you two," he says. "Blue built another path and opened another way, didn't he? The two lives—he took care of the path and the way for our side, didn't he? Right?"

Setsu nods.

When he speaks again, Gordy's voice reveals the anger he's controlling. His voice doesn't tremble or quaver, instead, it is the sound of waiting power, a bowstring drawn and held, or the steel hum of an unsheathed sword.

"A few questions, my monkeyman friend," he says to Setsu. "Could you have stopped Creel and Simon from throwing that rock? Did you let that baby die? Maybe let a child be killed in order to give the world a little 'balance'? Maybe to get yourself a little 'holy harmony'?"

Setsu stares into Gordy's eyes. "You know this," he finally says. His voice is thick and dark and weary, full of brutal notes. And for all the hurt he carries, for all the love that shows so clearly in his eyes, his voice reminds me that he, too, is a dangerous man. "I allowed nothing," he says. "I let no child die. Things happen as they happen. The battle always rages, the world is always at war. The threads unravel, and then are woven again."

As he speaks, some of the edge leaves his voice. He looks at Gordy, and I have the impression of a teacher standing over a student, reminding him of his lessons, reassuring him and telling him again, "You know this."

Gordy stares at Setsu. Then a few faint lines begin to wrinkle his face. Creases return to the corners of his mouth. And I know that his anger is fading, that he's becoming calmer, no longer looking for *something to strike right now*, for *something to blame and destroy right now*. He takes a deep breath.

"You're right," he finally says. "I *do* know." He looks around the table. "Now, let me tell you *how* I know."

FUELED WITH the urgency of shared purpose, our conversation moves quickly. Outside it is still early morning. The earth is warming and the breeze—not yet caught by the sun—still has a hint of coolness in it. This is the time of day when there's a feeling of limitless hours to enjoy, of endless minutes to unspool. Elsewhere, other people are just waking up, probably thinking of nothing more than the sun and the long day ahead of them. They have no thoughts about the full moon that will rise tonight, no doubts that they will see tomorrow's dawn. But those are our thoughts and doubts, and that is what we are doing: waiting for tonight's full moon, wondering if we'll see tomorrow's dawn.

And it is now, as we're talking and waiting for the full moon, that we are given a small gift—a gift which, for no other reason, I will gladly fight this war.

GORDY TELLS his story. It begins with "First, the phone woke me..." and ends with "Then I drove back here, knowing we'd need more guns."

As he speaks, our minds take in the bloody pictures he paints: Renny's body in the cage. The murdered people he found at the house on Salt Creek Road. His run through the woods, pursued by the beast...pursued by the twin. And when he tells about firing his gun, firing again and again at the thing, Elissa asks out loud what we all are wondering.

"How do we kill it? How does it die?"

And Setsu answers simply, "By blood. By love. And only on the hill."

When Gordy finishes, Elissa has other questions. "Why isn't he alone? He's strong enough. Why is he using the Glammerys? Why does he have the black cars? What *else* is he doing?"

"I do not know," Setsu replies. "He lives in a hole where I cannot see"—and at this, Gordy and I look at each other quickly, furtively, immediately knowing where that hole must be—"However," Setsu continues, "he has had time to make many plans. Plans with many parts to play." Setsu looks around the table, his eyes commanding our attention. "In this one thing, though, he and I have done the same: We each have gathered our tribe."

Tribe.

Yes, that's the right word for our group. I can feel the power of it. The correctness. The sense of something deep and strong joining us together. A mix of blood and spirit, of love and trust. A bond that has formed. We are, indeed, a tribe.

Gordy says aloud what I'm thinking. "Tribes—that's good. I like that," he says. "But tribes need names. What are we called? Something fierce, I hope. Something—"

Setsu interrupts. "We are the oldest tribe. We are the *Jo-Nah.*"

Gordy pauses. He considers what he's heard. "Okay—not exactly the bloodthirsty image I was hoping for, but still good. I get it. The Jo-Nah. But what about the bad guys? What do we call those bastards in the hole?"

It is now that we are given the gift. The gift we've all been wanting, the gift we've all been praying for, even as we were sitting at the table and talking. The gift is a voice—

The boy's voice.

"Riffraff," he says. "It's the Riffraff." He's looking at us over the arm of the couch, and now I wonder how long he's been listening, how much of our discussion he's heard. "The Riffraff killed my parents. The Riffraff killed my Nanny T." Then he begins to cry.

WE SURROUND the boy with a wall of protective words and caring eyes and gentle hands.

Elissa and Callista kneel beside him, stroking his face, catching his tears, listening to the words spilling in a torrent from his mouth, telling us what had happened to him. The rest of us unconsciously assume the four positions of guard, posting ourselves at his head and feet and shoulders. Elissa tips a glass of water to his lips, letting him sip as he speaks, and Callista pulls a blue cloth from her bag. She spills water onto it, then dabs the damp cloth around the boy's face and throat, calming him with its soft, cool touch.

Eventually his tears stop. And his words slow. And his eyelids flutter and close again. We hear the deep heavy breathing of his exhaustion as he sinks back to sleep—a sleep that I hope is dreamless. A sleep with no pictures or sounds, no memories or thoughts. I wish him a sleep that wraps itself around him like a soft, cool blue cloth, muffling him in its thick folds, holding him in perfect silence.

Even as he sleeps, we hold our positions. Elissa and Callista remain kneeling beside him. And Allasadir, Setsu, Gordy, and I still stand over him, keeping our watch. After a few minutes, Callista looks up at Gordy. "It was my sister's house, wasn't it?" she asks. She looks again at the boy. "His Nanny T. and his parents—that was my family there on the ground. Theirs were the bodies you saw this morning, weren't they?"

At first Gordy doesn't answer. Just lowers his head and stares down at the boy. Then he nods, closing his eyes against whatever memory he sees.

At his nod, Callista pushes herself to her feet, but she stays near the boy, gazing down on him. When she speaks, she doesn't raise her eyes, and her voice is quiet enough to not to disturb his slumber.

"They were family," she murmurs. "A part of this tribe. They should have been here with us." Her voice grows stronger. "And I'll be damned if we leave them to rot outside, becoming some snack for whatever else might go walking through that field! I want them buried and at peace—at her home, all of them together, right there in the middle of her wildflower meadow. And I want that *now*, before anything else can take a bite."

CALLISTA MAKES it clear: She is staying with the boy. But she wants everyone else to go. When Alassadir presses to stay with her, to protect her and the boy, she answers, "Bury your aunt. Bury her children. It's better that all of you to stay together, to guard yourselves while you work. Cole and I will be fine here alone. I think that Cole's Riffraff is back in his hole for the day, getting ready for tonight. Maybe only blood and love can kill that one, but for anyone else who visits? I think bullets will do just fine." She reaches into her bag and pulls out the gun she was holding earlier this morning.

"Like I said before," she says. "I travel with a carnival."

LATER, WHEN I see that the boy is awake, I notice that he's looking at me intently. He moves one hand, waving me over to his side. Once I'm there, he gestures again, still saying nothing, asking me to bend near. As I kneel down, he whispers in my ear, asking me for a favor. And asking for my promise.

I give him both.

CLETE. THE MATCHMAN

*THE FIREFLIES were floating in the dark outside his window,
keeping him company. Their tiny blue lights were comforting
and soothing. They made him feel less worried, made him feel
less afraid...*

RENNY WASN'T back yet. Last night, Clete had watched from the window, seeing Renny leave at midnight, his taillights disappearing up the hill. When Renny drove by, Clete smiled and waved from behind his unlit window, knowing his son couldn't see him, but waving anyway because he felt so happy and daddy-proud, knowing that Renny would be just fine. And that the red-haired man would be so pleased. He even felt—for a little while—that his belly was unclenching, that the ground-glass razors in his stomach were slowing their ribbon-cutting ceremony through his insides. Sitting by the window, he'd started thinking that things might turn out fine after all, that things were starting to look pretty good.

Now, though, hours later, he wasn't feeling happy. And wasn't feeling proud. Instead, he was worried. Worried about Renny, sure, but even more worried about the red-haired man. Worried what he'd think, worried what he'd do. Because Renny wasn't back yet.

Clete felt his gut pain again. Felt it twisting through him again, doubling him up and squeezing, making him breathe in little baby spoonfuls...reminding him that nothing was fine about anything, that nothing was any good at all.

LITTLE BLUE fireflies. He watched them, entranced by their lights. They hovered in place, glowing and blinking in the black night. The small, low cloud of them winked on and off, staying clustered around the trucks, never moving far from the cars...and then he knew: It wasn't fireflies. It was THEM. He looked closer, staring at the flickering lights. And he saw that they were staring, too—the bright blue eyes of the things sitting in the cars were staring straight back at him.

HE'D TRIED staying awake. Didn't want to sleep. Stayed up for hours, sitting at the window, watching for Renny to return. It was dark when he fell asleep. Was still dark when he woke—
—when he fell asleep, he fell back into his chair and dozed, only for a few minutes, but long enough to dream. In his dream, he was at the bottom of one of the truck ramps. He started walking up the ramp, could see the long black hole of the truck's cavern getting nearer and nearer. At the back of the hole was a blue light, a beautiful blue light. All he wanted was to walk through the blackness in the truck and into the warm, blue light. He went up the ramp and stepped into the dark tunnel. Took only a few steps and started coughing, feeling something moving in his throat, something choking him, scratching and digging inside of him. Then fingers and thumbs began wriggling out of his mouth, pouring in a torrent out of his throat. Some landed at his feet and then crawled back up on him. He could feel them under his pants, inching up his leg like little worms. More of them crawled out of his mouth and hooked themselves on his lips. They dangled there a moment, then they crawled up his cheeks, moving toward his eyes. At his eyes, the fingers arched over and pinched his eyelids shut. They held fast, closing his eyes to the blue light, trapping him alone and blind in a dark hole. He knew he'd be wandering in darkness forever.

Then he figured it out. If he wanted to see again, if he wanted to find the blue fire, he'd have to pluck the fingers and thumbs off his eyes and swallow them back down. He'd have to chew fast, eating them quickly, before they could slither away. So he reached up to his eyes and grabbed one of the pinching fingers. He squeezed it hard at the knuckle and it let go of his eyelid. Holding it out from him, the finger squirmed and flipped, its gristle and bones snapping like a click-bug as he popped it into his mouth. He felt it trying to crawl back out of his mouth, felt it gouging and digging at the inside of his cheek and tapping at the back of his teeth. He chewed harder, grinding the finger down into a slippery pulp, then swallowed the whole mashed mess. He reached up again. Squeezed the knuckle of another finger. Felt it writhe and twist as it unpinched from his eye. Felt it trying to catch hold of his lips as he dropped it onto his tongue. Then felt it curl and spasm as he ground it between his jaws.

HE'D WOKEN up scared, drenched in a clammy bath of sweet-smelling sweat. Awake, he saw what had changed while he napped. The red-haired man's car was gone. He'd driven away while Clete was dreaming. But Clete knew what else the red-haired man had done, knew it without a doubt. The red-haired man had stopped outside and he'd stood at Clete's dark window, peering in with his blue-fire eyes. He'd stood there staring, grinning and watching Clete sleeping—watching him pinch at his face, watching him pull the crawling dream-fingers off his eyes. He'd smiled at Clete's tiny sobs and cries, and he'd inhaled the damp reek seeping out of Clete's skin. And he'd pressed one hand flat against the window, whispering before he left, "Nighty-night, Clete. Sleep tight. Don't let the bedbugs bite."

He'd left then, folding into the darkness, leaving only the ghostly print of his hand on the window glass. A handprint tipped with pointed claws.

THERE WAS only the flicker of blue. He couldn't see their silhouettes, not in the deep night near the trucks. He couldn't even see the outlines of the cars they sat in. He could only see their eyes. And their eyes never left him.

CLETE WATCHED the dawn come up. The thin rays tried lighting the ground, pushing weakly against the dark that never fully left the hole, the darkness that was always chewing at the corners and edges of whatever runny daylight found its way inside. Finally, though, the sky grew light enough that he could see the shapes of the parked trucks and cars. And the shapes of what sat inside.

A car was coming down from the top of the hole. The red-haired man's car. It slid through the thick, layered coils of gray fog, disappearing smoothly into the mist, then slipping out again, suddenly revealed. It moved like a sleek, graceful predator, stealthily crossing the ground, leaving only shadow and mist behind.

Yes, the red-haired man was back. Clete watched the car's approach, thinking, *Renny isn't here, Renny isn't here, Renny isn't here.* He felt his stomach burning. Felt it spitting acid into his throat, filling his mouth with scorpion stings and bile. *Coming for me,* he thought, staring at the car. *Sure as shit, he's coming for little old me.*

THE RED-HAIRED MAN was smiling as he waved at Clete, beckoning him outside. From the window, Clete saw that he'd had a bloody morning. The red-haired man's black suit coat was gone. His white shirt was a red-soaked rag, a crimson bib plastered wetly to his chest. His hair was messed and spiked, tipped with blood and grease. More blood was smeared and dried across his face. He looked like he'd been swimming in a pool of viscera and gore, the way a dog twitches and rolls in something dead, wanting the smell and feel of it on his skin. Wanting to press the death into his pores.

But Clete didn't move. Wasn't sure he could move. Wasn't sure he could do anything at all but stand frozen at the window and watch the red-haired man smile and wave. But the red-haired man wasn't waving a hand. Not anymore. It had stopped being a hand. Wasn't even close to being a hand, not even a hand tipped with claws. Now it was something else—something black and yellow and scaled. It belonged to something else, too, something that still wore the red-haired man's face. Something that kept waving to Clete, inviting him to come outside and play. And now that Clete was invited, he knew he had to go.

When he got to the door, he coughed up a bubble of blood. A perfect red bubble that held full for a moment between his lips and then burst, misting a fine spatter of blood-specks across his cheek and under his eye. He wiped the blood off with the back of his hand, smearing the specks. Then he stepped outside.

CLETE. THE MATCHMAN

*T*HE BLUE-EYEDS *were still staring at him, their bright eyes following him, tracking him as he walked toward the red-haired man. They stared without blinking, watching calmly as the thing's black-clawed arm lifted above Clete's head as Clete walked closer.*

HE WAS going to die. He was sure of it. He wondered if it would hurt. Wondered if he should say something first—something about how sorry he was, about how he wished he could have helped more. About how he understood, though. That he knew how things worked.

After all, "fuck 'em." Right?

The red-haired man spoke first. "Hungry?" he asked, nodding at the black car. "Got some good old food in the backseat." Smiling and laughing—a quick, barking laugh, like he'd told a joke that Clete didn't understand—he raised his arm and stepped closer to Clete.

Seeing the black-tipped claws above him, Clete thought, *Gonna die, gonna die, gonna die.* Then, like the red-haired man, he smiled too. Closed his eyes. Thought, *Finally. Finally some sleep. Maybe in a warm blue fire.*

He stood still and waited—waiting for the cutting, waiting for the end.

The arm fell.

But it didn't cut him. At least not like he'd thought it would. And it didn't hurt. Not like he'd thought it would. No, it settled across his shoulders—pulling him close, pressing him against the red-haired man's blood-soaked shirt. Held close, snugged tight in the embrace, Clete breathed in the thick scents of copper and leather. The smells were smothering and nauseating, making him cough again, bringing more blood to his lips. After he stopped coughing, he heard a sound. A murmuring sound, seeming so very near.

The red-haired man pulled him over to the car, the two of them walking like drunken old chums. Clete could still hear the sound, louder and clearer now. Caught in the hug, he walked with his ear tilted toward the red-haired man's mouth, close to the rows of teeth that now filled his smile.

After a moment, Clete figured out what he was hearing. Singing. The sound was the sound of singing. *He's happy,* Clete thought. *The red-haired man is happy.* Then he thought that maybe he'd been wrong earlier. That maybe he wasn't dying today, after all.

The red-haired man was singing as they walked. "I see the moon and the moon sees me. The moon sees the somebody I want to see."

They stopped beside the car and stood staring for a few seconds into its black-mirrored windows. The red-haired man reached for the car door with his free hand. The reaching hand was the same as the clawed thing stretched across Clete's shoulders, its pointed tips piercing his arm, drawing blood and holding him fast. The red-haired man grabbed the door handle.

"Old food!" he shouted, pulling the door open. "Old food! Old food! Old food!" But he was so excited that he pulled the door open too fast, with too much strength. The door swung back hard against its hinges, then ricocheted forward, banging closed again. The force of the heavy door shook the whole car, rocking it on its wheels.

He's happy, Clete thought again. *He's just so damn happy.*

The red-haired man opened the door again. Slower this time. Slow enough that before Clete could see inside, he could hear the sloshing sounds—the splish-splash of liquids moving back and forth, rocked by the slamming door.

Then he saw the stacked, wet pieces. The piled things slipping and oozing off the seat, sliding down and dropping on the car's dark-pooled floor, landing and splashing in little ripples of red.

He recognized some of what he saw: an ankle, a rib, a splintered jaw. The worst was the hair—long curls of old, gray hair. Bloody silver strands of it were loosely wrapped around a jagged cap of still-attached flesh, rolling it into the shape of an uneven, matted ball wedged into the corner of the seat. *Old food, old food, old food,* Clete thought looking at the pillow of an old woman's hair. And he felt his mind start crawling away.

He heard more singing. Maybe had been hearing it for a while, maybe listening without realizing it. Might have been hearing other things, too, but he couldn't be sure. In fact, he wasn't sure what he'd been thinking about at all for the last few minutes. Had the detached feeling that he'd drifted away somewhere and then returned. All he knew, right now, was that he was still standing next to the open car door, still staring at the gray ball of scalp and hair.

The scaled arm was still draped over his shoulder, still holding him close. He realized that the singing was another nursery rhyme. Different than before, but still familiar. The refrain of it had wriggled into his thoughts, bringing him back from wherever he'd been.

It was the red-haired man. He was singing again, happily shouting his new song through an open mouth full of long, sharp teeth. "The ants go marching one by one, hurrah! Hurrah! The ants go marching one by one, hurrah! Hurrah!"

The red-haired man stared upward while he sang—"...ants go marching one by one, hurrah! Hurrah!"—clearly watching something Clete couldn't see. At least not yet. Before Clete saw what it was, the red-haired man stopped singing and stood silent. Then Clete saw it, too. And seeing it, he knew without a doubt that Renny was in trouble. It was a car—the little brown dot of a sheriff's car, way up at the top of the hole, crawling slowly down, cautiously coming down the steep road descending into the hole.

"Look at that!" the red-haired man said gleefully. "An ant, marching right down into our hole!"

And Clete couldn't help it. Had to say it. Had to shout, "Hurrah! Hurrah!" and then felt so happy, felt so blue-fire warm when the red-haired man began laughing at his joke. And as the claws dug deeper into his shoulder, flexing and gouging in rhythm with the red-haired man's laughter, even then, Clete kept smiling, feeling so very happy to have brought the red-haired man some joy.

THEY WATCHED the sheriff's careful approach, neither of them saying a word. The only sounds came from inside the black car, the same sounds Clete had already heard—the delicate *drip-drop* of a slow, bloody rain, and the thick dull *plop* of "old food" slowly sliding into the puddles on the floorboard, the meat landing with a flat, wet smack before it sank into those pools.

The red-haired man finally broke their silence, whispering to Clete after the brown car had stopped at the bottom and the sheriff was hurrying toward them. When the sheriff was almost to them the red-haired man asked, "What do you think, Clete? Is he a SLEEPER or a KEEPER? Is he NEAT or is he MEAT?"

SHERIFF TIM

THE SHERIFF was wondering how he was going to say it, how he was going to give Clete Glammery the news: "Your son Renny is dead." And he wondered what he would say after that, when Clete asked him what all civilians always asked, "How? How—?"

It didn't mattter that he'd already answered the question only seconds before. Didn't matter that he'd already said that somebody "was killed in a hunting accident this morning" or "died in a car accident on the highway." No matter what he'd already said, people always asked again anyway, always asking the exact same question. "How? How—?"

When he'd first started the job, he hadn't known shit. Hadn't been smart enough yet to know that words like "killed" and "died" absolutely mind-wiped civilians, erasing everything they'd just heard except the person's name and the word "dead." But eventually, like every cop, he'd learned the right way to tell people bad news. Learned the trick was to give them one idea at a time, in the order they could understand. But even then—even when you did everything right—they all still asked that same damn question, they all still had to hear it again. "How?"

This time, the "how?" was a problem. There were too many answers to the question and not a single good way of saying any of them: Renny was beaten? Then had his throat cut? Then got arrow-shot?

He decided to start off with something simple at first. Something all-inclusive, like "fatal assault." That would work, at least for now, and it was enough for Clete to begin understanding the big message: "Your son is dead." After giving Clete the first answer, he'd give Clete a little time. Time to get over the shock. Time to let him think about it. And then, after Clete settled down, it would be Clete's turn to answer a few questions—simple ones at first, like "What the hell was Renny doing in a monkey cage?"

DRIVING DOWN into the Glammerys' hole was no fun. He was in the cruiser, not the Jeep, and the cruiser's suspension was nonexistent. It should have been replaced last year, but the town board had told him "no money, no way," then said to wait another six months on any repairs. So now here he was, ass-bumping down the hill, teeth clacking together like a wind-up toy at every pothole, trying to concentrate on staying on the road at the same time that he was working on what to say to Clete.

Briefly taking his eyes off the road, he glanced at the bottom of the hole to see how much farther he had to go. Looking down, he suddenly felt that maybe he was the one who'd been mind-wiped, that maybe he was the one who couldn't remember the answers he'd already been told—answers to questions like what the hell were all those parked cars doing at the bottom of the Glammerys' hole? And who were the people sitting in the cars? And why were all the trunks popped open? And what were the two big, black semi-rigs doing parked down there? And—most of all—questions about who the hell was the tall, red-haired, bloody man standing next to Clete? And, finally, why were Clete and the red-haired man both standing so still, watching him drive down into the hole?

SHERIFF TIM

H E STEPPED QUICKLY out of the car. Shouted, "Hang on!" and jogged over to Clete. He'd decided to help the two of them first—before he told Clete about Renny, before he asked Clete any questions. He'd figured out that Clete must be helping the injured, bloody man into the back seat of the black car. From the look of things, blood loss alone would soon make the man pass out and fall.

He was almost to them, was about to slip his own arm under the red-haired man's other shoulder when he heard the man say, "Meat, I think," and saw him lose his balance and reach out fast, reaching for help. And he heard Clete shout, thought he heard him yell, "Hurrah! Hurrah!" except that made no sense at all, was just some crazy-ass shit, and he tried moving closer, wanting to catch the man before he fell, wanting to help ease him down—

—but he couldn't move. Couldn't get any closer. Couldn't move at all. His legs weren't working. They wouldn't walk forward. Instead, they suddenly felt like they were filled with hot sand. But he knew that was just more crazy shit that still made no sense. So he pressed harder toward the tall, red-haired man. Still trying to reach him. Still trying to help. And now he felt so weak, only now it wasn't just his legs. Now his whole body was weak. The hot sand was filling him, weighing him down. His head dropped, and now he saw his own chest. Saw his own blood spraying out from there. And then saw the red-haired man's arm slipping out from between his ribs (*crazy shit, makes no sense*). And last, he saw the curved black knives the man was holding, the blades that were now being rinsed in a bright red fountain.

Then he did it. Did what he had thought he'd never do, not even at the end of things. As he fell forward, he stopped—stopped being a cop. Stopped knowing how to give information one piece at a time and how to tell it to people in the right order. And stopped remembering what he'd said, and what he'd been told, and what he already knew. As he fell forward, he changed. Became different. Became like everybody else he'd ever given bad news. Because in the last bit of his light, in the last thoughts that he thought, he became someone who kept repeating the same old question, someone who wanted to know, just like everyone else always wanted to know: *How? How did I die? Please tell me. How? How—?*

BLUE 48

*W*E SHOULD *have watched the trees. We should have been more careful. We'd only bowed our heads for a moment, only closed our eyes in prayer for an instant. But an instant was all they needed. A moment was all that it took for them to appear.*

AS WE'RE GETTING ready to leave, I see Callista sitting with Cole on the sofa. The way they sit together, Callista's arm circling Cole's waist and him leaning against her, his head resting on her shoulder, it's like they've known each other forever. I watch them talking. Callista asks a question and Cole thinks for a second, then answers. Then he asks a question, and it's her turn to pause before she replies. They look so serious, and so sad. I didn't see them crying, but there are fresh tear streaks on their faces. Then Callista laughs at something Cole says, and as she laughs the boy smiles. And for a moment they share a bit of happiness, for a moment they are simply a young boy and an old woman sitting on a couch, trading family stories. And the beauty of it makes me ache.

ON THE WAY to Nanny Tinken's cabin, Gordy's truck is in the lead. Gordy drives fast, taking us to where he'd been before. To the site of the slaughter. Setsu rides with Gordy. Following behind, I see them through the cab window of Gordy's truck. They look at each other a lot, nodding, shaking their heads. I wonder about their conversation. I can only guess at what they might be saying, but I do have a suspicion about what they might be planning.

No such discussion takes place in my car. We barely talk. We stare straight ahead. Focused on following Gordy. Thinking about what we'll find at Nanny's cabin. Dreading what we are about to do. We're feeling anxious and tense, worried, like we're going to a funeral…which, of course, is exactly what we're doing.

After a while, Gordy signals and turns into a drive. A large rusted mailbox, painted TINKENS, tilts backward, slanted away from the road. I follow him up the drive. He's going slow now, taking time to see everything. Being careful to avoid any surprises.

It turns out that what we find isn't as bad as we'd worried about or imagined.

It's much worse.

Not far up the drive is the parked car he'd told us about. There are two things spilled beside it, and I know in my heart that I'm looking at Cole's parents, a mother and a father—and although I know that fact in my heart, I can't believe it in my head. There's nothing left of them to recognize. Nothing left of what they were. They don't look like people at all, not like anything that was once alive, that walked or loved or breathed or cried. No. The things near the driveway are empty. There is nothing beautiful left there, no holy spark, nothing that hints of grace or spirit or thought or song. All those things are gone, stolen from what lies in the grass. Those things have been ripped up and feasted upon, torn so small that they can no longer be seen.

Looking at the remains, I know this: it was right for us to come. Our dead need caring.

ALERT, READY to shout out warnings if we're attacked, we walk to the field behind the cabin. The field is perfect—a painted picture of wild flowers, lush with bright colors and life, surrounded by woods on three sides. Immediately I know: We will bury them here, in the middle of this field. This is where they will rest.

Except for the chair, it looks like there's nothing's wrong here. There's an overturned white wicker chair lying in the middle of the field. Cole told us about it. "Nanny's flying chair," he said, "where she'd sit and take her rides."

The chair is here. But Nanny isn't.

I lift the chair, setting it upright. Under the chair, scattered on the ground, little red circles glisten in the bent grass. I squat and carefully push the grass back to see what's there, fearful of whatever small horror I'll find.

Gordy is standing a little distance away, near an area where the grass is matted and slick. "He stopped here when he was chasing me," he says. "Her body was here, and he stopped beside her." He walks around the area, looking at the ground, studying the scene.

The field is different where he's standing, like it is part of a different place, or a detail from a different painted picture—a picture where the grass and wildflowers have been painted with a wet red brush. The red transforms them, makes them difficult to recognize. They seem exotic, like flowers of an alien landscape. I'm transfixed by a handful of ruby beads that have been thrown across the ground, but then realize what I'm seeing. Blood-soaked dandelions.

Gordy looks back at the road. "He took her with him. Like a goddamned animal dragging away its kill—"

"An important kill," Setsu says. He's kneeling at the edge of the wet ground. "A trophy kill. Worth keeping." He looks up, his eyes moving from one of us to the other. "As all of you would be." He stands up. "All of you can change the plans he's made. He knows that. And doesn't like it."

I find what was hidden in the grass, what was red and glistening where the chair had toppled. It's a spilled pocketful of cinnamon candies. I know why they're here—Cole had told us about Nanny T.'s cinnamon kisses. The candies are part of what

I promised him I'd do. But right now, knowing how they came to be here, I don't want to pick them up, much less hold them in my hand. As my fingers brush against them in the grass, the cellophane wrappers make small crinkling noises, like the sound of tiny, breaking bones.

Gordy starts walking toward the woods. "One more to find," he says. "Cole's Rockman."

"The Rockman." Cole had whispered the name to us. "That's who the Riffraff was killing at the stream. He was killing my friend—" and when he said that, we realized he'd been awake longer than we thought, that he'd been listening while Gordy talked about finding bodies, and being chased by the monster-twin, and about thinking he was going to die. Cole hadn't made a sound while Gordy was telling his story. He'd just lain quietly on our couch, putting things together in his mind, assessing his situation, all alone in a roomful of strangers, listening to the narrated details of his nightmare.

And I knew then that the boy was brave. Maybe braver than any of us.

WE FIND the Rockman lying near the water. What is left of him. We gather him up, gently laying him on one of the long blankets we brought along. When we're through, Alassadir and Gordy fold the blanket over the body, then fold it again. With Gordy at what's left of the head and Alassadir at what's left of the feet, they lift the blanket, and we take him back to the field. He belongs with the others. He is part of our group, a member of the small family that we're burying today...the family of people who were loved by Cole.

Alassadir and I dig the graves as Elissa and Setsu stand guard. Elissa paces with the shotgun while Setsu stands still. But his eyes are always moving, always searching. We dig three holes. Whether Nanny's body is here or not, she'll have a place in the field. A protected place, between her son and the Rockman. We will bury Cole's parents together in the same hole.

Before covering the blanket-wrapped bodies with the rich brown earth, I ask everyone to wait. I have promises to keep.

I go into Nanny's cabin to look for the things that Cole had asked me to gather. They aren't hard to find. In the upstairs bedroom, after finding what I was searching for, I also find a small black suitcase sitting on the dresser top. The suitcase is filled with jeans and T-shirts. The clothes are clean and packed for travel, ready for home. In addition to the other thing, I take the suitcase, too. It belongs in Cole's new home.

IT IS TIME to keep my promises.

Into each grave I carefully place what I've promised to put there, and I say what I've promised to say. Out of the treasure chest that I took from under Cole's bed, I set a small pile of geode crystals on the Rockman's blanket. As I stack the stones, I say, "These. Take these." Then, beside the geodes, I place the three apples I found in the kitchen. The apples are washed and polished, like Cole had asked me to do. Setting them down, I tell the Rockman, "The Gala apple. Your favorite. To enjoy forever."

We'd placed a blanket at the bottom of Nanny's grave. I now lay a small glass vial on the blanket. The vial is also from Cole's treasure chest. It's full of gold flecks that float and sparkle as they drift in glycerin. I also pour a handful of cinnamon candies onto the blanket—I'd found an open sack of them in the kitchen; I keep the ones from the field in my pocket. Then I speak Cole's message, just the way he told me to say it. "Nanny Tinkens," I say, "Cole says... Hello. He says that he certainly will not miss you every day. And that he never loved you at all. And that he won't love you forever. And he wants you to know that although you say 'Si! Si! Si!' he will always say, 'No, no, no.'"

I place nothing on the blankets holding Cole's parents. Instead, I take a wonderfully shaped, green glass bottle—Royall Lyme All Purpose Lotion—out of the treasure chest. When I unscrew the metal crown cap, the scent of spices and lime lightly rises from the bottle. I tip the open bottle over the grave, and as a sprinkle of scented rain falls onto the blanket, I say to Cole's parents, "Now you are swaying in an island hammock, dozing between lime trees, surrounded by tropical waters. And as you sleep, dream of pirates and treasure." When the bottle is empty, I return it to the small wooden treasure chest. The chest is the last part of my promise. "Please," Cole asked, "please, could you bring the box back to me?" And I gave him my word that I would.

THEY ATTACK, after—

—after we've filled the three graves.

—after we've put down our shovels and not yet picked up our guns.

—after we've bowed our heads to pray.

That's when I hear the thrumming sound of quiet running, so subtle at first that it doesn't register, so soft that it seems to be just a vibration in the air.

But it isn't a vibration. It's their sound, the sound of them racing across the open ground, a line of them coming from each of the field's wooded sides. Coyotes—gaunt, filthy, all bones and teeth. They are almost to us when we see them, are almost upon us before we begin to move. One of them isn't like the others. He has a black, scarred muzzle. He is strong and sleek and running in front of the pack. He reaches us first and leaps, fast and straight and high, flying at Gordy's throat, eager for the kill. And even though he's the first, he isn't so very far ahead of the rest. By the time his jaws are almost on Gordy, the others are nearly upon us, too.

CALLISTA. COLE

*T*HROUGH IT ALL, *she heard the screams coming from the other room. And after each scream, the heavy slamming of a body. A body crashing again and again against the wall.*

SHE WANTED to breathe, but it hurt to breathe; her ribs were cutting her up inside. And she wanted to move, but she couldn't move because her spine hurt too much. And she wanted to stand, but she couldn't stand, couldn't imagine her legs being able to hold her. Couldn't imagine her hands pushing against the floor and lifting her. She couldn't imagine any of it. Didn't think that she could do anything. She had no strength. Not enough to do what she wanted, not with her ribs grating and jabbing inside her. Not with her back in a stabbing fire of pain.

She wanted to find Cole. Wanted to save the boy. And wanted to kill the man on the floor across the room. Wanted him to be dead before she was dead. Wanted him to die in front of her eyes.

But she needed it to happen soon. Needed her wishes granted quickly. Because as she watched the man lying on the floor—

He took a breath.

He moved his head.

And she saw that he still had strength. Strength enough to rise.

She watched his legs draw up beneath him. Watched his hands push against the floor. Saw him trying to stand.

If he stood, she knew he would finish her. And then he would finish the boy.

She watched, willing him to fall down. Willing his legs to buckle beneath him. Willing his strength to fail. Willing him to slip and spin and tumble back to the floor.

But he pushed himself up. Then stood. And began walking toward her.

She watched. Still wanting to breathe, still wanting to move, still wanting to stand. Still wanting him to die.

THE SCREAMS grew louder. Louder, filled with rage. Filling the cabin with crazed waves of angry noise. The screams shook the walls, walls already trembling with the thudding slams that followed each scream, that were already vibrating with the crash of a body thrown hard against them...and then picked up and thrown again.

SHE'D BEEN so sure about this day.

Had known so much about this day.

And had been so wrong about this day.

She'd known she'd be part of it, a part of the "red, red day." She'd seen it in her teacup and had read it in the lines of her hand. She'd already known that she'd be hurt. Badly hurt. And she'd known that her blood would spill. The near-sight had given her hints, had provided clues about the day.

And she'd known other things too—things about which she'd been so sure. She'd been sure it would happen later. Had never thought it would be now, not now at all. And she'd been certain she'd be hurt later. At the Circle. When it tried to stop her from singing. Because with Nanny T. gone, it was just her now. Callista alone. She was the only one left to sing.

And she'd been sure she'd be alive at the end of it all. She knew she'd be hurt, but never believed that she'd die. Had been certain she'd live to see the new Stone. She'd been so sure that that was her fate. She'd been so sure about everything, but now she wasn't sure, not at all. Not while she watched the man walking slowly toward her, not while she waited for him to finish what he'd begun.

Now she wondered whose future she had seen in her teacup. Wondered whose fate had she read in her hands? Because although she'd been right in one way, she had been wrong in so many others. She'd been right about the blood. There was plenty of blood. But she'd been wrong about the "when" and the "where." The "when" wasn't later. It was now. And the "where" wasn't at the Circle. It was here. Her fate was here and now—it was shuffling toward her, advancing very slowly, but still advancing. Bringing death to where she lay.

And she wanted to breathe, but it still hurt to breathe—but she made herself breathe anyway, taking quick, shallow breaths. She felt the fresh oxygen brighten the room and push the dark edges away from her eyes. And she wanted to move, but it still hurt to move— but she made herself move anyway, curling herself slightly up from the floor. She barely raised her back, then felt surprised when the pain lessened, when the sharp pressing on her spine immediately began to ease.

THE SCREAMS were bad. But the crashing sounds were worse.

In the middle of her own pain, she shuddered at the thought of the pain happening in the other room, at the pain of flesh being hurtled time after time through the air, ending in brutal collisions of wall and bone. After each collision, she heard the body being picked up and flung again—flung without rest, without thought of bruises or blood or bones. Flung again and again and again, until the incessant crashing became a village drum pounding a violent tempo, beating a message on the walls.

EARLY MORNING had been wonderful. After the others left, leaving just her and Cole, they'd sat down together on the sofa, snuggling up against each other and talking like long lost friends. As they talked, Grendel's snoring was the only other sound in the cabin. For a while, they laughed at the snoring and watched the big cat napping, seeing the lynx through the open doorway of Blue and Elissa's bedroom as he rolled from one end of the bed to the other, wrapping himself into a lumpy ball of blankets and sheets as he stretched and turned and snored.

At first, Cole talked about his parents and told her about his father calling him Old King Cole and about his mother's smothering worries. He also told her about how his mom and dad fought sometimes, but lately they'd been fighting less than ever before. He told her how their fights were only with each other, never with him, and that he'd known they loved each other…and knew even more how much they loved him.

Then they'd talked about Nanny Tinkens, each one happy to hear the other's stories. Callista told him the little things she still remembered about her sister. Things like how her sister's name was Cassandra, and how the two of them, "Cally and Cassie," were so close that sometimes they traded names with each other. And about the childhood moments fixed in her mind, moments from the games they'd played—games with buttons, games with their cats, games played in the woods. And how, even after having to share everything—a room, a bed, their clothes—she still always thought, *How lucky I am, to have her always here.*

And Cole told her about his grandmother, about the games they'd played—about their "opposites game" and their burping contests and the "seeing game" they played in the field, sitting side by side in their flying chairs and taking trips to everywhere. He told her how, even though she was old, Nanny still wanted adventures, still wanted to explore, still loved to walk and laugh. And how he'd also thought, every night when he heard her snoring down the hall, *How lucky I am, to have her always here.*

COLE WAS telling another story when she heard a car coming up the driveway. She stood up without interrupting him and walked over to the open door. She looked outside and saw the black car. Saw *TURNING UP THE HEAT, NATURALLY!* in blue and yellow lettering across the car's hood. *Wasn't supposed to be here,* she thought. *Wasn't supposed to be now.*

Her next thought was about Cole, about keeping the boy safe. *My God—please, no, don't let them hurt the boy.* Without further thought, she closed and locked the door, then crossed the room fast, planning what to do—but she hadn't felt this coming, not now, and she hadn't seen this happening, not here—

So what else had she missed? What else did she not know?

There was no time to plan. No time to run. Which decided everything. Without flight, she'd fight. But the boy had to run. He had to get away. And he had to leave alone.

She heard the car stop. Heard a car door open. And she grabbed Cole's arm, pulled him up and whispered, "Go! You need to go, the Riffraff's here, another black car is here, you have to go right now!" and she rushed him to the back door.

But she saw that the cabin's back door and front door were in a straight line with each other, and what if the black car's driver looked through and saw Cole running away? So she changed her mind and pulled Cole into the bedroom. But the boy was struggling with her now. He was confused and frightened, clutching at her arm and stumbling as she kept pulling and whispering, telling him, "Now, go now, you have to go now" and she opened the bedroom window and he half-climbed out and she half-pushed him the rest of the way. He tumbled outside, then stood there stunned as she scream-whispered, "Run! Run! Run away! Run away far!" and slammed the window shut, then ran back to the front room, pulling the bedroom door closed behind her as she ran, so no one could see the window, so no one could see Cole standing outside. Then she heard heavy footsteps on the porch, and was rummaging in her bag for the gun when—

—she heard four quick, rapping knocks. And she crossed the room and opened the door and saw the man's bright blue eyes and his dark gray suit, and saw that he was a little short and a little round, and saw his big smile, and then, of course—

She shot him.

She extended her arm. Pointed the gun. Shot twice at his heart. Saw blood spurting out of the two small holes. Was going to shoot again, but he smacked her hand and the gun was suddenly gone, clattering to the floor. Then he stepped in close, wrapping his arms around her and lifting, squeezing her tight and crushing her. Her spine bent inward under the pressure, and she heard one cracking noise and then another. At first, she thought her back was breaking, but then felt a bursting pain inside her chest, and knew her old ribs were snapping. And she knew she was going to die.

He suddenly dropped her. Her feet were turned when they hit the floor, and her ankle twisted as she lurched backward, trying to find her balance and failing, landing flat on her back. Then she saw that he'd fallen, too, also landing on his back, his blue eyes open and staring at her. His shirt was streaked with the blood pumping out of the two red holes in his chest.

But now he was up and walking toward her.

She tried to lift herself up, but her chest was a bright orange agony. Her ribs filled her with a whirring pain, but she kept breathing, kept holding the darkness away. Her ribs were killing her, but her back felt...*better*. It somehow felt better with each tiny push up off the floor. So she tried again, rolling and leaning a little bit to the side, lifting her spine as she moved. *And oh, my God, and sweet Sonny Jesus, her ribs did punish her then.*

But it worked.

The back pain shifted and slid downward, now pressing in a different spot. A lower spot, where her back still touched the floor. Then she knew what she was feeling—

It was the gun.

She was lying on top of the gun.

SHE AND the man had said nothing. They'd only made the scuffling, grunting noises of fight. And even now, when they were both quiet in these final moments, the cabin was alive with the screams coming from the next room. The walls reverberated with the horrible, wrecking punishment being given there.

HE WAS almost to her.

Her death was so very near.

He was walking slowly, but walking straighter now, taking stronger steps.

She pushed up on her elbow, trying to lift herself high enough so she could reach under her body and pick up the gun. She heard another crack and more bright bombs of pain exploded in her chest. The flashes filled her eyes and blinded her, making her gasp. The gasp brought more bright explosions, and she collapsed back on the floor.

She couldn't do it. Couldn't reach under herself for the gun. So she tried reaching behind, awkwardly slapping at the floor and stretching her arm, her hand, her fingers at where she'd felt the pain. And found nothing. Then stretched her fingers again, felt them touch something. She slapped again, felt something hard under her palm and grabbed it, then brought it around to see. And was so happy when she saw the gun, because she knew she could kill him now. He was close enough that she knew she couldn't miss, no matter that her hands were shaking horribly, no matter the blood she could taste in her mouth. She couldn't miss. Didn't even have to aim. But she aimed anyway.

And fired.

And the bullet hit him.

A new hole in his chest began to bleed. But he didn't slow. And didn't stop walking. And then she knew that he wasn't going to die before she did. That he refused to die until he finished her. So she fired again and again and again and again, pulling the trigger until the gun was empty. He stopped walking while she fired, just stood still and looked down at her, watching her try to kill him.

When she was done, he looked down at his chest, looking where the bullets should have gone. Then he looked up, shaking his head and smiling. He ran his hand over his shirt, and she saw what was making him smile.

She'd missed. Entirely. There were still only three bleeding holes. The same three small red circles as before. Still smiling, he stepped forward. But now his step faltered and a flash of confusion crossed his smiling face. She guessed it was because he didn't understand the expression on her face, that he didn't know why she was smiling too. And she didn't think that he'd heard it yet, the new sound that was filling the cabin—

The sound of no screaming.

The sound of no crashing body.

The sound of silence in the other room.

THE BULLETS had missed him. But she hadn't been aiming at him. She'd aimed behind him, shooting at the bedroom door. And she hadn't missed—the doorknob was now destroyed, its lock completely shot through.

She saw the door swing open. And saw the furred rush of anvil-sized paws and bared teeth explode from the room—the room where Grendel had been throwing himself against the walls, launching himself again and again, roaring in frustration and bloodlust, wanting to break through and attack the attacker. Wanting to kill what he sensed was near.

She saw the big cat jump, leaping forward in a spear of fangs and claws, landing on the man's back before the man could even begin to turn. He ripped through the man's throat before the man even stopped smiling, slivered the man's flesh before the body fell down dead.

387

WHEN GRENDEL was finished, he roared again, a different roar this time, the roaring scream of savage victory. Then he padded over to the old woman lying on the floor. She reached out and he felt her stroke his ears. And he heard her telling him again and again the words he loved to hear, telling him, "Good boy, Grendel. You're a good boy, Grendel."

Purring loudly, he settled down beside her to sleep.

She lay still, letting Grendel warm her, feeling the rumbling massage of his purr. Blood dripped from her mouth, and she could feel the slick puddle of it growing on the floor where she rested her cheek. Bleeding and weak, she hoped her family would return home *before*—before another black car arrived, before she died, before she could no longer tell them what she needed to tell them... that Cole was still alive and they needed to find him right away, that they needed to save the boy. She also wanted to tell them that she was so sorry...sorry for what she hadn't felt and hadn't seen, sorry for what she'd thought she'd known. And sorry most of all for having been so sure, for having been so certain, and for having been so wrong.

COLE

COLE RAN.

At first he stood frozen outside the slammed-shut window, his ears still ringing with Callista's words—*Run! The Riffraff's here! Another black car is here! Go!*—knowing he should go, but he couldn't make himself move, couldn't think of what to do. He knew he should run, but he couldn't run. He could only stand there, thinking, *Not again, not again, not again.* And he almost started crying, but he didn't cry. He was tired of crying.

Then he heard two gunshots inside the cabin. The shots, startling and loud, broke his paralysis, making him understand what he needed to do: GO GET HELP. He needed to find the others. Needed to find them and bring them back. Back to kill the Riffraff. Back to save his friend.

So he ran, circling fast around the cabin, heading to the driveway. He wheeled around the front corner, his feet flying, running faster and faster—and then he stopped—scared and surprised, skidding in the gravel only a few steps away from the black car.

The car was so close he could touch it, so close that it seemed it might touch him. It crouched like a big animal in front of him, its black windows gazing at him, making him stand rock-still.

He knew two things.

He knew that if he moved, it would pounce.

And knew that he'd seen something moving inside.

So he waited, motionless and staring, waiting for whatever might come out of the car to devour him. Standing there, he could see a reflection of himself, floating in the car's dark shine. He watched the reflection for a moment, watched as it stood and trembled with fear. The cabin behind him was reflected there, too.

Then he realized he'd been tricked by his own eyes and his terror. No one was sitting in the car, nothing had moved in its black depths—he'd only seen himself, his own running reflection in the car's mirror of black glass and black paint.

Spell broken, he looked down the driveway. The reflected boy looked, too. Cole turned toward the road. So did the other boy. Then Cole raced away alone—no other footsteps following, no ghoul chasing close behind.

As he ran, he heard a scream behind him, something inhuman and piercing inside the cabin. He flinched and almost stopped, almost picked up a stone or a stick and ran back to the cabin. But knew in his heart that sticks and stones wouldn't help right now. Knew that he had to get the others. So when the next scream came soon after the first, he screamed too—screamed a killing scream, and kept running, faster than ever before.

At the road, he looked left, then right, then left again—frantically searching for a clue to tell him which way to turn, which way was the right way to GO GET HELP. But there were no clues except one. It was a small one, but it was all he had.

The mailbox. It was a little help. Not as much as it would have been if he'd known Nanny's address. If he'd known her address, maybe he could have figured it out. Maybe could have looked at the box's stick-on numbers and known that left was the direction he should turn. Or maybe could have quickly figured out that turning right was the wrong direction, maybe would have realized his error and turned back when he saw a lower number on the next mailbox—if he knew Nanny's address. But he didn't.

Even though the address numbers didn't help, the street name did. Sort of. Salt Creek Road—the name was spelled out letter-by-letter with more stick-on squares. Nanny's cabin was on Salt Creek Road, too—that was easy to remember, a real no-brainer because Salt Creek was the same stream he panned for gold in, the name of the same stream and road that circled the hill—

THAT CIRCLED THE HILL.

He knew what to do. Knew that he had to just guess—had to pick a direction and run. Had to run as fast as he could on SALT CREEK ROAD IS A CIRCLE. That he had to keep running until he saw Nanny's cabin and found the others and GOT HELP.

So he guessed.

And turned.

And ran.

BLUE

THE COYOTES ATTACK.

They run out of the trees and are almost upon us before we even know we're in danger. I step in front of Elissa, pushing her behind me and yelling, "Guns!" I face the rushing animals, hoping Elissa will have enough time to pick up a gun and shoot whatever breaks past me. Hoping she'll hand me a gun, too.

The pack has a leader—a black vision with open jaws and long teeth. It springs at Gordy, legs outstretched as it jumps, like a thrown spear aimed at Gordy's throat. Despite the speed of everything that's happening, time seems to slow for a moment and I see the finest details of the coyote, the criss-crossing white scar lines on its black muzzle, the thin cords of foamy drool streaming out of its red mouth, the flakes of dried brown mud on its legs, the tiny green burrs stuck on its chest. As its head floats past me I see its glazed white eye drift by—the eye's pupil is missing, rolled back in the coyote's head by the animal's fury, leaving only a glassy white marble in its socket.

I see all of this in an instant. And I see that Gordy is moving, too, ducking down as the coyote leaps. He sinks to one knee, dropping below its body and reaching up to grab the coyote's outstretched legs, planning to snap the bones as he pulls it down and twists, using the coyote's own momentum to help him break its legs—

Then I see the coyote die. But Gordy hasn't touched it yet, hasn't even placed his knee fully on the ground before the animal is suddenly dead, its neck instantly broken by a single, hammering blow—broken and killed by something I see in front of me, but something I don't understand or believe, by something impossible—yet, impossible or not, it's something that's somehow still standing in our midst, somehow making the ground actually tremble beneath our feet.

The coyote's body flops to the ground, making a loud, final *whumpf* as it hits. The other coyotes stop their attack and start skittering backward, yelping and scrambling away, terrified and surprised by what now stands towering above us, reared up on its hind legs. It bares its teeth and bellows at the retreating, confused pack, batting the air with its powerful front legs—

Ursus arctos horribilis: a sculpted mass of muscle and claw. A creation of blunt, brute strength and ripping, shredding power. Clothed in a coarse coat of gray and silver-tipped brown hairs—

A grizzly bear.

Standing at Gordy's side.

Standing where Setsu had stood only seconds before.

We are suddenly quiet. Quiet in the way of those who witness a miracle. Quiet like those who are present when the answer to a mystery is revealed, but then find the answer is a mystery, too. Quiet like those presented with a haunting and wondrous glance at larger things unknown.

As we watch, still transfixed by the impossibility of its presence, the grizzly bear begins shimmering. Its coat becomes indistinct and its shape folds in upon itself, transforming before our eyes. Then, as quickly as it had appeared, the bear is gone and Setsu again stands by Gordy. Gordy looks at Setsu. Then looks down at the coyote's crumpled body.

"Sweet holy Jesus," he says.

IT HAPPENED in seconds. In that small speck of time, everything became real—more real than old stories of ancient places, more real than tales of wondrous gifts and mythic battles. It became more than only physical, grisly facts and reminders of unspeakable acts, more real than the brutal, bloody deaths of those we had just buried.

Now we knew it was true.

All of it was true.

We'd already believed it in our hearts. Now we knew it in our minds. We'd seen it. Had been saved by it. The stories were no longer myths and legends. No longer only an old and treasured tapestry of symbols and metaphors. The stories were real: magic and evil and good were all around us—some of it fighting against us, some of it fighting for us. A living, breathing part of the magic now stood with us at these three graves, mourning with us for those who were lost. And in some way I didn't fully understand—watching Setsu bow his head with us, hearing him murmur his prayers with us, knowing that his love for us was real—that seemed like a sort of magic, too.

As we walk back to the cars, Gordy is behind me when I hear him call my name, telling me to wait for him to catch up. Before he reaches me, I know what he'll say. Before he even spoke my name, I knew. I'd known it as I followed him here, when I was watching him talk with Setsu as they drove in his truck. Before that, sitting around the table this morning, when we learned that the Riffraff lived in some deep, dark hole, and Gordy and I had looked at each other, both of us suddenly certain where to find the Riffraff's nest—that's when I first knew.

He isn't going back to the cabin with us.

He's going to the Glammerys' hole.

"Think of it as reconnaissance," he says. "Gathering information behind enemy lines. I'll take a quick look around, then leave."

We don't need "information," I tell him. We need him. "And don't bullshit me. We both know the real reason you're going."

"All right, now who's bullshitting who?" he answers. "All we know is that we don't know squat about what's going on down that hole. We have no idea what we're up against—not a single damn clue about what surprises are on the way."

He and I stop walking. The others continue toward the cars, leaving us alone.

"Blue," he asks, "were you listening to the story? I was—and I heard the part about that thing wanting to take out the entire fucking hill when he pulled this shit the last time. Who knows what his plan is now? Besides, I'll be fine. Don't forget, this is what I do every day: I spy in the woods. I sneak up on people. I watch what they do. Then I arrest them or shoot them or I just leave. But I'm not arresting anybody today—hell, I'm probably not even shooting anybody either. This is just a quick sneak and peek, that's all. I'll be back at the cabin before dinner. And even if I'm late, I'll find you guys later—up on the hill. And, Brother Blue, you're wrong about that other thing—I'm not going there because of that. It has nothing to do with this."

"Gordy."

"What?"

The only thing I know how to tell him is also the thing that will hurt him the most. "Gordy, you've always told people that she's dead. You even tell it to yourself. And everybody you've told believes it. Everybody but you. And you're the one who should believe it most of all. You should believe it with all your heart. Because she told you it was what she wanted, that it was the choice she was choosing. Sarah's gone, Gordy. Gone a long time ago. She let herself go away. She let herself disappear. So let her stay gone. Do what she asked you to do: Let her stay dead."

And just as I'd known what he was going to say when he called my name, I also know what he'll say now—because I know he can't say anything else. Because I know he has never stopped loving her, that he has never forgotten the color of her hair or the flower-print of her dress or the way she felt in his arms on that day so long ago at school.

"Can't do it, brother," he says. "I've gotta go there. Gotta go see." He smacks my arm. "You understand, right? You know I have to, don't you?"

I nod. He's right: I do know.

And as much as I know all of this, I know something else even more.

I know that I will never see my friend again.

LIKE I KNEW about Gordy, Elissa knows something, too. As we pull out of the driveway—we turn right, Gordy turns left—Elissa looks at me, her eyes worried, her voice tight.

"Something's wrong at home," she says. "We need to get home, Blue. We need to get home *right now*."

She speaks only once more on the trip, not turning to me but staying focused straight ahead, feeling something in her heart. She says it while I'm speeding through the narrow turns, pushing the car hard on the steep ups and downs, racing through the miles that lead back to our home.

"Faster," she says. "We need to go faster."

COLE

*H*E FILLED HIS *mind with the Very Most Important Thing and thought of nothing else, concentrating on it as he ran without stopping, willing himself to keep going no matter what—willing air into his lungs and out again. Willing his legs to keep pumping up and down. Willing his feet to keep moving step after step after step. Willing his pounding heart not to explode.*

A CAR was coming. It was somewhere up ahead, still hidden by the curves and hills, but he heard the engine revving as the car climbed an incline, then revving even higher as it sped downhill. It was moving fast, too fast for the narrow road, probably swinging out too wide in the turns, not leaving enough room for other cars. Still running, Cole swerved from the center of the road to its edge, where he'd be safe even if the car came too far over the middle.

He tried to stay focused, tried to keep thinking only about the Very Most Important Thing and nothing else. But concentrating was harder now because he was also listening to the approaching car. And he was hoping, too—hoping that whoever was driving would stop when they saw him, hoping they'd listen to him and would take him to GO GET HELP. And he was hoping for one last thing—that the pain would end when he finally did what the pain wanted him to do and he could finally STOP RUNNING NOW. He wanted to do exactly that. Wanted to stop running and double over and vomit and catch his breath. But he knew he couldn't stop, not yet. He wasn't done. So he kept running, side by side with the pain.

He slowed down only long enough at each driveway to see that it wasn't Nanny T.'s, then he sped up again, running as fast as he could to the car he could hear racing toward him.

The pain wanted him to quit. Wanted him to stop and fail. He'd felt it early, nudging and testing him. At first he ignored it—acted like he couldn't feel it, like there was nothing wrong. He ignored it as long as he could, just kept running. Kept thinking GO GET HELP and thought of nothing else. But he couldn't ignore it anymore. The pain was filling his head, making him pay attention, running alongside him, pace for pace. It whispered to him as he ran, telling him to slow down, telling him to STOP RUNNING RIGHT NOW. It bumped against him. Stuck needles in his side. And it kicked at his heels to trip him—his feet banged together and tangled, almost making him fall down, but he straightened out of the stumble and kept running.

He could feel the pain everywhere. It was cramping his legs— his thigh muscles were knotted and burning, and he hit his legs with his fists as he ran, pounding at the knots. And the pain was stealing his breath—his chest was bursting, he kept sucking in air, kept filling his lungs, but couldn't get enough air, couldn't swallow enough oxygen to give him back his wind. And the pain was filling his head—the bruise on his forehead was pulsing and throbbing, slamming a club into his brain, making his vision begin to blur and spin, unbalancing him so that he began drifting as he ran, drifting back across the road...

The car was close now, only seconds away.

Cole wiped at the sweat pouring down his face, rubbing his eyes with the back of his arm as he ran, trying to stop the stinging and see the road more clearly. The car's engine sounded like it was already right next to him. He started waving his hands in the air, wanting to be sure the car saw him when it made the turn up ahead, wanting to be sure that it knew to stop—

—but suddenly he felt too dizzy to stand. Felt his raised arms somehow floating away from his body and his center of gravity somehow rolling to somewhere low and behind his head, pulling him backward, yanking him down. As he tottered on his feet, trying not to fall down, trying to lock his knees and stay upright, the car appeared in front of him, and he saw that he'd guessed right, that the car was indeed going too fast, was swinging too wide around the turn—

—then the gravity pulling at him won, making his knees buckle as the blood rushed down from his head to his feet. He crumpled forward. As he fell, it seemed to him that he was floating slowly to the ground. He looked at the road as he fell, watching it come closer, but coming way too slow. And, as he looked at the road, he realized that something was terribly wrong, that somehow he'd made a mistake—

He wasn't at the edge of the road anymore.

He wasn't anywhere safe at all.

He heard the car's brakes squealing and tires skidding. Heard its engine whine, heard gears grinding, heard the engine shift down fast. Then he heard yelling, words screamed in teenage voices as the car drove by, screaming "STUPID, GODDAMNED IDIOT" and "GET OUTTA THE GODDAMNED ROAD," then laughter and another voice yelling "HAVE ANOTHER DRINK WHYDONCHA, ASSHOLE!" And the engine revved again and the car sped away.

Sprawled on the road, he listened to the car leave, thinking that it was still going too fast, that it was probably still swinging out too wide in the turns.

Minutes passed. He knew he should get up. Had to get up. That he shouldn't just lie there in the road. But it felt so very good to finally rest for a while, so good to feel the pain finally creeping away. He knew he was forgetting something—forgetting a Very Most Important Thing—but he was so very tired. And his eyes were so very heavy. And it felt so very good to finally breathe. It all felt so good that he was almost disappointed when he heard another car coming from the same direction as the first one. And he thought about staying right where he was, about not moving and hoping that the car would drive by without noticing him. But then he remembered the Very Most Important Thing that he had to do— had to GO GET HELP.

Lifting his head, he decided to stand up, or at least get up on his hands and knees and get out of the road, but had no idea what to do when he discovered that his legs weren't ready to do anything, that they weren't ready to move at all. And he didn't know what to do when the world started spinning again, when it started dipping and swirling right in front of his eyes.

The second car was coming closer, coming fast, but not too fast, not fast enough to worry him at any other time—but this time he was lying in the middle of the road. He looked at the turn where the car would appear. Another wave of dizziness swept through him, knocking his head back down on the pavement. He took some deep breaths and felt the dizziness ease a little. He waited a moment—felt his eyes clearing, saw the world stop spinning—then lifted his head again. The car was coming around the turn now, driving straight at him. But, almost instantly, it started braking, started slowing down and turning away from him, skidding to a stop only a few feet from where he was sprawled.

Seeing the car, Cole felt his eyes cloud up again, felt his vision blearing with tears. Only not bad tears this time, not the kind of tears he was tired of crying. These were good tears. Wonderful tears. Because things were finally better. Because help was finally here. And it could hardly be a better kind of help at all.

Because the mailman was here.

And the mailman would know exactly where to find Nanny's cabin.

The mailman would know everything Cole needed to know.

Cole felt so happy and lucky and saved. He watched the mailman get out of the mail truck and walk toward him. He wondered for just a moment about the large, empty mailbag in the mailman's hand.

The mailman squatted down beside him. "Well, aren't you a cute little biscuit?" he said to Cole. "Aren't you just porridge and pie?"

He snapped the empty mailbag up and down.

The canvas bag opened with the sound of a cracking whip.

CHICORY

THE COSMIC CYCLE. It was happening again—was swinging back around, coming full circle. He could feel it as he woke up. Could feel it in his bones. Felt it in his soul, too.

The wonderful wheel—

He'd heard its music while he slept, heard it winding through his dreams. He could hear the music even now (faintly though, barely at all) as he lay in bed, half-asleep. He lay still, thinking about last night. Thinking about what had happened at the monkey cage. Thinking about the padlock. Thinking about the arrow-shape under the shroud.

And thinking, most of all, about what Gordy had told him at the end.

He understood: It was about endings and beginnings. About everything flowing along in a mystical river of chance and opportunity. A river of comings and goings. Endlessly circling. Offering choices. Waiting for him to choose....

It didn't have to wait long. He'd already chosen.

He'd made his choice last night.

He got out of bed, rising unsteadily, last night's alcohol still coursing through his system. He was still tired. His body wanted to keep sleeping, wanted to stay cushioned in the soft blankets and pillows. But he stayed standing, rocking unevenly back and forth. He'd lie back down when he was finished—maybe fall back asleep again and dream some more. Maybe even hear the music again—the music of the universal rotation, the music of the eternal river.

He'd made his choice. It was time.

He walked through the house, opening drawers and cabinets. Looking everywhere. And at last he found what he was looking for. Found it where it had been tucked away for years.

LATER, STANDING in front of the bathroom mirror, he hesitated, reconsidering what he was about to do. As his thoughts wandered, the blade he was holding began slipping out of his grasp. He reflexively tightened his grip just before it dropped.

He stared at the blade. Thought that maybe he should wait a while longer, maybe sober up a little more. Maybe think things through one more time. But in his heart he knew not to wait—knew he'd already seen too much in this life, too much for him to bear: This life would always be haunted, would always be lit by pinwheel flashes of blue-green-white in front of his eyes (*even now he could see the tiny green sneaker, its loose white laces dangling down…and could see the bright blue eyes that gazed down at him*).

No.

He wouldn't wait.

He wouldn't think about it anymore.

He understood—

It was about endings and beginnings.

About things that were born, and things that died.

He'd done what he was supposed to do. He'd finished his task.

It had been a good life. But now it was time—

Time to ride the wonderful wheel.

Time to swim in the mystical river.

Time for him to die.

HARLEY 54

"THE BOY," the voice had said. Hearing it, he'd turned his truck around, knowing he was supposed to speed back the way he'd come. As he drove, he felt the eye moving behind his eyes, felt it peering out through his skull. It was looking everywhere, straining to see everything, scanning from the woods to the road to the stream—searching all the deep-shadowed places where a fleeing boy might hide.

Then he'd driven around a wide bend.

And he found what the voice wanted him to find.

And he heard what it wanted him to do.

He put the boy in the bag. It was easy. He just lifted the kid's feet and stuck them in, then worked the bag up inch by inch, pushing down on the boy's hips, rolling him from one side to the other whenever the canvas snagged or caught. The boy didn't fight, just flopped back and forth when he rolled—his legs and arms making little jerky movements, his voice making little jerky sounds.

It didn't take long to stuff him in, only a few minutes. As he pulled the bag over the boy's shoulders, he'd looked into the boy's eyes and was surprised by what he saw—or, instead, was surprised by what he didn't see: The boy wasn't crying. There were no tears on his face. Just confusion. And anger.

"Well, hello, Tom Terrific! You're sure a brave one," Harley said, making small talk, deciding there was no reason to be unfriendly. "I gotta tell you, though," he said. "If it was me in the bag, well, I'd be crapping my pants."

JUST BEFORE he closed the bag, he pushed the back of the boy's head down, forcing the kid's chin toward his chest to take up less room in the bag. But he paused when he touched the boy's hair and felt the young straw-and-fur feel of it, warm and soft from the road and sun.

For a moment—a moment when he heard only his own thoughts, a moment when he saw only through his own eyes—Harley almost stopped, almost took the boy out of the bag. Almost gathered him safely in his arms and took him to go get help.

Almost.

But then the voice spoke again. It spoke honestly and sincerely. And it made so very much sense.

The moment passed.

You almost got me, Tom Terrific! You almost spoiled the plan, he thought, pushing down harder on the boy's head. He pulled the bag's drawstrings and cinched the top closed, then wound the strings around and around the bag's neck, finally knotting them tight, thinking, *Just try to escape from that, Tom Terrific!*

Then he heard the voice laughing and the sound made Harley so happy, made him so glad he'd pleased the voice that he said the words out loud this time, yelling them at the boy inside the mail sack. "Escape from that, Tom! Escape now, Tom Terrific!" And the voice laughed louder, laughed so much that it made Harley start laughing, too, and Harley knew that it might all look a little crazy, that it might look absolutely nuts to anyone who didn't understand, but it didn't matter what anyone else thought, it didn't matter a single bit, and too bad for them if they don't get to share in the joke, too bad for them if they didn't know that laughter was good for the soul.

And right then, right when he was sure everything was as good as it could be—that's when it got even better! Their laughter had started trailing off, fading to a few last sniffles and snorts as things calmed down, and then Harley saw something so damned funny he started laughing again, even harder than before. He couldn't help it, the joke was that good, and jokes are for sharing between friends, so of course he had to tell.

"Look," he said, jabbing the bag with his finger, pointing at the big letters printed across the canvas. "Read that!" He was laughing so hard now he was crying, the joke was just so great. "U.S. Mail! U.S. Mail!" he said. "Get it? U.S. *Male*! U.S. Male! Get it?" Then, a moment later, he heard the voice "get it"—he heard its slow chuckles at first, then an explosion of hysterical giggles.

It was then—sitting in the middle of the road, listening to the good sounds of laughter—that Harley smiled and silently gave thanks, knowing he was both lucky and blessed. *This is what matters,* he thought. *This is all that's important. Friends and laughter. That's all a person really needs. That's what it's all about.*

But of course a person couldn't spend the whole day laughing. Not with work still to do. Not with a delivery still to make. He stood, yanking the top of the bag to set it upright in the road.

"Time to go, Tom Terrific," he said, "Time for you to meet the boys."

He dragged the bag to his truck, shuffling backward a step at a time, saving his strength, trying not to strain himself (*but, son of a bitch, the boy was heavy*). He could already feel the heavy heat in his arms and back, the early, deep-burning pain, and sure as shit, he'd be eating some pills tonight, eating them by the handful, and he already felt his muscles hurting now, but knew he'd feel worse even later, after he dead-lifted the bag into the truck and then after that when he lifted it again to dump it out.

He almost made it to the truck before he had to rest, needing a half a second to catch his breath and straighten his back. As he stood there, moaning and groaning a little, pressing his lower spine with his palms, a car came screaming around the turn up ahead. It came straight at him, accelerating until it was almost on top of him before it braked and swerved around, tires screeching, brakes squealing, the driver flipping Harley the finger, yelling at him "MOVE, MAILMAN!"

Harley watched the car speed away. He shook his head, thinking how sad it was who they let drive on the roads these days.

"Lunatics," he told the voice. "Buncha goddamned lunatics."

HARLEY

55

THE BOY still wasn't talking, still wasn't moving in the bag. *I bet he talks later*, Harley thought. *I bet he starts dancing and singing when he meets the boys.*

He'd never been to where he was driving. Had never gone near it, not once in eighteen years of delivering mail. In all that time he'd never gotten off of the roads, never turned onto any of the overgrown and forgotten trails. Until now. But this time he knew exactly where he was going. And knew exactly what he would see—the eye had already shown him. The eye was helping him see. The voice was helping, too. It guided him forward, whispering, *Turn here. And now here. And then turn again, just up ahead....*

He drove deeper into the woods, slowly up the hill. At some places the soft ground yielded so easily to the weight of his truck that sometimes it sank, almost completely bogging down before he felt the big tires bite into solid earth and then climb out of the troughs and keep going forward.

Other times, there was no path to see. Young branches full of leaves hung down from the trees and reached out from the sides of the trail. They pressed against the truck windows, entombing him in green, completely blinding him to the way. But he kept going forward. Because the eye still saw. Because the voice was always there.

Then the voice said one more word. *Here.*

He stopped the truck. Looked around. Recognized it all. He'd seen it before, had seen it through the eye like he'd seen everything else today, from beginning to end. Just like he'd seen the boy. And the bag. And the path up the hill.

What he now saw was exactly what he'd expected to see. It was what he'd already been shown: a small black hole in the side of the hill. A dark doorway slanting down into the earth. It was the mouth of a low, narrow cave—the place where Simon and Creel were waiting for the boy...the place where snakes slept among the Glammery bones.

Harley looked at the mailbag. The boy was still quiet, but he was moving now, pushing at the canvas with his hands and feet, testing the bag's strength. Harley watched the bulges where the boy pushed his fists against the canvas, and where the toes of the boy's tennis shoes pressed hard against the bag's bottom. He watched for several minutes, wondering how long the boy would struggle before he finally got tired, how long it would be before he realized that he wasn't ever getting out of the bag. Ever.

Finally, tired of watching the bag, Harley opened the truck's back door. "All right, Tom Terrific," he said. "Time for me to deliver the mail. Time for you to meet the boys."

He pulled on the bag, sliding it toward him and lifting it up to the lip of the cargo trunk. Once the bag was over the edge, he dropped it, letting it hit the ground hard—not really caring if the boy got hurt. Thinking that, at this point, it didn't really matter much at all.

HARLEY

56

THE BOY was yelling now, shouting and punching and trying to turn. The corners of his elbows and knees would suddenly angle out, pushing at the sides of the bag, then just as quickly pull back, then immediately push somewhere else. The heavy canvas muffled some of the boy's yells, but not much. Harley heard every word, heard every threat the boy made, heard every screamed, "Please...please!"

Told you, Harley thought. *I knew you'd start talking.*

He dragged the bag up a slight rise. The ground was rocky, making him step carefully. *Careful, Harley, don't want to twist an ankle here.* He moved backwards slowly, looking over his shoulder every few seconds, making sure that nothing was slithering out of the cave behind him. Snakes were supposed to rattle before they bit you, he knew that, but with his luck, sure as shit he'd step backward onto the only snake that didn't believe in firing a warning shot. Luckily though, there was no problem so far. Not for him, at least. But the boy sure wasn't having the best time he'd ever had. Every time the bag bumped over one of the bigger rocks, the boy screamed again—each scream a little angrier than the last, a little more pain-filled. And a little more afraid.

HARLEY COULD SEE the bones. They were at the base of the cave's ramped floor. The skeletons were lying close together, their ribcages like two white baskets set side by side. And the baskets were full of nasty surprises. As Harley's eyes adjusted to the gloom, he started seeing more than the pale white of the bones. Now he could also see the black shapes that were moving inside the skeletons' rib cages, the black masses pulsing and sliding upon themselves, slipping and flowing, yet somehow remaining coiled and contained. Unlike the floor—

The floor was alive.

The snakes were everywhere. They writhed and curved in every direction, gliding noiselessly...except for the hollow rattling sound beginning to fill the cave. The snakes were aware of him now, could sense his body heat at their door. The rattling got louder, spread across the floor, was soon coming from even the cave's farthest, darkest corners, the black places that Harley still couldn't see.

Harley poked the bag with his toe and laughed out loud. "Hear that?" he said, loud enough for the boy to hear him over the rattles. "Everybody down there says to tell you, 'Hi.' Everybody says, 'Hello!'"

HARLEY

THE RATTLING was getting louder, building and swelling as though the snakes sensed what was about to happen. Harley stopped at the cave's entrance, looking in as far as he could see, shivering with pleasure, enchanted by the two sounds surrounding him, sweeping him up in their music. The sounds were thrilling and frightening—the sounds of poison and fangs and nightmares, the sounds of death approaching.

Listening, he realized how perfect it was, the way the two different sounds blended together, creating a harmony more beautiful than either sound alone. It made him linger, wanting to hear more, carried away by the song. He knew that he should get to work, but he waited a little longer, losing himself in the wonderful music made by the rattling snakes and the crying, screaming child.

Finally, after a few minutes more of the music, he squatted down, dropping low and bending his knees as he wrapped his arms around the bag. The boy was squirming more than ever inside the bag, trying to drive blows and kicks into Harley's body. But the bag was too confining for him to build up any power.

Harley took four deep slow breaths, preparing to lift and throw. As he inhaled, he reminded himself, *Lift with your legs, not with your back!* He counted each breath, taking his time, saying, "One Mississippi. Two Mississippi. Three Mississippi. Four Mississippi." Then he grabbed the bag and stood, holding the awkward, shifting weight in his arms. He pivoted his hips away from the cave's entrance as he lifted, wanting to build up some power and speed in his throw, enough to send the bag rolling all the way to the bottom, enough for it to reach the pile of bones—

—now he twisted back fast, swinging toward the cave, simultaneously leaning forward and releasing the bag. As the bag left his grasp, he instinctively knew he was throwing it well, with strength and good timing. He watched it land and roll, seeing how quickly it was already almost to the bottom of the slanted floor, almost down to the bones. Then he suddenly felt his spine spasm and cramp, a bolt of pain folding him over, making him gasp with surprise at the shock of it. Bent and stumbling and surprised, he felt himself pitching forward, following the bag down into the cave. And as he fell, he heard a third voice adding itself to the musical harmony. A gasping scream that rose higher and higher. A different scream than the boy's, but still the sound of nightmares, still the sound of death approaching.

THE SNAKES filled him with their poison, striking first as he stumbled past them, reeling down the ramped earth, then striking him again as he swayed upright, teetering for a second before he collapsed to the floor. Then striking again as he landed.

He landed face-down on top of the bag, his arms and legs splayed out. He could feel the boy moving weakly under him, trying to push him off. But Harley didn't move. Couldn't move. Couldn't do anything, couldn't even keep screaming. There was too much pain inside him—pain so large that it demanded all of him, leaving no room for anything else.

He could only lie there, feeling the snakes continue to bite him. Feeling their fangs sinking into his hands and his arms. Into his thighs, and back, and shoulders. He even felt them biting his face—their fangs striking his cheeks and the venom pouring in, swelling shut his nose and his eyes, the poison burning so hot he was sure his skin had caught fire, was sure his flesh was crisping and turning to ash.

He could hear other sounds now. Sounds that joined the snakes' rattling. It was the sound of their striking bodies—the flat, smacking claps of their triangular heads hitting against his flesh. And another sound, too, like rain falling inside of the cave. At first this sound confused him, but then he understood—it was still the snakes. They were striking the bag beneath him, hitting it again and again, striking the canvas so often that it pattered and drummed with the beat of their attack.

AT THE VERY last, he heard the voice again, one more time. Heard it say, *Looking good, Harley. Looking good. Bye-bye, Harley*, and for a moment he saw himself through the eye—saw the dead weight of his swollen, motionless body collapsed across the mailbag, anchoring it forever to the ground. And he saw that the bag was no longer moving either, that even Tom Terrific seemed to have gone away.

Then the voice was silent.

And then the eye winked closed.

COLE

*T*HE SNAKES *kept striking, snapping their heads forward, driving their hollow fangs down onto the bag's thick canvas. Their fangs left spatters of venom all over the bag's surface, but they couldn't pierce the heavy material. Rivulets of the clear poison pooled and ran together, flowing down the bag's sides and dripping onto the floor.*

DARKNESS.

The rattling noise was everywhere. He'd known what it was as soon as he heard it. The sound had grabbed his heart and squeezed, making him cry out in terror. Now it was all around him, enveloping him like the bag, covering him and pressing down, freezing him with fear.

He felt the snakes striking. It was like being slapped again and again, not hard enough to hurt, just enough to make him wince. Even worse were the moments when nothing struck—when he waited, knowing the next strike was coming but not knowing from where, not knowing if it would be the one that finally sliced through the bag. Not knowing if it would be the one that killed him. Like they had killed the mailman.

Cole had heard the mailman die. Had heard him screaming, then felt him fall on the bag. Heard him say, "Bye-bye," just before he stopped twitching, just before the smells of poop and pee filtered into the bag.

Cole couldn't move. The mailman's heavy body was on top of him, pinning him down. The man's dead arms and legs bracketed the corners of the bag, like the bars of a cage.

He was lying face down, the right side of his face pressed hard against the cave's floor through the bottom of the bag, his right arm bent under him, caught under his stomach. His other arm was stretched flat along his side. His hips were twisted left, his knees drawn up close to his chest. *Like a little baby*, he thought. *A little baby, all curled up in the dark, hiding under the blankets, hoping that the monsters couldn't see him, hoping the monsters would stay away—*

And like a frightened baby, he knew something that most grownups didn't know, something most people forget when they grow old. But it was something he'd never forget, not ever: *The monsters were real.* And they were everywhere—they were waiting in the dark, waiting for the blankets to slide away. And they were there in the daylight, too. Driving mail trucks and black cars.

And the monsters didn't just kill children.

They killed everyone.

HE WAS GOING to die. He knew that. He just didn't know how. Didn't know if it would be from one of the good ways or if it would be from the very bad way. He hoped it would be one of the good ways. So he waited, hoping for one of the good ways to die—

—hoping the snakes would kill him, waiting to feel their poison enter his body, wondering how much it would hurt when it did, wondering how long he would writhe in the bag before he grew cold and still.

—hoping his air would run out and he'd suffocate, his lungs burning for air at the end, gulping breath after breath, needing more fresh air than what could seep through the sack.

—hoping he would starve to death, or die of thirst, or that maybe his heart would burst and stop.

—if he just hoped hard enough.

He waited, hoping one of these would be the way he died. Hoping one of these would happen first, before the bad way happened—

Before the blanket fell away.

Before the monster came for him again.

BLUE

I DRIVE recklessly, pushing the car hard, then pushing it even harder, wanting to get home quickly. Wholly believing Elissa's words: Faster, Blue. We need to go faster. Because now I feel it, too, the feeling that Elissa sensed right away. The certainty that something is wrong.

THE FIRST THING I see is the black car in my driveway.

Then I see the cabin's open front door.

And then…the feet sticking out of the door.

The feet belong to a dead man. Standing over him, I see that there's no doubt he's dead, and it's also easy to see that one of two things killed him—it was either the gunshots, or it was the other thing. There are three bullet holes in his chest. His blood has poured out through them, drenching him in red. Maybe the gunshots killed him. Or maybe it was the other thing—the other thing is that his head is almost completely torn from his body. The skin is flayed from his shoulders and neck, and his bloody neck bones are bare and splintered. They've been broken and chewed on with savage intent.

There are large, saucer-shaped paw prints in the blood around the body.

The prints lead across the floor, over to another body.

Over to my mother.

Grendel is guarding Callista. He's stretched beside her, lying so that she's between him and the wall. His face is blood-covered and he doesn't move when he sees us, doesn't even budge as Elissa and Alassadir rush over. He only stands up and leaves Cally's side at the last moment, giving her over to Elissa and Alassadir's care when they kneel and reach out to her.

"She's warm, Blue," Elissa says, cupping Callista's face. "She's alive."

Callista stirs at Elissa's touch. Her eyes flutter open. "Cole," she whispers. "Find Cole."

I see that Grendel has gone to a far corner and settled back down on the floor. He lies there, out of the way, watching things unfold. While watching us, he licks a broad front paw and rubs his damp foot over his face, beginning to wash the blood off his whiskers. I walk over to him. And I tell my friend once again what it seems like I am always telling him: "Good cat, Grendel. Good cat." Then I scratch his ears and hug him. And thank him for saving my mom.

COLE IS MISSING.

As Elissa and Alassadir speak softly with Cally, Setsu and I begin searching for the boy. He isn't in the cabin. And he's not outside. I search the dead man for a clue. We carry the body out of the cabin on a blanket, doing it that way to keep his head attached by what little skin is still holding it on. We put him down beside the black car, and I go through his pockets, having no idea what I'm hoping to find, unable to think of anything he might have that could help us, but I need to try everything, need to check for anything that can help us find Cole.

It doesn't take long to confirm what I expected: the body is only a body. It holds no answers, it offers no direction. Besides his car keys, the only other thing the man is carrying is tucked inside the blood-soaked pocket of his suit jacket. It's an advertising give-away:

a blue and yellow, flame-shaped, plastic pen. A smiling match flame character floats up and down inside a clear tube in the pen's center. The words printed on the pen are the same ones painted across the hood of the black car: *TURNING UP THE HEAT, NATURALLY!*

INSIDE THE CABIN, Elissa finishes checking Callista. "You're right," she says. "It's your ribs. If that's it, there isn't a lot to do except wrap them tight and give you pain pills. But it might be more than your ribs, I can't tell for sure. We'll take you—"

"Wrap me, then," Callista gasps. "Give me pills. And get me up off the damn floor. But don't even think about a hospital, not until this is over." She takes shallow breaths, inhalations that barely move her chest. It's easy to see that every word hurts her, that every movement is agony. "I'm going to be fine," she says. "And I'm certainly going to the Circle. I'll get all the help I need later," she says, still gasping at the pain. "Now, though, we need to find the boy."

She looks at the sofa where she and Cole sat and talked this morning. "Did he leave anything?" she asks. "Did anything fall out of his pockets? I need something from him. Anything that was his. Maybe I can use it to find him. Maybe I can use it to see."

At her words, everyone rushes to the couch—except me. I stand still, feeling puzzled and certain at the same time. Absolutely knowing that I have the best answer to what she's asking for, but unable to immediately remember what it is. I stand motionless, waiting for inspiration, looking wildly around the cabin. Feeling the answer is right in front of me, but only drawing a frustrating blank.

Then I remember. And run outside.

It's in the car trunk, right where I'd left it.

His treasure chest.

Running back into the cabin, carrying the small wooden box tight in my arms, I can hear the geode crystals and the empty green bottle clinking together. It sounds like a handful of dice being rolled, like a game of chance being played.

BLUE

ELISSA HELPS CALLY stand and they walk into our bedroom, where my wife binds my mother's ribs, brings her pain pills and a glass of cold water, wipes the blood from her face, and brushes her hair. When Cally walks back into the front room, she walks with a careful, brittle step, as if each tiny movement is breaking something inside her.

Cally sits stiffly in one of the hard, kitchen chairs. She holds the treasure chest on her lap. The box's hinged lid is open, revealing the jumbled collection of things that Cole finds precious. The geode crystals. The Royall Lyme bottle. Three old coins (a buffalo nickel, a Mercury dime, a copper wheat penny). Two peeled-off paper labels (one from a Heineken Beer bottle, the other from Green Apple Jones Soda). Two chess pieces, a castle and a knight, both pieces finely detailed and yellowed with age, like carved ivory. A single, dark green marble (it's a big "shooter" with a white swirl through the middle). And, finally, a long silky ribbon, rolled to fit inside the box, printed with *#1 Son, Happy Birthday!* in gold letters on a white background (there's a faint streak of dried, light-blue cake icing smeared across part of the ribbon). It is an innocent's treasure, a collection of neat stuff, found art, preserved memories. A box filled full of a child's gathered-up special moments.

Elissa stares into the box, then begins to cry, pressing her face against my shoulder. Then she pulls away and looks up into my face. "Blue, don't let the bastards take another boy. Not him too." I hold her, feeling her warm tears on my throat. And I know that she is right: They can't be allowed this theft. We won't surrender this boy. *And listen, Secret Jesus, I pray. If they do have him—if he's hurt, or if he's worse—I know another thing, too: They can't have him for free. And they have no idea how much they're going to pay.*

"HE'S ALIVE," Callista says. She is pressing her hands against Cole's treasure box, staring down at it, her eyes wide and unfocused. She's been this way for several minutes as the rest of us stand around her, quiet and waiting. "He's alive," she says again. She seems to be listening with her hands. "I don't understand this," she says a minute later, "I don't know how to say this—he feels surrounded, but he also knows that he's alone. And he knows that death is almost touching him—he feels its tight arms, feels it keeping him close, keeping him still and unmoving...but he isn't dying! And he's worried that he may not die in time, that it might be far too long before he's dead."

Callista closes the chest's lid and continues staring at the box. When she speaks again, her voice is filled with more than the pain of her broken ribs. We also hear the sound of her breaking heart. "I can't help at all," she says. "Not anymore. That's all I can see. And I'm so sorry, but I don't know what it means...I have no idea at all."

I quickly kneel beside her, grateful for her gift. "Mom, you've helped more than you know. Everything you've said is helpful. It all matters right now. Everything you said will help us find Cole."

Because I know enough—

He's alive, not dead. He's in one place. Isn't going anywhere, isn't being taken somewhere. He's alone, which means he isn't at the Glammerys'. And isn't where he can see anybody else, so he might be hiding somewhere—maybe in an empty cabin. And he isn't in danger right now, not yet, maybe not for days. But danger is coming, and when it comes, he knows it will be bad. So bad that he'd rather be dead.

It's enough. Enough for me to know what to do next.

I pull the keys out of my pocket—keys taken from the dead man. Keys to the black car.

I'm going for a drive.

IT HAS to be me. I'm the one who needs to look for the boy, the one most familiar with the roads. The one who knows the places to search and how to get to them. The one with the greatest chance of noticing something out of place.

Besides, no one else can leave right now. Elissa needs to stay and care for my mother. Alassadir needs to continue gathering the details of what happens—he needs to be here when it's over and done, so that the story remains alive. And Setsu needs to protect and watch over them all, needs to keep them safe from whatever else might visit.

So it has to be me. Only me.

I need to look for the boy.

Alone.

BLUE

I T IS CALLED MIMICRY.

Through the process of adaptation, an animal or insect evolves to mimic the appearance of a different animal or insect. By this purposeful redesign, the wardrobes of hunters and hunted become mixed. The hunters begin wearing the hunteds' garb, and the hunted don costumes that mirror the hunters' shapes and colors.

So clothed, each desires to fool the other. Each one hopes to escape notice, and—if seen—hopes that the other will pause, be deceived, and then look away. The process serves both predator and prey, ultimately advancing one of two simple outcomes for each creature: help it to eat more, or help it to avoid being eaten.

It's about survival, about allowing the predator to move closer to their unsuspecting prey. About allowing the prey to move unharmed among the predators.

Mimicry—

It is why I'm taking the black car to search for Cole. Because I want to move freely where the predators are roaming, because I want the chance to get close. Because, if I'm seen, I want them to pause, be deceived, then look away...because I want the chance to prey upon them.

BEFORE I GO, Elissa pulls me away from the others. "Find Cole," she says. "But come home, too. I need you here, for when all of this is done...for when it's more than just you and me...."

As she speaks, I realize the time is here. She's decided to tell me, to share the news that I've been wondering when she'd share, the news I've been acting like I didn't know, like I'd noticed no changes at all—like I couldn't see the wonderful swellings and darkenings that have begun shaping and filling her body. And like I haven't observed the small differences accumulating in her days: her trips to the bathroom, her naps, the ever-shifting prism of her moods.

I've been waiting for her to tell me. Waiting for when she feels strong enough, for when she feels the time is right—the time when her happiness overwhelms her sadness, when her joy surpasses her sorrow.

I've been waiting for today.

"Come back to *our family*," she tells me, taking my hand and placing it above the slight, round miracle within her womb. "Find Cole. Then come home. Home to the family we're going to be."

I TALK WITH Setsu last. Or, rather, he talks with me. He takes me aside before I touch the black car.

"Go search," he says, "but return before the moon. Under the moon, we must heal the Circle. Under the moon, it must be won again." He looks over at Elissa, who is watching us from the porch. When she sees us turn and look in her direction, she waves, then steps back inside the cabin. Setsu looks at me again. "If the battle is won, all of the children—found or not—might still be saved. All of them, Blue. But if the Circle is lost...."

We look at each other. It's hard to believe that we met only hours ago. His face is not a stranger's face—it seems to be the face of someone I've known all my life.

"Hunt well, my brother," he says. He reaches up, squeezes my shoulder. "Keep safe. And be back before the moon." Then without

426

a backward glance, he turns and walks into the surrounding woods. Watching him disappear, I wonder which shape he will take, what beast's skin he will wear as he prowls through the green shadows.

NO ONE is with me when I open the black car's door. No one is with me when I bend and peer inside. I'm the only one there to feel it—a sense of something stirring, of something coming to life. As I slip into the driver's seat and close the door, I have the feeling of being watched—of being considered, sized, and weighed.

Then I turn the key, put the car in gear, and begin to drive.

BLUE

I'M INSIDE the black car.

And I am not alone.

Something else is in here, and it has welcomed me. It wraps around and embraces me, settling heavily on my hands and arms. Another part drifts across my eyes, covering them in a veil of blue. I am still me, but now I feel like I'm being shared with something else. It isn't a haunting, the car has no ghosts. It's more of a...a possession, a small possession, by something filled with its own desires, something that revels in the scenes of its own memories.

It is my hands that grip the car's steering wheel, but another's hands are on the wheel, too. I feel them clenching and squeezing, filled with eager strength. And my arms, although they follow my directions to steer this way and that, they also follow the movements of the other's arms, reacting to the surprise of muscle impulses that command, *Turn here...now there...and now over there.* And my eyes, although they see the actual things that exist where I look, I also begin seeing other things—

Things that someone else once saw.

Things that someone else once did.

Bad things.

"FIND COLE." That is my mantra, repeated again and again, the two words drawing the map that I intend to follow. My plan is simple—to search the vacant and abandoned places scattered along the roads. To look inside all of the empty homes and buildings and barns, all the secret places where a boy might find to hide—all the empty rooms where he might curl into the shadows, hoping to evade what he fears is following him. All the piled, molding straw stacks that he might burrow into and fall asleep in, exhausted by escape and dread. And the low walls that he might peer out from behind, ever alert for his nightmare's approach.

I also need to check other places. Places that offer no haven. Dangerous places—under rotted, fallen beams that might be pinning him down. And down inside the deep, dry wells and rusted-through, buried tanks into which he might have fallen. And in the dark places below the floors and steps that might have collapsed under his weight, in the cellars and crawlspaces where he might be lying, broken and trapped.

Those are the places I intend to look. Those are the things I intend to see—

But those aren't the places I look.

And those aren't the things I see.

Because whatever is riding in the car with me begins showing me other things, begins showing me so much more. Driving past the houses along the road, I see some of the homes brighten and glow, suddenly identified and illuminated by the blue light that now wavers across my eyes. The car stops at those homes and, in that glowing blue light, I'm shown more than what exists, more than what is physically there—more than driveways, yards, porches, and doors. I'm shown what happened earlier within those walls. I see the memories of what happened when the black car visited its terrors upon these houses. Phantom images swim before my eyes, scenes playing out in the flickering blue. And as I watch each bright blue memory, the bright light invites me further in, making me a player in the scenes. Making me a participant in their horror.

Sitting in the black car, I stare at the blue, glowing homes, watching the scenes I'm shown unspool. As I watch, the car's other's presence is with me. It's a black thing, becoming more whole with each recalled slaughter. A thing that basks and revels in the cold echoes of silent, remembered screams.

The memories are terrifying. They fill the blue light and move like dreamt imaginings, littering my soul with their gruesome little pieces of hell.

I see children die.

And I see other children trussed and taken away.

If there is a worst kind of evil, it's the one I watch here—the evil that deceives children into believing that it is still their parents who inhabit the human shells that call them closer, the evil that allows a child's last thought to be the gruesome lie that it was his parents who betrayed him, that it was his parents who gave away his life.

At the end of one memory, I see a small girl pressing the perfect teardrop of her face against the rear window of a departing car. A fine, golden curlicue of hair droops across her forehead. Something that was once the child's mother is driving the car. I can see the girl's eyes perfectly—it feels as though she is staring into the future, as though somehow she sees me watching her. The girl looks at me through the window and through time. And through her frightened tears, her wide eyes are still lit with a hope that hasn't died, a hope she's held onto all her life: *It'll be okay. Mommy's here.* Even as the car fades from my view, the girl's hope remains alive in her eyes, the hope that her Mommy will make things okay.

But it isn't only children.

Others die, too.

And still more are simply taken.

I'm shown a doomed procession, an unfurling line of spectral men and women—husbands and wives, lovers and friends. In another memory, a man holds the limp form of a woman, holding her like a groom who has gathered up his bride as he brushes his cheek against her pale temple. His touch is loving and gentle, and he carefully avoids touching the claw hammer protruding from her forehead. He ducks down and slips her body into the back seat of the black car sitting in their driveway. Then, smiling and pleased, he stands straight, his hands clasping the blue plastic pen that he's been given. He is still smiling when the black car drives away. And he appears even happier as he gets into his own car and follows after it.

It doesn't stop. I'm shown scene after scene after scene. Before I see each one—just before the memory movie begins, just before I'm drawn back into the flickering blue light—just for a second, I think, *Cole. Find Cole.* But then I sense the Something Else in the car. "Just one more home," it says, "and then just one more after that." And I feel that it honestly wants to show me something, something that it sincerely wants me to see.

So what can I do but agree?

What can I do but keep driving?

So I surrender my arms to the Something Else's instructions. They now simply turn the wheel as directed. *Here…now there…and now straight ahead.* I drive slowly up and down the roads, stopping at home after home. At each one, I bear witness to whatever horror was done there before, to whatever tragedy unfolded.

And I get closer to the blue light each time, the blue light that feels so warm.

CLETE. THE MATCHMAN

C *LETE WAS STANDING outside, waiting on the other side of the clearing, trying not to stare at the red-haired man. The red-haired man was over by the trucks, ignoring the activity around him. He was listening to something that Clete couldn't hear. Something somewhere up the hill. Whatever it was, Clete decided that it must be a good thing. Why else would the red-haired man be smiling?*

CLETE WAS EXCITED. Things were happening in the hole, and he wasn't trapped inside the trailer anymore. It felt good to be outside, to be a part of things. What the hell had he been worrying about? The red-haired man wasn't going to hurt him; the red-haired man fucking loved him—that was clear enough from the way they'd laughed their asses off about "old food" and then about the sheriff. Hell, it was obvious they were friends from the way the red-haired man had trusted Clete's son to do something important, but then hadn't held it against Clete after Renny had obviously screwed things up.

Even the crowd of blue-eyeds didn't worry Clete anymore. Today none of them were even giving him a second look. Today they had jobs to do. They were working in pairs, walking back and forth from the cars to the trucks. Each pair walked to the trucks, climbed a truck ramp, then worked together to lift one of the cylinders. After lifting the cylinder, they'd carry it back down the ramp and over to a car, where they'd put it in an open trunk. Working in pairs was hard for them, especially the lifting and carrying parts—one blue-eyed was always either lifting higher or walking faster than the other, making the cylinder they were carrying slip out of their hands and drop. Then, while the two of them fumbled to recover their load, the other blue-eyes would stack up behind them, forming a long, silent line of laborers waiting for their turn.

The blue-eyes had started working after Clete had gone back to bed and taken a nap earlier this morning, when the fatigue of the last few hours had washed over him. It was the anxiety of waiting all night for Renny, the exhilaration of the red-haired man shouting "old meat!" and, finally, the simple pleasure of watching a cop sliced-and-diced in front of him. It had all suddenly come crashing down on him, making him need to shut his eyes and rest. He'd crawled back inside his trailer and collapsed, immediately falling asleep. It had been a fast nap—not long, but deep. When he woke, it was still only late morning. He felt refreshed and ready, looking forward to whatever the day might bring. By the time he stepped outside, the blue-eyes were already working hard. They hadn't loaded many cylinders yet, but they didn't stop working and didn't look tired, so, no matter how long it took, he guessed that eventually the car trunks would all be full.

Sure, he was curious about what was going on, but not enough to worry or care about it. It didn't really matter, did it? It was the red-haired man's business, not his. If he wanted Clete to know, he'd tell him. And if he asked for Clete's help, well, Clete would give it. Because that's what friends did for each other.

But the red-haired man hadn't talked about his business. And hadn't asked for Clete's help.

Which left Clete free to enjoy the day however he saw fit.

Maybe it was the fresh air. Or maybe it was the sudden joy of finally not being afraid. But the one thing he felt like enjoying most of all right now was a little slap-and-tussle happy-time with Renny's

Princess. Renny never minded sharing women with his Pop. And even if he did mind, from everything Clete could guess about what happened last night, he doubted Renny would ever be minding much of anything again. Shit, as good as Clete was feeling, when he was done with the Princess, maybe he'd hump his way through all the ladies in the other trailers, too. Right now his cock was pointing in his pants like a granite divining rod. As he was making the rounds, he'd check in on his other boys to make sure they were doing okay, remind them to stay hunkered down. And he'd tell them that Renny had died doing something brave and good, and how the red-haired man was helping to find Creel and Simon, and how, when that happened, when his two oldest boys were finally back home where they belonged, my God, what a party they'd have! And then, right after the coming-home party, what a goddamned massacre they'd visit upon everybody who was responsible for keeping his boys away.

It was then, while he stood thinking his jumble of good thoughts about slap-and-tussle fucking and sweet revenge, that he saw the red-haired man waving to him, calling him over to talk, maybe wanting his help. And as good as all of Clete's other thoughts felt inside his head, the idea of helping the red-haired man felt the very best of all.

"Do you hear that?" the red-haired man asked him, looking up the hill at the thick brush and trees near the top of the hole. "Do you recognize that sound?"

Clete strained to hear something, to hear anything at all that would let him agree with the red-haired man. Anything that would let him answer, "Yes, yes I do." But he heard nothing. And he didn't want to lie, didn't want to be untruthful. So he stood mute beside the red-haired man, his whole body seeking the vibration of a certain sound, his whole being aching to hear a familiar noise.

The red-haired man's smile widened. "It's the smallest hardly-even-a-sound. The sound of someone watching. Of someone walking on teeny-tiny feet." He looked at Clete. "You've heard it before. This morning. It was different then, but still the same. It's another ant. Another little ant marching one-by-one into our home." The red-haired man whispered at the hill, saying, "Hey, little marching ant, I cannn hear youuu walkiiinngg. I can hearrr youuu watchinng."

Staring where the red-haired man stared, whispering like the red-haired man whispered, Clete spoke softly then. "Hurrah, hurrah." And he stood perfectly still, listening for the sound of someone watching, for the sound of someone walking on teeny-tiny feet. Trying to hear the smallest hardly-even-a-sound.

GORDY

D AMN, he'd lost sight of them. Clete and the red-haired man had disappeared. He'd been watching them talking by the trucks. Saw them laughing and slapping each other's backs like old drinking buddies, both of them acting positively giddy. But then he heard a noise and swung the rifle scope over to look where one of the cylinders had been dropped and was rolling down a truck ramp, knocking over the line of people standing there like they were bowling pins. He'd looked quickly back at Clete and Red Hair, but they were gone.

He kept scanning the area through the scope, searching for either one, then saw Clete standing on some stacked concrete block stairs leading up to one of the trailers. Clete was at the top of the steps, about to step through the trailer's open door. In the crosshairs, Clete still looked giddy, like he had hold of the best secret in the world. As Clete held the door open, Gordy felt a shock of surprise when he saw someone else suddenly framed in the doorway, someone who made him stare at the door long after it closed, wishing he could will it open again, praying for only one more glance. But the door didn't open, no matter how much he wished or prayed.

Focus. He needed to focus. Needed to find the red-haired man. That was the thing he needed to do, the thing that demanded his concentration. After a few moments, he was able to pull his attention away from the trailer door…away from who he'd seen behind it. He started looking again, playing the scope back and forth across the area. But his red-haired target was missing—at least for now. It wasn't good that he was gone, but things would be okay. Red Hair would eventually be back. And Gordy would wait as long as it took. All day if he had to. All night too. Because he'd already decided: he was going to kill that prick where he stood.

He smiled, happy with his decision, wondering how many bullets he could put in the red-haired man before the bastard fell down. He hoped he could pull the trigger fast enough to make the nasty fucker's body do a bouncing little jig before it collapsed. Shape-shifter or not, monster or man—it wouldn't matter, not this time. Because after Gordy finished punching its head and chest full of high-velocity, 30-caliber, soft-tipped slugs, it wasn't ever going to stand back up and ask for more. Nothing ever did. Not after the last dance that they all danced before they died.

HE'D SPIED on the Glammerys before. Had crept close to their hole and looked down at the scattered trailers, peering through binoculars, always hoping to see a flash of strawberry blonde hair that glowed like sunlight at first morning. Always hoping for a faraway view of her brown eyes.

He'd spied on the hole during days and during nights, sometimes lying flat on a little ridge that was hidden in the scrub. Other times—at night, when the moon wasn't out—he'd lean back against the bumpy trunk of a half-dead elm. During the nights, sitting alone in the dark, he'd think of sneaking down the hillside. Think about finding her alone inside a trailer and convincing her to leave. To let him take her home. Home with him.

But he never crept down the hill.

Never found her alone.

Never offered her his home.

Instead, he always left the same way he'd come, slipping back through the thickets and the brush, hiking back to the little cut-out where he parked his truck. Each time, driving away, he'd felt hollow and dull inside, like he'd left the breathing, living center of himself behind on the ridge, still peering down, still looking for a flash of strawberry blonde hair that glowed like sunlight at first morning. Still looking for the brown eyes he'd stared into once so long ago.

AFTER LEAVING Nanny Tinkens' cabin, he'd driven straight to the hole. He'd sped along the roads, his senses still filled with the morning: still smelling the fresh-dug graves, still feeling the blood-slick bodies they'd buried, still hearing the sound of the coyote's breaking bones.

He'd parked where he always parked, pulling his truck off the road, hiding it behind a thick screen of hanging greenbrier. Being careful to make no sound, he'd followed the deer trails through the woods. The trails were narrow and smart, leading him the best ways around obstacles and through thorny bushes. At his spying ridge, he'd lain down and inched forward, scooting beneath low ropes of grapevines to get to his spying spot.

Looking through the rifle scope, he saw the cars first, parked in a pattern fanning out from the two big, black semi-trucks parked at the bottom of the hole. The cars' trunk lids were all open, making them look like a herd of metal animals waiting to be fed. But one car wasn't part of the fan-pattern. The sheriff's car sat apart from the others, separate from the open-mouthed herd. It was at the bottom of the drive, parked at an angle like it had stopped quickly. All four doors were open and the top bar of cop lights were flashing, but he didn't see Tim. From up on the ridge, the car looked abandoned, like something gutted and thrown away.

Then he saw the people.

At first he'd thought the other cars were empty. The thin, early sunlight drifting into the hole hit the cars' windshields and feathered across them, turning the windshields into silver mirrors that shielded the cars' interiors from his sight. He'd seen no telling movement beneath the light, no forms or shadows signaling that anything was waiting inside the vehicles. There'd been nothing. The people had all been sitting as still as corpses, staying so still that they'd been invisible to his spying eyes.

Then the car doors started opening.

All the doors opened at the same time, as though on command. Moments later, people began stepping out. He recognized some of them—almost. But there was something different about them now, something changed. Something he couldn't see clearly from where he was. A sense of wrongness.

Then they started walking, or at least trying to walk, except it wasn't really walking. Not regular walking, the way most people walked, with comfortable, familiar movements. It was more like riding, like they were balancing inside their bodies and thinking about every step before their legs took it. Some of them lost their footing when they leaned too far forward or too far back. After a few minutes they got better at it, though, as if now remembering the mechanics of walking. If he hadn't seen how they'd started, if he'd only seen them after they'd been practicing, he might not have thought there was anything odd, maybe wouldn't have even noticed the rigid tilt a few of them still had. Or the teetering steps that some were still taking.

Traveling in pairs, they slowly walked up the truck ramps and disappeared inside. When they came back out, they were carrying their treasure. Seeing what they held, Gordy felt a cold sweat bead across his face, chilling him and making him shiver as he whispered, "Sonofabitch. Sonofabitch. Sonofabitch."

C.N.G.

Compressed. Natural. Gas.

Cylinder after cylinder of it being carried from the trucks. Bastards. They were going to blow everything up. They were planning on destroying the whole thing—the hill, the Circle, all of the homes and people on Jonah's Belly. Whenever that blue-eyed, red-headed, monster-freak got whatever it was that he wanted, he was going to make damn sure nobody else ever took it away. He was going to wipe the playing field completely off of the map, leaving just a black smoking crater.

Well, fuck him. Fuck the red-haired man.

And fuck everybody down there helping him.

Gordy made his decision. It wasn't going to happen. Not here. Not today. Not ever.

He wiped his arm across his forehead to dry the sweat, then smiled as he immediately decided how all the shit going on down there was going to end. Deciding to end it his way, not theirs. He always felt good when he made these decisions, when he decided ahead of time how to bring a situation to its proper conclusion. It was always better, of course, when the other assholes didn't have a clue, when they had no idea about the ass-kicking he was about to bring down upon them. *A battle always rages. The world is always at war,* he thought. *You bet your ass.* And this battle was starting now. Because he'd just made his decision: He was bringing them a war—

—*there!* He saw him. The red-haired man. He was standing by the trucks, motioning Clete over for a visit. Gordy watched them talk for a few minutes, then thought, *Fuck it, shoot him now,* and put the final crosshairs on the man. He was feeling a little giddy, imagining Clete's surprised look when the red-haired man's head exploded in the middle of a backslapping joke. He took two deep, even breaths, letting the air out slowly, started squeezing the trigger—

—but in the scope's glass circle, he saw the red-haired man's attention snap away from Clete and over to the trucks. Gordy looked, too, wanting to know what had happened, and saw the dropped cylinder rolling down the ramp, rolling through the line of the falling, tripping people. After realizing it was nothing, he swung the scope back almost instantly to where it'd been, but wasn't fast enough because now the spot was empty.

That's when he saw Clete standing on the trailer steps by the open door. And that's when he also saw her, a flash of strawberry blonde hair and a pair of brown eyes, framed in the doorway for only a second, but long enough to answer every prayer he'd ever prayed as he'd lain searching all those times. And long enough to see that she was still beautiful. Long enough to feel the breathing, living center of himself clutch tight around his heart, making him gasp at the fast stab of memory and lost love, making him whisper, just once. "Sarah."

SARAH.

He'd held her tightly that so-long-ago day, trying to make her feel safe, falling more in love with her each second she was in his arms. He'd stroked her hair, comforting her after the Glammerys' game of Dots and Plugs was over. He pressed her face against his chest, hiding her eyes from the sight of Creel and Simon and also from the sweet, perfect savagery of Blue's horrific and wonderful attack on them. Holding her to him, he moved his mouth soundlessly, wanting to whisper his love, wanting to tell her he was with her now. That he'd always be with her. That no one else would ever hurt her again.

But he hadn't whispered anything—not then, and not before her parents had taken her out of the school and moved away, taking her from him, away from any way to find her. Taking her away before he could tell her everything he wanted to say.

It had taken him three years to find her, three long years to learn her family had moved to a city only five hours away. After learning where she was, he'd driven to her home the very next day, only to learn that she had died.

Her mother—answering the door he'd knocked on, in the city he'd driven to—had smiled a polite, brittle smile, but quickly grew distant when he asked about Sarah, nervously explaining that he was a friend from school. Her mother had listened to his mumblings, watched him shuffle and hesitate until, feeling anxious and so full of love, he politely asked, "Please, may I see Sarah?"

She'd shut the door then, telling him to wait. He stood still, expecting Sarah to appear. But when the door opened, it was her mother again, pushing a pencil-sketched map into his hand, telling him, "You can visit her at her grave."

The map led back to Brown County.

Back to the Glammerys—

Back to the brothers who'd found her again before he'd found her again. Brothers who had found a way to finally win the schoolyard fight, who sought out and laid siege to a broken girl who worried she'd done something to invite and deserve their attack, and whose embarrassed parents were certain of it. The same girl whose father had already broken and emptied her long before, sneaking into her little-girl room and her little-girl bed with his whispers and his hungry flesh, ruining anything hopeful or bright in her little-girl life. An already broken girl who withered and withdrew even further into her shame and pain, who heard the Glammerys say they wanted her, and who believed she deserved even less than them.

Gordy had tried to get her back.

He'd followed the map to the Glammerys' hole and found it empty and dark and rotting. He'd driven down into the depths of the hole, wondering, *She's here? My Sarah is here?* Getting out of his car, he'd seen no one, no signs of anyone at all. He'd started yelling her name, calling as he walked to each trailer, knocking on the doors. No one had answered, but women peeked out the windows at him, their pale, hollow faces rising from the darkness inside the trailers, then receding back down.

He knocked on four different doors before she walked out of one of the scattered school buses that were rotting into the ground. He walked straight to her, his determination and confusion defeating his nervousness, making him certain of what he must say. And he said it clearly, without shuffling or hesitating: "I've loved you forever. And I love you now. And I will always love you. I'm sorry it's been three years, but I've found you now. And now, please, won't you come with me back to my home?"

She looked at him with her hurt, brown eyes, the same eyes

he'd shielded on that long-ago day, eyes that had seen more pain since then. She moved close to him and circled his neck with her arms. She pulled him to her mouth, pressing her lips to his with the very same touch he'd imagined every single day. After kissing him, she kissed him again, helping him know that it was really happening. And then—as he'd wanted to whisper to her so long ago—she whispered to him, "I love you, too." Then whispered, "But I have died here, and this is where I'll stay. I am dead now. I am dead and you must leave me alone." Then she climbed the stairs to the trailer they were standing near, opened the door, turned back to him, and said, "Let me stay buried here. Let me stay dead. And, please, never visit here again." Then she stepped into the trailer's darkness, softly closing the door behind her. Like the women he'd seen earlier, he caught a glimpse of her through the front window, then watched her fade into the gloom, becoming only a ghost who'd left two kisses on his lips.

HE DID go back. Three more times. The first two times, he found the hole as empty as before, without Clete or his sons around. But she didn't answer when he called her name. And she didn't open any of the doors when he knocked again and again.

The third time was the last time. The hole wasn't empty that time. Creel and Simon were there, but they didn't fight him, didn't even bother to threaten or insult him. He walked up close to them, unafraid and ready for anything, ready for them to do anything except what they did, the thing that made it certain he'd never come back.

They called her to them.

They called her by the same name he'd called, only this time she answered. They called, and she came. And as he stood there, they began touching her. Started wrapping their fingers in her hair. Started sliding their hands into her clothes. Started touching their mouths against her skin.

And she let them.

She smiled through it all, bending her body to their pawing caresses, answering their grunting jeers with her own encouraging sounds. That's when he left, deciding to do what she'd asked, deciding to begin to believe what she'd said: *Sarah has died. Sarah is dead. Sarah, my Sarah, is gone.*

NOW HE WAITED and watched, methodically sweeping the scope back and forth, looking for the red-haired man but seeing only cars and cylinders and people. The people worked without rest, not stopping to talk or drink or eat, working with unstoppable urgency.

Even while he was watching and waiting, he couldn't stop himself from thinking, *Sarah*. Couldn't stop from letting the scope wander back to the trailer where she was inside. He knew he should clear her from his mind, that he should only think about the most important thing, about killing the red-haired man. He knew he shouldn't think about anything that distracted him from his killing plan, shouldn't dwell on anything that clouded his thoughts—

—and then realized that his thoughts *had already distracted him*. That they'd already made him much less than the hunter he needed to be. Because from behind the nearby elm came the unmistakable sound of footsteps, the sound that told him he was no longer hunting the red-haired man, that told him, instead—

The red-haired man was hunting him.

The elm tree was behind him and to the right. Hearing the soft footsteps, he rolled left, off of his belly and onto his back, crashing through the grapevines, pivoting the rifle down and across him as he rolled. The rifle barrel caught on the vines, but he easily freed it and swung it around and held it at his waist, low and close, pointing the gun at the sound, instinctively aiming where he knew the red-haired man would be, where he knew the attack would come.

He was right. The red-haired man was beside the elm, walking toward him and grinning, waving a hand that was no longer a hand but was now a thick, black-scaled nest of claws. The thing was singing too, grinning and waving and singing, "—*ants go marching one by one, hurrah! Hurrah! The ants go marching one by one, the littlest stops to suck his thumb—*"

And Gordy started pulling the trigger, pulling as fast as he could, firing the high-velocity, 30-caliber, soft-tipped slugs one after another straight into the thing coming toward him. He saw the bullets hitting it, saw their impact stop the thing in its tracks. He kept firing, only now he was the one grinning, was the one who felt like singing, because he knew was about to happen, knew what always came next—the jerking, crazy death dance the bad guys always did when they finally fell down.

But the red-haired man didn't fall down. And didn't dance a death-dance. He just stopped walking. Waited until the bullets stopped being fired. Then began walking forward again, still grinning and waving.

And Gordy knew he should move. Knew he should roll away and jump up and run. Knew he should swing the rifle at the thing's head, that he should poke the barrel into its blue eyes. But somehow, the thing with the claws was already standing right above him. And suddenly there seemed to be so little he could think of doing, so little he could think of at all as he saw the claws above him start swinging down.

GORDY

HIS LEFT LEG hurt the worst, even more than his head. His calf felt ruined and bleeding. He couldn't see it, but he felt it. Felt the blood flowing down over his ankle, seeping onto the floor, crusting to a sticky film under his bare feet. He wasn't quite sure what had happened at the ridge. Just remembered the surprise of knowing he'd been stalked and found. And he remembered the thing's arm—its claws—swinging toward his face. After that... nothing.

He didn't have a clue about his leg. It hurt enough that he wondered if he'd shot himself when he'd rolled onto his back, maybe had put a slug through his own calf. Or maybe ol' red-hair had cut him up a little. Maybe knocked him out, then slashed him with a handful of claws. Whatever'd happened, he wouldn't be able to stand on that leg if he got free. The only thing keeping him from collapsing right now was that he was tied so tightly to the metal post.

He'd woken slowly, feeling groggy, first feeling the awful pain in his leg, then the thunder in his head. Then realized that he couldn't move.

And then saw he wasn't alone.

The left side of his face was puffy and swollen, closing his eye so that all he could see was a thin, blurry slot of haze. But his right eye was fine. His right eye saw people walking back and forth in front of him. And saw three rows of stacked C.N.G. cylinders across from him.

He knew where he was. He was inside one of the black trucks. He'd been stripped naked, then bound standing up to one of the support posts on the rows of iron shelving. Four thick, silver circles of duct tape were wrapped around him—binding him at his ankles, knees, chest, neck. The tape held him tight, trapping him hard against the post's sharp metal edges. The edges cut into him, scoring his skin along the length of his spine and down his ass. He could feel something pressing into each butt cheek, something round and metal and cold, but the tape around his neck kept him from looking down. But when he looked at the shelving across from him, he figured out what was poking him—it was cylinders, on the bottom row, one cylinder on each side of the post he was bound to, just high enough that their nozzle tops stuck into him like blunt hypodermic needles.

HE DECIDED that the things in the truck weren't people, at least not anymore. Not after looking into their empty blue eyes. Not after watching their strange, alien movements up close. They'd been people before, but now they were something different. Something not human.

But whether they were people or not, he still called out to them. Still asked for their help. The tape around his neck made breathing hard, made his voice a dry-sanded rasp. But they ignored him and just kept picking up cylinders and taking them outside, paying him no attention, not answering his questions, not responding to his hoarse entreaties. They acted like he wasn't there, like they couldn't see the naked, bleeding man they were walking back and forth in front of. Like they couldn't feel it when he touched them. The duct tape around his chest and his arms pinned him above the elbows, but he could raise his hands, could reach out and sometimes brush his outstretched fingers against them if they walked by close enough to him. But they didn't respond, didn't do anything to acknowledge his touch. They didn't step away from him, didn't even bother turning their eyes his way...until later—

When something changed.

When he thought they started watching him.

It happened when he began feeling weaker, in the hazy moments just before the pain and blood loss made him drift off and begin to dream. That's when he had the feeling they were looking at him, looking but averting their eyes when he glanced their way. He also sensed a growing excitement in them, an anxiousness. *Anxious for what?* he wondered, fighting to stay awake, but feeling himself fading, feeling unconsciousness taking him down into its black and spinning world.

NAKED AND BOUND, he stood there, dreaming in a fog of exhausting pain. A fog in which his body sought escape and rest, a place between the edges of reality and hallucination. He dreamt of two separate visitors—one a man, the other an angel, each one appearing through the mist. The first gave him a message. The second gave him a gift.

The first dream-visitor was Clete. Clete, shouting at him, screaming in his face, yelling, "My boys, my boys, you bastards took my boys," then singing "Fresh meat! Fresh meat!" over and over again. Then the old man started talking quietly, acting almost friendly, leaning close enough that Gordy could smell his breath and his skin. Saying, "Listen, you gotta stay small, gotta not stir, gotta stay tucked tight away."

Next, Gordy saw an angel. His angel.

He saw her strawberry-blonde hair. Looked into her brown eyes. Felt her angel face press against his face. Heard her angel voice whisper, "...sorry, I'm so sorry." And then she gave him her gift—gave him back the flint heart he'd made and given to her so many years ago. She pressed it into his hand, wrapping the cord around his fingers so that it wouldn't fall from his grasp, telling him,

"I never let it go. I always kept it near." And she kissed him once, then kissed him again (helping him know it was really happening, helping him to know it wasn't a dream). Then she flew away on strawberry-blonde angel wings, wings that glowed even in the truck's gray gloom.

When she left, he was alone again, walking in the dream-mist, now wandering toward a brightening light. Noticing that even in his dream, he was limping, that even in his dream he was hobbled and groaning.

THE PAIN woke him.

It was new, fresh pain. Pain in both legs and both feet. Excruciating, raw pain. A bright, burning agony that was the light he'd stumbled toward in his dreams, that was the reason he'd been called back to consciousness.

Something had happened while he was asleep. Both of his legs were bleeding now. He could feel the blood running down his hips and thighs and knees, dripping on his bare feet. Unable to move or fight or fall, he yelled in helpless rage, and he would have dropped the angel's gift, would have let it slip from his grasp before he even realized it was truly there. But the cord kept his fingers curled around the hidden heart-shape of it, and he could feel its sharp, fletched edges when his hand clenched tight in anger. Feeling it cut into his palm, he suddenly quieted, thinking that maybe she'd gifted him twice—

Maybe once with the heart.

And maybe again with wings.

NOW HE KNEW the answer. It was an easy answer, the simplest one of all. He knew what they'd been waiting for, knew why they'd been looking at him so anxiously.

They were hungry.

449

They'd been waiting for him to doze, eager to begin their meal. And now they were eating him. Starting with his legs and feet, eating him bite by bite. Taking mouthfuls while he slept. One of them had probably bitten into his calf when he was first bound inside the truck. Maybe that's what had woken him. The others had begun feeding when he fell unconscious the second time, taking bites from both his legs. Maybe even biting off some of his toes.

He'd woken in pain, bleeding and helpless and angry. But even in his pain, he was still aware, was able to notice that things had changed. The blue-eyed things were acting differently now, were openly watching him, no longer averting their eyes as they walked past. A few even looked like they were trying to smile, but their faces didn't work right, not enough to smile real smiles. Instead, their faces bent and folded into grotesque, frightening expressions. Some were walking closer to him, too, closer than necessary, intentionally getting close enough to touch him. One walked up close and leaned over, below his line of vision. He felt the thing's hands on his thigh. Felt it pinching a roll of flesh between its fingers and thumb.

Then he felt its teeth.

The teeth carved through his skin, tearing off the mouthful the blue-eyed thing wanted. The thing stood there and looked at him, watching him while it chewed and swallowed. Then another one bent down and he felt it tilt his bare foot up, felt his toes being pulled free of the floor they were stuck to. And then, of course, he felt more pain, more than he'd ever known before.

But even as he was screaming, even as part of his mind reacted like an animal being consumed alive, another part was calm. The calm part of his mind quickly soothed and quieted the animal, sharing the secret good news it had found. Good news about his immediate decision. And about his angel's gift. News about why his hands were now working so quickly and deftly behind him.

The news was so good that his screaming stopped. Was so good that he smiled.

The blue-eyed things were still human enough to be surprised by his sudden silence, were wary enough to be confused by his smile.

And Gordy's smile grew even wider, because now things were exactly the way he liked them—when he knew something that the bastards around him didn't know, when they had no clue at all about what he was going to do.

BLUE

*E*VERYTHING ELSE *is gone.* Now there is only the black car and driving—from home to home to home—and all of the bright blue memories that I'm shown.

These are the only things I think of now.

These are all I know.

But they seem to be enough.

They seem so perfectly fine.

I know there are other things I should remember: important, critical things. But somehow I've forgotten them, somehow they are gone. The only hint of them that's left is my unsettling, wobbly sense that "something's missing"—a sense of absences and gaps in my thinking, of empty spaces that were once filled with thoughts I can no longer recall. Oddly, while I've lost the specifics of the missing things, I still have the feelings that came with them—the driven, anxious feeling that there are places I need to be going, that there are tasks I need to do. And there's an ache of something lost and needing to be found...and of a promise, too, the unsettled feeling of an unkept promise. But what is it? All these feelings give me no answers. I don't know which places to go or why I should be going to them, and I don't know any of the tasks that need to be done. It seems that whatever was lost will stay lost, and that my promise may already be broken. I can't remember any of it. It has all fallen into the bright blue fire I can see dancing on my skin, the blue fire I feel wrapping me in its flames.

The fire is all that remains now. Everything else is gone. Now there is only this black car. And driving from home to home to home. And all of these bright blue memories that I'm shown.

These are the only things I think of now.

These are all I know.

But they seem to be enough.

They seem so perfectly fine.

Now I'm sitting and staring at a home, watching a memory end.

It is the memory of a man and a woman. The man is short and walks with a rolling limp. He has long yellow hair tied back with a red bandanna, and a beard braided into four thick crinkly ropes that hang almost to his waist. Small, colored glass beads are neatly woven through his hair and beard. When he walks, his limp makes the beard-braids swing from side to side, and different beads appear and disappear with each step. The woman's hair is a close-cropped black fuzz that barely hides her skull. Her body is slender and muscled and tall. When she walks, she moves quickly and with strength and grace. Her pace only slows when she and the man are walking together, each with an arm wrapped around the other's waist.

When the black car parked in their driveway, it was the woman who strode out to meet the driver. She went to him the same way she walked everywhere, each step conveying confidence and health. I can see the scene. After she stands for a moment at the black car, after she reaches out and takes the bright blue and yellow yardstick the driver holds out for her, after they both laugh about the slogan printed along the stick—*MEASURING UP PERFECTLY! NATURAL GAS!*—she changes. I can see her change. I see her blink in blue-eyed agreement with what she just heard. And I see her accept entirely what she's just been told needs to be done: that she needs to ease her loved one's suffering, a loved one who cannot move in the same strong, straight strides that she can, a loved one deserving her help and strength to assist him quickly along his final way. I can see that she fully understands, that she seems so perfectly fine.

The short, limping man tries to run away. He saw her new blue eyes and immediately knew that it wasn't her, knew she'd become something else. But his uneven legs betray him, making him hop and lurch, and as he tries to run, his head dips and rises, making his braids and hair swing wildly around. I hear the little glass beads clicking and clacking together, making a delicate music that follows him.

She catches him right away. She sweeps his legs out from under him, then holds him in her strong arms as he struggles. When he's finally quiet, exhausted in her embrace, she wraps two of his braids in each of her hands, then loops them around his neck and pulls tight.

She smiles the whole time, feeling so happy to help him, feeling so grateful she can release him from his pain. As she's strangling him, she looks lovingly down at the beautiful beads in his hair, treasuring their shapes and colors as his head flips this way and that. The beads look like a small rainbow he's made for only her, like a last gift that he wants her to have.

Minutes later, the woman walks to her car. She doesn't look back at the man's body, doesn't slow her strong, straight strides away from him. She doesn't need to, she is holding onto all of the memories she needs—his four blond braids are still in her hand, pieces of a beaded rainbow that she's been given by her love.

Then, like all the other times, this memory is over and done.

And now it is time—

Time to visit another home.

Time to watch another memory.

THERE'S SOMETHING different about the next home. The home is small and beautiful, with cream-colored clapboard siding and gingerbread trim along its eaves. There is a tall, solitary oak in the front yard, and gracing its branches is a child's tree house that's painted the same cream as the home and decorated with the same gingerbread trim. Spread randomly across the front lawn, like marbles rolled from a giant's hand, are reflective gazing balls of all colors—a whimsical cluster of them is nestled at the oak's base, making the tree seem part of some fairy tale.

But none of that is why the home is different. Not the paint or the trim. Not the lawn decorations. Not the tree house or the row of short boards nailed up the tree, making a child's ladder to the hideaway. No, it's something else, some difference so big that even when I look directly at the home, at first I don't realize what it is. Then I see it and begin to understand. Unlike all the other memories, there is no blue light around this home, no tinted filter of memory through which to see what happened here before.

However, like all of the other memories, a black car is still parked in the driveway.

But this time the driver isn't walking toward the home.

This time he's standing in the driveway, looking directly at me.

I know that he's been waiting. Waiting for me to join him.

No, this home isn't like the others. The other homes were empty, already dead and dry, but this one is alive and full. Looking through the black car's windshield, I see three faces—two small boys and their mother. They're looking out through the front window, staring at me and the other driver. Their expressions are curious and wary, wondering about the two black cars in their driveway. About the two strangers who've come to visit.

When I see their faces, I understand what's going on. There are no memories here for me to see. No remembered scenes of earlier horrors will be played out in a warm blue light. Because this is happening now. This is real and here.

The other driver and I are here to gather this family.

We are here to make a new memory.

And making a new memory seems like such a good idea.

It seems so perfectly fine.

As I watch, the other driver opens his car's trunk, and even before he lifts anything out, I know what he'll be holding when he turns around: two blue and yellow basketballs, printed with a flame-lettered slogan across their pebbled-leather surfaces. The driver will smile and roll the balls across the yard. The balls will keep rolling until they both stop under the first rung of the wood-plank ladder that's nailed to the trunk of the tall, solitary tree.

Then the children will run out of the house to play with their new toys.

And then we'll make a memory.

GORDY

THE HUNGER had them in its grip, making them pay less attention to the cylinders and more attention to him. They formed a tightening semicircle around him, watching him with their bright blue eyes. Watching his face as they took their turns eating. Watching as they consumed him alive.

They watched him, and he watched them. And he waited, smiling at them, staring back into their eyes. Watching as they walked forward to feed.

He kept waiting.

He didn't feel the pain anymore, couldn't feel his legs at all. Barely felt it when one of the blue-eyed things bent down and fastened its teeth on the skin over his ribs, tugging and chewing till it tore a bite free.

Then he waited a little more, waiting until he could wait no longer. Waiting until the darkness around him grew even darker, letting him know that his wait was ending. Letting him know it was time to fly away on his hidden wings.

He hoped he'd waited long enough. He thought he had, but he wanted to wait a little longer. Long enough to be sure. But the darkness was coming fast, covering him quickly in its shroud. It dimmed everything, even the fire in all the bright blue eyes still staring back at him—the same blue eyes that hadn't paid attention to his hands moving behind his back. The same blue eyes that hadn't seen his fingers fumbling for the knobs on the cylinders pressing against his ass.

He'd worried that the blue-eyed things would stop him... either when they saw what he was doing or when they heard the gas whooshing out of the cylinder nozzles. But they hadn't been watching his hands, had only stared at his face, entranced by his expressions of pain. And after he twisted open the cylinders, he decided that they couldn't hear things, at least not the things he heard. He thought that maybe they were listening to something else, something only they could hear. Whatever they heard, the silent sound of it filled their minds and ears completely. It had stopped them from hearing his earlier cries. And it stopped them from hearing the rush of compressed gas now escaping into the air.

He knew not to cut himself free, not to use the knife-sharp edges of the flint heart in his hand to slice through the silver tape. If he cut the tape, he knew he'd fall down in a helpless heap, unable to even crawl. He'd turn into a naked and bleeding feast lying on the floor.

So he waited—

Waited for the two cylinders to empty.

Waited to use the heart his angel had given him.

Waited to unfold his wings.

He waited until he couldn't wait any longer. But if he didn't try soon, he knew the darkness would completely have him. He smelled the gas. It mixed with the rotting, fetid scent in the truck. The cylinders weren't entirely empty yet, he could still hear gas hissing through the nozzles, but he hoped they were empty enough—

The waiting was over.

Now it was time.

Time to spread his wings and fly.

He lifted his arms away from his sides and held them the way a priest welcomes a congregation. The silver tape around his chest held his upper arms and elbows, but his hands rose upward, pointing to heaven. In his left hand, he held his salvation. He clutched it sideways, his fingers curled over one curved, sharp edge, the heart's other half extending from his fist. In the last moment he thought of offering his blue-eyed flock a prayer, a few final words of either blessing or forgiveness, but then decided that a simple warning would suffice. Before speaking, he smiled and looked one final time into the circle of eyes around him, enjoying—as he always did—the secret of knowing how this would end, of knowing that they still didn't have a clue.

And even though he believed the blue-eyeds couldn't hear him, he said the words anyway, treasuring them, knowing they were his last. Knowing it was time for him to fly. "Fire in the hole," he said. "Fire in the fucking hole." Then he brought the heart down quickly, smashing its sharp, flint edge into the iron shelving behind him. And when rock met metal, it struck the spray of orange sparks that set him free, that was the fire that gave him his wings.

THE EXPLOSION shook the earth. Cylinder after cylinder instantly exploded. The expanding fireball swept over everything, incinerating all that it touched. The explosion's volcanic blast pounded out against the hole's steep walls and followed them up, rushing to the sky and carrying hell along with it. The blast reached into the clouds and became a mushrooming pillar of bright orange fire. Then the pillar of fire began to rain—

Molten metal and a white hail of burning debris began falling out of the sky. The debris rained down into the inferno still raging in the Glammerys' hole, and it disappeared into the fire's cleansing pool of heat and light.

Everything burned.

And then everything was buried.

The hole's walls began moving, rippling and sliding, breaking free of their anchors, slipping down. They became a rolling, boiling avalanche of scorched earth and stone, all of it tumbling into the deep, foul hole and filling it, closing the grave forever over what it touched—over the dead, and the dust, and the dark.

BLUE

I SEE IT before I feel it. It appears in the distance—an eruption of orange flame spearing up into the sky, a beacon of climbing fire that fills my eyes with its raging power. Seconds later, I feel the shockwave, the warm wind and the rumble of an incredible explosion—something so strong it must have left nothing behind but ash and ground. I stare across the sky, startled wide-awake by the spectacle of swirling red and orange destruction. And as I look at that distant, incandescent, and engulfing flame, the blue flames surrounding me begin to dim and flicker, as if they're being smothered by the larger fire in the sky. The blue flames fade with each new plume of orange fire, becoming smaller and smaller with each aftershock…until at last they wink a final time and then are wholly snuffed out, their heat quickly fading from my skin.

I feel the change, but it isn't just me.

The car changes too—

It dies. Or whatever I'd felt riding beside me dies. Whatever it was, whatever had rolled and smiled and squirmed in the dead, blue-lit memories, enjoying every drop of blood and tears—that thing disappears, burned away in the rising orange flame.

With the blue fire gone, my thoughts and memories come rushing back. I remember everything I'd forgotten. I see everything clearly again. And I now see that towering, faraway torch with new understanding—I see the direction it's rising from, and I can guess exactly where it touches the earth. Looking at it, a sense of certainty fills me—certainty about what happened, certainty about who was responsible for the fire…the fire that set me free. "Thank you, Gordy," I say out loud, also knowing with certainty that my good brave friend can hear me, knowing that he is with me even now.

FROM MY ARRIVAL, to the explosion, to now. Only scant seconds have passed, hardly any time at all. I'm still parked in this driveway—still looking at this home and this family, still watching the other black car and its driver.

The mother and her children are still looking out the window, wondering and worrying about these two strangers outside their home. The other driver is still standing at his car trunk. But he's acting different now. I've regained my memory, but he seems to have lost his. He stands in the drive, looking deflated and dazed, hesitant and weak—uncertain what to do next. He's holding the two basketballs, but he doesn't bend down and roll them across the ground. He doesn't move at all. He just stands there with his head tilted slightly to the side, like someone trying to hear the end of a fading song, or someone listening intently for the rest of an interrupted message. He stands, straining to reestablish contact with whatever he has lost.

Then I see him find what he's searching for. Or I see it find him.

He begins hearing the message again. Or he's hearing its faint-but-strengthening sounds. I can tell he's made contact because he straightens up, he tilts his head just a little more, turns a bit more in one direction, like he's fine-tuning his reception. As he listens, his body begins filling out again, begins getting stronger. Seeing this, I know that he's beginning to feel the blue flames again, burning against his skin. And I know that he's now remembering why he's here—that he's here to gather this family, that he's here to finish wrapping me in the fire.

When I turn the key and the car's engine roars, he turns his head at the sound. In that second, he's still not completely reconnected yet, still isn't completely strong. Then, in the next second, at the very last moment, his eyes blaze bright blue again. And in that moment, when our eyes lock, he understands what I've got in mind.

There's no time for him to react, no time for him to leap or dodge. And no time for him to avoid being crushed between the two big, black cars as I stomp on the accelerator and rocket forward. When my car hits him, he actually folds in half and his face slams down onto my hood. The two basketballs fly out of his hands, first hitting my windshield, then bouncing away. They ricochet over his body, arc back over the other black car, then bounce and roll across the yard. They roll to the oak tree and stop, ending up exactly at the bottom of the wood-plank ladder nailed to the tree.

I put the car in reverse and back up, releasing the man from the steel crush of bumpers and hoods, letting him spill down. Then I drive forward again. The car lifts and drops twice as first the front wheels and then the rear ones roll up and over his body.

I do it one more time, making certain his blue fire is truly and finally stamped out. Making certain he can hear no message that tells him it's time to get up and make another memory. As I drive over him, I hear screaming. But it isn't him. It's the children inside the house. Their eyes are filled with fear, their mouths are wailing in terrible surprise. Their mother is holding them. But she's not screaming. She's frozen with shock, staring at the man she's just seen killed in her front yard. She can't believe it. It is a horrible moment, and will become a brutal memory they'll never forget. And I'm the one who's given it to them, the one responsible for their next nightmares.

They're lucky—

At least it's their memory to weep at.

At least it is their trauma to recall.

And at least they're the ones who saw him die, not the other way around.

That's what I tell myself as I drive away.

I speed out of their drive and race back to my cabin, needing to get there immediately. I'm returning without finding Cole, without having any idea of where he might be. But more than anything else in the world, I need to go home, because now I also remember my promise: "Be back before the moon." Looking up, I see that I'm already late, that my promise is already broken—there's a full moon, ethereal, white, and glowing, hanging in the late afternoon sky, floating above the orange pillar of fire.

Other cultures tell stories of seeing a rabbit on the moon. I like those stories. But as much as I've tried, I can never see the rabbit. I always see a face—the face of the man in the moon. And the face I'm now seeing fills me with new fear—it is a face with no expression, with pale skin and closed, sunken eyes and thin lips pressed tight together.

It is the face of someone dying.

Or of someone already dead.

BLUE

I NEED TO GO FASTER. I need to be home.

The moon is larger in the sky now, shining bright as polished bone.

I've been gone too long. The black car and the blue flames and the memories stole my hours and covered my eyes, blinding me to the day-moon's rising and keeping me away from where I needed to be. I'm driving back to my cabin now, knowing I'm too late—too late to save my family, too late to protect them from the beast. Too late to do anything but bury the torn pieces that I'll find lying on the ground. Too late to do anything but mourn.

Even with the blue flames no longer dancing on my arms, even with the black car empty of everything but me—I know that the fight it isn't over, that we haven't yet won. Whatever it is, Gordy hurt it, but he didn't kill it. I know that it's still alive because I'd seen the other driver listening to its whisperings in his ear.

I stare straight ahead, looking only at the road, unable to bear looking up at the moon again. I'm afraid that it will no longer be a face, afraid that it will now be only a skull. A grinning skull shining down from a field of velvet blue.

I need to go faster.

I need to be home.

FROM OUTSIDE, the cabin looks empty. I don't see anyone, and at first I think they're all gone. Then I'm sure they're dead. There's no one on the porch. No one opens the door. No one is awaiting my return.

But before I can get out of the car, the *tink-tink-tink* of metal on glass makes me swing around. I'm suddenly staring at the barrel of a handgun, the gun that Alassadir is tapping against my driver-side window. He'd moved silently and fast, getting to the car without my seeing him or knowing where he stepped out from the line of trees. From his expression, I can see that all is well, and relief sweeps through me—an overwhelming, grateful feeling that I haven't lost them, that they are all still here and safe.

I step out of the car and hug him without a word. I can't talk, can't tell my Gypsy brother about all the things I've seen...and why I'm still shaking from the things I almost did. Hugging him, I look over his shoulder at the woods, and Setsu appears, forming from the green and shadows, stepping out of a hiding place that seems hidden itself, where one moment there's nothing there, then the next moment he's walking toward me.

He looks at me, and I can tell he already knows where I've been and what I've seen. He also knows what almost happened. Knows how very close to hell I came. He looks up at the sky, then back to Alassadir and me.

Without a word being spoken, we all know that it is time.

Time to climb Jonah's Belly.

Time to sing at the Stones.

AS WE WALK up the porch steps, I'm still anxious—still thinking about blue flames and children peering through windows, and about news that still needs to be shared...news about what I had not done. News about what was lost that I had not found.

But there's no one in the living room. The room's emptiness unnerves me, starts me thinking I'd believed a lie, that Elissa and

Cally weren't safe at all, that they'd been gathered and taken away, that they were now only memories veiled in blue. I almost call out Elissa's name, but before I can, she comes out of the far bedroom. She closes the door softly behind her, then hurries to me. I feel her concern and worry in the arms she wraps around me, in the kiss she presses on my mouth.

Holding her, I barely find the words. I don't want to say them, don't want them to be true. But I need to tell her, there's nothing else I can do until she knows. "Cole," I finally whisper, "I didn't find Cole. He's still lost. And still alone. Elissa, I don't have him...I didn't save him."

She doesn't pause. Doesn't step away or loosen her embrace. But there's a change—a kind change, a loving change—in her feel. A change in the way she makes me feel. Now her arms are full of comfort. Now her kiss is strong and healing.

"We'll find him, Blue." The words are a kiss on my lips. I feel them spill down my throat and into my chest, landing on my heart like warm, soothing rain. "When we're done at the Circle," she says, "then we'll find him." She takes my head in her hands and turns my face so I'm looking into the green world of her eyes, making me see the truth of what she feels, making me see the sureness of her next words. "I know we'll find him. I know it."

I believe her words. In her eyes, I see that she knows it with certainty, the same certainty I'd felt as I thanked Gordy. And, for now, her certainty offers me all the forgiveness I need.

"Okay," I say. "We'll find him then. We'll find him when we're done at the Circle. That's the plan."

And there it is, our two-point plan: First, we will go to the Circle. Second, we will find the boy. Two steps. They make things sound simple and easy. Almost simple enough to make me stop wondering which of us will die, almost easy enough to forget how much blood has already spilled. But I don't stop wondering. And can't forget. Not that simply. Not that easily.

Besides, there's already a wrinkle in our plan.

"But, we do have a problem," Elissa says. She nods at the three of us, beckons us to follow her to the closed bedroom door. "It's Cally," she says, opening the door for us to look inside. "It's her injuries. She can't go with us."

BLUE

70

"**C**ONSIDERING what happened to her, she's doing better than you'd think," Elissa whispers. "But she's still not good. Not for what's next."

Grendel and Cally are both asleep on the bed. Along with Grendel's snores, I can hear Cally's ragged breathing. She's lying in a too-rigid posture—the evidence of pain and taped ribs.

After a moment, Elissa lightly pulls the door shut again. "No matter what she thinks, she's not going up any hill, not like that." She's still whispering. "For the next few days, she shouldn't go any farther than the front door. Even driving her part way up won't work. The bumps and bouncing would be just as bad—or worse— for her than walking. She could start bleeding internally. Maybe go into shock. Or maybe worse—"

There's no doubt what Elissa means by "maybe worse." It means another grave in Nanny Tinkens's meadow. It means the two sisters lying forever side by side. It means I'll lose my mom.

But we need Cally. The plan doesn't work without her. We need her at the Circle, and we need her there *now*. We all have our parts to play, and Cally's is one of the biggest.

She's our singer. The only one. *The last one.*

She's the one who sings the shifting songs, the songs that call the spirits, the songs that shape the Stone. Without her song, the Circle will remain unguarded. It will be an open target for that horrible thing—the thing I heard laughing as I stared into the blue memories, the thing laughing at each shattered, crying child, the thing I felt growing stronger with every blow it landed. And, most of all, the same monstrous thing that had murdered my family, that had killed my wife and son, spilling their blood into the water and taking their lives so it could gather more magic in its bag, using their souls to scoop up the magic pouring so freely out of the ground.

Suddenly I know the solution. The solution to our problem—

Maybe the only solution.

And maybe it will work.

Maybe.

HEARING MY STEPS as I go into the bedroom, Grendel lifts his head and watches me through half-asleep eyes. He lazily swipes a paw over his whiskers as I carefully sit down on the bed beside Cally.

"Mom," I whisper, touching her shoulder. I can feel her shoulder bone through the blanket. She suddenly seems so old and fragile, like one of her pale, translucent teacups, so thin you feel nothing but warmth in your hand.

She stirs, then wakes up quickly. Unlike her bones, her eyes are strong and alive. She smiles at me. "Blue," she says. "Home again, home again, jiggety-jig."

It's good to see her smiling. Good to hear her voice. "Hey, Gypsy Girl," I whisper. "It's show time. Time for you to sing for your supper. Time to sing your songs on the hill."

The others don't know the answer to the problem yet, but I do—

Magic.

The answer is magic.

And I know exactly which magic we need. And where I've found it hiding before.

ACTUALLY, THE MAGIC isn't hiding. It's already here, already all around us. Everything is now in place—a full moon shines in the day's dark blue sky, a pillar of orange fire burns in the distance, and a battle is near at hand. Magic and power are flowing like rivers of energy through the air, rushing down from the Circle and then back up again. The magic feels strong and familiar, moving with the same heavy, building rhythm of a rising tide. Even within the cabin's walls, I can feel it —the undertow, the tug and pull of it returning to its center, circling back to an ancient heart.

Of all the other times, this is the truest time, the time to trust in magic: the time, most of all, to believe—

It will work.

I know it will.

Callista won't have to walk far, not even as far as the front door. We aren't going that way to the Circle. We're going a different way. A way I've traveled once before, when the Circle first drew me to it.

I STAND THEM in a line: Elissa, Cally, Alassadir, Setsu. Grendel is there, too, weaving his way through everyone's legs, inviting us all to scratch his ears. I tell them, "Follow close," then take hold of Elissa's hand and step inside the same narrow closet I'd walked into once before. The same closet with the path that once took me to the Stones. Walking slowly into the closet's dark, cluttered tunnel, I hear the expected sounds behind me: the hushed talk and whispers of the others, the uneven jangled music of bumping-together wire hangers, the muted rustling of brushed-against clothing. Soon though, those sounds grow fainter and fade to an indistinguishable hum and buzz, becoming a sound from somewhere far away. After a few more steps, they grow even softer still.

I continue walking into the darkness. Seeing nothing. Hearing nothing. Feeling only Elissa's hand in mine—the small, round bump of her severed finger presses into my palm, reminding me of the two most important parts of my life: The part that I still have. And the part that was taken away.

THERE'S SOMETHING ahead.
　　I hear sound.
　　I see light.
　　And then—
　　Here is magic.
　　Because we are suddenly at the Circle.
　　Because we are now standing with the Stones.

BLUE

*M*AGIC AND SERENDIPITY, *accidents and omens—these four forces have been my touchstones. They are the bearing walls of my life. The four are always present: In each blessing I've received and every lesson that I've learned, their influence and touch are there. And when I've had questions to ask, these four forces have answered them, have given me what I sought. They've given every answer that I needed to find…until now.*

Now I'm adding another source of answers, a fifth force— Miracles.

I'm adding miracles to my list.

I expected so much today, but I didn't expect a miracle. Not a real one. Not something holy and pure. Before today, whenever I prayed, I knew the power of prayer had limits—that there were places a prayer couldn't go, that there were thoughts it was futile to think. I knew that, even for prayer, there were rules, boundaries, acceptable expectations…which is why what happened is a miracle. It's a miracle because it breaks all of the rules, because it ignores all of the boundaries. Because it runs rampant over my puny expectations. It's a miracle because it answers a prayer I never even thought to pray.

WE STAND inside the Circle. No one speaks. No one points or nods. Instead, we turn slowly, silent and awe-filled, fully caught in the spell of the Stones. The Stones surround us and welcome us.

Among them, I have a feeling of reunion, of return and gathering. The Stones stand along the circumference of a perfect circle. Except for one wide and empty space, each Stone is equidistant from the others—their weathered white forms frame the green spaces beyond them. Through those tall frames, we stare out at Jonah's Belly, entranced by the lush tangle of beauty growing there.

There is only one wrong thing. It looks wrong and feels wrong, but it still powerfully draws my eyes, demanding my attention: the empty space where another Stone should stand. Though the Stone is gone, the empty space makes the missing Stone somehow seem to be as present as its fellows, maybe even more present—after all, its death is the reason we're here. We have come to fill its place at the Circle—and to leave one of our own here to die, to leave one of us behind forever. And as much as I know what must happen next—as much as I've now come to understand—that doesn't stop me from wishing there were another way, doesn't stop me from wondering "why?" But all of my wishes and wondering don't matter. In the end, the facts won't change—

The fact that Setsu will never leave this hill.

The fact that this is where he'll die.

It is foolish to wonder why. I know why he's going to die here today. It's because of blood and gifts. It's something I've known since Alassadir told the story of the second battle, the fight that the brothers began as beasts. And I understood it again while I was praying over the graves at Nanny Tinkens's home, when a bear suddenly stood among us, huge and powerful with the wild magic coursing through its blood.

Setsu will die for the same reason that Cally is needed here now: because we all have a part to play. Because we each have our role and we each have our gift—roles and gifts assigned by blood. *Alassadir*: He is here to keep and to tell the story. He'll make certain the People know, make certain that they remember. *Me*: I have both the lowliest gift and the easiest task. I'm here to join the battle. To fight and bleed. *Callista*: She is the only one who can sing the shifting songs. The songs that call to the spirits, the songs that allow blood to turn to Stone. *Setsu*: Like Cally, he is another "only one." The only one who can shift, the only one whose blood and flesh can turn to Stone—which makes him the only one who can fill the Circle's empty space, the only one who must live and die as Stone.

OUTSIDE OF the Circle's perimeter, the hill is ripe with life. The late sunlight, slanting through the overhead branches, looks like a new sort of illuminated forest—rather than spearing down, the rays of light seem to grow up from the ground like thin, gold saplings glowing in the spaces between the green trees.

Squeezing my hand again, Elissa murmurs, "It's what you said, Blue. It's magic...and so beautiful."

I recognize the look in her eyes. She's feeling the same thing I'd felt when I first found the Circle. The joy of it is filling her.

Without a word, Setsu steps away from us and walks to the nearest Stone. He begins to follow the circumference of the Circle, walking from Stone to Stone, pausing by each one. As he looks at each Stone, his face lights up with warmth and caring, with the recognition of familiar company. Watching him, I realize something. *He knows them. He knows the men they were. He knows and loves each one. And they love him in return.*

Only then do I truly understand: Setsu, too, is filled with joy.

He hasn't returned here as a sacrifice. And hasn't come here to be left behind and die. This is his homecoming. This is where he wants to be, home forever with his friends. To stand eternally with the other Stones. Seeing him visit with the Circle, I realize just how right it is for him to be here—how much, just like the trees and the ground and the light and wind, he is part of this place. This is where he belongs.

When he reaches the empty place in the Circle—where the missing Stone should be—he stops and stares down at the ground. I know what he sees, what it is that he stands considering. He is looking at the hole in the ground, the hole no longer sealed by Stone. It is an open well, dropping down to a hidden sea. It is the passage through the hill to the magic lying beneath, pooled and waiting.

Then, on this day of surprises, I am surprised again—

Setsu shifts.

It happens quickly, with no forewarning or delay. He simply shrugs off one shape and slips on another. One moment, we see a man standing next to the hole, the next, we see silver-gray monkey standing there. Then, just as suddenly, the monkey is gone, too. *Presto-change-o.* One second he's there, the next he's not. He disappears so fast that, for an instant, I think he's shape-shifted again, this time becoming the air itself, dissolving into the nothingness of wind and light. But he hasn't dissolved or melted away. As I replay the moment in my mind's eye, I realize that I saw where he went. He didn't *shift* into nothingness, he *stepped into it.*

The monkey had disappeared down the hole.

It was all miraculous, but none of it was the miracle—not our trip to the Circle, not the beauty around us, not the Stones that once were men, not even Setsu's shape-shifting. None of those things. The miracle was what Setsu had gone to find. The miracle was waiting below.

Standing near the hole, waiting for him to return, I felt a breeze rushing up from out of the ground. It was a cool breath of earth and water filled with scents of clay and rock and sea. But its touch wasn't what made me shiver, wasn't what made my knees buckle and left me kneeling on the fragrant, thick grass like someone at church. No, I didn't fall to my knees to pray. I knelt because of a sound I heard, a sound being carried on the breeze—

I heard the child again.

The child crying on Jonah's Belly.

72

THE WARRIOR, ALWAYS ONE MORE ARROW

A S HE CLIMBED down the narrow chimney, his long thin limbs instinctively found toeholds and fingerholds in the dark. Although he was descending, for a moment his perspective felt reversed, as though he was standing still and it was the black walls around him that were moving, rising higher and higher above him.

Looking up, he saw a small pane of floating, shining light, and the rising black walls were lifting the light farther and farther away from him, lifting it so high that it became a single glowing star at the top of the tallest night.

Only his hands and feet gave him proof that he was the one in motion. Without thought or direction, they automatically clasped and released the bumpy grips and crevices in the walls, finding one and then instantly seeking another, moving him as quickly and smoothly downward as though he was falling deeper and deeper into an endless abyss...falling until he could no longer see even that single star...until there were only the darkness and the walls and the wind.

The wind swept up from below, sometimes blowing so strongly that he felt like he was at the edge of a storm, other times blowing so gently that it barely ruffled the coat of gray hair covering the body he now wore. With each breath and gust, the wind spoke to him, whispering and beckoning...and carrying the cry of a child, a child held safe within the buried sea.

He continued down, descending until he felt the cool touch of water on his extended paw. He stopped then, holding motionless in the passage. In the darkness he began chanting prayers—first giving thanks to Father Hill for loving and protecting Mother Sea. Then he gave praise to Mother Sea for the life in her waters and the magic that she birthed. He thanked her for the gift she'd called to him to receive.

He turned in the darkness, his arms and legs moving easily, reaching out and finding the needed holds, turning himself so that his face was now nearer the sea. He moved closer to the water's surface and breathed in the wet, salt smell of it, filling his lungs with its heavy air.

He moved again, lowering himself even closer to the hidden water.

Then opened his mouth to drink.

BLUE 73

FOR WHAT HAPPENED at the Circle that day, I should have three separate memories, not just one—one memory is too small; it holds everything too close together, wrongly smearing everything with the same splashes of blood and horror. Yes, there should be three separate memories—each one isolated from the others, with two of the memories held close and treasured, and the third buried deep and forgotten. Buried so deep that it can only rise in nightmares.

The first memory should be of the miracle—the miracle that I'll always remember as beginning with a monkey's smile. That would be the first memory. A memory bursting with life and unexpected blessings. A memory of a sudden rip in the world's fabric through which I glimpse a benevolent god.

The second memory is the one I should see only when I sleep, when darkness and anguished dreams dig it out of its grave. In the second memory, there is no god or benevolence anywhere. There's just blood and death and loss.

The third memory is bloody, too, filled with its own death and loss. But within it are also sacrifice and courage and family—and those are their own sorts of miracles, the kind that give the clearest glimpses of God.

WE WATCH the hole, waiting for Setsu to return. We wait for so long that I feel worry starting to build among us, for so long that I sense the others beginning to think what I'm thinking. *Should I climb down after him? Should I hike home and get a rope? How long would that rope have to be? How far down is it to an ancient sea?*

But before our worries grow too great, a single gray-haired paw reaches up out of the hole and grasps a handful of grass. Then a second paw reaches up and grabs its own grass anchor. Then the rest of him nimbly follows.

He climbs out of the hole and sits monkey-hunched beside it, not waving or walking to us, just sitting quietly. Not knowing what else to do, we stare, uncertain whether to go to him or leave him alone, not wanting to interrupt some magical rite or thought.

And then he does something surprising, something I don't expect to see—

He smiles at us.

He shifts then, changing back to his man-form, changing as quickly as he'd done before. This time, though, one thing doesn't shift. One thing stays the same in the man as it was with the monkey. His smile remains. Only now I can tell that he isn't really smiling at the whole group. He's looking at Elissa. And it is to Elissa he now walks, holding out one hand.

The closer he gets, the surer I am that Something Is Happening. Something unplanned and unforeseen, making the air feel more alive. Something that pushes me forward. And pushes Elissa, too.

She walks to Setsu and reaches out, lets him take her hand. He steps backward, gently pulling her so she has to follow, leading her to the hole. I follow the two of them across the Circle, knowing that whatever is happening, it isn't magic—

It's something older than magic.

Something much, much older.

Then Setsu stops, standing so close to the hole that his heels hang over the edge. Without a word, he sits down, right there at the edge, and points to where he wants us to take our places.

Elissa is to lie on the ground in front of him, and he gestures for me to sit beside her. After we're settled, he cups his hands below his mouth and bows his head. A trickle of water begins spilling out from between his lips. He catches each drop, collecting them in the chalice he's made of his hands. When the water stops, his head stays bowed, and for the first time since he climbed out of the hole, he speaks. But he isn't talking to us. He's talking to the water, praying over it—

—and although I knew where the water came from and how precious and powerful it must be, as I remember that moment now, I realize that then, right then, I still knew absolutely nothing. Even while I was sitting so close to all of it—to Setsu, to the water, to Elissa, to the Circle, with everything about to completely change—I still had no idea, I still could not imagine—

Then I hear it. From the look in her eyes, I can see that Elissa hears it too.

The Circle's voice.

Not a song. Not a sound carried on the wind.

A voice.

I hear it inside me, inside my head. But more than merely hearing it, I feel it…the same way I felt my heart speak when I first saw Elissa, the way I heard it say to me, *This is true. This is forever.* It's the same sort of feeling now. And the same message, too. One felt in my heart, making me suddenly understand. *This, too, is true. This, too, is forever.*

The Circle's message. I listen to it. And feel it. And I believe what it says. It is more than water in Setsu's hands. It is also a life and a soul—a small life, one that's been kept safe below and within the hill, one that's been held safe within the sea.

Setsu slowly uncups his hands and the water pours like a thin silver chain onto Elissa's stomach. It slips across her skin and then disappears…delivering the small, found life back into her body, tucking the small, found soul back into her womb.

It's the child.

The child I heard crying. The child I searched for but couldn't find.

The hill and Setsu—they've given us a miracle.

They've returned what was taken from us.

They've given us back our son.

THAT IS HOW the first memory should end. If it ended there, it would be a memory I could hold close and study, feeling awed by the way it always shines, enthralled by how everything changed in a single brilliant instant. I could remember how thrilled I was that—for just that moment—I felt the touch of something perfect.

But that isn't how it ends.

It ends when the nightmare that is the second memory begins, when the woods around the Circle erupt with a crashing noise, and a man comes charging out from the trees. The man is enveloped in a blurry nimbus of blue fire. Guided by the tongues of pale blue fire that flicker from his body, he runs straight at us, the flames leading him to what he's been sent to find.

I know why he's here. I know what he wants.

He's come for the child.

He's come to take back our boy.

BLUE 74

A S THE MAN runs at us, for the briefest moment I again hear the blue fire's message. It reaches out for me and I hear it whispering in my ear, speaking to me, reminding me of what I was shown, telling me about what is yet to come…and inviting me back into its warm blue flames. But along with those blue whispers, I hear another sound—a high-pitched vibration that courses through me, filling my veins with a cold wind, filling my ears with the sound of winter hail pounding down against steel, the sound growing so loud it drowns out the blue fire's words. I recognize the sound—I've been hearing it for almost a year. I recognize it from all of my sleepless nights, from all of my restless, angry thoughts—

It's the sound of my rage, the sound of a falling rock hurtling down.

I am ready for this fight.

I turn to Elissa, telling her, "Go to the woods. Hide there. Stay safe." Then I rush forward into battle. I feel my skin humming, feel the hammering velocity of my blood. Racing toward the man, I ask myself, *Does he hear the sound, too?* And if he can hear it, does he know that it's coming from me? Does he know that I am the falling rock now dropping toward him, ready to collide and crash and crush?

When I'm almost upon him, I can see more clearly into the flames. He's another one of the drivers, like the one I'd killed earlier.

Within the flickering blue light I can see his dark suit and his bright blue eyes, his eyes glowing even brighter than the flames. As we near each other, he howls. I howl back. And as I throw myself into his fire, I hear gunshots and another eerie howling behind me, but I don't have time to turn around, there's no time to do anything but thrust my hands at his face, aiming at his bright blue eyes.

Afterward, when things were finished, I learned what happened behind me. They'd planned their attack so they could split our group apart. The gun was Alassadir's. He was firing at the second flame-wrapped figure that broke from the trees, attacking from a different place than the first, heading straight for my mother. And just like I ran forward to protect Elissa, Alassadir charged forward to keep the fight away from Cally. Running, he fired at the licking blue flames, sending bullet after bullet into the dark shape that howled beneath the blue fire.

Already separated, Alassadir and I charge even farther apart—acting on the adrenaline of an instant, attacking the threats that burst from the woods…and leaving someone unguarded behind. Focused only on our enemies, neither of us pauses or hesitates. Seeing nothing to the left or right of our targets, we simply run straight ahead, without even thinking to also look up. So neither of us sees the wings streaking down, or the talons carving through the sky.

Setsu is the only one who knows all the places from where danger can come. Only he sees the small spot of shadow that appears on the ground and then quickly grows bigger. Looking up, only he sees the owl that is now swooping down from the daytime moon.

BLUE 75

I'VE BEEN in the blue fire before. I've already seen through its veil, already felt its warm embrace and heard its promises of pleasure. The blue fire doesn't confuse or daze me, doesn't distract me from what I intend to do. I reach the man and charge into the swirl of circling blue flames, thrusting my hands at his face. And I blind him—my thumbs plunge into the blue infernos of his eyes, pop through the bright marbles of his pupils, then pull back fast, ripping out gleaming bits of dangling cords.

He howls again and pitches forward, sightlessly reaching for my throat. I grab his wrists and yank, pulling him closer to me, pushing him down. He stumbles. Still pulling, I pivot to one side of his unbalanced body, then release his wrists and draw my right arm around his neck. I close the noose, my left hand grabbing the wrist of my circling arm and locking my right forearm to crush his throat—

—and he feels his air suddenly gone. His hands flail up, trying to land a blow as I sink to the ground, simultaneously dropping down and leaning back, pulling up hard with my arms—

—and as the bones and hard tubes of his neck begin to crack and break, the blue fire dims. The flames crawl off me, slipping away from my skin and snaking slowly across his body. They worm into the ruined pockets of his eyes, and then they disappear, leaving no trace of ever existing.

At the same time, the owl screams—a sharp scream of

victory—and I look up, immediately understanding that it is the sound of the real battle beginning, understanding that the fight I've just fought and the one Alassadir's now finishing as he fires again at the flickering body on the ground...those fights have been nothing but diversions.

I rise at the owl's first scream and start running, already knowing I'll be too late, already knowing that Cally is going to die. The owl is going to kill my mother. Neither Setsu nor I can get to her in time, neither of us can save her.

The owl comes slashing down.

It is huge—so large that its shadow is like a dark sea rippling across the Circle. Its wings are feathered longbows, drawn and curved in the air. Its legs are extended to seize its prey, talons ready to clutch and shred and tear. Slanting through the sky, it arcs across the top of a Stone and aims itself at Callista. Setsu is running ahead of me, but I know he can't reach her in time, not in time to keep the talons from tearing Cally's skin, not in time to save her throat from the owl's razored feet and beak. And I'm so focused on the owl, so intently anticipating the sick, pounding sound of its strike against my mother's flesh that at first I don't recognize what I suddenly see—

—a shape appears so quickly that it seems to spring instantly from the owl's breast. The shape screams its own hunting scream as it covers the owl's talons with tawny fur. The shape's jaws open wide, snap shut, open again, trying to catch the owl's stabbing, piercing beak in a white clamp of long fangs. Then I see the shape clearly—

It's Grendel.

He's leapt onto the owl.

BLUE 76

I SEE THE OWL'S talons slice into Grendel's belly, ripping the skin from his bones, squeezing and cutting through the cat's soft tissues. Locked together, the cat and owl fall backward, knocking Cally to the ground beneath them. The owl's wings beat up and down against the cat and the woman, battering them both in a feathered storm. Its beak stabs at Grendel again and again, ripping up each time with a bloody wad of fur and meat. It swallows each raw piece, then knifes back down for more.

WHEN SETSU is almost to Cally, he shifts and changes...and a bear's huge paw suddenly swings into the owl's body, batting it off of Grendel and smashing it to the ground. Before the owl can spread its wings, the bear falls upon it, blanketing it in a mountain of muscle. The bear's claws rake the giant bird, and its broad tree-stump of a head shakes back and forth as it presses down, crushing and biting what it holds, spraying droplets of blood into the air.

While the bear and the owl are fighting, I run to Cally and Grendel. Alassadir is already there, and Elissa has also emerged from the woods and is coming back to us, running past the bullet-ridden body lying between her and the Circle.

Cally is lying on the ground, her eyes closed, her skin paler than ever before. She looks like a sculpture made of eggshells and tissue, a fragile figurine of a small, sleeping woman left on display.

But Grendel, bleeding and gasping beside Cally, ruins the illusion of art. His golden eyes are half-open and his paws move weakly as I approach. One of his tufted ears has been torn away, making his head look oddly round.

The bear suddenly rises into the air, heaved upward by the yellow-scaled, black-clawed thing that now rears up from where the owl had been only an instant before. Twisting clumsily in the air, the bear's tumbling bulk is suddenly unmoored from the earth and gravity. But when it falls, it falls heavily, and as it crashes to the ground, the bones in one of its front legs break with a loud snap.

Cally's gun is on the ground beside her still body. I've picked it up and am already walking forward as the bear falls, am already firing at the hideous, scaled creature as it lurches at Setsu. The gun's popping sounds are insignificant, like the sounds of a child's toy pistol, but I keep pulling the trigger, firing with each step I take, shooting at the reptilian head that swings around to face me, shooting and hoping for the beast to fall.

The thing turns toward me and steps forward, its black tongue flicking in and out of its mouth, slipping between rows of cruel, sharp teeth. The bear lies behind it, crumpled on the ground. I hear my gun still making harmless little pops and bangs in my hand as I keep firing, wondering what I'll do when the bullets are finally gone and the beast hasn't died…wondering what I will do when it reaches for me with its black claws.

COLE

H E THOUGHT the snakes had finally quieted. But maybe not. Maybe they were still rattling, still striking at him like before. Maybe he'd just gotten so used to the noise that he couldn't hear them anymore—like hearing the same chime of the same clock every hour of every day until you've heard it so many times that you don't hear it anymore. Or maybe—

—maybe there wasn't anything to hear anymore. Maybe he'd finally died. Or was dying now. Maybe he was so close to death that he'd floated free from the canvas bag he'd been shoved into. Maybe now he was drifting somewhere else in darkness, maybe in a quiet, safe place far away from the snake-filled cave. Maybe, at last, he'd escaped from the dead man's arms.

Maybe.

Wherever he was, it sure smelled good here...like limes. Limes and tropical waters.

And wherever he was, he noticed that it wasn't completely dark anymore. He could see specks of green and blue, tiny bits of color coming closer, getting brighter and larger with each black wave that he felt lifting and carrying him closer...closer to what he now saw was an island shore.

He drifted lazily on the sea, watching the island grow larger.

When his feet eventually touched sand, he stood in the warm, shallow water and waded ashore to a white beach that stretched for miles in both directions. At the inland edge of the beach, growing on the other side of a sloping, silky dune, he saw a grove of lime trees. And strung among the lime trees, he saw what he hoped he was going to see—

Two hammocks, swaying in a pirate breeze.

As he stared at the hammocks, the grove's leaves rustled with the dappling sound of dropped pennies, and then he watched his dad step out from the trees. His dad was tanned deep brown, and was wearing his favorite summer clothes—a pair of bright green, knee-length swim trunks and a Mr. Peabody cartoon T-shirt (**Mr. Peabody's Improbable History! Set the WABAC Machine!**).

Cole waited. His dad's feet kicked up little fans of sparkling sand as he crossed the beach. When he reached Cole, his dad knelt down and hugged him close, saying nothing as Cole took a deep breath and smelled the Royall Lyme scent on his dad's neck—the smell that told him this was real, that told him he was home.

"My little King Cole," his Dad said, giving him another tight squeeze, then leaning back, still holding Cole in his arms but moving so that they could look each other in the eye. His dad smiled, a sad kind of smile.

"Been a hard bit of bumpy road, hasn't it, son?" he asked.

Cole nodded, agreeing but unable to find any words. Instead, he moved back into his dad's tight embrace, again tucking his face into the curve of his dad's neck and breathing in the good lime smell.

His dad nodded. "You're doing fine, my little King Cole," he said. "And there's just a little more left to do."

BLUE 78

AS THE BEAST comes at me, the only thing left for me to do is throw the empty gun at its head, hoping for a David-and-Goliath sort of moment, hoping the pistol will hit exactly the right place on the thing's scaly forehead and kill it in its tracks. Or, at the very least, that the steel barrel might chip one of the thing's many, many teeth. Except that its teeth aren't what are worrying me the most right now—it's the claws, the black claws at the end of its thick arm. The arm now rising above my head.

Up this close, I can see the pebbled texture of the monster's tongue. The scarlet lining of its wide nostrils. With nothing else to try, I hurl the gun at it as hard as I can. It hits the thing's head and bounces away, not slowing it at all, not even making it flinch. Then it's standing in front of me, arm raised and ready to fall, ready to slice down with a hand of open claws. I'm close enough to see that every dull yellow scale on its body is striped with small red lines. Close enough that I could reach out and trace the wrinkled network of veins under its leathery, reddish skin. And close enough to know there is no escape.

Taking my last breath, I look away, deciding to fill my eyes with anything else but scales and skin—wanting the last thing I see to be anything but the beast's open mouth.

What I see is Setsu.

He's standing behind the beast, still too far away to stop the thing's arm from crashing down on me, too far away to stop the claws. At first, I think that Setsu has found two white, pointed sticks, two sharp new weapons that he's cradling in his arm. But then I realize what I'm seeing, what he is holding—and I know for certain that the black claws will soon fall, that even Setsu can't stop whatever is going to happen next...not with the two jagged stilettos of bone protruding from his broken arm.

But I'm wrong. Setsu does stop the claws. But he doesn't shift. And doesn't run forward. He doesn't attack at all.

Instead, he calls out to the thing. One word—

"Brother."

The thing's arm pauses above me, held fixed by the power of Setsu's single word. The thing swings its head around. It looks at Setsu, who doesn't move. Doesn't do anything except hold his shattered arm and stare straight into the thing's eyes.

Then Setsu drops his eyes.

And then he bows his head.

It's a universal gesture, meaning the same thing to man and beast—it means that he is surrendering. It means he is offering it victory, that he's offering his life.

I know what else it means—

He's offering it a trade: Himself for me.

I don't understand why he's doing it, but I don't need to understand. All I need to understand is that it's a shitty deal, making no sense at all. And it's something I can't let happen. We all have our parts to play and, right now, Setsu's part is to kill the thing, kill it the way that it has to be done—kill it on this hill, kill it with blood and love. Setsu is my only chance to keep Elissa alive. And my only hope of keeping the others safe, too. Only Setsu can kill it...and that's something he can't do if he dies first. Or if he trades himself for me.

So I do the only sensible thing I can do. I play my part—the part where I try to distract the beast, the part where I fight to slow it down.

I jump at the beast's arm.

I grab onto its black claws with both of my hands.

BLUE 79

THE CLAWS slice my hands.

It feels like I'm grabbing onto black knives, like I'm rappelling down the teeth of a ripping saw. Blood sprays from the cut flesh of my fingers and palms. The red spray slicks the thing's claws and scales, making me lose my grip and slip off of its arm. I stumble back a few steps, but immediately charge forward again, rushing low, shoulder down and elbows in, pressing my bleeding hands against my stomach, trying to hit the beast and knock it down, trying to give Setsu some time—

Trying to play my part.

I HIT IT hard. My shoulder rams straight into its leathery gut. But the beast doesn't even look down, doesn't turn its head away from Setsu. It just gives me backhanded swipe that sends me reeling and leaves me splayed on the ground, my breath knocked out, making short, barking gasps of noise.

All I can do is watch, my sliced hands still balled against my stomach.

The thing walks away from me and starts changing into something else. Its massive shape melts and shrinks. Its scales and skin flow together, turning into a milky-white layer of human skin. With each step it takes, the changing beast stands straighter. And it grows a head of bright red hair.

It becomes a man.
It walks toward Setsu.
"Brother," it says.

BLOOD AND LOVE. When I see Setsu and his brother standing together on the hill, I finally understand what it means—I know what it is…and what it isn't. It isn't the blood spilled during battle— it's the blood that's flowing through their veins, the blood they share, the family blood that joins them. And it isn't their love for each other—it's the love for what each of them has lost, the love for what each took from the other…the things that neither of them will ever allow to be taken from him again.

Setsu is still holding his shattered arm, the splintered bones poking out just above his wrist. From where I'm lying, though, I can see what Setsu can't. I can see the red-haired man's other arm, the one it is holding behind its back. The hidden arm hasn't changed. It's still covered with yellow scales and leathery skin, and it still ends in a nest of black claws. Still trying to draw a full breath, I push up from the ground. I want to shout a warning, but can only manage a weak, empty, wheezing sound.

Setsu's head stays bowed. He is making the trade. He is keeping the deal. As if to whisper in Setsu's ear, the red-haired thing bends toward him. But I see the claws begin to open behind its back, see the arm begin to move. Then, without looking up, Setsu reaches out with his unhurt arm and steps forward, moving closer to the leaning, red-haired man. His good hand catches hold of the bright red hair and pulls, yanking the thing's head down at the same time Setsu's broken arm spears upward, driving straight into the thing's face. The sharp, fractured bones pierce the red-haired man's bright blue left eye. The bones sink in, burying themselves so deep I hear the ending smack of Setsu's arm against the thing's cheek. It happens so fast that only after the bones have hammered through its eye does the red-haired man scream—a short, scream, ending almost as quickly as it begins, the sound of sudden pain and death. And as quickly as that—

It is over.

As quickly as that, the red-haired monster is dead.

Setsu holds the body tightly to him, keeping it from falling. The thing's clawed arm now hangs limply down, brushing against the ground, where the claws gleam like a cluster of polished black fruit. The thing's dead face is turned to me, letting me see its lifeless right eye. The eye is open and staring. It looks like someone has laid a bright blue coin on a corpse' face.

But then the eye blinks.

And then the black-clawed arm moves.

I lurch up, shouting a warning as the scaled arm rises from the ground and swings at Setsu. But Setsu doesn't have time to react, doesn't have time to drop the thing's body and raise his own arms in defense. For a moment—only a moment—the claws disappear. Then they reappear, slipping out of Setsu's chest, pulling back from deep inside him where they've been...still holding on to what they've ripped out of his insides.

THE THING drops Setsu's body, casually discarding him. Before I can think about what I'm seeing, the red-haired man changes back into the beast, a monster standing hunched and muscled. The monster watches me and waits, watching with its one bright blue eye. Waiting with its teeth and claws.

I am going to kill it.

I am going to kill it the way it needs to be killed—on the hill, *with blood and love.* With the blood that's running in their veins— the same blood that also runs in mine. And with love—love for what's been lost, love for what's been taken...love for what I won't allow to ever be taken again.

I shout "Brother!" as I charge.

And as soon as I'm close enough, I jump, punching my cut

and bleeding hand into its open mouth, feeling the rubbery length of its tongue beneath my hand, feeling its teeth shred my arm as I drive my balled fist deep between its jaws. The thing wraps its arms around me, squeezing me to it, crushing me against its scaled hide—

—and I open my fist inside its mouth, letting loose the things that I'm holding in my hand, the things I've been carrying in the bag around my neck. They are the things that weigh so little, yet hold so much—so much anger, so many memories...and so much love.

The things roll out of my grasp and tumble down the beast's black gullet. I feel them as they fall, each one thrumming with power, each one a perfect piece of love and loss. One by one, they fall out of my hand—the lightning-struck nugget of silver dog tag, the three small, polished bones of Elissa's severed finger, a red cellophane-wrapped piece of cinnamon candy, the pewter-colored crown cap of a bottle of Royall Lyme.

LIGHTNING FILLS the thing. The purple lightning of a summer storm. The flashing light explodes from inside of the thing, spearing out in a jagged, burning star that's so bright I can see it on the lids of my closed eyes. I don't feel the thing's clawed arms releasing me; instead, I feel its arms dissolve. And I don't feel its mouth open wider around my arm, or feel its teeth lift from my skin. Instead, its mouth and teeth are simply, suddenly gone.

I open my eyes. The lightning flashes don't blind me, and their heat doesn't burn. Looking through the bright nova, I see the monstrous thing die once again...and this time there is no doubt. I watch until the beast and the lightning both disappear, until there is nothing left before me.

That's when I feel a hand on my shoulder.

"Brother." It's Alassadir, standing behind me. "There is work to do. Work needing done now."

At the sound of his voice, I turn. But it isn't Alassadir I see standing there—it's me. I'm looking at a perfect reflection of myself.

The reflection stands on my legs. It reaches out to me with my hand. It speaks to me from my mouth. "Brother Blue," it says, "my identical-fraternal twin." Then, just as quickly as its hand touches my shoulder again, the mirror-reflection shifts...and turns back into my brother. And in the same way that I've learned so many other things in so little time, I suddenly behold another revelation: My brother's gift is more than that of a storyteller. He is more than a keeper of tales.

AT OUR BIRTH, our father hadn't been wrong or confused. His eyes had told him the truth. As he gazed down at his two newborn sons in the hospital's oversized crib, the babies had indeed been identical—each one a smooth, pink, perfect mirror image of the other. A moment later, though, he took two quick steps back from the crib, startled by what he'd just seen. Before his eyes, one of the babies changed its shape. For whatever reason—maybe because Alassadir was full of gas that needed to be burped, or maybe because he'd felt a painful colicky cramp—my older brother shifted back to his own true form and surrendered his copy-shape of me...the only other shape he'd ever known, the shape he'd felt growing beside him in Cally's magical womb.

That's what my father saw.

First, his sons were identical. Then, seconds later, we were fraternal, too.

We were his identical-fraternal twins.

MY BROTHER tells us good-bye.

First, he kisses Cally. (She's bruised and broken and can only whisper, but she's alive.) Next, he hugs Elissa. Then he stoops and softly strokes Grendel's fur, careful not to press hard against the bandages Elissa has made from our torn clothing.

Then he tries to smile at me. Tries to tell me that everything is fine. "It isn't because I have to, Blue," he says. "It's because I want to. I'm tired—tired of always moving, tired of all the different places. Even tired of being the Gypsy King. Growing up, I always thought you were the lucky one—the brother who lived in a place like this, who called these hills his home. I've always wanted to live here, to be anchored in a place that didn't move. That didn't keep changing. Waking and sleeping and waking again—always surrounded by the same trees, in a place where I could see the morning sun, and where I could watch the moon all night. Brother, I promise you," he says, now hugging me, too. "This is more than my gift. This is also my heaven."

We each have our role to play.

My brother is more than a storyteller. More than a keeper of tales.

He has another gift.

A gift that lets him join the Circle.

A gift that lets him shift and turn to Stone.

WE DIG a grave for Setsu. We dig the hole along the Circle's curving line, between two of the tallest Stones. We use branches to dig, and the rich brown earth moves easily. We bury him there, with old friends on both sides, where ancient magic flows beneath him, and where there's another sort of magic above. We lay him to rest where the tall pillars will give him shade.

Then I hear it.

The last bit of magic—

An ethereal song begins to fill the air, coming from nowhere and from everywhere. Its music folds around us, joining our mourning at the grave. I smile because I know who is singing—it's Cole. It's his voice. Somehow he's here. I know it's him, and I also know the song. I've heard it before, sung in my dreams of old men held suspended over holes in the ground, their blood falling into the waters below—

It's the shifting song. Cole is calling to the spirits. He is singing to the Stone.

It's time.

Alassadir and I walk to the open well where the missing Stone should be. We wrap our arms around one another, hugging one last time.

"Remember to come talk with me," he says. "Come to the Circle. Come and tell me about our family. Come and dance with the Stones."

As we talk, the song Cole is singing grows stronger. A breeze begins swirling around us. The breeze is warm and smells of limes.

COLE

A S COLE and his dad walked along the shore, small, peach-colored birds ran past them, following the dark stripe of wet sand at the water's edge. The birds squeaked as they ran, their thin, wiry feet leaving a trail of diamond-shaped tracks.

"Your mom's here, too, son. She said to tell you she loves you, that she'll see you next time. But, for now, she knows you and I need to talk about some things before you go."

Cole stopped walking. "Next time? Before I go? But I thought...." He let the sentence trail away, then tried again, but still couldn't finish. "I thought...." Unable to speak, he stood silently, watching as the birds began darting into the water, dipping their heads into the little waves, then running back to sand, holding glittering exclamation points of tiny fish in their beaks.

"Not this time, Cole. Not yet. This is just a visit. A chance for me to pass along a message from Nanny T."

Cole stopped watching the birds. "Nanny T.? She's here, too?"

"Not right now. She's somewhere else just now. Somewhere that smells like cinnamon." His dad smiled. "I'm sure we'll get together with her after we all get settled in—I've got the feeling that anything's possible here...even a visit with my boy. For now, though, I'm supposed to tell you two things. And honestly, King Cole, I have no clue what either thing means, but she said you'll know. She said to tell you to '*Si! Si! Si!*' at the Circle. That's the first thing. And the second thing is that she wants you to sing. She said that your stone will teach you the song."

His stone. The pendant.

Cole felt it then, still lying against his skin. It had been there all along, suspended from the leather cord around his neck. He reached under his shirt, wrapped his fingers around the stone... and he heard a song that began filling him, a song that made him think of white wicker flying chairs and yellow dandelions brushing against the bottoms of his feet.

His dad turned and looked down the beach, turning just enough that Cole could see only one side of his dad's suddenly worried face, only half of the pale, straight line his lips had tightened to. "Actually, son, there's a third thing she told me, too. Something I don't understand at all, something I'd rather not say. But I promised her. I promised I'd tell it to you exactly like she said it."

His dad turned back to him, knelt again, took his son into his arms. "She said to tell you that she doesn't miss you, that she doesn't miss you even the tiniest littlest bit."

And as his dad held him, Cole started laughing—laughing so hard his belly hurt, so hard that the small peach-colored birds turned to watch the boy and the man.

WENDELL

WENDELL MORRIS had been reborn. And now reborn, he heard the music calling him. It was the music of the wonderful wheel, the song of the cosmic cycle. The sound of everything swinging back around. It was all returning to him, spinning back in the universal rotation. The music was leading him now, was taking him back to the beginning. It felt good to be going back. All he had to do was listen. Listen and follow the music.

Follow wherever it led.

CHICORY DIRTFOOT was dead.

His vision had been fulfilled. His life was over and done—he'd cut off his long, braided hair, then had eased himself, body and soul, into the depths of the mystical river. The river of chance and opportunity, the eternal current of coming and going. The river accepted him and took his life. Its waters washed him clean and emptied him. It took away who he'd become and returned him to who he'd been.

Chicory entered the river. Wendell emerged.

Chicory was gone. It was time to forget him. Time to forget about white shoelaces and green sneakers and glowing blue eyes. It was also time to forget about monkeys and padlocks and dead bodies in cages.

He was Wendell again.

It was time to return to the beginning of things. Was time to take another ride on the wonderful wheel.

HE KEPT CLIMBING, following the music all the way up the hill. The music was louder now, so he knew he was getting closer—closer to where the conservation officer had told him he'd find what he was looking for. Closer to the beginning.

He'd driven part way up the hill, driving until the brush was too overgrown for his small car to go any farther. Stopping his car, he got out to look around. He heard the music then and knew it was calling him, that it was guiding him to what he wanted to find. The music was beautiful. It was sweet and pure and sad—the same music Chicory had heard as he'd disappeared into the river, the same music Wendell had heard as he dreamed.

He found the cave.

He followed the music and found it, the cave where Gordy had said he'd taken Wendell's snakes, the same snakes that had been present at the beginning, the same snakes that Wendell now wanted back. He'd decided last night: It was time to reopen the Serpentarium. Yes, it was time to again STARE DEATH IN THE EYE!

A mail truck was parked near the cave's entrance, its keys still in the ignition. The music was coming from somewhere down inside the cave, somewhere Wendell couldn't see, beyond the wedge of light that angled into the low, slanted doorway. The music was stronger now, clearer than it had been even a moment ago. He closed his eyes as he listened, realizing what he heard. It was more than simple music. It was a child. A child singing a song. It was a song that called to him, a song that beckoned him down into the cave.

Wendell stooped down and walked inside. He kept walking, even as the snakes began striking his legs, even as he felt their venom beginning to burn. The earth sloped down into the darkness and the sounds of rattles rose around him, joining with the song being sung. Past the edge of the darkness, his foot kicked against something heavy. Reaching down to move whatever he'd kicked, he felt more snakes strike him, their fangs sinking into his hands, their heads smacking against his arms.

Then he touched flesh. Dead flesh. He moved his fingers past the cool flesh and felt canvas. The canvas moved when he touched it. Then, at his touch, whoever was in the canvas stopped singing and cried out a familiar prayer. "Please," Wendell heard in the darkness. "Please. Please."

THE SNAKES bit him again and again as he dragged the heavy canvas bag back up the ramp. He felt his skin swelling and nausea building, felt thick sweat streaming out of his pores. At the cave's entrance, he stepped out into the day's last light. He pulled the bag out with him, then crouched over it and began untying the knots that held it closed. As he worked, he talked out loud, reminding himself what it was that he needed, what he needed to go find when he was done here. "Ice cream," he said, untying the final knots and unwrapping the cords from the bag's neck. "Lots and lots of ice cream."

BLUE

THE SHIFTING song has faded away, and the hill is quiet. Weary and silent, we sit in the center of the Circle, surrounded by tall Stones. One Stone is different from the others. It looks newborn and unblemished, with a gleaming, smooth, unweathered surface. Its sides are flat and unlined, glowing as white and liquid as fresh cream. Each angle of it is perfect. The new Stone rises straight and tall, neither slanted nor tilted. It stretches up, as if trying to touch the sky, as if wanting to see the sun and moon.

A sudden flurry of maple tree whirlybirds from a nearby tree spins around the Stone. The cyclone of whirlies lifts and descends, riding on a gust of wind that holds the slight, damp hint of rain. Then, moments later, the air is painted with a soft, falling drizzle. The beaded mist brushes against my face. The rain's touch is soft and comforting as it begins to wash the blood and dirt off my skin. And I feel something else in the rain, something healing and renewing that rinses the exhaustion out of my bones.

The rain is an elixir, and I can see the others are feeling it, too. Elissa and Cally turn their faces up to it. They're both smiling. Neither of them has ever looked more beautiful than they do just now. My bride is more radiant than ever. And the mist on my mother's face reveals the young Gypsy she once was.

The rain cleanses and fills us. It pours new strength into our arms and legs. Feeling stronger, I gather Grendel in my arms and stand. He begins purring. Beside me, Elissa helps Cally to her feet.

My mother stands quietly, then takes a few tentative steps on her own, growing stronger with each step.

It's time to go home now. As we leave, we hear a new song begin behind us. A song being sung by the Circle of rain-wet Stones. It is a song of welcoming and family...a song of blood and love.

THE RAIN follows us through the woods and all the way to the cabin. I'm surprised to see a mail truck parked in our driveway. I'm even more surprised to see two people sitting on our porch swing, swinging back and forth, their faces bent over their laps. Even after we step out of the woods and into the open, they don't look up from what they're doing. Their unbroken concentration gives me the chance to stare in wonder.

One of them is Cole. The other is a man I don't know, but he looks familiar, like maybe someone I've seen in town. Both Cole and the man have large bowls heaped full of ice cream in their laps. As they eat, their metal spoons tap against the sides of the cold bowls, making a fast rhythm that rings like bells.

EPILOGUE

ONE YEAR LATER.
    One year since an orange fire speared up into the sky. One year since all of those souls flew up into the flames. The town has a memory of that day—a memory containing enough truth to be believed, and enough details to stop most from trying to remember even more. It's a memory that answers all of the questions that everyone asked, until the questions were finally asked no more.

The people who were lost and the earth that was scorched left scars behind. Scars that even now are still warm and painful to the touch. They haven't cooled off yet, not enough to be forgotten or ignored. The people in town still talk about what happened, still worry and fret over it. But now the story is always repeated in the same words, and anyone who listens always nods and agrees at the same places where they've nodded and agreed before. When the town tells its story, it makes me wonder about the different kinds of magic that fill our days, the different ways that the very same moments are either cloaked or revealed to each of us. I think about how so much is hidden from us, how so little is truly seen. And how rarely we recognize the magic that brushes against our lives and changes the course of everything.

The town remembers the fire. It knows how so many died. It even knows why—

...natural gas explosion, that's what it was. An explosion at the traveling Wonders of Natural Gas display everyone was invited to.

Invitations came in the mail, along with the brochures about that new pipeline they wanted to put in. And, my God, I swear I almost went, but I just couldn't get up early enough that morning, not with my ankles and knees so swollen like they were. Thank the Lord they organized it up in the hills, far enough away that the whole town wasn't incinerated to a crisp. Well, no matter how it happened—either because of those Earth First! protesters like the gas company says, or because of a faulty exhibit like everybody else says—it don't change the fact that whole families was lost. All their souls just disappearing into the clouds, all their bodies buried under the rubble..."

The town remembers. And continues on.

Certain of its memory.

Sure of what it knows.

LIKE THE TOWN, I remember it, too. I remember, every day.

I remember it when I see Cally and Cole sitting together on the kitchen chairs they've carried out into our back yard. They sit out there for hours, talking and then being quiet, looking at the beauty around them, then closing their eyes. As they sit there, I'm not sure who's teaching who. I don't know where they go or what they're seeing, but at night Cole tells us stories about prehistoric mounds of earth and tall stands of ancient trees. He talks about places where no one goes—place hidden far away, yet somehow still nearby, places that are always close, but still unrevealed. I can hear in his voice that he wants to visit those places, that one day he'd like to stand near them and hear their tales. When I look at Cole, I know who I am seeing: I'm looking at the next King of the Gypsies. I'm looking at their Little King Cole.

The carnival will be there when Cole wants to join it. Cally sent it ahead without her, with Wendell leading it now. He decided he wasn't ready yet to STARE DEATH IN THE EYE! and left the snakes where they were in the cave. Decided that he wanted to go even further back in the universal rotation, to get even closer to the beginning—back to the rides and the midway where he'd first discovered his own gifts.

And I remember it every time my one-eared cat carries another small, hurt thing out of the woods and watches as we bind the animal's wounds and set its bones before he climbs back onto the porch to nap in a spill of sunlight. Before going to sleep, Grendel rolls over onto his back, letting the sun warm his stomach. The crosshatch of scars on his belly looks like a tawny, patchwork quilt, one that's been sewn together with thick white rope.

And I remember it, every single day, when Elissa touches my lips with hers and we stand together in the cabin's crowded nursery, both of us rocking gently back and forth, holding our twins in our arms. Our fraternal twins, a boy and a girl, both of them born with their own sort of gift. My daughter Cassandra has the same green eyes as her mother, a green capable of casting any spell. And when my son Gordon cries, his mouth opens wide enough for everyone to see the dark blue-black color inside.

And I remember it at the Stones when I sit with Alassadir and Setsu, telling them about my days, trying to give them a cabin to go with their hill. After I tell them everything I can think of, I sit and listen for their voices, for their tales of Jonah's Belly. And I ponder their ongoing discussion of the moon and the sun and the rains.

Sitting at the Stones, hearing their quiet, peaceful sounds, I realize that I am wonderfully surrounded, that there are Circles all around me. I live gratefully within them. They are the miracles in my life, the blessings and amazements that wrap and tie everything together as they weave through my life with their love. They are the Circles of family and friendship and stories...and they are the best kind of magic, the extraordinary magic of every day.

ACKNOWLEDGEMENTS

SPECIAL THANKS TO:

—My parents, Jim and Barb. For a childhood filled with a love of story, Saturday morning trips to the library, and—when every penny counted and there were no pennies to count—the glorious gift of an unlimited budget for each month's Scholastic Book order. Also, much love and thanks for a lifetime of art, curiosity, conversations, and encouragement.

—My son and my daughter, Aaron and Megan. No herd animals here. Your talents amaze and impress. No father has ever been more proud. I took the time to write the book because I wanted more time with you. It is an inspiration and a joy to see you using your gifts to make your own less-traveled ways through the green and dark woods.

—Elissa, my beautiful and brave bride. For going along for the ride, wherever the ride might go. None of the good things happen without you, and most of them happen because of you. I'm so glad that I've known you longer than I haven't.

—All the friends who read the many chapters and shared their thoughts and comments.

—Barbara Ardinger, Ph.D. When I threw an imperfect book at the universe, it threw back the perfect editor for the story.

AUTHOR BIO

ANTHONY WITTWER spent a year living in a small, log cabin in the middle of the same green, wooded hills that are the home of *Jonah's Belly*. While living there, he worked as a grapevine wreath-maker. Each day he walked through the woods, pulling vines down from the trees to weave into wreaths, and trying—at the same time—to avoid rattlesnakes, hunters, and poison ivy. During that year, he imagined the characters and stories that would eventually live on *Jonah's Belly*.

In addition to being a grapevine wreath-maker, Anthony has worked as a construction laborer, a toy store manager, a penny-per-piece craft-maker, a suit salesman, an office clerk, and president/CEO of two national companies.

He lives in Fort Wayne, Indiana, with his wife, Elissa.